THE SARA ELIZABETH MASON MYSTERIES

VOLUME 1

THE SARA ELIZABETH MASON MYSTERIES

VOLUME 1

MURDER RENTS A ROOM

THE CRIMSON FEATHER

COACHWHIP PUBLICATIONS

Greenville, Ohio

The Sara Elizabeth Mason Mysteries, Vol. 2
© 2018 Coachwhip Publications

Murder Rents a Room published 1943.
The Crimson Feather published 1945.
No claims made on public domain material.
Cover image: Rosemount Plantation House (Forkland, AL),
   by Iana Z.; feather © Evgeni89.

CoachwhipBooks.com

ISBN 1-61646-441-0
ISBN-13 978-1-61646-441-7

CONTENTS

MISS CONSTANCE MOCK
Civics

MISS REBECCA UNDERWOOD
Spanish

MISS MARGARET TURNER
Typing

MISS LOUISE WHEELER
Dietitian

MRS. JOHN R. LEATH
Biology

COACH L. L. NELSON
Football, Basketball

MISS SARAH CLOUGH PARKS
Dietitian

MRS. SUSAN GARNER
Retail Selling

MISS ETHEL HOUSER
English

MISS SARA ELIZABETH MASON
History

MRS. J. B. HAVARD
Physical Education

MRS. CATHERINE HURST
History

F A C U L T Y

Yearbook photo of Sara Elizabeth Mason as history teacher
at Gadsden High School, Alabama, in 1943

DEATH IN THE HEART OF DIXIE
(AND THE WINDY CITY TOO)
THE MYSTERY FICTION OF SARA ELIZABETH MASON

CURTIS EVANS

[Rosemount] plantation grew to be over five thousand acres, she said, and the [Glover] family fortunes grew with it. The *Allen Glover*, sidewheel
steamer, proudly carried its owner's cotton and tobacco down the Warrior River to the markets of
Mobile. A coach and four, outriders beside it, bore
visitors from Rosemount to the other Black Belt
houses. There was gay dancing and the drinking of
imported wines. Fox hunters rode to hounds and
spent the long evenings at poker. Slaves were plen-
tiful and happy. Milady walked in the garden with
a slave to hold her parasol and another to fan the
air into cooling motion about her. Life was full of
pleasant formalities.
— Carl Carmer, *Stars Fell on Alabama* (1934)

Carl Carmer (1893-1967), a charismatic and imaginative young
northerner who in the 1920s had been employed for a half-doz-
en years as an associate professor of English at the University of
Alabama in Tuscaloosa, attained enviable fame in 1934 with the
publication of *Stars Fell on Alabama*, his bestselling book about

the state. When during his six year sojourn in the Heart of Dixie Carmer took the occasion to visit Rosemount plantation in neighboring Greene County, the charming and gracious chatelaine who guided him around this aged yet still breathtaking relic of Old South domestic Greek Revival architecture was Amelia Walton Glover Legare (1869-1941), a granddaughter of the original builder and a first cousin, once removed, of Alabama educator, librarian, and Forties crime writer Sara Elizabeth Mason (1911-1993), the subject of this introduction.

Sara Elizabeth Mason published her entire corpus of mystery fiction—four novels to be exact—between 1943 and 1948, a period in American history when many white non-fiction writers, whether they hailed from the South or the North, tended to wax comfortably nostalgic over what they deemed the genteel living of the plantation aristocracy of the Old South, as can be seen in the fervid moonlight and magnolia mythography which perfumes the pages of such popular books about the South from the Thirties and Forties as Carl Carmer's *Stars Fell on Alabama*, J. Frazer Smith's *White Columns* (1941), and Clarence John Laughlin's *Ghosts Along the Mississippi* (1948). (For more questioning approaches to the subject see Clarence Cason's *90 Degrees in the Shade*, which was published in 1935, shortly after the author, an esteemed UA journalism professor fearful about what the local reception to his book might be, tragically committed suicide, and *The Mind of the South*, the classic 1941 study by Wilbur J. Cash, who similarly is believed to have killed himself, not long after his book was published.)

While the last of Sara Mason's mysteries, *The Whip*, takes place in Chicago, where the future crime writer in 1938 received a master's degree in history (her thesis was "Sectionalism in Alabama, 1840-1860"), her first three mysteries all are firmly rooted in Alabama soil. Yet all three books are mostly lacking in the Old South romance dreamily indulged in by the starry-eyed Carl Carmer and other of his contemporaries.[1] In the debut Mason mystery, *Murder Rents a Room*, the titular room belongs not to some bustling urban lodgment, but rather a remote and timeworn plantation house in rural Greene County, Alabama, where the descendants of the original owners are simply struggling to hold on to what they still have by taking in paying guests. They have little time to spare in their harried present for apotheosizing the leisured past of their ancestors—and they perforce carry their own parasols.

Nine decades before the publication of her mysteries Sara Elizabeth Mason's great grandfather Williamson Allen Glover (1804-1879) had erected in Greene County, on land given him by his father Allen Glover, Rosemount, one of the finest of the state's antebellum mansions. (Rosemount's design, which included a front portico with six ionic columns and a massive columned cupola adorning the top of the house, was devised by William Nichols, then the state architect of Alabama.) At this stately home, imposingly set on a star-shaped knoll in the heart of Alabama's richest agricultural country (dubbed the "Black Belt" for the color of its fertile alluvial soil), there grew to adulthood a dozen of Glover's children by his two successive wives, Amelia Tillman Walton (of nearby Strawberry Hill plantation) and Mary Sophia Haden. (An additional four Glover children died in infancy; neither of Glover's wives survived past her forties.) The most historically significant marriage made by one of the many Williamson Allen Glover offspring was that concluded in 1850 between Glover's eldest daughter, Amelia Walton Glover, and wealthy Mississippi planter James Lusk Alcorn, a bitter opponent of secession who during the era of Reconstruction which followed the Civil War joined the Republican party and served successively as governor of Mississippi and one of the state's U. S. senators (the other being Blanche K. Bruce, an African-American); yet it was younger Glover daughter Mary Willie Ann "Mollie" Glover's Reconstruction-era marriage to Greene County farmer John Stanhope Brasfield which ultimately gifted vintage mystery fans with Sara Elizabeth Mason.

Born on September 2, 1911, Sara Elizabeth Mason was one of two children (the other being her elder brother, Stanhope Brasfield Mason) of Mollie and John Stanhope Brasfield's daughter Fenton Amelia Brasfield and her husband, Edwin

Bolton Mason, a hardware merchant in the town of Demopolis in Marengo County, located at the confluence of the Tombigbee and Black Warrior Rivers about a dozen miles below Rosemount. In Demopolis had lived not only Sara's great-great grandfather Allen Glover, sire of Williamson Allen Glover, master of Rosemount, but her great-aunt Sara Serena Glover Lyon of Bluff Hall and her great-aunt Anne Gaines Glover Lyon of Lyon Hall, as well as her great-aunt Laura Davenport Glover Prout, wife of banker Daniel Fowler Prout, through whom the twentieth-century Glovers were connected, in a manner of speaking, with Hudson Strode (1891-1976), a celebrated English professor at the University of Alabama for nearly a half-century, from 1916 until 1963. (Although the second husband of Strode's mother, Hope Hudson, was, like Sara Mason's father, a Demopolis hardware merchant, Hope's third husband, William Sylvester Prout, was the only son of Daniel Prout and Laura Glover and his father's successor as bank president.) Both Glovers and Glover relations were interred in Demopolis in a white-stuccoed classical mausoleum, completed in 1845, which still stands in the town today, vainly warded by remnants of a Gothic Revival cast iron fence, upon a chalk bluff overlooking the Tombigbee River.[2]

Edwin Bolton Mason came of humbler social origins than the storied Glovers, being the son of Sumter County, Alabama farmer Edwin Francis Mason and his first wife, Jessie Bolton, who died when Edwin Bolton, the couple's only child, was less than two years old. Leaving his young son behind with his mother-in-law, Edwin Francis Mason left Alabama for Mer Rouge, Louisiana, where he became an overseer on Isaac Brown's cotton plantation. Shortly afterward he wed Brown's daughter Jennie and with her had three daughters, one of whom was named Sara Elizabeth and presumably was the woman for whom Edwin Bolton Mason and his wife Fenton named their own daughter.

Not long after the First World War, Fenton and Edwin Mason with their two children left Demopolis and the world of the Old South behind them when they moved to the rapidly developing

New South industrial city of Gadsden, perched in the highlands of northeastern Alabama, where Edwin managed another hardware store and the family resided in a one-story bungalow on 602 South 11th Street. Between 1900 and 1940 the population of Gadsden leapt by more than nine times, from roughly 4,000 to 37,000 inhabitants, as a slew of businesses, such as the Dwight Manufacturing Company of Chicopee, Massachusetts (a maker of cotton textiles), the Jefferson Lumber Company, the Alabama Steel and Wire Company and the Gadsden Car Works of the Southern Railroad, established plants in the area. During this same period the population of Demopolis grew much more slowly than that of Gadsden, increasing from around 2600 to 4100. The contrast between bustling Gadsden and somnolent Demopolis may have inspired Sara Mason's setting for her second crime novel, *The House That Hate Built* (1944).

Both of the Mason children attained distinction in life as adults. Sara's brother, Stanhope Brasfield Mason, graduated from West Point in 1928 and rose to the army rank of Major General in 1951, having served during the Second World War as chief of staff of the 1st Infantry Division (famously nicknamed "The Big Red One") and the V Corps. (He also commanded the ROTC at the University of Alabama.) For her part Sara between 1929 and 1938 attended Agnes Scott, a woman's college in Decatur, Georgia, and earned degrees from both the University of Alabama—she matriculated at UA just two years after Carl Carmer left the school under a cloud, the married yet dangerously sociable professor having developed what was deemed too intimate a relationship with a female student—and the University of Chicago before she was awarded an MS degree in library science from Peabody College in Nashville (now part of Vanderbilt University). When she was a student at the University of Alabama, Sara's distant relation-through-marriage Hudson Strode had not yet inaugurated his vaunted creative writing workshop, but then the late Pulitzer Prize winning *To Kill a Mockingbird* author Harper Lee (1926-2016), who attended UA some dozen years after Sara had graduated, would manage rather well without it.[3]

During the Second World War Sara returned to reside with her parents in Gadsden, teaching American history to students at Gadsden High School; yet after the war, Sara like her brother traveled to Europe, where she found employment as a teacher in Frankfurt, Germany with the American High School, which served the children of American government, military and civilian personnel. Returning to Alabama after a few years, she took positions at the University of Alabama at the Amelia Gayle Gorgas Library, built a decade earlier on the site of the antebellum Rotunda, burned during the Civil War; the Birmingham Public Library, where she was head of the catalog department and curator of the cartographical collection; and the Gadsden Public Library, where she was appointed Assistant Director. Her third crime novel, *The Crimson Feather*, the last of her mysteries with a southern scene, is set in Tuscaloosa among the local white elite, including members of the University faculty. Before her death in Homewood, near Birmingham, on August 15, 1993, she published *A List of Nineteenth Century Maps of the State of Alabama* (1973) and, reflecting her interest to the end of her life in her own family heritage, *The Glovers of Marengo County, Alabama* (1989).

During Sara Mason's short career as a crime writer, reviewers lauded the good writing and authentic *mise-en-scene* that graced her four mysteries, in the first three of which the author adhered to the tried-and-true romance and ratiocination formula of such hugely popular American authors as Mary Roberts Rinehart, Mignon Eberhart, and Leslie Ford. (The last of them, *The Whip*, veers more from traditional suspense to the manner and form of the psychological crime novel that such authors as Margaret Millar, Very Kelsey, Dorothy Hughes, Elisabeth Sanxay Holding, and Charlotte Armstrong were developing at this time.) Two of her novels, *The Crimson Feather* and *The Whip*, were reprinted in paperback, the former by Dell in 1947 (as part of their "mapback" series, beloved by modern collectors) and the latter by Bantam in 1950, but all four of them received good notices in the newspapers.

Murder Rents a Room, which introduces rural county Sheriff Bill Davies, was deemed by Isaac Anderson in the *New York Times Book Review* a promising first detective story, while William C. Weber in the *Saturday Review* declared that the tale had "plenty of zip" and influential crime fiction critic Anthony Boucher in the *San Francisco Chronicle* enjoyed the "pleasant romance about nice people in a timeless southern setting." Boucher found *The House That Hate Built*, set in the fictional mill town of Monroe, a "[m]inutely detailed small-town novel," while Weber praised it as "[c]apably plotted, with some rather surprising situations" and "interesting characters." Weber was similarly praiseful of

SARA ELIZABETH MASON
Four-Time Novel Winner

The Crimson Feather, wherein county Sheriff Bill Davis returns to investigate a murder, this time in nearby Tuscaloosa (though the town in the novel is not so named). Weber lauded *Feather's* "[a]bly concocted plot, enlivened by sharp pictures of southern small-town life and family squabbles," and he additionally admired the novel's "[u]nostentatious sleuth," who performed a "believable job" of criminal investigation. Anthony Boucher echoed Weber's words in his review of *Feather*, noting the "shrewd inspection of Sheriff Bill Davies" and the tale's compelling "family atmosphere."

After a lapse of more than two years (when she was living in Frankfurt, Germany) and a change of American publisher from Doubleday to Morrow, Sara returned to print in January 1948 with *The Whip*, structurally her most unusual crime novel in that it relies heavily on a flashback narrative and the analysis of disordered emotional states (the hero is a psychiatrist); reviewers found the author had not lost her touch in the interim. In the *Saturday Review* a pleased William Weber judged that the psychological crime novel, which he colorfully termed a "believable brain-prober," presented a rare "case where [the] flashback method of narrative" did not "retard action." In the *New York Times Book Review* Isaac Anderson, obviously impressed with Mason's new tack, declared that the "excellent novel" was "a moving narrative of unfeeling cruelty practiced upon a sensitive young girl by a selfish old woman and her relatives." For fans of Sara Mason's mysteries it is disappointing to see that her interesting and entertaining fiction writing career came to an end after so brief a span of time, with places like Birmingham or even Frankfurt, Germany, left unexplored, but it is pleasing to know that she went out on a high note.

NOTES

[1] Which is not to say that Carl Carmer did not have clear-eyed, or even cutting-edged, moments in *Stars Fell in Alabama*. To the outrage of reactionaries in the Heart of Dixie, Carmer in his book dared to afford space to the distinctly

unromantic matters of the lynching of black men and the menaces of the Ku Klux Klan. (During the half-dozen years in the Twenties that Carmer resided in Alabama, white mobs murdered five black men in the state.) Concerning Tuscaloosa, home of the University of Alabama, Carmer witheringly observes that the city "prides itself on its culture. But culture in Tuscaloosa is generally rather a tradition than an actuality. The prevailing sentiment seems to be that it is a quality that one inherits from distinguished ancestors."

[2] Yet another of Sara's great-aunts, Mary Amelia, married James Innes Thornton of Thornhill plantation in Greene County, a near neighbor of Rosemount, and another of the finest antebellum Greek Revival mansions erected in Alabama. Certainly the Glover girls had a knack for wedding well, or at least lucratively.

[3] The very picture of a mid-century southern literature professor, Hudson Strode was a surpassingly adept promoter of his creative writing students—*Forrest Gump* author Winston Groom was a Strode student ("Strodent") during the professor's final year of teaching in 1963—and he has been ballyhooed in Alabama for many decades. (After my father came to teach at UA in 1968, my mother, a schoolteacher who taught and had majored in English in college, was met with the incredulous exclamation, when she queried a woman who Hudson Strode was, *"You were an English major and you never heard of Hudson Strode?!"*) However, Strode's own publication record consisted of numerous name-dropping travelogues (culminating in his memoir *The Eleventh House*, which has to be read to be believed—or not) and a multi-volume, would-be magnum opus biography of Jefferson Davis which has been dismissed for "superficial research and extreme pro-Davis bias" (see *Civil War Times Illustrated* 11, 1972, p. 56). ("It's trash," a prominent historian once pronounced to me

bluntly.) Harper Lee's biographer Charles J. Shields spec-
ulates that Strode did not invite Lee to take his creative
writing workshop because he realized that Lee, who had
taken Strode's Shakespeare class, did not hold him in respect. "[Strode] was a disappointed actor who declaimed
passages from Shakespeare in class, probably thinking his
students would enjoy seeing scenes performed; but Miss
Lee [recalled a former student] dismissed him as 'pomp-
ous. She would be almost rude to him.' One day, as he was
holding forth in his mellifluous voice, she drew a carica-
ture of him as Hamlet addressing Yorick's skull. It was so
good that the class secretly passed it back and forth, sputtering with laughter." See Charles S. Shields, *Mockingbird:
A Portrait of Harper Lee, from Scout to* Go Set a Watch-
man (2006; rev. ed. 2016), 61-62. Around the time Lee
attended UA, Hudson Strode served as one of three judges
for the O. Henry Memorial Award Prize Stories for 1946.
Competing for prizes were, among others, Eudora Welty,
Patricia Highsmith and Lee's old friend Truman Capote,
none of whom even placed. First Prize went to John Mayo
Goss, who, as it happened, was a student in Strode's creative writing class. See Curtis Evans, "Hudson Strode
and Highsmith: The Tale of 'The Heroine' and the 1946
O. Henry Prize Stories," 23 July 2015, *The Passing Tramp*.
After *To Kill a Mockingbird* became a smashing success,
the resourceful Strode told his students that Lee, though
she had not taken his writing workshop, had "learned a
lot from him through Shakespeare." (Shields, *Mockingbird*,
156).

PREFACE TO
MURDER RENTS A ROOM

MURDER RENTS A ROOM (1943)

CURTIS EVANS

Rounding the gradual bend in the road, they drew up before an old plantation house. There was nothing unique in its plan; it was square, almost box-like in shape. Six fluted Ionic columns supported the two-story roof to the veranda. At one end a vine was being trained to curl around stout wires leading to the roof. Shallow steps of uneven rose-colored bricks led to the porch and to large wooden double doors whose severity was lightened by a graceful fanlight and glass side panels. Across the front of the house the tall narrow windows were flanked by sagging blinds. The house was gray with age, and at least fifty years had passed since it had known paint. In a few places new boards had replaced old ones, and the wind and weather had turned them all the same neutral gray. The Georgian simplicity of the architecture was marred by a square observatory placed in the center of the roof and surrounded on all four sides by a wooden railing and short, slender pillars.

Opening the door of the car, Kate stepped quickly to the ground, and the young man followed her up the short moss-grown brick walk.

"This is Cliff's Edge," she said. "The site was chosen by the first Leigh who came to this section

*when it was still a part of the Mississippi Territory.
It was the second Leigh, Charles Henry, however,
who built the house in 1830. If you look that way
you get a splendid view of the river." She pointed,
and he turned to see a broad expanse of water moving rapidly between high banks. "That's where the
house gets its name. It's built on a rise of ground that
slopes down to the riverbank. There's a pretty steep
bluff over there. Won't you come in?"*

> —Kate Frazier lands a lodger, Alex Dexter, at
> her Alabama ancestral home, Cliff's Edge,
> in *Murder Rents a Room* (1943)

Explicitly placed deep in the Alabama Black Belt in rural
Greene County, once one of the richest counties in Alabama,
Cliff's Edge, the menacingly-named locus of death in Sara
Elizabeth Mason's *Murder Rents a Room*, seems an amalgam
of at least a couple of antebellum homes associated with the
author's Glover ancestors: Williamson Allen Glover's Green
County plantation house Rosemount and his brother-in-law
Francis Strother Lyon's Bluff Hall, a white mansion with a massive square-columned portico fronting a fanlighted doorway
that was built on a high chalk cliff overlooking the Tombigbee
River. (Before completion of the Demopolis Lock and Dam in
1955, the White Bluff—or *Ecor Blanc* as it was known to French
settlers—was nearly 80 feet high, but since has diminished to
less than half that height.) Bluff Hall still stands today, about
a dozen miles south of Rosemount plantation in the town of
Demopolis, where it is now a house museum. However, the
Cliff's Edge of Sara Mason's novel is, like the Rosemount of her
ancestors, very much a plantation home—though one which,
having been defaced by the fleeting hand of time, possesses
only fragments of its former grandeur.

Kate Frazier (nee Leigh), the focal character of *Murder
Rents a Room*, has only recently returned to Cliff's Edge, after
the death of her husband, Pete, with whom she spent four bliss-
ful but all-too-brief wedded years in New York City. Having

been "brought up in a land of sagging houses," as Sara Mason picturesquely puts it, Kate, like Carl Carmer and other real-life spinners of "moonlight and magnolia" tales of the Old South, sees beauty in southern decay—and she is willing moreover to do the hard work necessary to stave off ultimate dissolution. Once many years ago Kate's grandparents had lived at Cliff's Edge, but her father, a physician, resided with his family "in town," presumably meaning Eutaw, the seat of Greene County and the only habitation of any numerical significance within its borders. On one of the few occasions in the novel when she discusses her past in New York, Kate explains to Alex Dexter, a wanly handsome off-season guest at Cliff's Edge:

> "That's been the story of the last two genera-
> tions of Leighs. We went to other places to make
> enough money so we could afford to live here. My
> bother Jack's in the navy [recalling Sara Mason's
> career army brother, Stanhope Brasfield Mason],
> and I went to New York."
> "You lived in New York?"
> "Yes, I went there to study commercial art
> and married and—well, stayed."
> "You married a Yankee?" Alex sounded scan-
> dalized.
> Kate turned her face toward the window. Her
> eyes had taken on a lost look. There were times
> when Pete seemed very close.
> "Yes," she said simply.

Like the late rural Alabama author and onetime Truman Capote confidante Harper Lee, Kate clearly loved her life in New York, but she also, like her Leigh kinfolk (with one no-table exception), feels intense and abiding loyalty to the old family home in the heart of Dixie; and she is prepared to sac-rifice a great deal on its behalf. "We're a funny family," she re-flects to Alex of the Leighs of Cliff's Edge, "We all come back to this place. It's in our blood—the land and the cotton and the sun." This observation recalls the life of the author herself, who came back to Alabama after spending several years in graduate school in Chicago, though she returned not to the Black Belt countryside of her ancestors but to a factory city in the Appalachian foothills.

Determined to keep Cliff's Edge from becoming, by their lights, yet another graceful Old South casualty of the crassly vulgar New South, which in its headlong rush after immediate material profit heedlessly places little value on the decorative past, however charming traditionalists deem it, Kate and the extended family members who currently reside with her at the ancestral mansion—her "Uncle" Brock Curtis, a former hardware store owner (recalling Sara Mason's father) from Birmingham, and her widowed Cousin ("Cu'un") Lucy (Leigh) Allen, "Cliff's Edge's animated antique"—offer fifty-cent house tours as well as lodging during hunting and fishing seasons, at the rate of three dollars a day or fifteen dollars a week.

Though he is a gaunt Yankee recovering from an unspecified illness, Alex Dexter makes a welcome addition to the company at Cliff's Edge, but acrimony soon commences at the house with the unexpected arrival of the Leigh family trial: drop-dead gorgeous, much-married, and man-devouring Kitty (Leigh) Bolling, currently come to Greene County to get away for a spell from the attentions of her wealthy third husband, Ralph. "Kitty couldn't have been around the archangel Gabriel without being personal," we are wryly informed of the incorrigible vamp, who has "already made two profitable trips to Reno." As is her wont, Cu'un Lucy expresses herself more bluntly: "Kitty was always vain and a scheming hussy too. I declare, I'm glad her mother's dead so she can't see her now."

Vain and scheming Kitty arrives by train, in all her feminine finery ("I can't vouch for what Kitty will wear," explains Kate to Alex, "She may come down in a sensible dress or she may come prepared for the Stork Club"), at the tiny station at Eutaw, a small town with a population of under 2000 souls in the year of 1940, around the time when the novel is set. "Once the town had been the thriving market center for the large plantations which covered the county," writes Sara Mason, "but it had lapsed into a dreamy, dusty village, almost forgotten in the present-day rush of industry and progress." Nevertheless, "going to town"— even a town as little as "dreamy, dusty" Eutaw—was an occasion for Alabama country folk on the eve of the Second World War, as Kate plaintively acknowledges when she drops Uncle Brock off at the bank: "You'd think we lived a million miles from town. . . . Everybody has given me a list of things to get. . . . How do they expect me to do my own errands?"

Tasked with doing Cu'un Lucy's grocery shopping, Kate makes her way to "the stores lining the four sides of the town square which held the white plaster courthouse," a building, Sara Mason observes, "saved from mediocrity by its wrought-iron railings and balcony. In its own way it was a gem of Southern architecture of the ante-bellum period." This "white plaster courthouse" still exists today. Originally completed in 1839, a year after Eutaw was surveyed and laid out as the new seat of Greene County, the building three decades later was partially consumed in an 1868 fire said to have been set in order to destroy indictments brought against local white citizens by Alabama's Reconstruction-era Republican government. The next year the courthouse was itself reconstructed, the builders economically making use of the first-floor walls, cut down, and adding a bracketed Italianate second story graced with four small cast iron balconies.

Uncle Brock, Kate Leigh, and Kitty Bolling return to Cliff's Edge, where they periodically are visited by a pair of Kitty's former Bama beaux (both of whom seemingly remain bedazzled by Kitty's siren charms): town relation Leigh Randall and neighboring run-to-seed gentleman farmer Jeff Gaines of the Laurels (whose surname recalls Francis Strother Lyon's uncle, the once-famed Choctaw Indian agent George Strother Gaines). Tiresomely for Kitty, Leigh Randall's figuratively green-eyed wife, Alicia, is on hand at Cliff's Edge as well, keeping a watch over her errant husband. Soon fireworks begin to fly . . . and it is not even the Fourth of July! Yet it is not Kitty whom a horrified Kate discovers dreadfully done to death on the grounds of Cliff's Edge, but another member of the household, one whom is vastly more missed by most Greene County locals, white and black, than the viperish Kitty ever would have been. This foul murder brings to the scene Bill Davies, "a hard-working small-town sheriff—tall, lean, angular, and loosely strung together," whose "shrewd eyes were skeptical and entirely disillusioned, as though he was very tired of people and knew only too well their human frailties." As the keen-minded and clear-eyed Sheriff Davies determinedly digs up Leigh family secrets and turns ghastly skeletons out of perfumed closets, Kate finds to her fright that not only can the truth hurt—it can, and indeed most certainly does, kill!

* * * * * * *

Inevitably, perhaps, many readers of *Murder Rents a Room* will be most interested in, along with the novel's intriguing tale of murder and mystery, its rural Alabama Black Belt milieu and the complex relations between the two races enmeshed in sometimes uncomfortable proximity within it. Sara Mason writes sympathetically about the various black dependents of the Leighs of Cliff's Edge plantation, but also with what many today likely will deem a falsely idealized paternalistic attitude, similar to that which is often found in the portrayals of gentry and servants in British detective fiction from the same era.

"They bickered with the Negroes, argued with them, ignored advice they were given, but frequently followed it," writes Sara Mason of the Leighs, with some defensiveness in her tone. "And, strangely enough, they loved the black people and worried about them." Clearly conscious of contemporary northern criticism of southern treatment of blacks, Sara Mason in *Murder Rents a Room* is palpably desirous of painting something of a different picture of Alabama race relations—at least within the Black Belt, as it concerns white "aristocrats" and the black people who work their farms and care for them and their homes. Mason's black characters (usually referred to as Negroes, but also sometimes as "darkies")—cook Ella, maid Fancy and the various males, young and old, Zack, Eph, Will, Ben and Link—stand out, in contrast with blacks in much of the crime fiction from the period, as individual characters and they are afforded some respect, though the maid Fancy, young and light-skinned (or "high yellow" to use the terminology of the novel), is several times faulted by Kate (and implicitly by the author) for her lackadaisical attitude toward her work, Kate going so far as to declare that she would have fired Fancy long ago but for the inconvenient fact that she is Ella's grand-daughter. Unlike her black elders at Cliff's Edge, Fancy clearly is less content (or perhaps less resigned) with her lot in the life fashioned long ago by Leighs for her and her like; and she accordingly is castigated with that derisive adjective *sullen*, long employed by southern paternalists against any "negro" deemed insufficiently subordinate.

Within the narrow ambit of paternalism Kate seems a kind and considerate employer, one who is willing, for example, to promote the musical ambitions of her young employee Eph, even though this could result in his taking leave of the Black Belt (and Leigh employ). Among other things Eph pumps the antiquated organ at Sunday church services at the lovely little Gothic-style wooden church in the nearby village (presumably St. John's Episcopal Church in Forkland, where some of the author's Glover relations presented several of the house of worship's stained glass windows and are eternally resting in the tiny cemetery).[1] Eph rides with the Leighs in Kate's station wagon on the short trips to and from the church, on this particular drive with "four white people crowded on the two front seats" (Kate, Cu'un Lucy, Uncle Brock and Alex) and Eph "in luxury in the back." He also is tasked with playing his precious mouth harp (harmonica) while Ben and Link draw bows across their fiddles (violins), on those festive occasions when

Kate—bowing not to tradition but to modern misapprehension as Sara Mason wryly explains—requests the trio to serenade her guests at Cliff's Edge:

> She knew that tourists expected the Negroes to come up to the house and serenade them. Movies and novels had firmly implanted this idea in their minds as an old southern custom. . . . Kate made a practice of giving them a small glass of wine and a little money. If they wondered why they were allowed to sing only spirituals and church hymns instead of the latest swing music, they put it down as another peculiarity of the white people.

One day Alex finds Kate working with Eph in the garden and he overhears the following conversation, which alights on the future employment prospects of the "little negro":

> "Lissun, Mis' Kate." Eph pulled the harmonica from his pocket and began a melody of steady beats and throbbing undertones. "Mis' Kate, do that soun' lak what yo' hear in them clubs?"
>
> Kate sat back on her knees. "That's very good, Eph. It is something you made up yourself?"
>
> "Naw'm. I lissun'd to the radio t'other day, and they kep' playin' it ova and ova." He dug one ragged shoe into the ground.
>
> "Well, you keep on trying, and one of these days maybe you can get a job with a good band. But you'll have to study. They don't play by ear." Kate measured her string, drove another stake into the ground, and tied the string to it.
>
> Eph dug earnestly at the dirt, carefully picking up the large earthworms that rose to the surface with each spadeful and putting them into an old tin can.

"Mis' Kate? When yo' goin' give me that fiddle of yo' grandpa's? That'd 'scourage me a whole lot."

"Why, you little devil! That's what you're angling for. Well, I'm not going to give it to you till you learn to do the job you're supposed to be doing now. I never told you I'd give you the violin, did I?"

Kate rose and pulled off the clumsy cotton gloves that protected her hands. She stuffed them into the pockets of the red sweater which already bulged with string.

"Naw'm. But I 'spec's yo' will." Eph grinned up at her and went on with his work.

Young Eph negotiates his place in Black Belt society more diplomatically than Fancy by skillfully playing on Kate's sense of paternalism—and her liking, perhaps unconscious, of playing the role of a plantation Lady Bountiful. (When, after the first murder, Kate, understandably "[n]ervous and out of sorts," loses her patience and speaks "shortly to the Negroes," she immediately feels remorse, being unable to "bear the hurt, bewildered look in their soft black eyes.") Yet Fancy, as readers will see, has more forceful ways than Eph of extracting favors from someone who has rejected the paternalistic tradition of reciprocal obligation in favor of modern mercenary methods of getting what one wants. Cognizant of these changes even in Black Belt society, the author, like many another privileged white southern "aristocrat" in her day, offers the following lament when noting the intensely close relationship between Uncle Brock and the black farm hand Will: "Such loyalty and faith are rare, indeed, between the black and white races today."

Murder Rents a Room succeeds in providing readers both with an entertaining tale of murder and mystery and an interesting look at a place and time which is alien to most of us who have grown up in the post-Jim Crow era. With the novel Sara Mason followed in the lucrative path of native Georgia journalist Medora Field, a close friend of Margaret Mitchell of *Gone with the Wind* fame who herself probably is best known today for her nonfiction study of Greek Revival domestic architecture, *White Columns in Georgia* (1952). Inspired both by Margaret Mitchell's massively popular regional romance and the bestselling suspense fiction of Mary Roberts Rinehart, Medora Field's lucrative mysteries, *Who Killed Aunt Maggie?* (1939) and *Blood on Her Shoe* (1942), were, like *Murder Rents a Room*, set in old mansions in the Deep South.[2] Yet it is the milieu in Sara Mason's novel, rather than Medora Field's, which has the greater air of authenticity. "Sara Elizabeth Mason's first mystery shows a capacity to handle background," noted the publisher's description on the front flap of the novel's dust jacket, which depicts a sinister trench-coated and fedora'd man emerging in the foreground before an old plantation house. This capacity would similarly reveal itself in Sara Mason's later trio of mysteries, including one which would again feature Sheriff Bill Davies. Yet only in *Murder Rents a Room* would the author portray the culture of Black Belt Alabama in the years shortly before the vanquishing of Jim Crow. Even with its author's glosses the novel, like Cliff's Edge itself, affords a most interesting view.

NOTES

[1] Writes Mason: "For the first time in years [Alex] found himself in a church, seated beneath a richly colored stained-glass window that bore the inscription: *For God So Loved the World That He Gave His Only Begotten Son*. And beneath it, in smaller letters, 'In Memory of Charles Henry and Katherine Prudhomme Leigh.' Glancing about in the semigloom he saw that the other windows bore the names of Leighs, Randalls, Brockways and Allens." This sounds much like the church in Forkland, though most intriguingly at this church one of the windows, depicting the *Ten Mitzvot* (Ten Commandments) in Hebrew, was presented by merchant Simon Levy, Reconstruction-era postmaster of Forkland.

[2] After going through multiple hardcover printings, *Who Killed Aunt Maggie?* sold 125,000 in paperback, while *Blood on Her Shoe* did even better, selling 175,000.

LIBRARY CARD PLEASE — Miss Sara Mason, Demopolis-born author of four mystery novels, is now working at the Public Library. Here she checks out a copy of one of her novels to mystery-fan, Edward Beaumont.

MURDER RENTS A ROOM

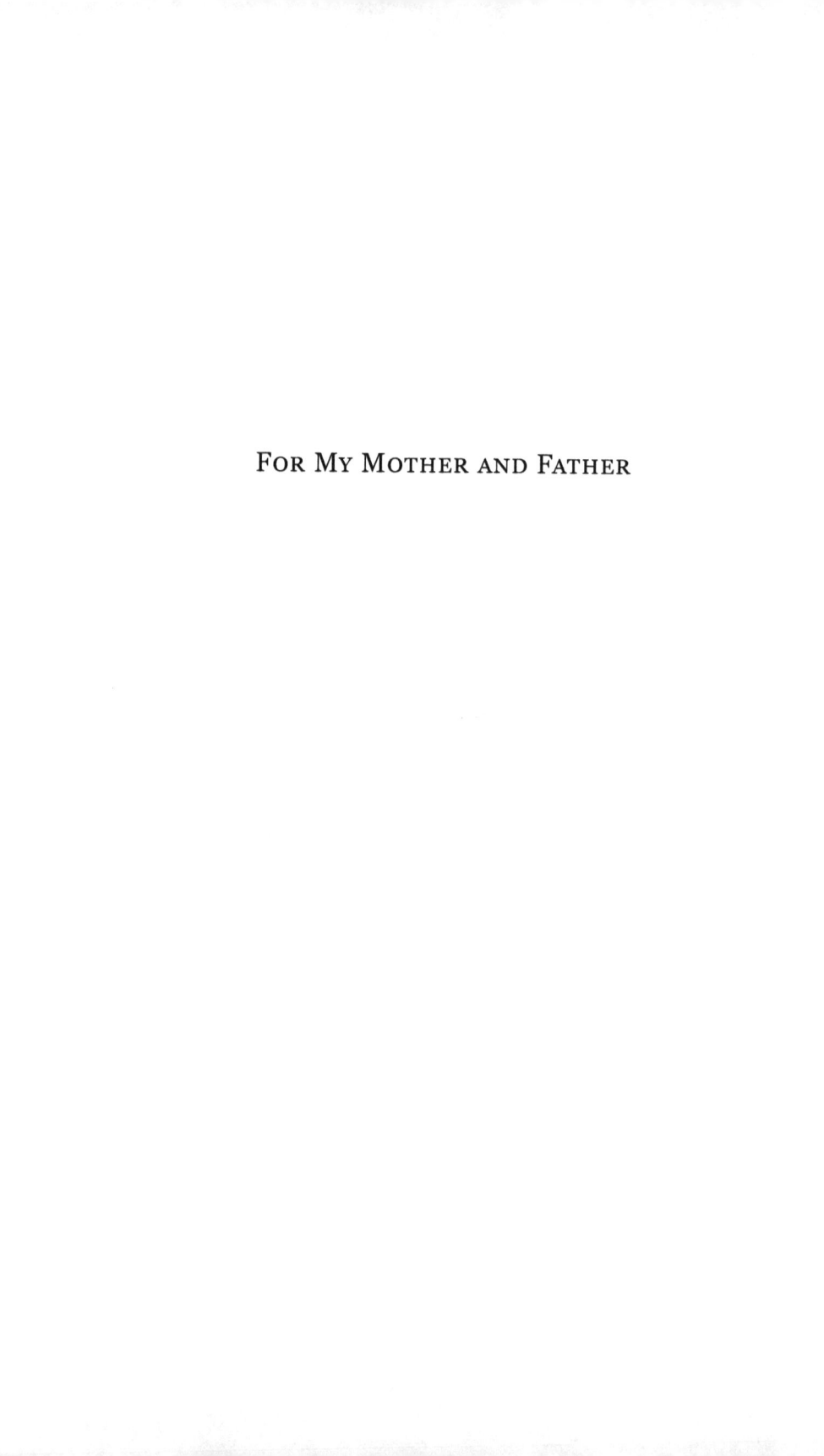

FOR MY MOTHER AND FATHER

1

The March sun shone brightly through the gnarled old cedar trees that bordered the curving driveway, casting blue-green shadows on the rutted road. Here and there clumps of grass and weeds were pushing their way up toward the sun. A few dogwoods struggled under the shade of the older trees; some had given up hope and had died, but occasionally a few showed signs of life.

The girl trudging down the road paid little attention to her surroundings, for the scene was a familiar one. She had seen many springs come and go, turning gradually into a blazing Southern summer, so that now she was scarcely aware of this newest awakening.

Kate Frazier was slender and long-limbed, though not really tall. Her features were cleanly cut, yet she was not a beautiful woman. It was her eyes that drew attention first—large, black, serene, dreamy. The wind whipped a tendril of dark hair across her mouth, and she brushed it back impatiently with her hand.

She wore faded blue slacks, soil-stained at the knees from the work she had left in the garden. Her fists were rammed deep into the pockets of a bright red sweater, for despite the sun's warmth the wind was chilling. With a much-scuffed oxford she kicked a clod of loose dirt and thought: Next fall I'll get Will to move some of the dogwoods from the swamp over here. If we can get them to grow the drive will look so much better, especially in the spring.

She pushed open the heavy wire gate that hung from crumbling brick posts. Ignoring the car drawn up at the side of the road, she took a rusty key from her pocket and opened the loaf-shaped tin box. The mail was disappointing: a rolled newspaper, a seed catalogue, two letters. Thrusting the newspaper and catalogue under her arm, she tore open one of the letters.

"I beg your pardon."

Kate looked up to see a strange man seated in a long sleek coupé. Apparently he had been just sitting there, watching her.

"Yes?" she said coolly.

"I'm sorry, but is that sign right?" He pointed to a wooden sign wired to one of the posts.

CLIFF'S EDGE
Admission 50¢
Hunting—Fishing—Rooms

Kate turned back to the man in the car. "Yes, that's right. Do you want to see it?"

"Yes, if you please. Is it very far? I don't see a house."

"No, you don't see it from the road." Kate smiled wearily. "It isn't far, only about half a mile."

"If you'll get in I'll drive you back. That is, if you're going back."

"Yes, thank you. I'll have to take you through." Kate walked toward the car, and the man reached over to open the door for her. She pushed aside a road map and sank into the deep leather cushions.

The few minutes it took to drive back over the road which she had so recently walked gave her a brief opportunity to study her companion. There was little enough to see, for his soft gray hat was pulled low over his eyes and his coat collar was turned up against the brisk March wind. He was very pale, and there were greenish shadows under his eyes and about his mouth. His face was thin, emphasizing the prominent bone structure.

Rounding the gradual bend in the road, they drew up before an old plantation house. There was nothing unique in its plan; it was square, almost boxlike in shape. Six fluted Ionic columns supported the two-story roof of the veranda. At one end a vine was being trained to curl around stout wires leading to the roof. Shallow steps of uneven rose-colored brick led to the porch and to large wooden double doors whose severity was lightened by a graceful fanlight and glass side panels. Across the front of the house the tall narrow windows were flanked by sagging blinds.

The house was gray with age, and at least fifty years had passed since it had known paint. In a few places new boards had replaced old ones, and the wind and weather had turned them all the same neutral gray. The Georgian simplicity of the architecture was marred by a square observatory placed in the center of the roof and surrounded on all four sides by a wooden railing and short, slender pillars.

Opening the door of the car, Kate stepped quickly to the ground, and the young man followed her up the short moss-grown brick walk.

"This is Cliff's Edge," she said. "The site was chosen by the first Leigh who came to this section when it was still a part of the Mississippi Territory. It was the second Leigh, Charles Henry, however, who built the house in 1830. If you look that way you get a splendid view of the river." She pointed, and he turned to see a broad expanse of water moving rapidly between high banks. "That's where the house gets its name. It's built on a rise of ground that slopes down to the riverbank. There's a pretty steep bluff over there. Won't you come in?"

She opened one of the doors and led the way into the broad hall. The man got the impression of great space, for the room was nearly twenty feet wide and the ceiling at least fourteen feet high. At the back and to one side rose a graceful curving stair, and on each side were wide double doors. The hall was open and led to a cross hall through the center of the house. A cold draft of air swirled through these hallways, and apparently no effort was made to heat them.

"If you'll sign here, please." Kate indicated an open ledger on a heavy marble-top table. "And you'd better keep on your coat, as the house isn't all warm," she added candidly.

"I'm afraid there's been a mistake. Of course," he added hastily, "I'd like to see the house some other time. I wanted a room."

"You want a room?"

"The sign did say rooms, didn't it?"

"Yes. But it's too late to hunt and not warm enough to do much fishing."

"Do I have to do one or the other to get a room?"

"Of course not." Kate gave him a searching look. For the first time she noticed that his clothes hung loosely from his gaunt frame, though they were well cut and of good material. His eyelids drooped and he looked tired and sick.

"The room will be three dollars a day or fifteen a week."

"That will be satisfactory," he replied without hesitation.

"In advance." Kate was grimly determined.

A smile appeared fleetingly on the man's face. "Of course," he said, taking out his wallet, and handed her three five-dollar bills.

"My name is Alex Dexter. And now if you'll show me where, I'll sign your book."

"I'm Kate Frazier. Would you rather come in the parlor, where there's a fire, before I show you your room? I'll have Zack light the fire in it now."

He followed her into the room to the right of the hall, and after telling him to make himself comfortable Kate left him.

Alex Dexter seated himself gingerly on a low oval-backed chair beside the fire. It was too hard to be exactly comfortable, and the springs creaked under his weight. Loosening his coat and still holding his hat in his hand, he took time to gaze about the room.

A fire blazed brightly on the hearth beneath a simple white marble mantel. He raised his eyes to the portrait of a really beautiful woman. Her black hair was parted in the middle and smoothed back into a low knot at the base of her neck. She had the same luminous eyes of the girl who had just left the room. The woman smiled at him from her place of eminence, and some trick of the artist made her eyes follow him as he rose and moved closer to the fire.

He slipped off his coat and looked about for a convenient place to put it. The room was filled with the massive antiques. of the early Victorian period: hard sofas, a solid-looking square piano, and a variety of small tables and chairs. Two long mirrors in heavily carved gilt frames hung on either side of the painted double doors through which he had entered. Before he had time to examine the place further the girl returned.

"I'm sorry I've kept you waiting," Kate said as she came in. "I've had Zack light the fire, but I'm afraid the room isn't warm yet. Would you like to see if it is all right? You can still change your mind."

"Thank you, I'll wait here. I'm sure it will be satisfactory."

Kate eyed him with curiosity. He seemed almost indifferent about the room. He hadn't objected to the outlaw price either. She was accustomed to having people pay those prices for the inconveniences of the old house in order to take advantage of the hunting facilities of the plantation. But he seemed uninterested in that too.

She walked over to the fire and extended her hands to the blaze. With a whisk of her hand she brushed off some of the loose dirt that still clung to the knees of her slacks and with the toe of her shoe pushed it toward the fire.

"Please sit down," she said. Mr. Dexter looked shaken and awkward, standing there holding tightly to the back of the chair. His eyes were bright and seemed to watch every move she made, and his face was flushed with the heat from the fire. At her suggestion he sank quickly into the chair.

"Zack will take your bags to your room. If you'll give me the keys to the luggage compartment I'll have him take them up now."

"It isn't locked," he replied.

Kate sat down then, uncertain whether to leave him alone or to watch him. For a moment both of them were silent.

From the back of the house came the sound of a rhythmic tune played on a harmonica.

"Is that some relative of yours?" he asked, finally breaking the quiet and nodding toward the portrait.

Kate looked up and smiled. When she did that there was a marked resemblance between them.

"Yes. She was my great-great-grandmother, the first Katherine Leigh. She's supposed to have been a great beauty in her day. You know—the lovely Southern belle. Since then all the girls in the family have been named for her in the fond hope that we might be beauties too."

Alex Dexter did not smile at her pleasantry but continued to stare vacantly into the fire. If she had not had such a regard for her property in the room Kate would have left him.

There was a draft of cold air as the door opened and a tall stoop-shouldered man entered. Kate looked up at him thankfully.

"Uncle Brock, this is Mr. Dexter," she explained unnecessarily, for she knew the Negroes had already told him and that he had come to see if everything was all right. "This is Mr. Curtis," she finished the introduction.

Uncle Brock had the absent-minded air of a scholar. In reality his education had been cut short when he was a boy. He had had to make his own way in life. His thick white hair stood up in stiff, aggressive bristles over a rounded head. Shrewd eyes peered out beneath jutting brows, and his face was lined and weather-beaten, though it had the healthy glow of life spent in the open country. The rough hands were square, and the blunt fingers were edged with a dark, oily rim.

Alex Dexter looked up to acknowledge the introduction and then shivered violently.

"Uncle Brock, will you take him up to the middle room? I expect it's warm enough for him by now. I've told Zack to take his bags, but perhaps if you'd—"

The old man nodded and motioned the younger to follow.

Kate drew a sigh of relief when the door had closed behind them. She was vaguely disturbed about this unusual guest. He did not fit into the types that had been coming to Cliff's Edge since she had opened it to outsiders. Shrugging uneasily, she drew from her pocket the letter she had found in the mailbox. In a moment she had forgotten the strange appearance of Alex Dexter.

She was still reading it when the door opened and Uncle Brock peered in. She looked up and smiled.

"I've a letter from Josie Travers. You've heard me speak of her so often. She thinks she can get off for a couple of weeks after Easter and visit me."

"That will be nice for you. But what I came to tell you was that that Mr. Dexter is sick."

"What?"

"Sick. He practically collapsed when he got to his room. Finally he told me he had just got up from a serious case of pneumonia and that the doctors had told him to come South for a rest."

"Why in the world is he driving around alone if he's sick?" Kate asked.

"I don't pretend to understand you young people." The old man smiled sardonically. "But the fact remains that he's still sick. I told Zack to put him to bed."

"Isn't it just like me to take in a lame duck?" Kate frowned. "Well, it's done now. I'll see Ella and get her to fix him a hot toddy. Do you suppose we'd better call a doctor?"

"I don't know. Has Lucy come back?"

Kate glanced at her watch. "No, not yet, but it's time for her. Maybe we'd better wait until she comes before we do anything. I'll go see Ella now."

Drawing the red sweater again about her shoulders, she hurried through the cold halls to the kitchen.

The kitchen was a large room to the right of the dining room. It had once been a master bedroom in the days when the kitchen was a separate building in the yard. When Kate had decided to make her home at Cliff's Edge and found it necessary to make the house self-supporting the bedroom had been converted into a kitchen, and the old kitchen and pantry were turned into an office and additional bedrooms.

The room was heated by an old wood range, its pipe disappearing up the wide chimney back of it. A large old-fashioned kitchen safe stood next a more modern kitchen cabinet, and shelves had been added for convenience. In a split-bottom cane chair was seated a large black woman, a mixing bowl clutched between fat knees. She was dressed in a faded green calico Mother Hubbard, and her hair was done in a multitude of crinkly plaits. She was humming to herself, keeping time to the rhythm with her stirring.

"Ain't Mis' Lucy back yit?" Her open mouth showed a row of gold-crowned, snuff-stained teeth. Ella was not an exhibit shown to visitors when they came to see the old house, but her cooking was welcomed at the end of a day spent in the open and had brought many a hunter back for another season. She was a Leigh Negro and owned them body and soul.

"She ought to be back any minute. Ella, we've a new boarder and he's sick. Zack's upstairs now, putting him to bed. Don't you think we might fix him a hot toddy?"

The colored woman gave Kate a look of disgust, and the words poured from her thick lips in a garrulous flood. "Mis' Kate, ain't yo' neva learn no discreshun? Yo' jist like yo' pa. He usta bring all sorts of things home. I bet Mis' Lucy would've had more sense." With a grunt she heaved her heavy body out of the chair.

"Stop fussing, Ella. He's paying for it at my price."

"I ain't neva unnerstood why yo' gits so much. It's highway robbery; that's what it is, Mis' Kate."

"Some of them are buying sentimentality, Southern moonlight, and magnolias. And some of them are buying my birds and deer," Kate explained petulantly, though she knew Ella would never really comprehend.

The two worked together to the accompaniment of a quarreling undertone from the old woman, which Kate heard distinctly but ignored. When they had finished she took the glass and went out into the hall.

Lucy was just coming in, followed by small Eph, who was weighed down under two large paper bags. Kate explained briefly what had happened.

Lucy accepted her story with equanimity, rearing back so that she looked more like a pouter pigeon than ever. She was a short, stout woman, with a mass of soft white hair which she wore piled up in a thick knot on the back of her head. She

had the family dark eyes and long thin nose, flaring slightly at
the nostrils. Despite her shortness of stature she held herself
regally, the result of early training with books balanced on her
head and boards slipped between her arms.

She was provincial in her outlook, having spent her entire
life in a rural section, but there was about her an arrogance
that boded no good when she fancied an insult, real or imagined. She was never fashionably dressed but somehow always
managed to look well groomed. She was the sort of woman
who fills in the neck of her dresses with bits of lace. Once Kate
had heard her described as "Cliff's Edge's animated antique,"
but Lucy never heard it. Small diamonds suspended on thin
gold wire glittered in her pierced ears, but they were no brighter than her small eyes which snapped, sometimes with humor,
sometimes with anger.

Lucy Leigh Allen had spent her early years protected first
by her father and then by the cousin she had married. She had
given every evidence of being the typical clinging vine, a tradition, however erroneous, in the family, but with the death of
her husband she had taken over the management of the small
property he had left and to the amazement of friends and relatives alike managed it well and efficiently. The bank had once
made a mistake in her statement, an error never repeated, for
she had left the president mopping his brow after her visit.

Indeed it was Lucy who had suggested the opening of Cliff's
Edge. When Kate, unhappy and lost after the death of her husband, returned to Alabama, Lucy had suggested that they pool
their resources and reopen the old house. In the four years
that had passed Kate had come a long way from the bereaved
widow, though she was still remote, satisfied with old friends,
guarded with strangers. She had achieved contentment but not
forgetfulness.

Four years of marriage to a successful advertiser had taught
Kate more than happiness. And it was this knowledge, applied,
that had made Cliff's Edge a happy hunting ground for wealthy
sportsmen. The sight-seeing part was Lucy's idea, and with a
little publicity of the right sort it, too, was proving profitable.

"Let me just put these bags down," Lucy said now in answer to Kate. "I'd better go up and see what should be done."
She carried a bag of lemons to the kitchen and after a few instructions to Ella rejoined the girl in the hall.

Together they climbed the steep back stairs and knocked op the door of the room at the head of the steps. It was immediately opened by Zack. This room was dominated by an enormous four-poster bed, the headboard heavily carved with a design of acanthus leaves. Four posts rose almost to the ceiling and supported a white canopy with a ruffled flounce.

"This is Mr. Dexter, Cu'un Lucy. Mrs. Allen. I'm sorry you're ill." Kate's clear eyes regarded the man propped up on the two larger-than-average pillows. "I brought you this. You'd better drink it now." She gave him the glass and turned to Lucy, disregarding the patient, as though he had no right to be consulted.

"What about a doctor?" she asked.

"Please don't go to any trouble," Alex put in anxiously. "I'll be all right. I was just weaker than I thought. I couldn't sleep very well last night, so I got up early and started on my way. I'd been driving around in no particular direction when I saw you. All I need is rest and quiet," he added with a significant look at Kate. "And I thought I could get it here as well as anywhere."

Kate looked down at him sharply. There were bleak lines about his hard, thin lips. New gray which had not been there a year ago showed at his temples. His eyes were dark, the color of gun-barrel blue steel, and the lids sagged as though it were an effort to keep them open. His body was excessively thin, and the hand that held the drink shook.

"Of course," said Lucy, "the country is the best place for quiet." She placed a small plump hand on his forehead. "You haven't any fever. I'll give Zack a bell for you so that you can ring for him if you need anything. The room is still chilly, Kate," she said, turning slightly. "Has the fire been lit long?"

"I sent Zack up to do it when he said he wanted a room. It takes a long time to heat this room." She walked over to the small grate and added two lumps to the bright blaze.

Alex Dexter finished the drink and lazily watched the two women. The hot whisky had relaxed him and he was drowsy. The room in which he had been placed seemed newer than what he had seen of the house. The paper was clean, and one wall looked entirely new. In this he was right, for Kate had cut off some six feet of the room, which, added to the depth of the chimney, had made a bathroom and closet space. It had made no appreciable loss in the size of the room, and the massive furniture did not look out of place.

The fire crackled pleasantly in the grate. Alex gazed at it as though it had been a long time since he had seen a really workable open fire. He shifted his body so that he could see it better. His eyelids drooped. Kate was sure he did not know when she closed the door softly behind her.

2

The days passed swiftly; days of rain and sunshine, of cold and warmth, for a Southern spring is more changeable than a woman. The river swelled with the spring rains, and the midstream grew more rapid as the big creeks joined it and flowed on its eternal way to the Gulf. The black earth took on new life as the early forsythia and jonquils began to bloom.

At first Alex was unaware of the changes around him. He was content to sleep in the great bed or to sit close to the fire. But gradually he began to take an interest in the people and the place. He had known few Southerners so intimately and he found them utterly unlike his imagination had pictured them. They bickered with the Negroes, argued with them, ignored their advice when given, but frequently followed it. And, strangely, they loved the black people and worried about them. They were charming, these Southerners, aggressive almost to the point of belligerency, passionate, and, above all, proud. They were not really so different from the people he had always known, but somehow, here in this remote section of the black belt, they had preserved a way of life that was different.

Alex was even beginning to understand the soft blurring of their words, the rolled vowels, and the chopped endings which were the language of the white people, though the Negro dialect was still largely unintelligible.

He found himself in a world of relatives, very old and very young, always addressed as cousin or aunt or uncle. Although he met many people he learned very little about them, even about those at Cliff's Edge. They were politely friendly, but always there was a reserved dignity about them.

Strange things, also, were happening to him. For the first time in years he found himself in a church, seated beneath a richly colored stained-glass window that bore the inscription: *For God So Loved the World That He Gave His Only Begotten Son.* And beneath it, in smaller letters, "In Memory of Charles Henry and Katherine Prudhomme Leigh." Glancing about in the semigloom, he saw that other windows bore the names of Leighs, Randalls, Brockways, and Allens. The quiet of the nave was broken only by a rustle of silk as the people rose or knelt. Each pew was carved with the trefoil of the Trinity, and the brass cross and candlesticks gleamed dully on a carved altar. Lucy stood next to him and forced his attention on the small prayer book in her hand, pointing to the place when his attention wandered, so that he could follow the responses.

In the small churchyard after service he met the people who crowded about Lucy and Uncle Brock, curious to know the stranger. He was bewildered by the unfamiliarity of his surroundings and was relieved when Kate blew the raucous horn of the station wagon which had brought them all to town.

Kate turned the car from Church Street into High, and soon they were bumping over a rough plantation road, the four white people crowded on the two front seats, while Eph rode in luxury on the back. The little Negro had been brought in to pump the antiquated organ which had wheezed out the anthems and songs during the service.

On the Tuesday following his church experience Alex wandered out of doors to find Kate working in the garden. Eph was spading the moist black earth while Kate worked with strings and stakes, trying to lay the space into geometrical beds.

"Lissun, Mis' Kate." Eph pulled the harmonica from his pocket and began a melody of steady beats and throbbing undertones. "Mis' Kate, do that soun' lak what yo' hear in them clubs?"

Kate sat back on her knees. "That's very good, Eph. Is it something you made up yourself?"

"Naw'm. I lissun'd to the radio t'other day, and they kep' playin' it ova and ova." He dug one ragged shoe into the ground.

"Well, you keep on trying, and one of these days maybe you can get a job with a good band. But you'll have to study. They don't play by ear." Kate measured her string, drove another stake into the ground, and tied the string to it.

Eph dug earnestly at the dirt, carefully picking up the large earthworms that rose to the surface with each spadeful and putting them into an old tin can.

"Mis' Kate? When yo' goin' give me that fiddle of yo' grandpa's? That'd 'scourage me a whole lot."

"Why, you little devil! That's what you're angling for. Well, I'm not going to give it to you till you learn to do the job you're supposed to be doing now. I never told you I'd give you the violin, did I?"

Kate rose and pulled off the clumsy cotton gloves that protected her hands. She stuffed them into the pockets of the red sweater which already bulged with string.

"Naw'm. But I 'spec's yo' will." Eph grinned up at her and went on with his work.

Catching sight of Alex at the end of the garden, Kate waved and came toward him.

"I think he can do the rest by himself," she said. "Want to come with me to the office and help me do some figuring?"

He nodded and fell into step with her as she led the way to the office.

Kate had come to accept him as a member of the household. There were no other guests, and after the first few days he had joined the family group. He seemed content to sit and talk or to wander aimlessly about the house and grounds. Rest and quiet were restoring his strength, but he showed no signs of leaving. One day he had followed Kate as she conducted a party of tourists over the house and the next day appointed himself as guide. But he had told such outlandish tales, even adding a fine ghost story to the legends, that Lucy had refused to let him repeat his performance.

The office was a sagging frame building some fifty feet back of the house. Kate inserted a large iron key and pushed open the door. The place was crowded with ledgers, art supplies, and shelves of junk that was just too good to throw away. A heavy iron safe stood in one corner, and a battered roll-top desk occupied another between two windows.

"We'll need some fire if we stay here long," Kate said. "Give me some of that paper and I'll get one started."

"You sit down. I'll build a fire for you." He knelt on the brick hearth and shifted paper and wood in the iron grate.

For a time there was no sound in the room except the sharp crackle as the paper caught fire. Alex watched it, then rose and brushed the dust from his knees.

"Push some of those papers off that chair and sit down," suggested Kate without looking up from the paper on which she was busily copying figures. "Check these figures for me, will you?"

Alex took the paper she handed him and quickly added the row of numbers.

"That's right," he said as he gave it back to her.

"I was afraid so. I thought I might have made a mistake."

There was a wistful note in her voice. "We had hoped to paint the outside of the house this summer. But I'm afraid it will have to wait till next summer—or the next."

She took the paper from him and stuffed it into an already overcrowded pigeonhole.

"One year won't make much difference." Alex tried to console her.

Kate laughed wryly. "That's what we say every year. Everything we've done so far has been inside. Bathrooms cost so darn much!"

"You mean there weren't any in that big house?"

"Not when it was built. Grandfather had one put in for that downstairs bedroom. You see, he and Grandmother lived out here, but my father was a doctor and we lived in town. That's been the story of the last two generations of Leighs. We went to other places to make enough money so we could afford to live here. My brother Jack's in the Navy, and I went to New York."

"You lived in New York?"

"Yes, I went there to study commercial art and married and—well, stayed."

"You married a Yankee?" Alex sounded scandalized.

Kate turned her face toward the window. Her eyes had taken on a lost look. There were times when Pete seemed very close.

"Yes," she said simply.

"You must be the one who paints." Alex, changing the subject, pointed to the dusty easel propped against the wall.

"Yes, but, frankly, I wasn't very good. I use my talent now in painting the house. Uncle Brock and I have done most of the interior decorating that's been done so far. We've painted the woodwork and scraped the floors and things of that sort."

Alex drew a pipe from the pocket of his coat and after fumbling in the other pockets found a thin leather pouch. He cupped his hands around the charred bowl, struck a match, inhaled, and blew out a puff of smoke.

There was a knock on the door.

"Come in," called Kate.

The door opened, and a chocolate-colored man in faded overalls came in. He took off his battered hat and stood there, uncertain of what he wanted to say. There was a sheepish grin on his face.

Kate pushed her chair around to face him.

"All right, Tom. What do you want?" She was accustomed to the darkies visiting her for a "tetch."

"Mis' Kate, I tho't yo' might wanta put me in 'at book."

"Put what in the book, Tom?"

"I'se gonna git ma'ad, Mis' Kate." A row of very white teeth showed between purplish-red lips.

"But you're already married, Tom. I wrote it down last fall."

"Naw'm, I ain't to say 'zackly ma'ad. That black gal ain't neva git her de-vorce, so we ain't been ma'ad."

"I see. Floss is going to get her divorce and then you're going to marry her again."

"Naw'm, not 'zackly. Floss, she goin' back to town, an' I'm gonna ma'a Penny."

"But Penny's no older—" Kate checked what she was going to say. "What does Fancy think of this?"

"Fancy say she ain't gonna live with no more stepmammas. She gittin' too big for her britches," Tom mumbled.

"Well, maybe we can find some place for her to stay up here at the house."

"Yas'm. I reckon so." Tom cast a side glance at Alex. "Yo' gonna put me an' Penny in 'at vile-sticks book now?"

"Not yet. When you get married come back and tell me. Then I'll put you in."

"Mis' Kate"—Tom lowered his voice to conspire with Kate alone—"gimme a cigarette."

"That's all you really wanted, Tom." Kate opened a drawer of the desk and found a crumpled package which she gave him.

With a grin that almost split his face Tom thanked her and left.

"Behold the conquering bridegroom." Kate turned to Alex and laughed at the utter confusion on his face.

He shook his head, rose, and knocked the bowl of the pipe against the side of the fireplace.

"Will you please tell me what a vile-sticks book is?" he demanded.

"It's a book of vital statistics," Kate explained, laughing. "I found an old slave record book when I first came here, so I just continued it. The county officers sometimes telephone me to get these records, so they really are useful."

"I see. But it still sounds strange."

"What's so strange about it? It happens nearly every day. They come and tell me when somebody dies or is born or gets married, and I write it down. It helps Uncle Brock keep a check on the Negroes on the plantation. There's the dinner bell. Come on, Ella'll be madder than a hornet if we keep her waiting."

As they closed the door and came out on the narrow gallery a man rode up on a powerful horse. Kate spoke to him.

"Hello, Jeff. It's been a long time since you came over to see us. Won't you come in and have dinner?"

"I brought you some fish I caught this morning." Jeff slid gracefully off his horse.

He was a tall, gaunt man with bloodshot gray eyes and sandy hair. His skin was sallow and puffed under deep-set eyes. He wore khaki trousers and shirt, faded almost white with many washings, and none too clean at the moment.

"I reckon I won't stay this time. I'll just give these to Ella." He held up a string of three large brook trout.

"This is Mr. Gaines, Mr. Dexter. Jeff's a cousin of mine."

Alex was surprised by the strong grip of the freckled hand, for though Jeff was lazy he spent much time out of doors, and under that lank frame were strong and powerful muscles.

"I reckon I won't stay, Kate," he repeated. "The others aren't too anxious to have me around." Jeff's voice was thin and reedy and irritated.

"Nonsense, of course you're coming." Kate slipped an arm through his and pulled him along with her. "Jeff helps me a lot with my hunting parties. He takes them out and sees that they don't shoot each other. I don't know what I'd do without him," she said to Alex.

"What she means is that I'm too lazy to do anything else," Jeff said.

"Oh, drop your grudge against the world for a little while, Jeff, and come on in and let's enjoy our dinner." She led them to the kitchen door. "You can wash up in Uncle Brock's room while I give these to Ella."

"I'll wash my hands here in the kitchen." Jeff followed her, and Alex went on down the hall and up the back steps.

"Here's some fish we can have for supper. You'd better clean them right after dinner." Kate gave the fish to Ella. "And, Eph," she added to the little Negro who crouched close to the range, "you go tie up Mr. Jeff's horse right now."

She washed her hands at the sink and with Jeff went into the dining room, where the other three were already seated and waiting.

Uncle Brock frowned when he saw Jeff, and Kate laid her hand on his arm as though to prevent him from some act of violence.

"Jeff brought us a mess of fish for supper, and I asked him to stay for dinner," she said quietly. "Zack will set another place for him beside me."

The room was still, and Kate realized that even Alex, a stranger, would feel the undercurrent of emotions and wonder. Then Lucy nodded and there was a polite, subdued murmur of voices. Kate closed her eyes and breathed a private prayer while Uncle Brock repeated the words of a conventionalized grace.

In this strained atmosphere Kate tried to make the conversation natural, but Uncle Brock was silent, and Jeff did nothing to help her. Alex was too engrossed in his food to be of much help. To him each meal was a revelation. It was the most amazing thing he had found in the South; vegetables cooked with meat which looked most unappetizing but which were wonderfully seasoned; hot bread, especially the coarse, unsweetened corn bread; beans they called peas, and always a heavy meat course. These people seemed inordinately fond of rice too. They ate it at least once a day and often more than once.

He was learning to like the highly seasoned food, and Kate told him that he was fast becoming a gourmand. Once when he had told Lucy he had enjoyed a meal she sent him back to tell Ella. Since that time he had become a favorite in the kitchen, and Ella had confided to Kate that she was determined to "put some meat on dat bag o' bones."

"Jeff," said Kate, "I'm expecting a visitor after Easter and I'd like to have her see your house while she's here. She's a decorator and is interested in antiques and old places." She lifted the heavy silver pot beside her. "Will anybody else have coffee?"

She poured out black coffee for herself and Jeff.

"I don't think your friend would be interested in coming to The Laurels."

"I don't wonder you're ashamed to show anybody that place. It's little more than a pigsty," growled Uncle Brock in an undertone, and Kate sent him a pleading look.

Fortunately the telephone shrilled two short rings, which was their signal, and presently Zack came back to the dining room to tell Kate she was wanted. She was gone only a few minutes and when she returned there was a worried frown on her face.

"What was it?" asked Lucy, and all the others waited expectantly.

"It was a telegram from Kitty. She's arriving this afternoon and wants me to meet her."

There was an absolute stillness in the room when she made this announcement. Jeff stiffened in his chair, and his eyes narrowed craftily; Lucy's eyes glittered, and the hand that held her glass of water paused momentarily in mid-air. Alex stirred uneasily, as though he sensed the antagonism of these people.

The rest of the meal was eaten in complete silence. Each seemed preoccupied with some obscure thought of his own. The hostility between Uncle Brock and Jeff was almost forgotten in the light of the newer event.

When dinner was over Alex went to the parlor and drew a chair close to the window. From it he watched Jeff ride away, man and horse somehow looking as though they belonged together, the lines of one flowing into the lines of the other. From a distance it made Jeff look like some reincarnated centaur.

Seated as Alex was, screened from the door, he became the unwilling eavesdropper as Kate and Lucy came into the room.

"Why did you have to ask Jeff to stay to dinner?" demanded Lucy.

"Cu'un Lucy, you know why. He doesn't get half enough to eat at home. He looks positively starved all the time."

"Well, if he had any ambition or any energy he'd do something with that place of his. He just hasn't the gumption to help himself."

"Jeff's pitiful somehow, Cu'un Lucy. Maybe we wouldn't amount to much if we had to live with that stepmother of his."

"Always drunk, always lazy. A more worthless man I never saw," grumbled Lucy.

"He wasn't drunk today. And he *did* bring us the fish."

"He'll never amount to a hill of beans. He had a chance, and look what he did with it. Coming home from Auburn because

he said it interfered with his hunting. And that father of his!
The only man I've ever known who drank himself into a stupor
regularly. Never saw him after Louisa died when he wasn't so
drunk he couldn't hit the floor with his hat. Jeff's going to be
just like him. He is already."

"Hush, Cu'un Lucy! You don't know what Jeff's had to put
up with. And he's a big help to me." Kate spoke quietly but
emphatically.

"Well, I'll have to admit that you're the only one that can
get him to do a thing. I only wish you'd use your influence to
make him look and act more decently."

"I can't do that. I know Jeff's on the downgrade, but I can't
stop him. He doesn't want to be stopped."

"I hate for folks to see him."

"He's kin to us, you remember. And I won't send him away
from any house that's mine." Kate's eyes flashed with anger.

Lucy snorted, undaunted by Kate's reply, and threw back
her head so that the small diamonds in her ears glittered.

"You're only making trouble for yourself. Associating with
po' white trash is making Jeff one of them." Lucy changed the
subject abruptly: "What time are you going into town?"

"The train gets in at four, so probably leave a little after
three. There are one or two things I want to get. Is there anything I can do for you?"

"If I think of anything I'll let you know. Brock wants to
go with you. He says he has some business to attend to. Call
him when you're ready. I have to get Fancy and straighten up
a room. Why didn't Kitty let us know sooner? She'll complain,
regardless of what we do for her. Why she wants to come down
here is more than I know."

Lucy bustled out and Kate followed her. Alex, who had
been acutely embarrassed throughout the conversation, whis-
tled thinly. He was catching a glimpse of the undercurrents of
the family, the skeletons that were beginning to rattle fitfully
in the closets.

3

When they reached the town Kate dropped Uncle Brock at the bank.

"You'd think we lived a million miles from town," she told him as she parked the car on a side street. "Everybody has given me a list of things to get: Cu'un Lucy wants groceries; Ella wants snuff; Alex wants pipe tobacco. How do they expect me to do my own errands? I hoped I'd have time to run by and see Mary's new baby."

"You've got an hour at least," Uncle Brock assured her absently. "You ought to be able to do most of those things in that time. I've seen you get things done in a jiffy when you're in a hurry. I'll try to be ready so I can go to the train with you, but if I'm not on the corner don't wait for me. I'll meet you at the courthouse when you're ready to go back."

"I'll see you later." Kate slammed the car door and made her way toward the stores lining the four sides of the town square which held the white plaster courthouse.

This building was saved from mediocrity by its wrought-iron railings and balcony. In its own way it was a gem of Southern architecture of the ante-bellum period. It was old, but it had aged gracefully, and the town had slowly grown up around its four sides. Once the town had been the thriving market center for the large plantations which covered the county, but it had lapsed into a dreamy, dusty village, almost forgotten in the present-day rush of industry and progress.

Kate paused to speak to most of the people she passed but hurried once she was in the stores. The clerks were familiar, so she gave Lucy's list to one and told him she'd pick it up on her way home.

The pipe mixture gave her some trouble. Alex had given her an order for a special blend, and she had to telephone him to see if some substitute would do.

"I'll never promise to shop for other people again as long as I live," she told the druggist as she hung up the receiver. "He says this will do."

"Oh yes, you will, Kate," he replied. "You're just like your father. He'd come in here to get prescriptions filled for his patients and then take the medicine out to them."

He gave her a small package, and she turned to leave. Two men who had been playing checkers in the back of the room interrupted her.

"Kate, how about letting us have a fox hunt over at your place pretty soon?"

"Why, of course, Mr. Bob. You know you're welcome any time. You want to have it right away?"

"Nope. Say in about two weeks. Sure it'll be all right?"

"The roads are pretty muddy, but you're welcome. Let me know when you plan to come. Some of the darkies get scared when they hear the dogs if we don't tell them to expect it."

"I'll telephone you when we want to come. And thanks a lot, Kate," he called to her retreating figure.

Kate hurried, for she was a little late. She heard the train give its signal as she reached the car. Just about time to get to the station, she thought, but I'll be out of breath.

Uncle Brock was not at the appointed corner, so she got into the car and drove quickly to the station, parking the car just as the train steamed by, coughed, and came to a stop.

Kate walked down the track toward the Pullman, where a colored porter was setting an array of smart luggage on the sidewalk. These were soon followed by a small and beautiful woman. The conductor was deference itself, and Kitty accepted it as only her due. She tipped the colored man, smiled pleasantly to the conductor, and came to meet her cousin. The two women embraced coolly, and Kitty laid a soft, scented cheek against Kate's.

They were alike and yet very unlike. A fashionable coiffure of ebony hair framed Kitty's oval face, and her dark eyes, though smaller than Kate's and surrounded by incredibly long sooty lashes, looked out appealingly beneath neatly arched brows. Her features were like those of a cameo: a slender nose, high cheekbones, and a soft, petulant mouth above a firm, rounded chin. It was not the face of a strong character, for it too plainly betrayed her temperament—shallow, vain, willful. But in its way it was beautiful, and Kitty was pleased. Her figure left nothing to be desired, and she adorned this shell with simply cut though daringly designed clothes, which always drew the attention she so avidly craved.

"It's good of you to meet me," murmured Kitty with tears in her eyes.

"We're glad you could come."

"Kate darling, I just couldn't stand it another minute."

She seated herself beside Kate and turned the rear-vision mirror so that she could readjust her small blue hat at just the right angle.

"Couldn't stand what?" Kate asked bluntly.

"But Ralph, of course. He's getting old, positively ancient. And he is so disagreeable." She tossed her head just as a thoroughbred horse does when he knows he's on display.

"Does he know where you are?" Kate was amused and curious at the same time.

"Of course not," Kitty replied with annoyance. "He's such a beast. He might actually try to beat me." Her eyes narrowed so that the soft contours of her face sharpened with an almost feral look.

Kate took the time to wonder fleetingly if Kitty had come to Cliff's Edge in order to give Ralph Bolling's temper time to cool. After all, he was a very rich man, and she would think twice before divorcing him. She had already made two profitable trips to Reno, and Kate shuddered to think that she might be planning a third. But on second thought she decided she was wrong. Kitty's life was easy and luxurious, and she intended to keep it so. All she wanted was absolute control, and she probably thought a little worry on Ralph's part would hasten that day.

"We have to pick up Uncle Brock at the courthouse. He came into town with me. He had some business to attend to or he'd have been at the station to meet you."

Kitty looked about her at the streets teeming with Negroes who had come in from the country. "How you can bury yourself in this place is more than I can understand," she remarked.

"Oh, I like it here. It's peaceful and quiet and—well, it's home."

"But it is so provincial. I'll never understand why you didn't stay in New York where there were some opportunities. You look as countrified now as the rest of these people." Kitty opened her purse and drew out a slim silver-gilt cigarette case. "Have one?" she offered.

Kate shook her head. "There's Uncle Brock now."

She parked the car at the curb, and Uncle Brock opened the door.

"Well, Kitty, my dear, this is a surprise." He leaned forward and kissed the cheek she turned toward him.

"I have to pick up the groceries Cu'un Lucy ordered, but I'll be back in just a minute." Kate got out quickly, pushed the door to behind her, and crossed the street.

"Kate could spend a little more time on her appearance, couldn't she?" Kitty flicked the ash from her cigarette.

"Kate has other things to occupy her time," Uncle Brock replied dryly, with a slight emphasis on the name which brought a frown to Kitty's placid brow.

Before anything else could be said Kate came out of the store, followed by a little boy covered in a long white apron and carrying a large paper bag.

Uncle Brock held open the door and helped the boy as Kate slid back into her seat.

"Did you finish your business?" Kate asked, noting the stoop of his shoulders was more pronounced and that he looked tired.

"Most of it," he replied, and a frown corrugated his fore-head.

"Isn't that Alicia Randall?" asked Kitty. "What a horrible, fantastically ugly hat."

"She'll probably be coming out to see you, Kitty," said Uncle Brock, the frown extending to his weary blue eyes.

"Oh, all right." Kitty shrugged her trim shoulders. "But you know we never cared for each other even when I was here as a child."

As the car turned off from town into the highway Kitty gave her full attention to the man on the seat behind her. It did not matter that he was old and tired; he was a man, and Kitty couldn't have been around the archangel Gabriel without being personal. She told him of her troubles, of her husband's mis-treatment, and Uncle Brock responded with a sort of preoccu-pied sympathy. If Kitty noticed his inattention she gave no sign of it but went on with her list of woes until Kate wondered if so much fiendishness could be found in one man.

When they turned in at the gates Uncle Brock got out and opened them, closing them as the car passed. They rocked on over the rutted muddy road to the house.

There was some confusion as they drew up before the steps. Lucy came to meet them and greeted Kitty cordially, though there was a sour droop to her mouth. Zack and Fancy began to take the numerous bags out of the car.

"You'd better put the heavy ones in the elevator, Zack," ad-vised Kate. "There're too many for you to carry upstairs to her room."

As she started toward the door Uncle Brock put a hand on her arm.

"Is the office locked?"

"I think I locked it when I left this morning. Do you want to get in?"

"I'd like to put some papers in the safe."

"All right. Come on in and I'll get the key for you. I think I left it in my room. Let me see about Kitty first and I'll bring it down to you."

Kitty was busy giving orders to Fancy, the high-yellow up-stairs maid, so after a moment or two Kate went down the hall to her own room. The key was on the tall old-fashioned marble-top dresser.

"Here it is, Uncle Brock." She leaned over the last banisters and gave it to him. "Do you want me to put the things away for you?"

"No, thanks, just some papers I got from the bank. I'll put them in the safe myself. I want to make a call on that phone, anyway."

Kate watched him go through the dining room. There was an outside door there which led directly to the office. He seemed depressed, and she wondered if he had got bad news in town. His gait was slow and dragging, unlike his usual springy steps. His bristling hair hung limp and bedraggled on his forehead. Kate turned away and went to the parlor, where Alex was sitting before the fire, a book laid over his knees.

"Did your cousin arrive safely?" he asked politely.

"Yes, and here's your tobacco. Sorry we can't provide the kind you wanted, but you should remember we live in a country town, not in a big city that can cater to special tastes."

"Oh, that's all right. I'm sorry I put you to so much trouble. Sit down, you look tired." He smiled up at her, and there was a friendly warmth in his dark blue eyes. "Here, have a cigarette. That'll pick you up."

He offered her his case and, cupping his hands about the flame, watched the light of the match reflected on her face. She sat down and looked up at the portrait of the woman over the mantel.

"Well, we have three Katherine Leighs under the same roof now. Two live ones and a painted one." She grinned at him engagingly.

"Is your cousin very much like you?"

"Like me?" Kate was startled. "Good lord, no. Here we are both named the same thing, yet she's called Kitty and I'm just plain Kate. That ought to tell you the difference. You'll see for yourself at supper." She glanced up at the tiny clock set in the middle of the mantel. "I had no idea it was so late. I'll have to clean up or Kitty will think we've become uncivilized down here in the sticks."

"Does this new arrival call for a dinner jacket?" Alex asked, rising with her.

"No indeed. I can't vouch for what Kitty will wear. She may come down in a sensible dress or she may come prepared for the Stork Club. The rest of us will dress as usual." Her eyes went over him appraisingly. "You stay here and read if you want to. What have you found to entertain yourself?"

Alex held up a heavy brown volume mildewed on one corner. "Scott," he said ruefully. "It was all I could find."

Kate laughed, and her face was almost transformed. It was so different from the still, immobile look with which he was so familiar. Alex was surprised to find that there could be fun, even gaiety, in those clear black eyes. It was like meeting someone he had not seen for a long time.

"God pity you," she said. "The first winter I was here I read them all. My great-grandfather must have admired the writer very much. As for me, it was the lesser of the evils. All the other books are heavy religious tracts or small-print biographies. I'll leave you to your romance." Her eyes mocked him as she spoke the last words over her shoulder.

Alex turned back to the flyleaf and read the signature, a flowery, fine script, the ink turned a pale brown with age: "Henry Prudhomme Leigh, October 1848." He turned back to his place and tried to interest himself in the chivalrous exploits of the characters. He had been reading most of the afternoon and had hardly made a dent in the book which could only be described by the word "tome." He came to a paragraph of solid print and flicked the page over, and the next. He read again and discovered that he had not lost the thread of the story. It became a game, then, to see how much he could omit and still get a sense of the theme. He was as delighted as though he had discovered something new.

He turned the pages absently until Lucy opened the door and joined him. She moved restlessly about the room, picking up some needlework she did at night, and finally settled into a chair opposite him. Alex made several efforts at conversation, but she quite evidently wasn't listening and only replied absently. When Uncle Brock came in she jumped as though she were startled.

"Oh, it's you," she said. "I wonder what can be keeping Kate and Kitty. Ella wants to get off early tonight. There's some sort of big church meeting down at Ebenezer."

"It's not late. They'll be along any minute." Uncle Brock sought to reassure her.

As though waiting for a cue, Kate opened the door, and she and Kitty came toward the fire. Kitty had not dressed formally, but the severe black wool dress she wore was subtle and breathed an exclusive designer with every flick of the skirt. It was unadorned, but she had added several heavy gold bracelets which jangled as she moved her hands, and matching gold clips were fastened to her ears. Kate offered no competition in her simple blue crepe which reflected blue shadows on the warm-colored skin of her face.

"Kitty, I want you to meet our only guest at present. This is Alex Dexter, Mrs. Bolling."

"Why, Alex darling! Fancy meeting you down here. What ever dragged you away from the bright lights of the city?" Kitty came toward him both hands extended.

Alex took her hands in his. "This is a surprise. I had no idea that you were the cousin they expected."

"This is sort of out of my setting, isn't it?" Kitty gave a bell-like laugh and turned to the others. "Alex and I are old friends. I met him several years ago and saw a great deal of him when I was in Philadelphia last fall." She slipped her arm through his and clung to him, the long red nails clawing hungrily at his sleeve.

"Suppa's on de table," Zack announced and held open the door.

It was a strange meal. The fried fish, the hot corn bread, the field peas, and finally the strawberries with thick cream were tasty, but Uncle Brock ate as though it were sawdust. Kitty kept up a running chatter with Alex about people and places with which the others were unfamiliar Alex made one or two attempts to include them, but Kitty had no idea of letting the conversation with him become anything other than intimate. She was so vivacious and attentive that the young man soon forgot everything else. Kate watched them with amused detachment before retreating once more into her own private world of impersonality.

With the meal over, Lucy took control of the situation. Her lips were drawn into a thin line of determination, and there was an angry glint in her beady black eyes. Even Kitty was forced to bend before the older woman's will. A bridge table was set up in the parlor, and they got out the cards. Kate would have liked to sneak away, but only Brock was allowed to leave when he told Lucy he had to go to the office to look over some papers.

Kitty was a shrewd and daring player, and she and Alex scored heavily after a series of intricate bids. Lucy's eyes snapped with pleasure. She was possessed of that rare thing, a sense of cards, which had been intensified since she had deprived herself of the weekly bridge club during Lent. The fact that she had forced two Methodists and a Presbyterian into observing her church season only added to her pleasing sense of martyrdom.

Kate herself was not a brilliant player, but she was steady, not given to the erratic bidding that sometimes guided Kitty's playing. In this way the scores maintained something of an even level. Alex was tired, and Kitty's constantly whispered words soon became irritating. Playing bridge with three women was not his idea of pleasure, especially as Kate seemed to smirk at his discomfiture, and he made a firm resolve never to be caught again.

Once when she was dummy Kate, with a murmured "Excuse me," left the room. She hurried through the cold hall and into the dining room, where the dim remains of the fire still smoldered in one of the fireplaces. Skirting the table, she went to the door opening into the yard.

There was a light in the office, and Kate could see Uncle Brock at the desk. While she watched he turned to somebody in the room, and she saw him wave his arm toward the door. A moment later the outside door was thrust open, and Jeff strode angrily down the steps, swung quickly onto his horse, and galloped away as the door banged loudly.

Kate watched him, her hand frozen on the doorknob. For some reason she was frightened.

But there is no reason to be frightened, Kate tried to reassure herself. It was not the fact that Jeff and Uncle Brock had been talking, even quarreling, but there had been such an urgency about Jeff as he left. The shadows in the room seemed to loom larger as the glow on the hearth became dimmer. Kate turned and fled.

She opened the parlor door breathlessly and slid quickly into her chair.

"We made it, pardner," said Lucy in a satisfied voice.

"You were gone long enough," Kitty said. "What in the world were you doing?"

"I wondered if Uncle Brock had shut the back door," Kate lied. "Whose deal is it?"

"It's mine," Alex told her. "Will you cut?"

"I don't suppose there's a chance we could get something to drink?" Kitty inquired.

"I'm afraid we haven't what you want," Kate replied smoothly, and Alex looked up with a knowing glint in his eyes. "There's some sherry here, though, and when Uncle Brock comes back I'll get it."

Before the hand was finished Uncle Brock came in, and Lucy asked him to bring the decanter and glasses from the sideboard. When he returned with the tray Lucy poured out the wine. For the moment conversation became general as they sipped or twirled the stems of the small glasses between their fingers. The tiny clock on the mantel tinkled ten o'clock, and Uncle Brock turned on the radio for the news.

Kitty was bored and, making little effort to conceal it, tried to draw Alex aside. But he was weary and, with an adroitness that surprised and amused Kate, avoided entangling alliances.

Uncle Brock clicked the radio silent, and Lucy immediately declared it was time for bed. She ruthlessly overrode Kitty's protests and herded them up the stairs. When Kate had gone about halfway Uncle Brock called her back and gave her the office key. The others had already disappeared when she reached the second floor, and she hurried thankfully to her own sanctuary.

She had just slipped off her dress and sat down on the low slipper chair to take off her shoes and stockings when there was a light tap and Lucy opened the door.

"Kate," she began without preamble, "Kitty is up to her old tricks. She may be married again, but that isn't keeping her roving eye at home. Well, what's the explanation for this visit?"

"Some sort of quarrel with her husband, I gather. I think she came down here to give him time to come round to her way of thinking."

"Is she getting another divorce?" Lucy questioned sharply.

"No, I don't think so," Kate replied slowly. "She has more to gain by staying married to Ralph Bolling."

"Kitty was always vain and a scheming hussy too. I declare, I'm glad her mother's dead so she can't see her now."

"Kitty lived out here more than I did, you remember. Maybe it seems like home to her."

"Nonsense," Lucy retorted. "She don't want a home. She'll have this place upside down in a week. You saw how Jeff looked when you told us the news at dinner. And she had Leigh hanging around her all one summer if I remember right. And now she knows Alex." Lucy looked broken, almost old.

Kate rose and put an arm around her. "Cheer up, nobody's dead. Kitty won't stay long," but her voice lacked conviction.

"Fiddlesticks!" Lucy regained some of her asperity. "She's a troublemaker. And the situation here is made to order. Kate"— Lucy laid her hand on the girl's arm—"I don't want her to get Alex. He's a nice boy."

"Alex can look after himself. It's Jeff I'm worried about."

"No need to waste sympathy on him. You like Alex, don't you?" Lucy came back to the point she had in mind.

"Why, of course." Kate's clear eyes regarded the older woman seated on the other side of the fireplace. "Don't get any fancy notions, Cu'un Lucy."

"I'd like to see you happy again. You're still young." Lucy's face softened with affection.

"I'm happy enough."

"No. I think you're perhaps content, but that isn't the sort of happiness I mean. You're too self-satisfied, Kate."

"You always were an incorrigible matchmaker, Lucy Allen. That's why I had to go to New York to pick a husband for myself."

"There's been too much happening here today; it's enough to upset us all. But, Kate, I do mean what I said about Kitty. If she starts wrecking any more homes and lives I'll choke some sense into her with my very own hands." She tossed her head, and the diamonds in her ears caught and reflected the angry red of the firelight.

"Go to bed. Goodness knows we all need some rest."

4

The day after Kitty arrived Leigh and Alicia Randall drove out to the big house. Kate, walking up from the river bluff, met them as the car drew to a stop.

"You're getting to be perfect strangers. You haven't been out here in a month of Sundays." She smiled with real affection at Leigh, and he threw an arm around her shoulders and gave her a warm hug.

Alicia watched them with compressed lips. She was a thin woman on the wrong side of thirty, with angles where there should have been curves. Her blonde hair was bleached-looking even in winter, though its color was natural. The remains of a permanent crinkled the ends, but since she made only erratic efforts to care for it, it always looked like what Lucy called a "hurrah's nest." Her fair, translucent skin and pale blue eyes finished the picture of a washed-out blonde.

"Come on in out of the wind." Kate took Alicia's hand and pulled her up the step. "I think the others are in the parlor. How did you happen to get off this afternoon?" she asked, turning back to Leigh.

"There aren't enough law cases in this county to keep me busy every afternoon. I decided I might as well come out here, and when I called Alicia she said she'd come too."

I'll bet she did, thought Kate. She wouldn't risk you coming out here alone to see me, much less Kitty.

"Alicia," she said aloud, "look at my wisteria. I've got a bud or two and I believe it will be in full bloom in a week." She pointed to the vine climbing over the wires at the end of the veranda, where yellowish-green cones were turning a faint purple.

"Mine's already in bloom." Alicia turned myopic eyes in the direction of Kate's pointing finger. "You ought to train that on the end column."

"I'm waiting to get it painted first"—a rueful smile twisted the corners of her lips—"but the Lord only knows when that will be."

She opened the door and led them to the parlor.

Alex and Kitty were seated on one side of the fireplace with a backgammon board between them, and Lucy flanked the other side, a determined duenna. They rose when the door was opened.

"Leigh darling!" Kitty threw her arms around his neck and pursed her lips for him to kiss.

"Here's Alicia too," said Kate.

"Oh, hello, Alicia," Kitty replied and then turned back to Leigh, as though she had not been interrupted. "I'm so glad you came out to see me. I've been asking all about you."

Alicia's eyes were as hard as agates and she was actually trembling. She was a possessive woman, and the fact that Kitty had practically stolen Leigh from under her nose the summer they were engaged was known to everybody in the room except Alex.

All Alex actually saw was a stockily-built man of average height with thinning brown hair and a weak receding chin. Leigh was an easygoing young man, always pleasant, always agreeable.

"It's good to have you back," Leigh said to Kitty and doubtless would have liked to add that she was more beautiful than ever. But he knew his wife and kept silent.

"Yes," Alicia cut in, her fingers creasing a sharp pleat in her skirt. "Are you on your way to Reno again?"

Kitty's eyes narrowed angrily, but she replied smoothly enough.

"Why should you think a visit here intimates a divorce?"

"It usually has in the past." Alicia's voice dripped venom. "And how can we judge the future but by the past?" She took a cigarette from her purse and lit it. Her fingers trembled slightly, and Kitty smiled.

"How rude you are getting, Alicia, not to offer any of us one," she said pleasantly.

Both men drew out their cases and offered them to Kitty immediately. She chose a cigarette from Alex and let Leigh light it for her.

"Thank you," she said, looking up through her long lashes.

Leigh lit a cigarette for himself, and Alex pulled out his old brier pipe. He dipped the bowl into a leather pouch and pressed the tobacco firm with his thumb.

Alicia arose abruptly. She rested her arm on the mantel, her back turned, as though she could not face the people in the room for the moment. A few short puffs and she threw the half-smoked cigarette into the fire.

"Then why have you come?" she demanded, turning to face Kitty.

Kitty let the smoke from her cigarette curl sensuously from her nostrils before she replied.

"I came for a nice quiet rest in the country." She spoke slowly, letting each word cut through the breathless stillness of the room.

For a minute Kate thought Alicia would strike Kitty. There was a blazing fury in her pale eyes. It was plainly written on her face that she wanted to destroy this antagonist, destroy her with a jealous frenzy.

"Why don't you play something for us, Kitty?" asked Lucy, her face flushed with anger at what she considered an ill-bred scene.

"Perhaps that is best." Kitty shrugged her rounded shoulders delicately and rose with the lithe grace of a tigress.

Alex went with her to the old piano and, laying aside the pouch which he was still holding, opened it for her. Leigh cast a contemptuous glance at his wife and followed them. Under his gaze Alicia whitened.

Kitty smiled demurely. She seated herself on the old-fashioned stool, twirling it once to adjust it, and smoothed the soft green wool dress which clung to her body like the sheath of a rosebud. Drawing two heavy gold bracelets from her wrist, she laid them on the piano and ran her fingers lightly over the yellowed keys.

"I'm afraid you'll find it terribly out of tune," said Kate.

"I don't doubt that, but maybe we can get some sort of music out of it. It used to have a tinkling tone something like a harpsichord," she explained with a glance at Alex.

Kate turned her face away quickly. Her eyes were unhappy, and her face was drawn and worried. Even then she did not realize that she was slowly coming back to a world of emotions and that the impenetrable stillness that had encased her like a hard shell for the past four years was broken.

Alex spoke softly to Kitty, and she answered with a quickening laugh.

"This?" she said.

She had a natural talent for music and, had she really worked, might have done something with it. Instead she had been content with skimming the surface, improvising where memory failed. Nevertheless, she played with verve and some skill.

Lucy was becoming more irritated. Kate stared vaguely out of the window and was of no help. All her attempts to distract Alicia were useless. Alicia replied, answered questions, but her eyes continually returned to the trio at the piano. Her hands clenched, and there was a tenseness about her thin body that was antagonistic. Alicia was a good hater.

Kitty had no real interest in Leigh; he lacked the virility and strength that she desired in her men. She only played with him to see how far she could goad Alicia, and the pleasure she derived from it was immeasurable.

Kate's thoughts were jerked back to the present with an alarming suddenness. Through the window she could see Jeff riding swiftly over the lawn toward the house. Without a word of explanation she left the room. The others watched her leave in surprise, and Kitty raised her eyebrows until they were almost perfect arches over her bright, malicious eyes.

Kate was beyond caring about the abruptness of her departure. She only knew that she had to prevent Jeff's entering that room. It would be like throwing kerosene on a smoldering fire. For Kate knew positively what Lucy did not, that Jeff had left college not because of the hunting season, but because he had thought Kitty was going to marry him.

She opened the front door as he slid from his horse and went forward to meet him. He stood unsteadily, holding tightly to the bridle for support, and his voice was thick and slow, as though he formed each word deliberately before he allowed the sound to leave his throat.

"Well?"

"I'm so glad you came this afternoon, Jeff. I wanted to ask you something about the horses. Come on in and I'll get a coat and we can go straight to the stable." She spoke hastily, the words tumbling over themselves.

"Came to see Kitty," he mumbled and stumbled on the lowest step.

Kate caught his arm and steadied him. "You can see her in a little while. I need you." She looked up at him pleadingly. "Please, Jeff."

He searched her face as though he expected to find some devious cunning there and then, still holding to her, followed her inside. The music came faintly through the heavy doors and he stopped.

"Came to see Kitty," he repeated.

"Not now. You must come with me." Kate picked up a coat which had been thrown over a chair in the hall and drew it carelessly around her shoulders. She half pulled him through the cross hall and into the dining room, where he stumbled again over one of the chairs, upsetting it. Kate drew a sobbing gasp and jerked him toward the back door.

Eph was sweeping the hard-packed dirt of the back yard, a cloud of dust rising from each dragging whisk of the old broom. Kate nodded to him that he was to follow, and the little boy's eyes opened so wide that the whites were like circles in his coal-black face. Kate needn't have bothered, for, with a Negro's intuition for impending tragedy and an innate curiosity, he would have followed anyhow.

Will was in the stable, piling hay into the cribs, when they opened the heavy wooden door. He looked up in surprise at this sudden intrusion.

"I want Mr. Jeff to see that scratch on Star's foreleg. He's just the one to tell us what to do with it."

"Sho is," replied the startled Negro.

Will took off his torn felt hat and scratched the kinky wool behind his left ear. It seemed to Kate that each kink rose in a doubtful question mark. All farm management was in the hands of Uncle Brock. The fact that he wasn't, and never would be, a farmer was borne out by the poor fields and meager crops. But Kate knew, and so did Will, that he would not want her to consult Jeff even on a minor injury to one of the animals on the place.

"Star's right here, Jeff. Will, you bring him out to the light so Mr. Jeff can see."

"Sho will." The Negro turned a large black horse out into the narrow open space and, catching the dangling forelock, pulled the horse toward the open door.

As soon as Jeff's attention was diverted Kate beckoned Eph.

"Run up to the house," she whispered, "and get Ella to send me a pot of coffee quick. If she hasn't any get me something else quick."

She gave him a shove and the boy was off, his thin legs leaping over the hard ground. There was a large snag in his ragged overalls, and the black of bare buttocks showed as the tear flapped with his movements.

"Nothing wrong with the horse," Jeff said, advancing toward the door.

"Sho ain't," agreed Will.

"Jeff, are they getting enough exercise?" Kate asked desperately. "I never have time to ride, and there's always something to do at the house or somebody comes in."

"Look al' right." Jeff turned to the four stalls again.

"Do you think we're feeding them the right kind of hay?"

"'S all right," Jeff said.

"Well, look at this one, will you? Uncle Brock was riding her over the field the other day, and she kept jerking the bridle out of his hand. Is there something wrong with her mouth?"

Somehow Kate managed to hold Jeff there with the horses. Afterward she didn't know how she did it. It was a cold day, and the March wind was damp and penetrating. It whipped color into her cheeks, and the tail of the coat was slapping her legs. She slipped her arms into the sleeves and only then realized she had picked up the lightweight brown overcoat Leigh had worn. It drooped sadly over her smaller body.

At last Eph returned, hurrying in with a teapot and a cup and saucer on a small tin tray. A trail of brown liquid had sloshed over the side of the pot, but Kate took the tray as though it were manna from heaven.

"Here's some coffee, Jeff. It's so cold I knew you'd like it," she said pouring the steaming coffee into the cup.

Jeff took it and drank greedily. He sat on a bale of hay as he drank, but his eyes never left Kate.

"Go on back to your sweeping, Eph. Thanks for bringing us the coffee."

Jeff handed his empty cup to Will and then, with head bent, ran his blunt, reddened fingers through his hair.

Kate watched him silently, pity shining through the dark of her eyes. Yet she knew that was the last thing he wanted; pity was the one thing he could not stand. So when she spoke her words were flat and toneless.

"You had better not go up to the house this afternoon, Jeff."

"I know you brought me down here to sober me up, Kate." He looked up at her with a bleak smile. "That's all right. You needn't worry. I won't go up to the house." He buried his head in his hands.

"You'll have to see her sometime. You can't always avoid her." Kate sat down beside him and brushed away a stiff spike of hay that clung to her coat. "But not this afternoon, please.

You see, Leigh and Alicia are up there now, and Alicia had just created the most God-awful scene. You know what she can do when she gets started."

"I'm glad you headed me off then." He pushed back the long sleeve and took her cold hand. "Why do I have to see her? Why does she come back here?" he demanded and then went on before Kate could answer: "I know her and I hate her very guts. And still I can't stay away."

"That's Kitty, Jeff. You can't change human nature. Do you remember how she always had all of you around when she came here as a little girl? Leigh started helping me carve *Cave Canem* over the doghouse that summer I was a freshman in high school. And then Kitty came, and it was never finished." Kate gave a short laugh. "I was so very jealous of her then. She had you and Leigh and Jack, and I didn't have anybody."

"You aren't jealous of her any more?"

"No." She spoke thoughtfully and as though her own words surprised her. "I don't think I am. She lives on surface emotions and sensations. She's shallow and vain and—determined. Somehow, though, I don't think she's ever known what it is to be really happy. Maybe I'm a little sorry for her."

"I don't love her any more." Jeff half whispered the words.

Kate shifted her position and caught sight of Will, his eyes enormous in his black face. She had forgotten him, but she knew that every detail of this conversation would be broadcast to every Negro on the place over the devious route of their grapevine telegraph before nightfall. The strange doings of the white folks would be common gossip in every town kitchen by morning.

"Will," she said, "go around to the front of the house and bring Mr. Jeff's horse back here. He'll be riding back over the fields."

Will hesitated, hating to leave, but finally ambled out of the stable, the soles of his worn shoes softly slapping the ground. Jeff did not look up; he seemed scarcely aware of the presence of the Negro, but he was silent until the door had closed with a creaking bang.

"That's all over, Kate," he said at last. "That's why I came. I wanted to see her once so I could tell her she didn't mean anything to me."

Kate moved closer, for the wind was swirling through the wide cracks of the frame building and there was a minor gale sweeping through the open passage. She didn't answer him, but she wondered if anything people did was ever finished. Didn't it usually go on and on, like some snowball rolling down a long slope, growing larger with each revolution? So reticent herself, it was painful to listen to Jeff, and she hoped that he would not remember how much he had said, so that their next meeting would not be embarrassing to both of them.

"It hurt unbearably at first," Jeff was saying. "You were gone; Jack was gone, and I was left here. I was so afraid that people would pity me if they ever found out what a fool I had been. God in heaven! That would have been the last straw!"

"I know. But it's over now, Jeff. You said so yourself."

"Yes, it's over. I did say that, didn't I? Well, it's true. I only hate her now. She's got plenty coming to her, and I hope to God she gets every bit of it."

"Please, Jeff." Kate was alarmed by his vehemence. "Promise me you won't quarrel with her. Cu'un Lucy is in a nervous state as it is, and I don't know what's the matter with Uncle Brock, but he's been acting funny these last few days."

Jeff looked at her sharply, as though he were trying to read something in her face.

"You don't know what's the matter?"

"With Uncle Brock? No. He's quarreled with everybody all day. He even got mad with Will this morning, and you know Will has always been his shadow."

"Maybe it's just spring fever," Jeff replied casually.

"Maybe, but he's been so irritable all day. He went to his room after lunch and hasn't been out since."

"Here's Will with my horse. I'll get along home. Forget I ever came over here today, will you, Kate?"

She watched him swing easily onto the smooth back of the horse. He gave her a brief salute and was off over the newly plowed fields as though Tam o' Shanter's witches were behind him. Drunk or sober, Jeff could ride. She saw him jump some low bushes that grew at the edge of the field, horse and man rising briefly, as though they were of the same flesh. Then she turned and walked back to the dining room, swinging along with the easy stride of a country woman, shoulders back, head up.

As she reached the door it swung open, and Kitty blocked her way.

"We wondered where you were," Kitty greeted her. "Wasn't that Jeff?"

"Yes." Kate did not elaborate.

"Why didn't you bring him in? He came to see me, didn't he?"

"Not this time," Kate lied. "He came to see about a horse of mine."

"You should have brought him in." Kitty's eyes were angry, and her voice was cold and hard. If she had been younger she would have stamped her foot or even beaten her head on the floor.

"He couldn't come in," Kate repeated quietly.

"Well, of course, if you wanted him all to yourself out there in the yard—"

Kate caught Kitty's shoulders and spun her around. "I don't like your insinuations." Her face was white and her eyes blazing. "As long as you're in my house I won't have them. You try some of your nasty tricks on me or on anybody in my house and I'll telephone your husband to come for you immediately."

"I really believe you would."

Kitty watched her cousin closely, realizing she had gone almost too far. She had never been able to manage Kate as she had all the others, and deep down inside her she knew she never would. Kate was quiet, but there were strength and courage in her, and Kitty did not doubt that she would carry out her threat.

It angered her to realize that she faced a will as strong as her own, and she knew that Kate was in a position to enforce hers. So she shrugged off the grasping fingers and opened the door. Kate followed, shaking with reaction. For four years she had been living in a world of peaceful dreams, but she knew that now, unwillingly, she had been swept into the stirring, vital lives of living people. She had been asleep, but her dream had been shattered and she was awake. There was no going back.

As Kate closed the dining-room door she became aware of angry voices. Kitty stopped, too, and there was a cat-and-mouse look in her eyes. The thick walls blurred the words, but undoubtedly they came from Brock's room.

"Where are the others?" Kate asked quickly.

"Alex went out soon after you did, and when Alicia got a little too catty Leigh left. I can't see how on earth he's stood being married to her so long. She would make anybody's life miserable," Kitty replied silkily.

Kate thought the same thing, but she didn't say it. This was no time to express her views, so she propelled Kitty toward the front room.

Alicia was very busy explaining some slight she had received, her voice high and shrill with indignation. Lucy threw Kate an angry look, but she welcomed the interruption to Alicia's tirade. Kate was sorry and bent her efforts to placating her sensitive guest.

She offered a bland and plausible apology for her absence and kept the conversation running on oiled rollers. Kitty, sulking in her chair, made no effort to join them, but her silence was better than her chatter. Lucy did her part, so the time passed as pleasantly as could be expected.

When Leigh came back there were deep furrows along his forehead. His face was flushed and he looked tired and worried. Alicia's eyes rested on him for a moment and then darted to Kitty, and there was an angry glitter in them. Kate wondered if Leigh would have to endure another jealous scene when Alicia got him home. She thought it quite likely.

In the electric tenseness of the room Alicia rose and said that they must leave. It was a relief to the others, and once the departing pleasantries had been said, they relaxed. Lucy sank into a chair in the cold hall and vowed that she would not have the strength to walk back to the fire.

5

Kate watched Lucy's collapse into the chair with alarm. She knew the older woman had had a trying afternoon, but it wasn't like her to give way to her feelings like this. Lucy had a fighting spirit and remarkable resilience and vitality for her age. Now her eyes were dull and her plump cheeks sagged.

"Let's all go up and rest for a while and then really dress for dinner tonight. We can pretend that we are quite stylish. I could tell Ella to fix something extra, and Zack will adore wearing his swallow-tail coat," Kate said and gave Lucy her hand. "We're getting positively gloomy, and it's been getting much warmer for the past few days. You run along upstairs and rest now." Her voice had a lilt, and she gave Lucy an affectionate push toward the steps.

"What shall we wear?" She turned to Kitty. "I'm sorry we can't do much in the way of entertainment. But you know it's Lent, and Cu'un Lucy would never permit a party. And even the country-club dances are off for the present."

"I thought you said this was your house." Kitty's voice was cold and bitter. "A more gloomy household I have never had the privilege to see. It didn't use to be that way." She turned on her heel and mounted the steps in injured dignity.

The fifth step creaked a light accompaniment to the click of her high French heels. Alone in the hall once more, Kate sighed. Kitty was so plainly bored, and Kate wondered again what emergency had brought her back to Cliff's Edge. She would never have left the excitement of a city except in some great urgency. The house seemed too quiet, and Kate turned quickly and hurried across the bare floors of the halls to the kitchen.

At least the kitchen was warm and bright and redolent with the cooking food. Broad black Ella stood before the wood range like some vestal priestess tending her sacred fire. Zack sat in a chair propped against the wall at a dangerous angle. He was enjoying his corncob pipe for which he had appropriated some of Alex's special mixture.

"We've got work to do," Kate told them as she shut the door. "We're going to have dinner instead of supper tonight."

The two watched her face, waiting to see just how much extra work they would have to do.

"We haven't much time," Kate went on, a note of desperation creeping into her tone. "Get the Haviland china, Zack, and I'll expect you to serve the meal. You can wear that dinner jacket I gave you."

Zack's face broke into a million wrinkles of pleasure. Kate had given him her husband's old dress suit but only allowed him to wear it on special occasions. Zack's own opinion was that it gave him more dignity than the colored preacher, who owned a cutaway which he wore for Sundays, funerals, and weddings. Zack would have liked to wear his coat every day but was restrained by the white folks.

"Where's Fancy? She'll have to help you," Kate continued. "Use the silver pheasants for a centerpiece and the silver candelabra. And, Zack, we'll want some wine. I'll ask Uncle Brock to get it for you. Maybe it will help him too. What's the matter with him, do you know?"

"Naw'm." Zack's wide mouth opened in a toothless grin as the excitement of the approaching evening coursed through his veins. He was envisioning a nice little "drap" before he went to bed.

"Where's Fancy?" Kate asked again, and this time Ella answered.

"She pro'bly upstairs with Mis' Kitty. She say she her pu'sonal maid."

"Well, she's no such thing as long as I'm paying her," Kate replied shortly and lifted the tops of the pots and pans on the stove. "This will be all right just as it is, Ella. Just try to make it look as fancy as you can. Whip the cream for the strawberries, and we'll put them in those glass dessert dishes. Is there any cake we can add?"

"Yo' all et it las' night."

"All right. We don't have cake then. You get Fancy to come right down now and help you. Kitty is perfectly capable of dressing herself. If dinner's a little late tonight it won't matter. And, Ella," she added as she put her hand on the knob of the door, "please be careful with the china and glassware. Don't let Fancy get her butter fingers on it."

Kate opened the back door and closed it quickly behind her. The sky was overcast and gray clouds hung over the river. The wind was tossing the newly leafed branches of the trees, which had now become black hulking silhouettes against the sullen sky. There was a rumble of thunder in the distance, blending with the murmur of the river and the faint sigh of the wind. The stillness was broken by the sharp bark of a dog in the run back of the stable.

She hugged her arms close to her body as the cold wind pierced the thinness of her dress, and ran through the growing darkness to the Negro cabins set at a distance from the house.

"Eph," she called, "Eph."

The door opened to show a crack of light from an oil lamp, and a head appeared.

"Eph, how would you like to come up to the house tonight and play your harp for us?" Kate was breathless from her run.

"Rat now, Mis' Kate?" Eph felt in his pocket where the precious harp lay.

"No. After we have supper. And, Eph, will you go see if you can get Ben and Link to come play their fiddles too?" Kate was thinking furiously. Music would be better, no matter how bad it was, than conversation.

The fiddlers had been one of her own inspirations. She knew that tourists expected the Negroes to come up to the

house and serenade them. Movies and novels had firmly im-
planted this idea in their minds as an old Southern custom.
Knowing this, Kate had found two of her tenants who could
play a little and had organized a small group of singers.

The Negroes enjoyed their own performances, more so as
Kate made a practice of giving them a small glass of wine and
a little money. If they wondered why they were allowed to sing
only spirituals and church hymns instead of the latest swing
music, they put it down as another peculiarity of the white
people.

"Yas'm. I'll tell 'em," Eph replied. Will had come to the door
and he stood behind the boy.

"I may need your help too, Will. Everybody has a touch of
spring fever, even Uncle Brock." She knew she was playing on
his sympathy, but she was past caring. Will's devotion to Uncle
Brock was accepted, and where the old man went, the black
one was not far behind. Such loyalty and faith are rare, indeed,
between the black and white races today.

"Sho will," he promised solemnly.

Kate turned and raced back to the house. She had no as-
surance that her entertainers would come, but she had done all
she could. As it was, she had little time to dress. Thoughts of
a nice relaxing warm tub gave way to a quick shower. And she
must warn Uncle Brock and Alex of the planned festivities.

She opened the door and hurried through the dining room,
taking no heed of a sullen Fancy who was helping Zack wipe
china and glasses as the table was set.

She knocked on Uncle Brock's door and received a gruff
grunt in reply.

"We're having a party dinner tonight, Uncle Brock. I promised Kitty we'd dress," she called through the keyhole. "Supper
will be a little later than usual. I've told Zack you would get
some wine out for us. Oh yes, and Ben and Link will be up
later to play."

She climbed the steep back stairs, and Alex opened the
door at her knock. He kept staring at her in surprise as she
explained her errand. Her hair was wind-blown and tousled;

she was breathing fast, and the wind had whipped high color into her cheeks.

"There'll be music afterward," she said. "At least I hope so. I've sent word for some of the Negroes to come up and play for us. You haven't heard them, have you? I thought not, but we usually have them come to the house and play for our guests. You can dress or not, just as you like. Uncle Brock won't."

"I will. Such lovely ladies deserve no less." He bowed gallantly, and the light fell directly on the white threads of hair about his temple, and his eyes, usually so steely, were a warm blue. "Shall it be a white tie or will black be sufficient?"

"Oh, black by all means; we aren't really having a party. There will only be the family," she flung back over her shoulder as she hurried on to her own door.

She opened the wardrobe door and pulled down a long cellophane bag. Unfastening the snaps, she took out a sapphire net dress with full bishop's sleeves. It was fairly new—in fact, she had bought it just last Christmas—and it was very becoming. Kate was grimly determined to look her best. The skirt was crumpled, and she screwed up her face in a grimace. There was no time to press it; she'd have to keep her back to the wall for the evening. It was already there, figuratively speaking, she thought.

She laughed to herself and, slipping off her clothes, threw them over the chair in front of the fire. The bathroom was empty, so she turned on the shower. The warm sprays beat hard on her skin, and she hummed softly to herself as she covered her body with suds and watched them melt away in the water. She rubbed herself dry and fastened the strap of her rubber bathing cap over the shower rail.

Putting on the old blue flannel bathrobe, she crossed the hall to Lucy's room.

"I hoped I'd catch you before you finished dressing," she said when Lucy responded to her knock. "I thought I'd better do some explaining."

Lucy sniffed but did not reply. She hugged her injured feelings like a mother protecting her young.

"Jeff came over this afternoon," Kate went on to explain, and Lucy turned to her with a look of surprise. Her back had been to the window, and she had not seen him as he approached the house.

"I had to keep him from coming in, so I met him on the steps. Jeff—well, he'd been drinking, getting up courage to come over and face Kitty, I reckon. That's why I was gone so long. It would only have made bad matters worse if I had let him come into the parlor."

Lucy lifted her eyebrows and puckered her small mouth into a silent whistle. "I'm certainly glad you didn't. There was no use adding more fuel to the fire."

"What happened after I left?" Kate asked.

"A lady's vocabulary couldn't describe it," Lucy said piously. "Kitty made some remark about people becoming mannerless down here in the country, and Alicia lit into her."

"A real fight?"

"Well—no, they didn't tear each other's hair. I was there. But the words were pretty blue. Maybe not so outspoken, but you know both of them are masters of sarcasm and—insinuations. I guess that's the word I want." Kate nodded, and Lucy continued:

"It must have been about then that Alex sort of drifted off. I didn't see him go. He's awfully elusive. Anyway, I noticed he wasn't in the room."

"What did Leigh do?"

"Nothing. He got real red in the face, and once I thought he might slap Alicia. But no," she said disgustedly, "he just went out of the door. Didn't even bang it."

"How did you ever get them to stop?" Kate inquired curiously.

"I told them both to shut up. After all, I was their only audience and I was disgusted. Then I sent Kitty to find you. She took plenty of time about that too."

"Why, she had just come into the dining room when I met her."

"No such thing! She had been gone at least ten minutes before you came in."

"I wonder what she could have been doing. I thought she had just come in the room—at least that was my impression."

"Something ought to be done about women like that. They give the rest of us a bad name. If you're going to dress for dinner"—Lucy changed the subject abruptly—"you'd better get started. It's seven-thirty."

"I'll have to hurry. Something must be done to amuse Kitty. Thank goodness Lent will be over next week!"

"I don't know that all this dressing tonight will be much use, but if it is I'm willing to do my part." Lucy shook her head doubtfully.

"Just help me keep the conversation going. I've seen Ella and Zack, but if you have time will you go by the kitchen before we eat just to be sure everything will be all right?"

At the door Kate paused and turned back to Lucy. "I've sent for Ben and Link to come up and play for us. It was about time we did some of the old Southern-hospitality stuff for Alex, and the music will relieve us of the burden of conversation. Not very high tone, is it?" A gamin grin quirked Kate's mouth. "Not what she would expect in a smart club but the best I could do on the spur of the moment."

Kate hummed to herself as she dressed. She felt almost giddy as she sat on the low slipper chair and pulled on her stockings. Kitty had come without asking whether it was convenient, and if things weren't to her liking she could take it or leave it.

She pulled the taffeta slip over her head and listened to its stiff rustle as she moved and the swishing sound as the net fell over the skirt. She jerked up the zipper and, fastening the narrow wristbands, went over to the dresser.

A small oval mirror reflected her face mistily in its watery depths as she combed the thick black hair from her face and watched it fall into soft waves down to her shoulders, where it curled upward. Moving a small lamp closer, she applied a thin film of powder and drew the lipstick over her generous mouth. Then, stepping back, she surveyed the effect in a standing mirror next her bed.

She nodded her satisfaction and at last went to the mantel and unhooked the painted glass that hid the mechanism of the old clock which had long since ceased to run but was kept as an appropriate touch for the tourist trade. In a dark corner beneath the pendulum her hand found the small key. With this she unlocked one of the drawers of the high dresser and drew out a worn leather case. She snapped the lock and looked at the old-fashioned set before selecting the heavy bracelet. These were the same jewels that had adorned the first Katherine Leigh in the portrait downstairs—necklace, earrings, and bracelet of sapphires and pearls set ornately in yellow gold.

They were too heavy for most occasions, but they were things that the family had clung to through the years—a symbol of past elegance. Kate jangled the bracelet on her arm and shut the case. She relocked the drawer and returned the key to its hiding place. It wasn't a good place to keep such valuables, but it was just as good as the rickety safe in the office. And since Fancy never overdid herself in dusting upstairs, the key was likely to remain safely hidden forever. If the lock was a hundred years old it was still a good one.

Alex came out of his room just as Kate crossed the hall.

"Wait a second for me and we'll make a grand entrance together," he said.

Kate turned, and a smile of pleasure lit her face. She caught her wide skirt and curtsied.

"How elegant you look, sir," she murmured, dropping her eyes.

"The girl's flirting with me!" Alex sounded delighted. "Stand over here a minute." He took her hand and twirled her. "You're beautiful!"

"You sound surprised."

Alex looked embarrassed, and Kate took his hand. "Come along," she said.

She ran her other hand along the curving rail of the stair. The hall was dim, and as they reached the lower steps they could hear voices raised in anger.

"I will not give it to you!"

"You have it, and I don't see why you can't let me have just what I want!" Kitty's voice was clear and angry.

"You don't see fit to tell me why you want it and then you expect me to just hand it over to you." Uncle Brock's words were harsh and gruff.

"I must have it!" Kitty sounded desperate.

"If that's what you wanted you can go away again. Haven't I enough worries—?"

Kate's shoe came down with a loud thud on the next step, and the voices stopped abruptly. She opened the door and went into the room ahead of Alex, fearful of what she might find.

Uncle Brock's shaggy brows were drawn in an angry scowl, and his short white hair stood up stiffly over his head. Kitty had her back turned, but she faced them in a minute. Only the thin line of her mouth and the blaze in her eyes were evidence of the quarrel.

"Hasn't Cu'un Lucy come down yet?" Kate asked.

"She went to the kitchen," Kitty replied, her voice steady and already calmer.

"Kitty, you have outdone yourself tonight!" Alex stepped forward and took both her hands. "They should do this more often, shouldn't they, Mr. Brock?"

Kitty had indeed achieved a dazzling effect. Her dress clung at just the right places and flowed over her slender body in soft folds, like those of a Grecian statue. It was daring and subtle, this dress, so that to Lucy and Brock it was only a lovely dress which thankfully covered most of her beautiful body, but to Kate and Alex, whose eyes were more sophisticated, it bordered on the indecent. Its soft gold color added a tint of ivory to her skin and contrasted nicely with the black hair and eyes.

Kate was piqued. She had enjoyed being called beautiful again, even if it had been a rather left-handed compliment. But no woman liked to hear that compliment repeated to another only a minute later. She didn't have time to give it much thought, for Lucy opened the door, and Zack was just behind her.

"Suppa's on de table," he announced solemnly.

Alex offered his arms to both girls impartially. With a malicious glance at Kitty, Kate accepted and they followed the old colored man into the hall, Lucy and Brock behind them.

Zack walked with exaggerated dignity; his swallow-tail coat drooped from his shoulders, and the cuffs were somewhat frayed at the edges. He threw open the door and waited for them to enter, then closed it quietly behind them.

The dining room was dim, with only the candles spilling their light over the table and reflecting in the glass and silver. Perhaps it was the dimness of the light that gave the room an air of mystery. Only one fire had been lit, and though the table had been lengthened and pulled to the center, the room was warm.

As the meal progressed the diners relaxed pleasantly under the influence of full stomachs. It was no better food than had been served on other evenings, but Zack's flourishes added zest to the occasion. When the strawberries had been served Uncle Brock produced a bottle of white wine and filled the slender-stemmed glasses himself.

"This is some scuppernong wine Will and I made last summer. We had a good crop on that arbor down at the end of the garden, and I think it's the best we've made in years."

Kitty sipped the wine with appreciation. "This *is* good. Maybe you'd give me some of *this*." The last word was emphasized.

"If you remind me I'll get you some before you leave." The scowl had returned to Brock's face.

"You made the wine yourself?" asked Alex.

"Yes sir. We have plenty of muskadines and scuppernongs, so Will and I put up about fifteen gallons every August."

"I don't know that I've ever tasted any better."

Uncle Brock's face cleared somewhat under the compliment.

"If you've finished"—Kate laid aside her napkin—"we can go back to the parlor. I think the Negroes I asked to come up and play are here. Kitty, I don't think you've heard them. I've been working with them for the best part of two years, and though they aren't musicians they do pretty well." She added to the others, "Ask for what you want. They'll play anything by ear, and if it's not exactly true, it's recognizable."

In the parlor two brawny Negroes were huddling over violins, and little Eph, his eyes brighter than diamonds, was slapping his harmonica against his overalls. There followed a concert such as Alex had never imagined.

The fiddles played fast jigs, pieces he did not recognize except when they went into "Turkey in the Straw," and the little colored boy did a fast shuffle on the bare space of the floor, supplying his own music.

Soon all of them were making requests, and with wide grins that displayed numerous gold teeth the Negroes complied, their bodies swaying with the rhythm of the music.

Alex sat beside Kate on the sofa that had been pulled back under the front window. Her eyes were bright, and there was more animation in her face than he had ever seen. From time to time he stole sly glances at her, as though he were seeing her for the first time. Across the room Kitty brooded, and the lovely oval face was marred by the sullen droop of her mouth.

Sometimes they joined in the choruses of the familiar songs, especially when Lucy and Brock began to call for the sentimental ballads of their youth, or they just listened with a nostalgic smile. Later the tempo grew faster, and one of the Negroes discarded his violin and, catching Fancy, whirled her into a fast dance.

Alex danced once with Kitty and once with Kate. But it was Kate that intrigued him. He had known a dozen Kittys, but Kate was new to him. She was as light as a feather in his arms, and the snatches of conversation they had that evening had been like dancing a minuet: sometimes she advanced with a smile, then she retreated with a formal bow.

Finally Lucy put an end to the merriment. She glanced at the clock and exclaimed, "That's enough for tonight! Ben and Link have to be in the fields tomorrow, and it's time they got to bed. Bring us some wine, Zack, and give the others some too. And mind you, not too much; you all have plenty to do in the morning."

"Aw, Mis' Lucy," Ben wheedled with a guffaw, "a little drap ain't gonna hurt us."

"Not one little drap," Lucy replied, "but several little draps certainly will."

Kate followed them into the hall, where she paid them before they went to the kitchen for their own refreshments.

"Be sure to lock the back door when you leave, Zack," she cautioned.

"Yas'm, I do dat."

Back in the parlor Lucy was saying:

"I don't see why we shouldn't get to bed too. It's after eleven, and Brock has missed his news broadcast."

"Oh, it's still too early to think of bed, Cousin Lucy," Kitty protested.

Lucy's small eyes bored into the girl. "You haven't been sleeping well, have you?" she asked. "You don't look as though you get half enough sleep ever. And usually this country air works just like a sedative."

Kitty shrugged, knowing she was defeated before she began the argument. She took Alex's arm, and they walked toward the stairs, Lucy dogging their steps.

Brock banked the fire, and Kate lingered with him to put out the lights and to see that the house was locked. When they were in the hall Kate caught his hand and swung it in hers.

"Are you worried about something, Uncle Brock?"

"Well, not exactly worried; it's past that. But I have been upset."

"Is there anything I can do?"

"There's nothing anybody can do now," he replied with a heavy sigh. "Maybe everything will turn out all right. You run along to bed and let me do my own worrying."

Kate blew him a kiss and ran up the darkened stairs with light, tapping steps.

Opening her door, she was surprised to find the light on and Kitty sitting in the chair before the fire.

"Hello. I didn't expect to find you here. I thought you had gone to bed."

"I wanted to talk to you." Kitty rose and walked over to the dresser. "Haven't you any cigarettes?"

"They're on the table." Kate unfastened the bracelet and took it off. "What did you want to say to me?"

"I wanted to tell you to quit throwing yourself at Alex."

"Quit what?" Kate swung round in astonishment to face her cousin.

Kitty lit the cigarette and threw the match into the fire. "I mean just what I said. I met Alex Dexter two years ago in Philadelphia and I saw quite a lot of him last fall."

Kate regarded her in silence. She did not know quite what to say.

"I also knew his wife," Kitty went on, unperturbed.

"His wife?"

"Yes. Eleanor Dexter was killed in an automobile accident last December. Alex was driving."

Kate sat down quickly on the steps beside the bed, her dress spreading in a deep blue pool about her body. Her eyes were wide and dark in her white face. The blood pounded madly in her head. What she had heard echoed vaguely in her mind.

"Yes," Kitty continued, watching Kate through narrowed lids, "she was killed instantly. I think Alex was in the hospital for some time afterward. She had just come back from Reno. That's right," she replied to Kate's unspoken question, "she had divorced him. But she was a very beautiful woman, and he was still in love with her. He wanted her back and he killed her."

"No, what a horrible thing to say, Kitty," Kate mumbled through stiff lips.

"Oh, it was an accident all right." Kitty tossed her cigarette into the fire. "But it was probably his fault. Everybody knew he was still wild about her. She was very rich and belonged to an old Philadelphia family. Ralph knows her father. He's a banker or something of the sort. So is Alex's family. And they had known each other always." Kitty moved toward the door but paused with her hand against the frame. "I just wanted you to know so you wouldn't get any foolish ideas."

Kate undressed slowly. Automatically she hung up her dress and put away her slippers, her mind feverishly turning over what she had just heard. It explained so many things, his silence about his family, his weakness when he arrived. She was surprised and unutterably shocked by Kitty's story but more so by her own reaction—that sudden unhappiness that had risen to the surface.

6

Thursday dawned clear and warm. The sun beamed down from a cloudless sky. Despite the brightness of the day Kate was depressed. She was so acutely aware of Alex after Kitty's revelations of the night before that she carefully avoided him.

She spent most of the morning in the office, ostensibly writing letters, but most of the time she gazed absently out of the window. She could hear Uncle Brock in the yard outside, tinkering with the tractor and swearing at its mechanism but thoroughly enjoying himself. What he lacked in farming knowledge he made up in mechanical ability, for all the plantation machinery ran smoothly and efficiently.

The morning was not without its interruptions, but Kate was reluctant to return to the big house when the luncheon bell was rung.

Outside her room, on the way back downstairs, she met Alex.

"Wouldn't you like to go for a ride with me this afternoon? After all, I haven't seen much of the town, and this section is entirely new to me." He smiled at her.

Kate was panic-stricken, and her words came quickly. "I'm sorry, I can't go with you today. I promised to ride over to some of the quarters across the big field this afternoon."

"Perhaps I could go with you. . . ."

"Oh no, you wouldn't be interested in what I have to do. I have to see Aunt Pleurisy. She's been sick, and I promised her I'd come over and see about her."

Alex looked at her without saying anything, but the lines about his mouth were hard and tight. Kitty joined them at the top of the steps.

"You might go fishing this afternoon," Kate suggested. "It's warm enough, and I know Will would be delighted to take you. We have the brook dammed not very far from the house."

"We could go out to the country club and play some golf," Kitty said. "They used to have a fairly decent course there."

"No, thank you," Alex said hastily. "Fishing is just what I want to do. It will give me a chance to just sit idly in the sun for a while."

"Just as you like." Kitty went on down the steps ahead of them.

In the dining room they found Lucy already seated, and Uncle Brock came in a few minutes later.

"I think I'd better begin the spring cleaning next week," remarked Lucy.

"You'll never get this place clean until you put some paint on it," Kitty said.

"Did you finish fixing the tractor, Uncle Brock?" Kate interposed, fearing the conversation was getting on dangerous ground.

"It was nothing. Ben can drive it on the east field tomorrow."

"I thought if you can spare Will I'd get him to take Alex fishing after lunch. They could go up the brook to the dam."

"You go with him, Kate." Lucy poured herself a second cup of coffee. "I'll need Will to drive me to town. Unless Kitty will do it?" She looked up expectantly. "This is the afternoon the Altar Guild meets."

"Not on your life," Kitty replied rudely.

"That's really all right," Alex put in quickly. "There's no need to plan for me. If it isn't far and Mr. Curtis will show me where to go, I'll be all right on my own."

"I have to go over and see Aunt Pleurisy," Kate explained.

"He might go with you instead," Lucy suggested tentatively, and Alex put his napkin up to his mouth to hide a smile.

Kate so obviously didn't want him, and when she caught his eye she knew he could sense her mental squirming.

"No," she said but did not explain, and Lucy let the matter drop.

"What are you doing this afternoon, Kitty?" asked Brock.

"I offered to take Alex golfing"—Kitty shrugged—"but he turned me down. I have some letters to write, and I'll get Fancy to come up to my room and wash some clothes where I can keep an eye on her."

"You'll be around the house in case anybody comes, won't you, Uncle Brock?" asked Kate, and Brock grunted in such a manner that she took it for an affirmative answer.

When luncheon was finally over Uncle Brock took Alex out to the storeroom across the hall from the office. As she changed clothes Kate saw them in the yard below, Brock evidently giving Alex instructions.

When she saw Alex leave, following the narrow footpath, she slipped on a leather jacket and went down the steps. She had to saddle Star herself, but he was accustomed to her handling and put his cold nose against her hair as she tightened the girth.

On the whole her afternoon was not successful. She rode to the far end of the plantation and talked to the Negroes, but she had come to escape her own thoughts, and they dogged her all the way.

The sun hung low over the river, its orange rays reflected in the swollen waters below. She turned back toward the house. Hundreds of insects hummed in a dreary monotone as she picked her way through the swamp. She pulled in her reins as she reached the sluggish stream and patted Star's sleek black neck. As the horse plunged into the shallow ford a large moccasin slid silently into the water from the opposite bank and, holding its head rigidly erect, slithered its way down the stream.

Scrub cedars and stubby pine brushed against the horse's flanks, and he slowed down to a walk. Kate had her mind on other things but came to with a start when he halted abruptly.

"Go on, Star. It isn't far," she said.

Star jerked his head, and the reins almost slipped from her cold fingers.

"What on earth is the matter with you?" Kate dug her heels into his sides. "Come on, I want to get home."

But Star began backing away from the low bushes that lay ahead, and no amount of coaxing could make him go forward. Kate was uneasy as she dismounted and drew the bridle over his head. It must be a rattler, she thought and picked up a dead limb that lay beside the path. She had on heavy boots, but she had no idea of attacking the snake; she only wanted to threaten it so that it would go away. She walked quickly around to the open space and stopped.

Afterward she thought she tried to scream, but only a hoarse sound came from her throat. Her eyes dilated with horror and she put her hand to her throat to ease the choking there.

Uncle Brock lay on his side, partly concealed by the low bushes. His body was twisted, his arms flung violently apart. There was a dark red stain on his left side, and a gun lay close to his feet.

"Uncle Brock," Kate whispered.

The sound of her own voice seemed to break the spell which had held her, and, throwing down the stick, she stumbled forward and raised his head. His body was still warm, but she knew she had come too late.

"Uncle Brock, Uncle Brock!" she whispered again, and realization began to reach her dulled senses.

It was then that she screamed.

Cliff's Edge was partly in sight but too far for her to be heard. The wind wrenched the words from her mouth and carried them even farther away. She clung to the quiet figure, and the tears streamed unheeded down her cheeks. Kneeling there beside him, his head still cradled in her arms, she looked about her, searching for help.

Finally she put his head back on the leaf-covered earth, gently, as though not to disturb his final sleep. As she did this she saw the small leather pouch which had been hidden under his body. It was stamped in gold with the initials A. D.

A new horror seemed to clutch her. This was something she knew. It was undoubtedly Alex's; she had seen him take

it from his pocket so many times and dip the bowl of his pipe
into it. Her hands were clammy. Kate was horribly afraid. The
implication was clear even though she tried to close her mind
to its meaning.

She stared at the evidence in her hands while her mind
fought frantically for some explanation. It was all wrong; this
had no reasonable place here, for already she knew that this
was no accident. Quickly she put the pouch in her pocket, as
though to hide it from her own eyes.

Rising, her heel struck the gun, and she glanced at it but did
not touch it. She looked about her again, but she was utterly
alone. Then she stumbled forward, her feet clumsily slipping
on the ruts and brambles. The sharp briers tore at her boots,
but she pushed them aside. Her breath came in short gasps as
she cut across the newly plowed field back to the house.

There was a man coming toward her, and she redoubled her
efforts when she recognized Alex. Reaching him, she clung to
him, sobbing, her grief unleashed in a sudden torrent.

Alex stroked her head. "There, there. What's the matter?
Were you frightened?"

"Uncle Brock. Out there. . . ." Her words were stifled against
the roughness of his coat.

"Don't cry." He held her in his arms almost awkwardly,
clumsily trying to soothe her.

"You don't understand." She raised her head, the shadow of
remembered horror in her eyes. "Uncle Brock's out there. He's
dead, Alex."

"All right." His voice was gentle. "I'll take you back to the
house and then I'll go see what frightened you."

With an arm about her he led her around the back of the
house and into the side door. She shrank against him as they
passed the closed door of Brock's room.

Halfway up the stairs she stopped him and, clutching the
rail for support, drew away from him.

"I'm all right now," she said. "You go back—back to him. I'll
be all right now, really." She turned to face him as he stood on a
lower step. She was pale and she gripped the banister so firmly

that the knuckles of her hands were white even in the fading light. "You go back," she said again, "and take one of the men with you."

Turning, she fled up the remaining steps.

Alex watched her uncertainly but made no effort to follow her. At the foot of the steps he met Lucy.

"Was that Kate who just came in?" she asked.

"Yes. She's hysterical. She was badly frightened on the way home. I'm going now to see what was the matter." He hesitated, undecided whether to tell her what Kate had said, but, deciding not to, he went out of doors again.

As he closed the door he stopped suddenly. Jeff was standing at the bottom of the steps, regarding him with a cunning look in his bloodshot eyes.

"I didn't hear you," Alex said, coming down the steps. "But I'm glad you're here. Kate was frightened this afternoon and I'm going to investigate."

"Can't come." Jeff's words were indistinct, sliding off his tongue like the muffled roll of a drum. He swayed unsteadily, and Alex caught his arm.

"Kate says Mr. Curtis is dead." Alex clipped his words sharply, as though he were driving nails into the other's befuddled brain. "If it's true I'll need you and one of the Negroes."

Jeff blinked his puffy eyelids and tugged at his collar which suddenly seemed tight. He clutched the other's arm for a moment and then threw back his shoulders, as though he had at last comprehended what Alex was telling him.

"I'll come with you."

Alex let his eyes rest on him doubtfully. For a moment he thought of sending him back to the women in the house; then he shrugged his shoulders, for, after all, if Mr. Curtis was badly hurt Jeff's physical strength would be needed.

As they came to the stable Jeff called to Will.

"You'd better come along with us. Miss Kate says Uncle Brock's been shot, and we're going to see what was the matter."

Will put down the tool he was mending and came with them immediately. His face was bland and expressionless. Alex had no way of knowing what the Negro really believed.

The three men walked single file on the edge of the cotton patch. Once or twice Jeff stumbled but on the whole managed himself well, considering the amount of corn liquor he had drunk. Once he hiccupped loudly and swore softly under his breath.

Without warning they came upon the bush with its hidden secret. For a time no one spoke; then Will knelt down beside the body.

"Mr. Brock. . . . Mr. Brock," he murmured. "It's Will."

"It's too late, Will." Alex put his hand on the Negro's shoulder and felt it quiver under his touch. "He's dead."

Will looked up at him, his eyes blurred with unshed tears. His face was crumpled, misery in every line.

Alex dropped down beside the Negro and placed his hand under the coat. But the body was already growing chill and stiff.

"Let's get him back to the house," Jeff said. Unconsciously all of them were speaking in whispers.

"We mustn't move him." Alex's eyes were on the gun which lay at a peculiar angle.

"The hell we can't!" Jeff swore and bent down and lifted the feet.

"Stop it!" Alex commanded. "We mustn't move him."

"And why not?" Jeff was belligerent.

"The police must be notified," Alex answered wearily.

Jeff dropped the feet, and they hit the ground with a dull thud. The three men looked at each other in silence. Alex's words had the driving impact of a boxer's blows, and two pair of eyes were riveted on him. A swift, chilling horror swept over them; horror not so much of what they already knew but of what they didn't know.

"Will you go back to the house and notify the police?" Alex asked Jeff.

"Who'll I call?"

"Your coroner, chief of police—I don't know." Alex was looking at the gun, but he didn't touch it.

"The she'f's the one mostly comes out this way." Will spoke for the first time.

"Hurry, Jeff." Alex couldn't keep the impatience from his voice.

Jeff stood still for a minute, biting his lips as though to shut back the words he wanted to say. Then he turned and almost ran back to the house.

Left alone, the white man and the Negro were silent. Alex moved about slowly, searching the ground, but he found nothing. He fumbled in his pocket and drew out a crumpled package of cigarettes. He lit one and offered the pack to Will, but the Negro shook his head. The wind was growing cold, and the damp earth seemed a ghastly resting place for the man who lay there. It seemed an interminable time before Jeff reappeared, and Alex started forward in relief.

"I talked to the sheriff and explained what we had found. He'll be out just as soon as he can get here. It ought not to be long. And I called the family doctor, just in case we need him." Jeff was nervous, and his movements were jerky and uncontrolled. After a while he added, "What makes you think he didn't do it himself?"

It was Will who replied. "Mr. Brock neva do a thing lak that."

"He's right, Jeff. He couldn't have done it. You can't hold a gun that far off and shoot yourself. There aren't any powder burns on his coat."

"You mean it's murder?"

Alex nodded silently.

Jeff watched him closely, his eyes narrowing, shifting slowly from Alex to Will and back again.

"Whose gun is it?" Alex asked.

"It's hisn," replied Will. Alex turned to him with renewed interest. A more violently unhappy face he had never seen, and he wondered if the Negro, less inhibited perhaps than the white, showed his emotions more easily.

"Are you sure?"

"Yas sir. Him an' me went huntin' togetha all the time."

"You told the sheriff where to come?" Alex turned back to Jeff.

"Who gave you the right to take charge around here?" Jeff's voice was truculent, and his face was flushed an angry red. "You're only an outsider. It's none of your business."

Alex drew back as though he had been slapped, but his eyes were like steel. "You aren't in any condition to take charge of anything. Drunk as you are, you'd be no help to those women up at the house."

The color drained from Jeff's face, leaving it a dirty white. His nostrils flared angrily, and his lips parted in a snarl. The moment was tense, and it seemed that the two men would be at each other's throats, stripped bare of civilization in their anger.

"Hello there. . . ."

Both turned to see two men approaching across the field. Sheriff Davies scarcely gave them a glance as he reached the spot where they were standing. Instead he gazed at the man lying on the cold ground at their feet.

He was a hard-working, small-town sheriff—tall, lean, angular, and loosely strung together. His shrewd eyes were skeptical and entirely disillusioned, as though he was very tired of people and knew only too well their human frailties.

He knelt down on the ground and opened the jacket, pulling it hard where the blood had stiffened; then he turned the body slightly.

"Which one of you found him?" Up until that time he had not spoken, and the men stood aside watching him intently. The stumpy man who had accompanied him was breathing hard. His short legs had been no match for the sheriff's long, easy strides.

"Kate did," Jeff answered in a sullen tone.

Alex looked up at him, and the thought came clearly to him. Jeff had known that Uncle Brock had been shot. Kate had not said that. Jeff had already known.

7

Without a word in reply Sheriff Davies turned back to the man on the ground.

In low tones he conferred with the man he had brought with him. They seemed to argue over one point until the sheriff again turned to Alex, instinctively questioning him instead of Jeff.

"Did any of you touch anything?"

"We only raised the body to be sure he was dead," said Jeff.

"None of us has touched it." The sheriff looked up at Alex sharply at this reply. It was as though he sensed something evasive in his tone. He waited a moment, but Alex added nothing to his information.

"Can't we take him back to the house now?" asked Jeff.

"I s'pose you might as well. Here, Tom, you give them a hand. Nothing we can do out here, and the coroner ought to be at the house by now."

Tom helped Will lift the shoulders, and Alex took the feet. A more ineffectual man could hardly have been chosen for a sheriff's deputy. He was later to be always remembered as the sheriff's stooge, a sort of Sherlock's Watson, who made the right comments at the right time.

They made the trip back to the house as quickly as possible. The sheriff followed slowly, bringing the gun, holding it carefully in his handkerchief. Lucy met them at the side door, and though she gasped when she saw them, she remained in full control of herself and led them to the door of Brock's room.

"Kate told me," was the only thing she said.

"Miss Lucy"—the sheriff began giving orders—"you stay here with me and we'll see about things. The rest of you go to the parlor. Tom, you tell Fred Williams to come in here just as soon as he comes."

Before they could leave the door was thrown open and Ella waddled across the room. She put her large black arms about Lucy and held her for a moment comfortingly.

"They jist tell me 'bout it, Mis' Lucy. I wouldn't let Mis' Kate come in, but I knowed you'd need me."

"Thank you, Ella." Lucy's eyes glistened, and tears spilled slowly over her soft plump cheeks.

Alex held the door for the others to leave. Will, his face still twisted with grief, went down the hall to the kitchen. He looked like a grotesque gargoyle snatched from some far corner of Notre Dame. His thick lips trembled, hung lax, as he began to realize the empty spaces in the days to come. Will had lost a friend and comrade and knew it.

The deputy paused in the hall where he cranked the telephone bell and then talked with evident familiarity to Central, whom he addressed as "Miss Susie."

Jeff opened the parlor door, and Alex followed him inside. Kitty sat huddled in a big chair beside the fire. She rose quickly as the men entered.

"What's happened, Jeff?" Her pointed fingernails dug into his coat sleeve like sharp claws. "Nobody ever tells me anything."

"Uncle Brock's dead. Shot." There was no gentleness in his voice, and he pushed her hand from his sleeve.

Kitty's black eyes blazed, but she showed no shock at the brutal truth. There was something cruel, almost venomous, in the tilt of her head, and her slender throat seemed to rise from the severe collar of her dress like a snake waiting to strike.

"Murdered?" she inquired.

"We think so," Alex replied.

"Oh," she said, her eyes cold and watchful.

"Where's Kate? The sheriff told us all to come in here." Jeff kicked a log in the grate viciously, sending a shower of sparks up the chimney.

"She must be upstairs. I'll get her." Kitty moved quickly, her steps sounding loudly on the bare floor of the hall.

She tapped lightly on Kate's door and without waiting for an answer opened it. She gave a small scream. Kate was standing by the fire, a poker in her hand. The draft from an open window blew the door shut with a bang, and both girls jumped.

"What on earth are you burning?" Kitty demanded. "It smells terrible."

"Nothing," Kate replied shakily.

Kitty glanced at the fire, but whatever Kate had been burning was beyond recognition. Kitty sniffed disdainfully and, walking across the room, slammed down the window.

"You're wanted downstairs."

"Very well," Kate said and put the poker, which she still held, through the handle of the painted coal vase.

Kitty gave the room a long and searching look before she closed the door and followed Kate down the front stairs.

In the parlor the men sat in silence. The unobtrusive little deputy had joined them and was perched stiffly on the horsehair sofa before the front window. Alex and Jeff pulled a brocaded love seat to one side of the fire, and the women sat down.

A heavy silence brooded over the room. Each was preoccupied with his own thoughts, not caring to interrupt their continuity, dreading and at the same time trying to anticipate the inevitable questions.

A car drew up outside, and they heard the rumble of the sheriff's voice as he greeted the newcomer. Presently there was a shuffling of feet outside the door and then absolute quiet.

In the parlor the people sat still, listening. They recognized the sounds and knew that Uncle Brock had left Cliff's Edge. But still they did not speak. The eyes of the deputy hovered from one to the other, yet they ignored him and seemed hardly conscious that he was in the room.

Kate heard the voices of Dr. Brady and Lucy in the hall, but that, too, was quiet and subdued. She had to strain her ears to hear the soft closing of the door. When Lucy joined them her eyes were red-rimmed, but her face was calm. Jeff rose and gave her his chair by the fire. Kate went to her at once, sitting on the rug and placing her head in Lucy's short lap.

Cars began to arrive, drawing up before the door with a screech of brakes, and the sound of strange voices could be heard in the hall. Occasionally Lucy spoke to Kate, but her words were low, and the others could not hear what she said. Kate nodded slowly, and Lucy stroked the cloud of black hair in her lap.

Jeff stood by the side window overlooking a part of the drive which led from the highway, but if he was conscious of those who came and went he gave no sign.

Twilight had come rapidly after the sun had set, and already the outlines of objects had melted dimly into the dusk.

Suddenly the door was thrust open and Leigh, followed by Alicia, entered like a rush of fresh air. He was hatless, and the wind had blown his hair so that it stood up in wispy peaks over his head.

"Kate, why didn't you call us at once?"

Kate rose and went to him immediately. His arms were about her, and she clung to him, sobbing softly.

"It's been so sudden," Lucy answered his question. "We didn't know what to do. I couldn't think."

Leigh released Kate and went over to kiss Lucy's damp cheek. "It'll be all right now. I'll tend to everything, Cu'un Lucy."

"It's been so perfectly dreadful." Kitty dabbed her dry eyes delicately with a scented handkerchief. "I'm so glad you've come."

Her silky words did what was needed. It made them momentarily forget their grief. Kate turned away and went back to her place on the love seat.

"Jeff," she said, "will you and Alex get some chairs from the other parlor? Alicia can sit here."

The little deputy followed them out, and when they returned he was not with them.

"I'll appreciate it if you'll make all the arrangements for us, Leigh," Lucy said. "Mr. Kenny should be called."

"You just leave it to me, Cu'un Lucy. I'll see Davies and I'll call Mr. Kenny." He patted her shoulder solicitously. "Don't worry another minute."

He smiled encouragingly at Kate and went out into the hall. She watched him go, and a sense of security and sanity flowed through her. The clock on the mantel tinkled musically and struck the hour.

"I'll have to see about supper," she said, rising at once. And, turning to Alicia, "Will you help me? Of course we'll expect you and Leigh to stay with us."

"Of course." Alicia was conventionally sorry, but there was no depth of emotion reflected in her face.

In the kitchen the Negroes were utterly demoralized. Death was an occasion to them.

Alicia, given something to do, went about helping Ella prepare the food. She worked silently but swiftly, and Kate caught herself almost liking her. Kate's hands were covered with flour when the sheriff came to the door and spoke to her.

"Can I see you for a moment, Mrs. Frazier?"

Kate stood very still, her hands poised lightly over the marble slab that served as a biscuit board. She was cold, breathless, as though she had suddenly plunged into an icy stream. Sheriff Bill was calling her Mrs. Frazier! He who had known her all her life and called her Kate. She had even played with his daughter Jenny, had gone through school with her.

"Of course." Kate made her face calm, but she felt frozen as she washed her hands at the sink.

"I'll get Cu'un Lucy to bed and send up a tray, Kate. I think the doctor gave her something to help her sleep," Alicia volunteered. "And Ella can take you something to your room, too, when you're through. Don't worry about the rest of us. I'll see to everything in here."

"Thank you." Kate followed the sheriff out into the cold hall.

"We'll go in here," he said, leading her toward Uncle Brock's room, and then he added as he saw the question in her eyes, "It's all right. We've taken him to town."

He held the door for her, and she took the seat he indicated. There was only one other person in the room, Tom, the deputy who had come with the sheriff.

"Sit down, Kate," Sheriff Bill said kindly. "I just want to ask you a few questions. It's too late to do much tonight. I thought you might tell me what you know, since you found him."

Kate watched him, her face expressionless. His keen, intelligent eyes were fastened on her, and she steeled herself to answer his questions. He was no longer her friend's father. He was The Law.

"S'pose you tell me where you had been and how you—how you found him."

Kate felt the breath come back to her lungs. She had not been aware before that she was holding it.

"I rode over to see some of the Negroes." Kate told him where she had gone and whom she had seen, wondering suddenly if he would check this for an alibi.

"Do you know what Mr. Brock was planning to do this afternoon?"

"No. He was in the office when I left. He had just explained to Alex—Mr. Dexter—where he could go fishing."

"He didn't say he was expecting anybody, had anything special to do?"

"No."

"Now then, tell me about finding him."

Kate told him how Star had backed away from the spot, how she had urged the horse forward and then finally dismounted to see what was the matter.

"I thought it was a snake, so I picked up a stick and circled the bushes. Then—then I—then I saw him."

"You mustn't get so upset." Sheriff Bill leaned forward, and his rocker squeaked on a loose board. "Try to tell me what you saw."

"Uncle Brock was lying there on his side under some low bushes. There's a lot of scrub pine on the edge of the field. That's why I couldn't see him from the other side."

"Hu'um. Yes, I remember the bushes. You're sure he was on his side?"

Kate nodded, and the sheriff rocked forward, picked up the poker, and stirred the fire. A red glare covered Kate's face. The ceiling light was on, but the bulb was small, so that the light was dim.

"Where was the gun?"

Kate was startled by the question. She had been lulled by the silence.

"Why, at his feet. Wait a minute, I think my heel struck it when I got up. But I don't think it could have been moved much."

"You didn't touch it? Pick it up?"

"Oh no. No, I couldn't have touched it."

"Hu'um," said the sheriff again. "And you're sure he was lying on his side?"

"Yes, his face was turned away from me. I knelt down and lifted his head. I thought he was just hurt. I didn't—see the gun."

"Did he look as though he had been pushed back there?"

Kate was remembering, seeing in every horrible detail the climax of her ride through the field.

"I don't know. He was very close to the bushes, and there are low branches. You mean he wouldn't have been standing so close to them?"

"It just struck me that a man wouldn't deliberately stand with branches and briers pushing at his pants legs. He'd just naturally stand off from them. Especially when there was room."

Kate was silent, trying to digest what he was saying. Did he mean that Uncle Brock had been moved? That he didn't die where he was found?

"Did it look as though he had been moved?" she asked.

"Well, now, Miss Kate, I don't know that. People had been walking around the place before I got there, and the ground is pretty soft. I can't tell. I thought you might be able to help me." His eyes met hers, but there was a question in them.

"I don't remember." Kate brushed a hand across her eyes. "I—I lifted his head and when I saw he was dead I called for help."

"Nobody came to you?"

"No. They couldn't hear me. I thought I screamed loud enough to be heard in town, but the wind was blowing the other way and nobody heard me. I could see the trees and the observatory, but I was pretty far away after all."

"Then a shot couldn't have been heard up here?"

Kate shook her head slowly. "I don't think so."

The sheriff rocked back in his chair. After a moment he asked:

"And then what did you do?"

Kate did not reply at once. She was remembering that she had picked up the pouch and had hidden it in her jacket pocket. Then, lest he make too much of her hesitance, she said:

"I ran toward the house and met Alex—Mr. Dexter."

"Who is this Mr. Dexter, Kate?"

"He's renting a room here. I guess he's been here about three weeks now."

"How did he happen to come here at this time of the year?"

"He'd been ill and his doctor sent him South." Kate was growing more and more uneasy at the turn of the questions. "He saw our sign and took a room here until he was better."

"You never knew him before?"

"No. But, Mr. Bill"—Kate dropped back into her childhood name for him and spoke earnestly—"we need the extra boarders out here to make ends meet. So much of the land's worn out."

"Yes, I know."

He rocked back and forth, meditating, and Kate thought she would scream as the rocker hit the loose board with a sort of rhythmic sound.

"That's all for now, Kate. You get some supper and a good night's rest. I think that's all we can do tonight, Tom. We'll come back in the morning and talk to the others."

Kate rose, holding the back of the chair to steady herself. The ordeal was over. She hadn't mentioned the incriminating tobacco pouch! She didn't understand, herself, why she had concealed something that might be important. The whole thing was bewildering, and her mind, racing lightly from one thing to another, was confused. She only knew that something alien was closing around the little group, that something was terribly wrong, almost sinister.

At the door she paused and turned again to the sheriff. "You're sure—you're sure it's—?"

"It's murder? Yes, I'm quite sure," he replied evenly.

8

Friends and relatives poured relentlessly into the house the next morning. Kate had Zack build fires in both the front parlors, and in the dim green one, so little used, Lucy received the cloying sympathy that Kate could not have stood.

The rector had come the night before and with Leigh's aid had made all the arrangements. He was a young man and seemed to understand that while Kate needed only a firm handclasp Lucy needed words.

The sheriff was an early arrival, and Kate took him to the office back of the house, where he lit the fire himself.

"I guess this is the best place for you, Mr. Bill," she said. "The house is naturally upset, and people will be coming in all day. And could you—will you let Cu'un Lucy stay up at the house?" she added a little wistfully.

"I reckon I won't need to talk to her today." The little crow's-feet about his blue eyes deepened. "You get the others down here now and I'll talk to them. Maybe we can figure this thing out." He held an old newspaper in front of the fire to make it draw better. "That's got it," he exclaimed and threw the paper into the fire, where it blazed brightly.

Kate left him and went back to the house but returned almost immediately. The sheriff was standing with his back to the fire, gazing out of the window toward the back of the house. Together they worked silently, pulling chairs to the fire and moving some of the debris which always collects in a farm office.

"I told Kitty, Alex, and Will that you wanted to talk to them out here. They'll be here as soon as they can."

"Thank you, Kate. Now haven't you remembered anything you forgot to tell me last night?"

The man's eyes were boring into her mind and Kate hugged her secret more tightly. Uncle Brock might have picked up the pouch, intending to return it to the rightful owner.

"No, I haven't thought of another thing," she answered after the briefest of pauses.

"You haven't any idea who might have done this?"

"No, I haven't. Uncle Brock was kind to everybody. He's run the farm here for us ever since Grandfather died. He looked after the tenants, collected rents, paid the taxes—all those things that neither Jack nor I could have done." Kate turned to the sheriff and faced him with candid eyes, glad to be on the firm ground of truth. "He was worried lately."

"Worried?"

"Yes. I asked him what was the matter once, but he only shook his head and said it was his worry, not mine." Kate remembered the drafty hall, the dim lights, and the tired smile with which Uncle Brock had dismissed her.

"When was that?"

"Oh, a night or two after Kitty came."

"Hu'um. Pretty recent then, this worry?" And when Kate nodded he asked, "Been quarreling with anybody lately?"

"With everybody," Kate answered simply. In her mind she heard again the irritation in the words she had heard outside his bedroom door and saw again Jeff angrily slamming the door of this very office and riding hastily across the moonlit fields.

But the sheriff was hardly listening. The door had been thrust open and Alex stood there, waiting for Kitty to enter. Her heels made a thin staccato sound on the floor. She was dressed carefully in black; the only color about her was the red gash that was her mouth. Complacently she seated herself on the one comfortable chair in the room and waited for the others to speak.

"Will had to finish doing some things. He was helping Zack and told me to tell you he'd be here as soon as he could," Alex explained, and the sheriff nodded understandingly.

"I can see him later. Right now I'd like to know what happened up there at the house yesterday afternoon." He looked at Alex.

"I went up the brook and did a little fishing after lunch. I didn't go very far, and when the sun began to set I came back. Mrs. Frazier hadn't returned, and Miss Lucy was worried. I had just started to meet her when—I saw her running across the field."

"Did you see anybody come to the house after you left?"

"No. I did see Miss Lucy come back from town not long before I started back myself."

"Cu'un Lucy went to town yesterday to the Altar Guild," Kate explained. "She must have left soon after I did. Alex had already gone then."

"Then who was here at the house?"

"We have to see that somebody's always here on account of the tourists. There aren't many at this time of the year, but somebody has to be here all the time. Uncle Brock said he'd be here and—well, Kitty was here too."

"If you imagined I'd take people over the house like a common guide—" Kitty began.

"No, I didn't expect you to," Kate said in a tired voice. "Zack was here and would have done that."

"You were at the house all afternoon?" the sheriff asked quickly, interrupting what might have developed into a quarrel.

"Yes," Kitty conceded grudgingly.

"What did you do all afternoon?"

"I wrote a letter and saw to it that that worthless Fancy didn't ruin some clothes she washed and pressed for me."

"You saw nobody go toward the swamp?"

"Only Kate."

There was a moment's silence broken only by the snap of the fire as the wood shifted on the hearth. Alex drew out his pipe and felt around in his pockets before finally returning it.

Kate watched him nervously, but apparently she was the only one who noticed his automatic gesture.

"You didn't see Mr. Brock go out?"

"No, I didn't." Kitty was defiant. "My room is in the front of the house, and I was there most of the time."

"What time did Mr. Brock leave?"

"I don't know." Kitty's voice was growing shrill. "Why do you keep asking me questions? Ask Kate. She knows more that goes on here than anybody else."

"I'm only trying to find out what happened at Cliff's Edge," was the matter-of-fact retort. "Kate wasn't here."

"Well, I didn't shoot him." Kitty had regained some of her poise. "Give me a cigarette, Alex."

Kate also accepted one and was grateful for the short break in the questions while Alex lit theirs and his own.

"Nobody's accusing you," said the sheriff. "What time did you hear the shot?"

"I didn't hear a shot. I told you my room is in the front of the house, and with the windows all closed I couldn't have heard anything less than dynamite." Kitty inhaled and blew out a long streamer of bluish-gray smoke.

"Hu'um. We'll have to see if we can get some of these times straight." He fumbled in his pockets and finally brought out a dirty envelope and a stubby pencil which he moistened with his tongue. "Now let's see. What time did you have lunch?"

"About one o'clock," Kate told him and watched with a sort of fascination as he slowly wrote on a clean space on the paper.

"Who was the first to leave?"

"I was," Alex spoke up. "I got away as soon as I could. I must have left a little after two, maybe a quarter past."

"Got a license for fishing, young man?" the sheriff asked, reverting to his usual role.

Alex squirmed uncomfortably in his hard chair. "Well—no."

"How did you happen to go fishing?"

"Kate suggested it," Kitty replied, her words as soft and smooth as a silk thread. "He wanted to go with her, and she said she'd better go alone. Then she suggested that he might fish in the brook."

Alex swore under his breath, and only the sheriff's keen ears caught his "Damn that woman!" But the sheriff was watching Kate. Her face was frozen and her black eyes stared with repugnance at her cousin before the lids dropped like curtains, concealing a mounting hatred. When she spoke her lips were stiff, her mouth almost rigid.

"It's my fault. I did suggest that Alex go fishing. I—I forgot about the license."

"Well, you see that he gets one before he goes again. Now then, you left about two-fifteen?" the sheriff came deftly back to his questioning.

Alex nodded, and the sheriff pushed the stubby pencil across the paper.

"Who left next?"

"I suppose I was next to leave," Kate replied.

Alex looked at her strangely, as though he sensed some change in her. He seemed to guess that she was fighting, fighting with all the weapons a woman possesses, for something she wanted very much.

"I left about two-thirty. After lunch I changed clothes and went to see about Star. I rode him because I had to cross the swamp. Alex had left a few minutes earlier."

The sheriff turned toward Kitty, as though expecting her to contradict this, but she only took one last draw on her cigarette and threw it into the fire.

"Do you know what time Miss Lucy left?"

"Cu'un Lucy was dressing when I went downstairs," Kate told him. "The Guild meets about three, I think, so she must have left a little before that time."

"And what time did you see her coming back?" The sheriff turned to Alex.

"I can tell you that exactly. I looked at my watch because I wondered if it was time for me to be getting back too. It was only five minutes after four, so I fished a little longer."

"Did you see Mr. Brock before you left, Kate?"

"Not exactly. He was in the office when I left. I could see him talking over the telephone as I went past on my way to the stable."

"Did any of the rest of you see him?"

The others shook their heads.

The sheriff digested this information slowly. Deliberately he pushed back his chair and, rising, put another stick of wood on the fire. The room had warmed and the sun streamed brightly through the uncurtained window.

"And what time was it that you found Mr. Brock?" Sheriff Davies settled himself again in his chair.

"I—I don't know. It was getting late. The sun was setting. But I don't know what time it was."

"Maybe I can help you." It was Alex who spoke. "I got back to the house about a quarter of five. Miss Lucy told me that Kate hadn't come in and she was worried. So after I put my things down I started out to look for her. I got as far as the stable when I saw her horse. I thought there had been an accident, so I hurried on and met her on the edge of the field. She told me what had happened, and I brought her back to the house. I met Jeff Gaines on the side porch, and we got Will and went down toward the swamp. As soon as we got there, or pretty soon afterward, I sent Jeff back to call you."

The sheriff made no comment. His gnarled fingers wrapped around the short pencil and he wrote painfully on the envelope. He wrote for some time, and the other three watched him as though he were writing ghost letters on a wax tablet.

Suddenly he raised his head. "You were in your room all afternoon?" he asked Kitty.

"Yes, I was. Almost all the time."

"Suppose you tell me what you did."

"At lunch Kate said she had to go see some old Negro woman who was dying, and Cu'un Lucy insisted that she ride because it meant going through the swamp. Alex wanted to go with her, but she wouldn't let him." Kitty paused dramatically to let her point sink in.

"Cu'un Lucy said it was the Guild afternoon and that she would have to have Will drive her. After lunch I went upstairs. I had Fancy wash some things for me up there where I could keep my eyes on her. It would be just like her to boil my things in an iron pot if I didn't watch her. I made her bring up the ironing board too. While she was doing that I wrote a letter. I saw Kate leave and a little while later I heard Cu'un Lucy. Will brought the car around to the front door, and I heard her go down the front steps."

"Do you know what time that was?"

"Of course not. I don't go around with my eyes glued to a clock!" She shot a malicious look at Alex.

"And then?"

"After I had finished my letter I went downstairs to get somebody to mail it. I gave it to Zack, and he said he'd take it down to the gate right away."

"Did you see anybody downstairs? That is, anybody but Zack?"

"There wasn't anybody else. Ella had gone to see a cousin, and Zack had been washing the woodwork in the front hall."

"You didn't see Mr. Brock?"

"No."

"How did you know Ella wasn't in the house?"

"Zack told me." Kitty sounded as though she were explaining something very simple to a rather stupid child. "He said if he had to go mail the letter somebody should be in the house and that Ella had gone."

"And did you stay downstairs then?"

"Yes. Fancy had finished the important things before I left her, so I went into the parlor and played the piano."

"Did you see anybody come up toward the house?"

"No, but my back was to the windows that look out on the road. I'm sure I would have heard anybody though. And certainly I would have known if anybody came to the door. Give me another cigarette, Alex. If I'm going to be third-degreed I might as well have a smoke."

The sheriff's face was furrowed with a frown as Alex gave Kitty another cigarette and lit it for her.

"This is certainly no third degree. That's just for books, anyhow; it don't really happen." He pushed back his chair and appeared to think: That damned woman sure can rile a man. "Did you see Zack leave the house?"

"No, but I heard him slam the door. I had just put another log on the fire. It was cold in the room, and the fire had practically died," she said in an aggrieved tone which seemed to imply that she held someone responsible for her discomfort.

"Did you see him come back?"

"Why, no, I didn't," she replied slowly in some surprise. "I played the piano only a little while. When the sun goes down it gets dark so soon. I went upstairs to dress. They eat so ridiculously early out here in the country."

"Hu'um. Any idea of the time?"

"I have not," she snapped.

"Did you see anybody in the halls while you were downstairs?"

"No. How many times must I tell you that? Fancy was still in my room. She had scorched a handmade blouse, and I sent her downstairs and got dressed by myself."

"Didn't you hear the others come back?"

"I heard Cu'un Lucy come in while I was dressing. She was talking to somebody in the hall. In a little while there was a lot of commotion, and when I went out to see what it was Kate told me what had happened."

The sheriff merely grunted, and Kate, who was sitting closest to him, saw him add whiskers to the crude animal he had been drawing. It looked like a fierce cat.

"I reckon that's all for now. You and Mr. Dexter can go back to the house. Kate here can help me a little more, but you can tell Miss Lucy I'll send her back in a few more minutes."

Kitty rose from her chair hastily but gracefully. She threw her half-smoked cigarette into the fire, and when it fell instead on the rough brick of the hearth she crushed it with her foot. Alex picked up her coat and held it, but she took it from him and threw it carelessly around her shoulders. At the door she paused and turned back to the sheriff.

"You might ask Kate what she was burning in her room last night." A smile curved her lips, but the eyes she turned toward them were hard and mirthless.

Kate sat perfectly still when the door closed. There was no use pretending she wasn't frightened. She was. The palms of her hands were wet. The sheriff watched her closely. He knew that she was frightened and that there was something she was hiding. Her face was immobile, her mouth set in a grim line. Oh, he knew his Leighs, stubborn, arrogant, quick-tempered. All this with a soft voice, seldom raised, even when their seemingly mild faces were flushed in anger. He stared at the squared jaw and decided against questioning her then. She was primed and ready now and would look him in the eyes and lie until hell froze over if there was something she didn't want him to know. Better wait and get it from her when she least expected it.

"I wonder if you can show me any of Mr. Brock's papers."

Kate stared at him, speechless, a look of surprise spreading over her tense face.

"Uncle Brock did bring some papers out here the other day." She could hardly grasp this reprieve he was giving her. "He brought them out to the office. guess he put them in the safe." She nodded toward the battered iron hulk beside the desk.

"When was that?"

"We went to town together. It was last Tuesday, the day Kitty came. I went to get her and picked up Uncle Brock as we came back through town. He had some papers under his arm with a rubber band around them. I'd almost forgotten it. When we got home he asked for the office key. I guess that's where he put them." She rose and knelt down before the safe. Twirling the nickel knob right and left, she pulled open the thick door.

Sheriff Bill came and stood behind her. The safe was filled with papers stuffed untidily in pigeonholes: a broken watch, a small bag marked "seeds," some old ledgers, and several boxes. Kate poked about a minute, dragging out papers and stuffing them back. Finally she pulled out a few and handed them to the man behind her.

"These look like they might be Uncle Brock's. But I'm sure he had more than this that afternoon. Do you want me to go through everything?"

"Yes, I guess you'd better. This is his will, I think. Who's his lawyer?"

"Leigh, I'm sure. He's handled all our legal affairs ever since he began to practice. Shall I go through these now?"

The sheriff pulled out a heavy gold watch which looked as though it might serve as an anchor in his vest pocket.

"You might as well, unless you want folks crying over you up at the house." Kate shook her head emphatically. "It kind of needs straightening anyhow," he added.

Kate set about going through the safe methodically. The sheriff hitched his chair over and sat beside her. She pulled out papers, sorted them, occasionally throwing one into the trash can. Others she handed to him. She opened one drawer in which were some broken pieces of jewelry and a package of letters tied neatly. She closed it quickly and without looking at the sheriff said:

"Those are mine, from—from my husband."

Swiftly they went through the papers, and the pile on the sheriff's knee grew—letters, bills, advertisements, an insurance policy, a perfect conglomeration of papers. They had been working for some time when they were startled by a knock on the door, and Lucy stepped inside.

Her eyes were red and her soft cheeks were covered with a multitude of finely etched wrinkles. Here was the one who would perhaps grieve the most, Kate thought. It's terrifying when your own generation begins to go. She looked at Lucy with pity in her eyes, and the thought came to her that age should by all rights have its just compensations of peace and quiet.

"You've been out here so long, Kate."

"Miss Kate's been helping me," the sheriff quickly interposed.

"We're almost through now, Cu'un Lucy. I was just going through the safe to collect Uncle Brock's papers for Mr. Bill. Sit down for just a minute and we'll go back to the house together." Kate threw her a wistful smile.

Lucy sat in the chair so recently vacated by Kitty and pulled at the somber black skirt that dipped over her plump knees.

"I think we've been through everything now." Kate rose and stared down at her dirty hands. "Is that all you want?"

"Are these the papers he had that afternoon?"

"I can't tell. They were long papers, sort of bundled together like some of these. But whether he put them all in here or whether he took some of them out again I don't know." She gestured vaguely with her hands.

"Who knows the combination of that safe besides you?"

"Uncle Brock knew it, of course, and Cu'un Lucy. Then probably Leigh, and maybe Jeff knows it too. It really isn't secure, and Uncle Brock used to say a baby could open it without any trouble. It's old, and we kept it mainly to keep prying black hands off some of our things."

"Hump!" grunted the sheriff.

He gave Kate his handkerchief, and she wiped some of the dust from her hands and slipped on her sweater.

"Miss Lucy, as long as you're out here, I wonder if you'd help me a little with the time people came and went yesterday."

Lucy had risen, too, and now she faced the sheriff, her mouth set in the same grim line that had marked Kate's earlier in the morning.

"Of course," she said. "I want you to find out who did this. Somebody killed Brock, and whoever it was must pay."

Kate slipped her hand in Lucy's and thought, She's like the avenging angel and she might as well be repeating those Bible words, "an eye for an eye, a tooth for a tooth."

"You left the house a little before three o'clock?"

"Yes. I didn't have much time, and Will drove me straight to the Parish House."

"And you got home a little after four?"

"No. . . . No." Lucy hesitated, her brow puckered. "The meeting lasted until after four. We sat around and talked. It must have been four-thirty or maybe even later before I got back."

"But Mr. Dexter says he saw your car come down the road and heard it at just four o'clock." Sheriff Bill's voice rose with excitement.

"That is entirely impossible," Lucy replied emphatically. "Will drove me to the short cut and put me out there. I sent him down the road to get Ella. Alex couldn't have possibly seen the car if he was fishing on the creek."

9

On the Saturday before Palm Sunday they buried Brock in the family plot at Cliff's Edge. It was high ground, far from the cruel approach of the river. The cedar trees and live oaks cast a funereal shade over the scene as the minister's words rose above the somber hush.

For Kate it had been a harrowing day. If Alicia had not taken over the management of the house it might have been worse. She had been so efficient, in fact, that she and Kitty had quarreled long and violently just before the funeral.

With a troubled look in her eyes Kate watched Lucy, her face puckered with misery. And always, there in the background, was the sheriff, his eyes cold and watchful.

Back at the house Kate took off her hat and quietly slipped through the side door. She crossed the garden and made her way toward the river's bank. From childhood this had been her place of refuge, and now she came to it automatically. She leaned against the rough bark of the tree that hung dangerously over the bluff.

The wind caught her hair and tossed it about her face, and the long slants of sunlight fell over her back, warming her shoulders through her light tweed coat. She closed her eyes against the glare of the afternoon sun on the water below.

She didn't hear Jeff's steps and was startled when he touched her arm.

"I didn't mean to frighten you, Kate. But I saw you come out this way and I wanted to talk to you."

"I'm glad you came," she said. "But I warn you, I'm not very pleasant company these days."

"I know." His gray eyes were steady as they met hers. "I didn't go out to the grave this afternoon, Kate. Uncle Brock hated the ground I walked on. Oh yes, he did." He spoke quickly at her protest.

"He thought you were capable of doing so many things. He wanted you to do so much."

"What's the use?" Jeff stared down at the water. "I'm lazy. I haven't any ambition. . . ." His voice tapered into the air. "But I'm really sorry about Uncle Brock, Kate. I wanted you to know."

"Thank you, Jeff." Kate caught his hand in hers.

"If you need me ever, I'll be here, plain Kate," he answered and then, turning, walked away through the trees.

Kate watched him go. He had been without his usual braggadocio and bluster, as though the chip which he eternally carried on his shoulder had been shifted. But back of all this was a nagging suspicion, the opening gun of everything that is evil on this earth. She remembered the quarrel, whose end she had so nearly seen and . . . Alex had found Jeff at the side door when she had sent him to Uncle Brock.

Though the spring wind was not cold she shivered as she turned back to the house. In the garden she saw Leigh, evidently waiting for her.

"I've been looking for you," he said. "I'm reading the will to the family. Come in by the fire. It's still too cold to stay out so long."

Kate took off her coat and threw it over a chair in the hall. Leigh held the parlor door open and followed her inside. The scene would easily have passed for a friendly family gathering, but the strangeness of the atmosphere, the tenseness of the people belied it.

Kate took a vacant chair in the shadow by the square piano, and Leigh drew a straight chair up to the table by the window.

"I think we're all here now. I'll have to notify Jack, so, Kate, be sure to give me his exact address before I leave." Leigh opened the brief case which lay on the table.

Kate looked about the room. Yes, they were all there, all the family. Lucy's face was a little blurred by the tears she had shed, but she sat rigidly erect in her chair; Kitty's intense eyes watched Leigh's every move with a catlike eagerness; Alicia nervously picked at a handkerchief and looked more washed out than ever, and of course there in the shadows sat the sheriff, inconspicuous, but she could not forget him.

Leigh shuffled some papers and began reading slowly. At first Kate hardly heard him, but suddenly she knew why the sheriff was there. The will. He would already know what was in the document, but he would still want to know their reactions when they heard it. Kate bit her lips to keep from crying out a warning to the others and then forcibly fixed her attention on the words.

But there was nothing extraordinary in the will. Uncle Brock, having no family of his own, had left a small gift to Lucy and the rest to be divided equally between Kitty, Kate and her brother Jack, and Leigh.

When he had finished reading Leigh put the papers back on the table and turned to the others with a sigh.

"And just what will we get, Leigh darling?" Kitty asked softly.

"I'm not sure, but I imagine between four and five thousand apiece."

"There ought to be more." Kitty's lips were pressed into a thin red line that gave her face a sharp look, and her eyes narrowed shrewdly.

"Well, Uncle Brock had made some investments that went bad." Leigh took out a carefully folded handkerchief and mopped his brow.

Alicia had watched Kitty in silence, but now her eyes smoldered, as though she believed Kitty was implying that Leigh was personally responsible for Uncle Brock's financial status.

"Of course I haven't had time to go through everything in detail," Leigh continued, "but Kate seems to have found practically everything he owned out there in the office safe."

"He was worth a lot more than that. What about the royalties from the gadget he invented? I've heard my father say that alone would net him a small fortune."

"You ought to be ashamed of yourself, Kitty!" Lucy threw back her head and regarded the younger woman, indignation in her small black eyes.

"The Leighs took him in as an orphan, didn't they? And when he got tired of working didn't he come down here and just live on you?"

"Kitty!" Kate was shocked.

"His great-grandmother was a Leigh," said Lucy. "And we were the only kin he had after his family was wiped out in that yellow-fever epidemic. And I can tell you, Brock held up his part at Cliff's Edge. What we would have done without him I don't know."

Kitty's pretty face was sullen, and her mouth drooped petulantly, but she gave no sign of feeling the anger the others were pouring over her.

The sheriff stirred slightly, so slightly that only Kate caught his movement. Instantly she was stiff with fear, for she knew that this was what he had come to hear, and the others seemed to have forgotten he was even in the room. If she had been nearer she would have touched Kitty's arm and reminded her, but she was too far away.

"It may be more, Kitty," Leigh was saying wearily, and Kate thought that at least he hadn't forgotten the sheriff and was trying to keep them from a quarrel. "As I've said, I haven't had time to examine all his papers, but he lost some money several years ago through bad investments and of course he hasn't been adding to his capital in recent years."

"I know he hadn't been doing any work. But neither had he been spending money. Cliff's Edge isn't exactly the place for riotous living. I tell you he had more than that. I swear it!"

"Please, Kitty." Kate forced the words, and they all turned toward her, suddenly remembering there were others in the room, and they saw then, too, the sheriff standing in the dim corner back of her chair.

Sheriff Bill cleared his throat, and the sound cut the stillness of the room like a sharp knife. "Just what is this gadget you're talking about? I knew Mr. Brock came back here about fifteen years ago, but I never heard he was an inventor."

Nobody volunteered the information, and the sheriff searched one face after another without success.

"Suppose you tell me what you know, Miss Lucy," he said finally.

"I'll do the best I can." Lucy folded her hands primly on her short lap. "Brock's father and mother and little sister all died in a yellow-fever epidemic in Mobile when he was a little boy. Cousin John, Kate's grandfather, went down and brought him back to Cliff's Edge. This was just as much his home as Kate's father's and Kitty's mother's. They all grew up here together. Brock was always handy with tools, and he started working in a hardware store in town. Then he went to Birmingham. When Cousin John was too old to manage everything here Brock came back to help."

"And the gadget, Miss Lucy?"

"I don't know anything about mechanical things. Brock invented some kind of improvement, a pin, a belt, a catch—I don't know what exactly. He never talked about it. But it seemed to be an important part of some farm machinery. He patented it long before he came back here to live."

"Any of the rest of you know anything? You, Leigh?" The sheriff turned to the flushed man still seated at the table.

"I'm sorry, but I don't know any more than Cu'un Lucy has told you." Leigh shook his head.

"You ought to know something about it. You took care of his affairs, didn't you?" Kitty interrupted.

"Uncle Brock handled his own business." Alicia's voice cracked, and there were two spots of color burning in her pale cheeks.

"If he kept his papers back there in that old safe anybody could have stolen them. A child could open that old iron box without half trying," Kitty persisted.

"You think something was stolen, then?" The sheriff almost purred.

"I'm positive of it."

"You!" Alicia's word rose in a hysterical crescendo. "You viper! Everybody was getting along fine until you came. You always have caused trouble, even when you were a little girl and came down here to visit. You depraved, malicious—"

"That will do, Alicia!" Kate broke into her tirade swiftly. "We're all tired and upset."

"But she's accusing us—"

"No, Alicia, Kitty isn't accusing anybody. It's just that we're tired and overwrought."

"That's right, Alicia, I'm not accusing anybody—yet." Kitty's mouth curved, but her smile went no farther. Her eyes slid from face to face with a sort of secret calculation buried deep behind the black irises.

Kate, watching her, thought suddenly that the sheriff was not the only one waiting for reactions. Only Kitty had the advantage in that she knew how to drop her bombs expertly.

"I think we've done all we can this afternoon, anyway." Leigh sounded helpless, but he was the first to break the circle.

Lucy caught this like a straw on the open sea and rose to meet the emergency with her old vigor. Even the sheriff gave way to her and climbed into his rattletrap Ford and followed the more modern coupé down to the gate. Once he looked back at the big white house, its edges blurring now in the half-light of early evening. It was so silent out in the open country, and the house seemed strange, almost eerie, brooding, lonely.

Left alone in the parlor, the three women scattered quickly. Kate went to the kitchen to be sure that supper would be served. Lucy was in no state for such practical actions now.

Ella was mixing the biscuits when she opened the door. A frown spread over her broad black face, and Zack shuffled nervously about the room. Silence in the same place with the garrulous Ella was so strange that Kate looked at them in surprise.

"What's the matter with you?" she asked.

"Ain't nothin' the matta," Zack muttered.

"Then what are you pouting about? Your lip's poked out a mile."

"Go on an' tell her," Ella commanded, and Zack looked up, his eyes accusing her of treachery.

"You might as well tell me right now what is the matter." Kate pulled out a chair and seated herself, facing both the Negroes.

Zack cast one last look of despair at Ella and then plunged into his story.

"Well, yo' see, Mis' Kate, Mis' Kitty, she give me a letta to mail that attemoon Mist' Brock—Mist' Brock—" Kate nodded and he continued: "I wus cleanin' in the hall lak Mis' Lucy tole me, an' she give me the letta to mail. I tuk the letta an' I start out, but Mis' Kate, I neva mail dat letta."

"You didn't mail it, Zack?"

"Naw'm. I got a—a pa'tridge trap ova t'uther side o' the road down side o' the river, an' I went down there to see 'bout it."

Kate's eyes were on the old darky, but she was remembering other things: Kitty telling the sheriff about giving Zack a letter to mail; Alex saying he saw a car on the road; Lucy denying—a car.

"Has the sheriff asked you about these things, Zack?"

"Yas'm." Zack's shoulders drooped despondently.

"What did you tell him?"

"I tole him I went down the road an' mail dat letta at the gate. An' Mis' Kitty, she ast me, too, an' I tole her I mail it. But, Lawd, Lawd, Mis' Kate, I forgit dat letta, what with so much happenin' round here."

"Zack, did the sheriff ask you if you'd seen a car on the road?"

"Yas'm. An' I tole him there warn't no car on it all atternoon."

Kate closed her eyes and tried to blot out the course her thoughts were taking. Alex again. Why had he claimed he had seen a car? It hadn't been Lucy, so why . . . ? And there was the tobacco pouch. But there couldn't have been any connection between Uncle Brock and Alex. . . . Or maybe there had been a car. . . . Kate opened her eyes.

"You must tell the sheriff the truth, Zack." Kate had made up her mind.

"But, Mis' Kate, I cain't tell the shelf 'bout my traps," wailed Zack, his lower lip trembling with fear.

Kate patted his ann. "Tell him anyway, Zack. I don't think he'll do anything to you this time. But you certainly know better than to trap quail at this time of the year. You go get those traps first thing in the morning. If the sheriff does fine you I'll pay him this time."

"Yas'm. An' what I goin' to do 'bout Mis' Kitty?"

"What about Miss Kitty?"

"She got a telegram dis mornin' what make her awful mad. An' she ast me did I mail her letta. . . ."

"And you told her you did?"

"Yas'm. But I ain't." Zack drew a very soiled envelope from his coat pocket and showed it to her.

"You'd better go mail it right now, and then we won't say any more about it."

"But it's dark, Mis' Kate!"

"Zack ain't goin' down dat road atter dark by heself. 'Tain't safe," Ella interrupted her husband.

"No." Kate was thoughtful. "Perhaps you're right. Mail it in the morning."

"You take it, Mis' Kate. It near 'bout bu'ned a hole right thoo my pants pocket, an' I don't want to keep it no mo'." Zack thrust the letter into Kate's hand.

"Suppa'll be ready in 'bout fifteen minutes." Ella was anxious to be rid of Kate now that the pressing business had been taken out of Zack's hands. He had made his confession and had been absolved.

Kate hesitated at the door.

"Do either of you know anything else you haven't told?" She searched their faces, but they told her nothing. "Where was Eph that afternoon?"

"He warn't here." It was Ella who answered. "He went down to Link's to play that harp of hisn."

"Did he see or hear anything?"

"Naw'm. Us cullud folks don't know nothin' a-tall."

Kate still wasn't sure. "If you learn anything you'll come to me right away?"

"Yas'm, we sho will."

Kate crossed the hall toward the front of the house but stopped short. From the parlor came the sound of angry voices. She recognized Kitty's, angry, demanding, and the reply in a deep masculine rumble that could be nobody's but Alex's. She heard something hit the floor with a loud thump; then the door was opened, and Alex slammed it behind him. Before she could move he had plunged headlong into her.

"I beg your pardon." His words clicked like coins dropped on a metal surface.

Kate gave him one look and, shrinking, fled, panic-stricken, up the broad flight of steps.

10

On Monday morning Kate woke to find the sun streaming through her window. A breeze blew the ruffles of the white curtains, but it was a warm breeze, and the day promised to be one of those pleasant, lazy days that come sometimes even in early spring.

The others were already up, all except Kitty, who seldom appeared before midmorning. Kate found Lucy and Alex seated at the table, lingering over their second cups of coffee. She took her seat and accepted the cup which Lucy passed to her.

"This is really spring," she said. "If this weather keeps up summer will be here before we know it."

In spite of her bright opening the others did not continue the conversation. Alex was morose, sunk so deeply in his own thoughts that Kate was doubtful whether he really heard her or not. And Lucy was still lost and without her former spirit, so the meal was spent in almost complete silence.

As they rose from the table Alex fumbled with the button on his coat, and Lucy aroused herself sufficiently to say to him:

"That button's nearly off. If you'll leave it for me sometime soon I'll sew it on for you."

"Cu'un Lucy"—Kate placed a delaying hand on her arm— "you'll see Ella about lunch today?"

"Lunch?" Lucy seemed startled for a moment; then she smiled down at Kate's face. "Of course, Kate. I'll take over my part now. It will be the best thing in the world for me. It's just somehow been so hard to remember he's gone. I keep expecting him to come in and ask me where something is."

"Thanks." Kate took the hand and pressed it against her cheek. "There'll be so much for us to do now, and I reckon you're right. The sooner we get down to it, the better it will be for us. I'll try to take over the office and see if I can learn to be a farmer—a really good farmer too."

Pushing back her chair, she followed Lucy into the kitchen, where Lucy immediately began giving brisk orders for the day. Fancy was sent scurrying to open windows, and Ella was consulted about the meals. Kate picked up a piece of toast and munched it as she listened; then she added an order for Zack.

"Light the fire in the office. I'll be there all morning. I'll give you the key and then go down to see about the mail. I'd like to have it fairly warm when I get back."

"Yas'm."

Kate went back to her room to get the old red sweater. Descending the stairs a few minutes later, she gave Zack the key and went out the front door.

As she trudged over the narrow road she was reminded of another day when she had walked this road, the day she had found Alex at its end. Since his coming life had been accelerated in the sleepy household. Things had begun to happen, terrible things. But Kitty had come, too, Kate reminded herself, and wherever she went she sowed the wind and let others reap the whirlwind. Kate pulled a piece of bark from one of the cedars along the drive and shredded it with nervous fingers.

At the gate she eyed the sign with distaste. She thought of taking it down for a time at least, then shrugged her shoulders and decided to leave things as they were. Opening the mailbox, she took out one letter, noticed that it was for Kitty, and put it in her pocket.

The driveway was still attractive, although the dogwood was no longer in full bloom; here and there white blossoms showed between the dark green of the cedars, like ghostly women flitting from tree to tree.

Abruptly she turned off the road. This would have been the place where a car would have turned and parked—if Alex had actually seen one.

There was a space between the trees wide enough for a car to have been driven through, but the soft carpet of grass showed no imprint of wheels. She moved about slowly, brushing the grass and low bushes aside with her scuffed oxfords. Once she thought the grass was bent enough and that a car might have stood there, but she couldn't be certain. She did find a partially used paper of matches under some fallen leaves and picked it up with quickening excitement. It was identical with some she had recently bought at the drugstore, garishly decorated with a bright red-and-yellow advertisement of some patent medicine. It was damp and dirty, and there was no way of knowing how long it had lain there. She put it in her pocket, however, thinking there might be a time when it would be useful.

She was disappointed that there was nothing else of interest along the road. If Alex sticks to his word, she thought, they can't prove that a car didn't pass or wasn't parked here.

Alex was driving his car around the side of the house as she came up the road. When he saw her he stepped on the brake and called:

"Come along with me to town. Miss Lucy gave me a long list and commandeered my car to get them immediately."

For a moment Kate was tempted. It would be grand to get in with him and drive away, away from the worries of Cliff's Edge, even if for only an hour.

"I'd love to go with you, but I can't this morning. I've got to straighten up the office and I'd better start now if I expect to get it done today."

"Can't you leave it till later?"

"I only wish I could, but it's really impossible. This is planting time on a farm."

"Very well, just as you please." Alex shrugged and, shifting the gears, moved off down the road.

From the veranda steps Kate watched the car until it was out of sight. Alex was really better; he had gained a healthy color in the weeks he had been there and seemed perfectly well again. The lines which had made his eyes and mouth seem hard had softened, if they had not entirely disappeared. His body had come to Cliff's Edge emaciated and flabby, but now it had filled out, and the dark hollows under his eyes had gone. Though youth had returned in some measure to his face and body, time could not change the white hair about his temple, but it added a distinguished look which otherwise would have been lacking.

As she turned toward the door Kate glanced up at the windows. Kitty was standing in hers, watching. In spite of herself Kate shivered, for there was something malicious about that vigilance. It was as though Kitty were watching all of them, watching and waiting.

She opened the door quickly and went through the house to the office. In the back yard she caught sight of Eph and sent him to bring Will to help her. With the addition of their four hands she set to work with a vigor which Eph, at least, did not appreciate. They stacked ledgers, filed papers in boxes which Kate neatly labeled. They burned trash and worked on until some sort of order began to grow out of the chaos.

Kate moved a box of papers off a chair and sat down. Dirt streaked her face and hands; her hair was disheveled.

"What time is it?" she demanded.

There was a brief knock, and Alex opened the door.

"Is there anything I can help you do now?"

"You were never more welcome," she declared, smiling. "How good are you with a hammer and nails?"

"If I don't hit my thumb too often I usually get the nail into the right spot."

"Then will you please help Will knock those boxes apart and fix me some shelves, so I can put these things on them?"

"Give me a hammer and I'll try. Can you stand the noise?"

"I can stand anything if I can just get this place in some shape, so I can really go to work. Uncle Brock knew where everything was, but I'll have to find out for myself how to manage now."

For a while there was the din of hammering and sawing as Will brought some old boards from the barn which had been converted into a garage. While Kate sorted papers a series of shelves were nailed to the wall, and though they might not have been a carpenter's idea of perfection Alex stood back and surveyed them with undisguised satisfaction.

"Those are undoubtedly the best shelves I ever built," he informed Kate pridefully.

"They're probably your first," she laughed in reply, "but they're just what I wanted."

"What if they are my first effort? They're still damned good shelves. And don't you disparage my work, either." He turned to her, a mock scowl on his flushed face.

"When better shelves are built, Dexter will build them," Kate paraphrased.

"You're tired. Sit down and have a cigarette with me. It's lunch time now, and you won't be able to do anything more."

Kate took the cigarette he offered and drew a chair closer to the fire. "That's all for now, Will. After you finish lunch you can come out here and move all those old boards back to the barn, and I'll get Ella to scrub this floor this afternoon."

"Yas'm, sho will." He retreated through the door through which Eph had escaped some minutes earlier when Kate's back was turned.

"That's been real manual labor." Kate sighed contentedly.

"You just removed the dirt from the room to your face. Here, let me clean it for you." Alex picked up his coat, which he had draped over the back of a chair when he began working, and produced a clean handkerchief. Cupping her face in one of his hands, he gently wiped her cheek. "There, just see how dirty you were. All dirt, no rouge, no lipstick."

"Are you sure you've finished? Give me that handkerchief. I'd better make sure." Kate took it and wiped vigorously at her face.

"Now that you've cleaned this room, just what is it going to do for you?" Alex asked as he pocketed the soiled handkerchief.

"I hope I can learn to manage as well as Uncle Brock. The land is pretty much worn out, but he made it pay the taxes and a little more. I'll get Jeff to help me. He could do a lot if he would. The house is supposed to take care of itself. All those modern improvements put us in debt, and it just takes time to clear it."

"But didn't your family live here before—?"

"Oh yes. My grandfather put in the droplights in all the rooms. But the only convenience the original house boasted was its elevator, and that's hardly been a convenience since Lee surrendered."

"What on earth are you talking about? I've never seen an elevator in the house."

"It's a very primitive one, I'm afraid. You ought to know where it is—there between the dining room and the kitchen. It was put in when the house was built and works on pulleys. In the old days slaves used to pull the ropes and move some of the things upstairs that way. Leigh and Uncle Brock put it back into working order for me so that we could move the heavy baggage upstairs. But really it's less work to carry them up the steps." Kate threw her cigarette into the fire.

"Was Mr. Curtis your mother's brother?" Alex asked after a moment's silence.

"Oh no," Kate replied promptly. "He was distantly related, but he was left an orphan, and Grandfather brought him here to live. We're a funny family. We all come back to this place. It's in our blood—the land and the cotton and the sun. I can't remember a time when there weren't several of us living here. That's why so many of us are buried over there on the hill." Kate's eyes were fastened thoughtfully on the fire. "Uncle Brock came back when he was needed. He helped my grandfather, my father, and finally me." She looked up at him and rose. "We'd better get back to the house if we want anything to eat. I'm starving."

Alex picked up the red sweater and held it for her. As she slid her arms into it she asked, "Do you ride?"

"Yes, why?" Alex switched his thoughts quickly at this abrupt change of subjects.

"I thought I might ride over to Jeff's this afternoon and get him to come over and help me. He knows about farming. Would you like to come with me?"

"After you turned me down this morning I ought to tell you I'm busy, but I won't. I'd really be delighted to go with you. But I warn you now that it's been months since I was on a horse, so let's take it easy."

"It's not very far, and we'll take the highway."

They hurried across the back yard and into the dining room, where Lucy and Zack were putting the finishing touches to the table.

"Lunch will be ready in a minute, so go wash your hands, both of you. I don't know when I've seen you so dirty, Kate. Anyway, work seems to agree with you."

"'Member what you used to tell me about idle hands and the devil's workshop, Cu'un Lucy? We'll hurry, and I'll bet we're down before Zack gets the food on the table."

They raced up the back steps two at a time, arriving breathless but laughing at the top. Kate hurried on to her own room, where she jerked off her sweater and went on to the bathroom to wash her hands. Back in her room she ran a comb through her damp hair and dusted powder lightly over her shining face.

She moved the slipper chair and saw that the match paper had fallen from her sweater pocket. She picked it up and turned it over in her fingers, uncertain what to do with it. Then she opened one of the small drawers of her dresser and placed it far in the back.

Zack was just ringing the dinner bell as she hurried down the steps. Alex was already in the dining room with Lucy, and Kitty came in immediately. Three appetites had been whetted by the morning's work, but Kitty ate her meal in silence, barely making civil replies to their queries and now and then casting contemptuous looks at Kate and Alex. In the middle of the meal Fancy came in to tell her she was wanted on the phone.

"It's them telegram folks agin."

Kitty threw down her napkin, and her chair scraped angrily on the floor.

"That's the second one she's got today," Lucy said when Kitty had left the room.

Kate looked up, a question in her eyes, and Lucy nodded.

"She's been in a bad humor all morning. She's been hitting the piano keys so hard for the last hour I'm afraid she'll break the strings."

Kitty offered no explanation when she returned, but the others could see that she was furious. Her lips were drawn down at the corners, and even Fancy and Zack waited on her in strained silence. As soon as dinner was over she went to her room and slammed the door with such vigor that the floor shook.

"We'll go over to Jeff's in about an hour," Kate told Alex.

"What are you going over there for?" asked Lucy.

"I want Jeff to help me with the plantation. I don't know anything about farming and he knows a lot."

"His place doesn't show it," Lucy replied acidly.

"I need some practical advice, and he's the only one I can ask. Leigh couldn't help me."

"How you can be so blind about that common—" Lucy walked away without completing her sentence.

Alex, who was feeling wholly unnecessary during this bit of conversation, said he would see about getting the horses saddled and hastily went out through the back dining-room door.

Kate's broad forehead was puckered as she went slowly up to her room. It was such a pity that Jeff couldn't get along with any of the others. She was honest enough to realize that it was largely his own fault, but she knew that there were hidden qualities in him.

She had no way of knowing that Kitty watched her through a crack in her door and that she would slip silently down the steps and pick up the telephone when the hall was clear.

It was nearly two-thirty when Alex and Kate went to the stable. Will had saddled Star and had chosen a chestnut mare for Alex to ride.

"He's given you an easy mount," Kate told Alex. "We named her Deirdre because she's so slow and looks so mournful. Come on; if we take the road it will be a little longer, and I want to catch Jeff at home."

The horses settled into an easy trot, and Kate was pleased to find that her companion really did have some knowledge of the art of riding. The day was warm and the trees along the country road cast a pleasing shade over the riders, dappling the roadway with sunshine and shadow.

Alex was totally unprepared for the state of dilapidation which met their eyes as they rode up the avenue to The Laurels. Beside it, Cliff's Edge seemed in an almost perfect state of preservation.

The house, though not so pretentious as the Leigh home, was of a more classic symmetry in its lines and proportions. Kate, brought up in a land of sagging houses, saw it only in her mind in its former beauty. Alex saw the rotting Doric columns at one end of the gallery where the roof sagged dangerously, the crumbling brick of the chimney, the unkempt yard. Viewing it from the front, he was amazed that it didn't disintegrate before his eyes.

Had he been a little more informed, he might have noticed that the columns were solid logs, that the house was built firmly, that any house that could stand up for more than fifty years without any repairs must have been well built.

As they approached a timid little girl in a faded pink dress peered out at them from the side of the porch. Kate checked her horse and called to her.

"Lillie Mae."

"Yes'm." The child came closer. Her face was thin, and she had pale blue eyes and such light hair that it was almost white.

"Is Jeff here? I'd like to see him."

The child ducked her head but was saved from a reply when the front door was thrown open and a plump woman came out on the porch. She was short and dumpy in appearance. She wore a faded cotton dress belted at her middle with a twisted sash. Her frowzy hair gave evidence of having been under the influence of curl papers, but nature had intended it to be stringy, and nothing she could do would change nature's course.

"Well, it's been a long time since you came to see us, Kate."
She spoke through her nose, so that all her vowels had an added twang. "Come right in, and your boy friend too."

Kate could feel the blood rush to her face and, to hide her
embarrassment, dismounted quickly. "Thank you, Mrs. Gaines.
I came over to ask Jeff for some help." She recovered her poise
and, motioning to Alex, said, "This is Mr. Dexter, Mrs. Gaines.
He's a guest at Cliff's Edge."

"Pleased to meet you." Mrs. Gaines held open the door for
them. "I'd heard you had a Yankee staying over at the house.
Willie," she called to another towheaded child lurking in the
hall, "you get us a scuttle of coal. We'll just build up the fire in
the parlor a mite."

She ushered them into a room that was clean but crowded
with such incongruous pieces of furniture as to be indescrib-
ably confusing. Clothes were strewn over the chairs, and an
overturned darning basket spilled socks and stockings onto the
floor.

"Lillie Mae, you run find Jeff and tell him we've callers.
Hurry," she added to the scurrying figure. "Now you all just sit
down and make yourselves comfortable. I'll just move this off
so you can sit here."

She moved a pair of dirty overalls from a chair to a sofa
as Alex murmured a polite reply. He was too amazed by his
surroundings to talk. A chair in one corner had a leg missing
and was propped up with three large books; all the upholstery
was worn, and several pieces were torn. Kate could have told
him something of the value of this furniture which had been
imported from France during the Empire period and that it
would have sent decorators and antique dealers into an ecstasy
even in its present state.

While he was occupied with staring Kate asked Mrs. Gaines
some questions, and the woman went into a monologue concerning her "ailings," though her health appeared excellent.

She broke off abruptly when Jeff strode into the room, a
scowl on his face, and for a moment she seemed embarrassed.
Jeff frightened her.

"Kate wanted to see *me*." Jeff stressed the last word, and Mrs. Gaines stood up immediately, stammered a few words, and hurried from the room.

"Why did you come here?" he demanded.

Kate went toward him and placed her hands on his arms.

"You told me to come to you when I needed help," she replied, holding his eyes with her own steadfast ones. "And, Jeff, I do need help. Uncle Brock took care of the land. He told the Negroes what to plant and when to do it. I can't do that; I don't know where to begin and I'll have to learn. You will help me, won't you, Jeff?"

There was a moment's silence. Both of them seemed to have forgotten Alex. But when Jeff did speak his voice was softer and the scowl had left his face.

"Of course I'll help you. Though why you think I can do anything to help you—" His words trailed as his gaze wandered through the window to his own neglected acres.

"Of course you can. You know more about farming than you let folks suspect," Kate said. "Alex, you look at those pictures over there. They're real Currier and Ives. Then we can discuss business." She turned back to Jeff. "I know some of the fields have been planted. The Negroes are plowing some of the south field today."

"I wish we could turn part of both these plantations into cattle land. There's no more profit in cotton. I made that proposition to Uncle Brock—" Jeff's mouth hardened.

"It sounds like a good idea to me," Kate said. "We have all the farm machinery and if we could start on a small scale we might do something with it."

"There's eight hundred acres left in The Laurel's lands, and you have about six hundred. If we put some of it in oats and corn—I know where we could pick up a small herd to start with." There was a new light of interest in his eyes.

"Could you manage both places that way? The high ground might make good pasture land."

"We can't do so much now. You've already got a lot of cotton planted, but we could turn the rest into corn and get some of the cattle."

Alex had his back turned, but he heard the plans. Snatches of the conversation came to his ears. A hundred head . . . mortgages . . . a thousand dollars . . . corn . . . lespedeza . . . oats . . . silo . . . capital. They were completely absorbed.

"We'll figure it as your time and my money," Kate said.

"I won't undertake it unless I can put up some of the backing." Jeff's jaw was set.

"Come over to the house tomorrow and go through some of the papers. Something can be worked out, I know. Cliff's Edge has just been paying its taxes, and you sound as though it might do something really good. Then I'd like for you to talk to the Negroes about what has already been done."

Alex moved and Kate turned to him.

"We've been very impolite, Jeff. But I did tell you I had to talk business, didn't I, Alex? Did you like the pictures? They're really mine."

"Yes, very much." There was a doubt in his tone. He couldn't see very much in the slightly stained prints which represented the four seasons.

"Jeff's grandfather cheated mine out of them. They used to hang in the dining room at Cliff's Edge." She rose and smiled at the men, pleased that her business had been successful. "It's quite a story involving a bet and a pair of gamecocks."

"Don't believe everything she tells you." Jeff sounded relaxed and pleasant. "She's told some—well, very tall stories about the house. And the pictures are legitimately mine."

"One of these dark nights they're going to quietly change places," Kate told him with a laugh.

"When they do I'll know where to look for them."

As they reached the porch there was a sound of hoofs on the drive, and in a moment Kitty reined in her horse at the steps. She wore a smart new habit which contrasted dramatically with the haphazard clothes of the three who stood watching her. Without moving she surveyed them in arrogant silence, and then her laugh rang out thin and clear and high.

"Who would have expected to find the very elegant Mr. Dexter, the scion of the Philadelphia Dexters, in Shantytown?"

A sound, half growl, half roar, tore from Jeff's throat and he stumbled down the steps and grabbed at Kitty as though he would tear her asunder. She shrank back, terror in her eyes.

"Take your hands off her." Alex caught Jeff before he could drag Kitty from her horse.

Kate, who was watching him, saw that his face was white and that his eyes were like cold steel.

11

"Let me go!" Jeff jerked away from Alex and lunged again at Kitty. "I'll wring your little neck!"

"Yes, and have one more murder on your conscience!" screamed Kitty.

Jeff's hand dropped from the bridle, and the two on the steps were shocked into silent amazement.

"I think that needs some explanation. *Now!*" Jeff's face was a pasty gray, and he spoke through clenched teeth.

Kitty laughed shrilly, regaining some of the confidence she had lost in her first fright.

"You were there, weren't you? You never have told us how long you'd been there, either. And you were sodden drunk too—as usual."

"Kitty!" Kate put out her hand as though to stem the accusing words, but the other turned on her, fury in her eyes.

"You! You're a nice one to talk! Don't think I don't know you were burning evidence that afternoon I caught you in your room." Her lips curved scornfully. "And let me remind you of something else. I haven't forgotten I found you alone in the dark in the dining room the night before he was killed."

"But who would have had a better opportunity for it than you, Kitty?" Jeff inquired slyly and with narrowed eyes watched her. "You were there all afternoon."

Kitty caught her lower lip between her teeth, and her expression altered from hunter to hunted. "I have an alibi for the afternoon. Fancy was there in the room with me," she said nervously.

"Not all the afternoon. You were downstairs a part of the time, you remember. And didn't you send Zack away? As for Fancy, she'd lie if you made it worth her while."

Kitty surveyed the three hostile faces before her. She was like a cornered fox with the dogs baying madly and she fought back just as ferociously.

"Uncle Brock was the only one who ever treated me decently down here. Besides, I had no motive. Whoever shot him stole his money. And who needed it more than you—and Kate?"

"And you, Kitty," Alex said slowly.

The others did not hear him. He had relaxed his hold, and Jeff again lunged forward savagely at Kitty. But Kate was quicker. She gave the horse a sharp slap on its rump that made him rear and then gallop madly down the road.

The remaining three watched her disappear without speaking.

"Get rid of her right away, Kate, or, by God, I will!" Jeff's rough hands clenched and unclenched suggestively.

Kate did not reply at once. She walked over to the small tree in the yard and untied Star. Only when Alex had helped her mount did she turn to Jeff.

"Much as I'd like to, I doubt if the sheriff would let her go." The words were flat and hard. "Come on, Alex."

Not once on the way home was the silence broken. Kate made no apology for the scene, and neither was in a mood for light conversation. The sun was already sending late-afternoon shafts of light through the trees, and shadows were lengthening toward the east.

Will took their horses when they reached the stable. "The she'iff's up at the house, Mis' Kate."

"Has he been there long, Will?"

"Yas'm. He come pretty soon atter you lef'."

Kate nodded and walked thoughtfully toward the house.

"What does he want now?" asked Alex.

"I don't know."

"Do you want me to come with you?"

"No." Kate gave him a wan smile as he held open the door.

Ella was waiting for her, her usually placid face ruffled with vexation. In her hand she held a large old iron key.

"Here yo' is, Mis' Kate. I done tole 'em an' told 'em I ain't gonna let 'em in de office. Dey'll mess up my clean floo's. Fust Mist' Leigh come an' then the she'iff. An' my floo's as wet as can be. Naw'm, I ain't gonna let 'em go trackin' dirt in there atter I spend a good hour scourin' it."

Ella rustled her apron indignantly.

"What are you talking about, Ella?"

"I wa'n't more'n halfway throo when Mist' Leigh come an' wanted to git in there to see 'bout some papers. I tole him he couldn't come in while my floo' was all wet, an' he git pow'ful mad an' said he had to git at those papers, an' I tole him he could jist as well possess hisself with patience, 'cause I wasn't gonna let him in twell you come back." Ella paused for a much-needed breath and then plunged again into her story: "An' the she'iff come along an' want to git in, an' I ain't gonna let *anybody* track my clean floo's. I tole him so too," she muttered.

"You wouldn't let him in?" Kate was incredulous.

"Naw'm. I lock the do' twell yo' git home. I ain't gonna be 'sponsible. An' I ain't gonna wash that floo' agin."

Kate thrust the key in her pocket and looked about for Alex, but apparently he had slipped out of the room during Ella's tirade.

The sheriff was waiting in the hall as she opened the kitchen door, his feet planted sternly on the boards.

"I've been waiting for you to come home," he said, his jaws set in a grim line.

"I'm sorry I've kept you waiting. We can go into the parlor and talk." She led the way into the room which, fortunately, was empty.

The sheriff stared out of the window for several long minutes after they had seated themselves. Kate's fingers beat a nervous tattoo on the arm of the chair as she waited, braced for what was to come.

"I've talked to the Negroes this afternoon," he said, turning at last, "Will and Zack."

"Zack has told you about the letter?" Her words were low, but he heard them clearly.

"Yes, he told me."

"Then somebody might have been on the road."

"Yes." He drew the word out in a long drawl. "Kate, what are you trying to hide?"

Kate was frightened, terribly frightened, as she had been that first time he questioned her. Her hands gripped the chair, but she could not reply.

"This is murder, you know—cold, premeditated murder," he continued, deliberately holding her eyes on himself. "Murder don't just happen." He paused for his words to have an effect. "I thought you loved Mr. Brock—at least that you and Miss Lucy did. But you're not doing a thing to help bring his murderer to justice. Maybe Miss Lucy don't know anything—but you do."

"What do you want to know?" Kate asked quietly, trying to prepare herself for the question she knew he would ask.

"What were you burning in your room that afternoon before I had a chance to talk to you?"

"Kitty," she said bitterly. "All right, I'll tell you. It was a tobacco pouch that belonged to Alex."

"Why did you burn it?"

"It was lying there beside—beside Uncle Brock." Kate's hands were clammy.

"Why did you bum it?" he repeated.

"I—I don't know. He couldn't have done it." She flung the words at him.

"We have only his word for it that he was fishing in the creek that afternoon."

"But why?"

"I don't know." The sheriff shook his head.

"He might have seen a car, just as he said. Zack wasn't on the road, so one could have come up the drive part of the way and parked somewhere out of sight of the house."

"Yes, it's possible but not so probable. Neither Kitty nor that house girl of yours saw anybody come up to the house. And the gun came from that rack in the back hall."

"Zack should have told you right at first, but he was afraid of you and Kitty. I mailed the letter for him yesterday and told him to tell you just as soon as possible."

"His story don't help much. It only complicates matters."

"I told him I'd pay his fine if he had one."

The sheriff's eyes softened somewhat, and there was a suspicion of a twinkle in the corners. "I didn't fine him. I just explained that they were your birds and that he wasn't helping you any by killing them out of season. I don't think," he added, "that he'll do it again soon. You'd better watch him, though. If it had been anybody else you'd have been in my office raising merry hell and demanding immediate arrest."

"Yes," replied Kate meekly.

"Now then, what about Jeff Gaines?"

She was on guard again.

"I had a little talk with Miss Lucy before you got back. She tells me that you don't know when he came over that afternoon. What was he doing? Just hanging around?" he asked.

"Jeff comes over sometimes in the afternoon. He hasn't much companionship at home."

"Who'd he come to see? Kitty? Everybody was pretty well scattered that afternoon."

"I don't know. Probably he came just to see us all, but he hadn't seen Kitty since she came this time. Why don't you ask her?"

"Hu'um." The sheriff was noncommittal. "Had he been quarreling with Mr. Brock?"

"Uncle Brock had quarreled with everybody those last few days." She evaded the direct question.

"But they never did get along together, did they?"

"Jeff isn't a person it's easy to get along with," Kate replied wearily.

"Drunk most of the time, isn't he?"

Kate thought of the decaying house, the shabby furniture, and the unkempt rooms, but she only said, "Yes."

"Now look here, you're not trying to protect him too, are you?"

Kate felt the blood rise to her cheeks at his implication.

"No, of course not. Jeff could have done it. Any of us could. I could have, or Kitty, or Alex. None of us have good alibis, have we?"

"No, you haven't," he said. "We figure he was killed sometime between two-thirty and four-thirty. Doc can't be certain. Now you listen to this: You were out riding—alone; Kitty was downstairs—alone; Fancy was upstairs—alone; this Dexter man was out fishing—alone; Zack was first downstairs and then out in the woods—alone; Miss Lucy walked back that short cut— alone; and Will was fetching Ella—in the car, alone."

"But there's no reason, no earthly reason, for any of us doing such a thing." Kate rose restlessly and kicked a log on the fire to hide her nervousness.

"There never is a real reason for murder," the sheriff told her. "But some folks evidently think there is, 'cause folks are getting killed every day in the year. I liked Mr. Brock and I intend to find out who killed him."

Kate sat down again. "That's what we all want," she said earnestly. "But you're accusing one of us, and there seems no valid reason for it."

"You listen to me a minute, Kate. I'm not saying it was one of you, but it might have been. That gun we found beside him was his own, and it had just been fired."

Kate stared at him, her dark eyes wide and bewildered.

"That gun was kept in the hall, Miss Lucy says. Mr. Brock may have had it with him. If he did he was afraid. But just the same, anybody could have taken it from the hall. Don't remember when you saw it last, do you?"

"Why, no. It was always there in the hall with the others."

"That's what Miss Lucy said too. It could have been taken several days ago. Or it could have been taken that afternoon. Anybody could have come in through the side door and got it if he was familiar with the house. Kitty was upstairs part of the time, and Zack was in the front hall."

"But—"

"Somebody got Mr. Brock away from the house so the shot wouldn't be heard. There weren't any signs of a struggle where you found him. That points to the fact that Mr. Brock knew whoever it was."

"But why—?"

"Kitty says money was the reason. She went out of her way to point out how all of you could do with a little cash."

"Kitty will say anything that serves her purpose."

"Yes. I remember she was always a little hellcat. But she keeps on saying there ought to be more money."

"It wouldn't surprise me if she didn't need some herself," Kate said spitefully.

"You Leighs never were known to bite your tongues," was his dry comment.

"I'm sorry. No, I'm not. She's just been particularly un-pleasant this afternoon."

"What was that?" The sheriff made her go over all the de-tails of the afternoon, asking questions, prompting when she would have stopped.

"Accused one of you of doing it, did she?"

"Yes. And I'd like to know how long I have to keep her here. I'd be glad to send her away tonight." Kate glared at him defi-antly.

"Hu'um."

"Why do you keep on harping on one of us? Why couldn't it have been somebody else? Somebody could have come up here and not been seen."

"Mr. Brock didn't have many outside contacts. And you folks and Leigh Randall are the only ones that benefited by his death." The sheriff stared at the cracked plaster of the parlor wall.

He waited for Kate to speak, but she was silent. His words had unleased a new train of thought, and they frightened her.

"Where would Mr. Brock get so much money?" He sudden-ly took up a new kind of questioning.

"Whatever he had he made himself," Kate said. "He owned the hardware store in Birmingham and sold it when he came back here to live. Then there was the invention. . . ." Kate was vague.

"Wouldn't have thought it would have been so much," the sheriff mused.

"Neither would I," Kate said frankly.

"It's getting kinder late, nearly suppertime. Can I have Mr. Dexter come in and talk to me for a little while?"

Kate got up. "I'll get him," she said. As she reached the door the sheriff cleared his throat, and she hesitated.

"Oh yes, I forgot to tell you. I sent the gun to Montgomery to be tested. It didn't have any fingerprints on it. Wiped clean."

Kate shut the door quietly and hurried up the stairs. Crossing the hall, she knocked on Alex's door. As she waited for his reply she heard another door close softly, but when she looked all of them along the hall were closed and she couldn't be certain after all.

As Alex opened the door the sheriff called:

"Kate? Kate? Just one more thing."

"He wants to talk to you," Kate told Alex.

She hurried down the steps, and Alex followed.

"Why did Kitty come down here?" asked the sheriff as she re-entered the parlor.

"I don't know." Kate was puzzled.

"Were you expecting her?"

"No, she wired from the train, and I drove into town that afternoon and met her."

The sheriff nodded and took out his corncob pipe and lit it. "Sit down," he invited.

Kate looked at him and then took a seat beside Alex, facing him.

"Smoke your pipe if you want to." He waved his own toward Alex.

Alex put his hand in his pocket. "Sorry," he laughed, "I must have left my pipe upstairs. I'll take a cigarette, though, if it's all the same." He took out a slender gold case and offered it to

Kate. She shook her head, knowing the questions that would follow. Alex took one, lit it, and returned the case to his pocket.

"I haven't had much chance to talk to you," the sheriff opened the conversation.

"Just what do you want to know?"

"Mostly something about yourself," said Sheriff Davies.

"About me?" Alex frowned. "I don't know what to tell you. My home is in Philadelphia and I work in a bank there."

"Know any of these people? That is, before you came?"

"No. I had met Mrs. Bolling, Kitty. She spent some time in Philadelphia last fall, and I met her several times then."

"Did she tell you about Cliff's Edge?"

"No. I had never heard of it when I came here. I was distinctly under the impression her home was in Washington."

"How did you happen to come here?"

"It was purely accidental. I had been sick and my doctor sent me South for a few months."

The sheriff's shaggy brows lifted skeptically.

"He collapsed the day he came, and we had to put him to bed," Kate interrupted, and Alex threw her a grateful smile.

"I was headed for Florida," he explained, "but I missed the main route somewhere in northern Georgia. It didn't seem to matter which way I took. I saw the sign out there on the, gate, and as it seemed peaceful and quiet I thought it would do. One place was just as good as another as far as I was concerned then."

"Hu'um." The sheriff pulled on his pipe thoughtfully. "In a pretty bad accident last winter, weren't you?"

"I see you've done a little investigation," Alex said sarcastically.

"Have to," the sheriff responded grimly. "Suppose you tell me about it."

"What earthly bearing on this case can an accident that happened in Philadelphia have?"

"Never can tell. You were hurt pretty bad?"

"You seem to know all about it. Yes, I was in the hospital for nearly a month; then I had pneumonia."

"Your wife was killed, wasn't she?"

Kate felt rather than saw Alex stiffen. To her the room seemed stifling and hot.

"My ex-wife. We had been divorced for over a year."

"Weren't they afraid to let you drive all the way South—alone?"

Alex let his eyes flick over the other man curiously. "No."

"You still say you heard a car on the drive that afternoon Mr. Brock was killed?"

"I not only heard it; I saw it."

Sheriff Bill looked up quickly. "You saw it?"

"Yes. Not the whole car, only the top. I was sitting on the creek bank, facing the road, and when I heard the car I looked up. There's a sort of ridge all along the creek, but it levels off in one place, and I could see the top of a car."

"Can you describe it?"

"No, I didn't pay much attention."

"Miss Lucy didn't come back that way. She arrived much later than the time you say you saw the car."

"Then it was another car." Alex crushed his cigarette in the tray beside him.

"Has Kitty ever told you why she came here?"

Alex hesitated, as though weighing his answer. "No," he said. Somehow, thought Kate, I know he's lying. She clasped the arm of her chair more tightly.

"Hu'um. Did you know she and Jeff were thick as thieves down here one summer? Folks thought they were engaged."

Alex looked from the sheriff to Kate. She turned her face away, for there was something in his eyes that seemed to say he had just begun to understand something that had puzzled him. But there was a question, too, in them.

"You met Jeff outside the door after you brought Kate back to the house?"

"Yes." Alex stirred uneasily, and Kate thought again that he was concealing something.

The sheriff must have felt it, too, for his eyes studied the two younger people who sat like culprits before him. Then as though he suddenly realized what was happening, he threw up his hands and laughed mirthlessly.

"My God!" he said.

He got up then, his long legs propelling him upward with one sweeping movement.

"One more thing, Mr. Dexter, and then I'm through. Do you have a tobacco pouch?"

Kate was rigid, and Alex must have realized the change in her, for he turned toward her. It was the thing she had been dreading all afternoon, the reason she had stayed in the room.

"Why, yes." Alex sounded surprised at the question.

"Where is it?"

"I don't know. I must have misplaced it. I've looked for it, but I can't find it."

"When was the last time you remember having it?"

"I don't know." Alex seemed genuinely mystified. "Not for several days though. Have you found it?"

"Kate burned it," the sheriff said and closed the door.

12

Holy Week was a prolonged nightmare for the people at Cliff's Edge. The house was too remote and the Leighs too unimportant to attract much outside interest. There had been no reporters and the Greene County *Express*, the town's weekly, merely carried an obituary.

Lacking publicity, town gossip died down, and only those in the house were aware of the sheriff's persistence. He came and went, talked to the Negroes, asked questions, searched, watched.

Despite doubts and suspicions the family was drawn closer, seeking each other's company and avoiding outsiders. Only Kitty went into the town, but she was silent about her visits. The house itself seemed to brood, and the Negroes began to shun it. Leigh and Alicia came out occasionally, and Jeff was to be seen in the office talking to Kate, but otherwise they were left alone.

Except for the sheriff.

On Thursday, while Lucy and Kate were at church, the sheriff talked to Alex alone. They sat on the bank of the river, talking, until Alex was lulled by the drawled words. Before he realized it he had told the tall man that Jeff had known about the murder when he met him outside the door.

The sheriff left soon after getting this information, and as nothing happened that day, Alex was left to conclude that it wasn't important after all.

Kate woke early Friday morning. She sat up in bed and let the cool spring air, fragrant with the scent of magnolias, sweep over her bare shoulders. The sun was already warming the day, and through her open window she could hear the early-morning stir in the yard below.

She dressed quickly and hurried down the steps to the dining room, where she found Lucy arranging the day's meals with Ella. Kate poured herself a cup of coffee and walked with it over to the fire.

"You're early this morning," Lucy commented dryly.

"It was too much like real spring to stay in bed, so I didn't even wait for Fancy to come in and light my fire."

"You haven't forgotten it's Good Friday, have you? You'll go to church with me?"

"Good Friday? Heavens, I can't realize Easter's so near. Yes, I'll go with you."

"Remind me to tell Mr. Kenny that we'll have some flowers if he needs them for the Easter decorations." Lucy looked down at the pad in her lap and picked up the pencil she had laid on the table. "I want Eph to polish the silver this morning, and Zack should air the downstairs rooms thoroughly. Thank goodness Alicia had the sense to get Brock's room thoroughly aired and cleaned right at first." Her chin quivered, but a moment later she bustled out of the room.

Kate sighed when the door closed, and Zack took the empty cup from her hand.

"Yo' set down, Mis' Kate. I'll bring yo' breakfust in right away. Mis' Lucy ain't eatin' nothin' today."

Alex joined her while Zack was speaking.

"Isn't Miss Lucy well this morning?" he asked as he unfolded his napkin.

"She's all right. It's Good Friday, and Cu'un Lucy always fasts. I'm not so good, you see. I'm putting away a meal that would do credit to a field hand."

But in spite of her brave words she ate very little.

As she left the dining room she found Lucy standing outside of Brock's room, her hand still on the doorknob.

"Have you been going through Brock's things, Kate?" she asked, a frown bringing her eyebrows closer together.

"No, I haven't been in that room since— Has someone been in there?"

"I don't understand," Lucy replied. "Alicia straightened that room last week, I'm sure. But someone has been going through the dresser drawers."

Kate linked her arm through Lucy's. She didn't understand either. There was absolutely no reason, but there had been no reason for the other things that had been happening. It was all so strange.

"Maybe we're just imagining things," she said.

The diamonds in Lucy's ears bobbed indignantly. "I'm not an imaginative person. Someone has searched that room.

Kate did not answer, and Lucy started heavily up the steps, her breath coming in short gasps.

As Kate turned toward the side door Eph came from the kitchen and called her.

"Mis' Kate?"

"What is it, Eph?"

A sheepish grin spread over his black face, and his teeth gleamed whitely in contrast.

"Kin I go to chu'ch with yo' this mornin'?"

"You'll miss your lunch if you go with us, Eph."

"I kin take a little snack along with me."

Kate smiled in spite of herself. She knew that the religious significance of the service was missed by the boy. It was the rhythmic cadence of the chants and the minor key of the music which reached his ears; the solemn words from the Cross which struck some chord buried deep in his soul. And after all, she thought, what more could one ask?

"All right, I'll take you if you can finish the things Miss Lucy wants you to do this morning and clean up a little more."

"Yas'm, I sho will." Eph fell back on his father's favorite phrase.

Kate was still smiling as she went down the low porch steps and crossed the brick walk into the garden by the river. While

the people at Cliff's Edge had been sorrowing the warm sunshine had opened the flowers. The white flags marched bravely
along the borders like an Easter parade, and here and there
were clumps of purple and blue and yellow. The forsythia
spread its long branches on the black earth, and the clusters
of white and lavender lilac scented the air with a delicate perfume. New shoots filled the brick-bordered beds that Kate had
planted a few weeks earlier, yellowish green against the dark
soil.

Alex joined her in the garden and, lighting a cigarette,
listened as she explained that this was the azalea which her
great-grandmother had planted; that was a pink camellia which
would bloom later in the summer. She turned toward him once
and found him watching her with a smile that was half wry,
half tender, but she knew he had given her words only half of
his attention.

"You love this garden, don't you?"

"Yes, I do." She broke off a spike of the forsythia. "I think
this was what I missed most when I lived in New York. It
seemed such a pity to have to go to a park to see living things.
Even then the flowers didn't bloom until it was almost summer."

She turned as she said this, hearing the patter of feet running along the path.

It was Lillie Mae, barefoot, breathless, her stringy hair
blown in lifeless wisps across her face.

"Miss Kate, Miss Kate!" She half gasped the words, breathing hard. "Can you come over to our house? Mamma said I was
to fetch you if you'd come."

"What's the matter? Is Jeff—?" Kate was instantly frightened and she clutched the child's thin arm.

"Yes'm." Tears spilled out of the watery blue eyes and rolled
unheeded down anemic cheeks. "They came and arrested him
this morning."

"Arrested him? For what, Lillie Mae?"

"I don't know. They came a little while ago and took him
to town. Mamma said I was to come tell you, that you was the
only one who'd do anything for him."

Kate dropped her hand from the child's arm with a helpless gesture. "Of course I'll come with you."

"Do you want me to drive you over there? Or would you rather have my car?" asked Alex solicitously.

"Please let me have your car. Cu'un Lucy will need ours. And this is something I must do myself."

"Go on to the car, then. I'll run upstairs and get my keys."

Kate watched him go. Nervously she twisted the narrow gold band on her left hand. Four years since Pete died, she thought. And I'm falling in love again. I *am* a fool.

Alex brought her the keys. She knew he wanted to go with her, but she pushed the thought out of her mind as she waited for the sniffling Lillie Mae to climb in beside her.

She drove the car down the country road with as much speed as she dared, and Lillie Mae clung to the seat with all her small strength as they bounced and splashed through mud-holes too deep to have dried.

Kate made no effort to question the child further; her whole attention was bent on getting to The Laurels as quickly as possible. When they reached the unkempt driveway leading to the house she speeded up the car and came to such an abrupt stop that she was thrown against the steering wheel, momentarily knocking her breathless.

Mrs. Gaines met her at the door, her eyes red and swollen.

Her frizzled hair stood out wildly from her face, and she dabbed ineffectively at her cheeks with a cotton handkerchief.

"What happened?" Kate asked as she came up the steps.

Mrs. Gaines beckoned her inside. The house seemed tragically quiet and empty to Kate as she entered the hall.

"What happened?" Kate repeated her question.

"The sheriff came here this morning and took Jeff back to town with him. He brought that little man with him." Kate nodded, remembering the quiet shadow that usually trailed the sheriff.

They went into the parlor, where a small fire glowed in the grate, and sat down on the stiff sofa. A broken spring creaked in protest of their weight.

"Tell me everything that happened," Kate said.

"I don't hardly know myself. It was pretty soon after breakfast that the sheriff came, and he wanted to talk to Jeff. They talked in here, and I could hear them. Jeff was shouting something at the top of his voice."

"What did he say?"

"I couldn't hear the words. I just know both of them were talking loud. After a while the sheriff came to the door and called me, and he said he was taking Jeff to town. I tried to ask him why, but Jeff shut me up and told me to mind my own business."

Kate looked at the woman beside her. Ungrammatical and common she might be, but she had a heart and had been deeply hurt by Jeff's ruthless manners. Kate patted the hand that held a sodden handkerchief.

The woman looked at her in surprise. Tears rolled down her cheeks and washed away the last barrier to all the pent-up feelings she had nurtured through the years. The words came quickly then.

"Miss Kate, I know Jeff never even liked me. I ain't the lady his mother was, and he resented me marrying his father. But I was good to the major and I kept him from being so lonely. He never loved me like I did him, but I did things for him and made him comfortable. I'd have liked to do them for Jeff too. He was such a sweet kid. But he wouldn't let me. He hates me, but he's sorry for the kids." She twisted the handkerchief into a rope. "Jeff won't let nobody help him, unless it's you." She turned her face, haggard and bloated, toward Kate in mute appeal. "Will you do something for him? Go to town and bring him back. If it's money, I got a little put by I can use. He'd only hate me more if he knew where it come from."

"Of course I'll go," Kate promised. "Did the sheriff say he was arresting him?"

"No. He just said he was taking Jeff to town and we wasn't to worry if he didn't come right back."

Kate rose and tried to put some hope into her reply, but she knew she wouldn't fool this woman.

"I'll go to town right away and see what can be done. I'll let you know just as soon as I find out anything. Don't worry too much," she added.

Kate was thoughtful as she drove back to Cliff's Edge. See Leigh, she counseled herself. A lawyer is what we need. He'll do something, even if he doesn't like Jeff.

She parked the car in front of the house. Zack met her in the hall.

"Where's Cu'un Lucy, Zack?"

"Lawd a mussy, she done gone to chu'ch. She sho was mad when she foun' out yo' done gone. Mist' Alex done took her an' Eph in the stashon waggin." He wagged his head as she hurried up the stairs to her room.

She dragged a light tweed coat off its hanger and pulled a hat from the top shelf of the wardrobe. Rummaging in a bureau drawer, she found a clean handkerchief, stuffed money and checkbook into her purse. There were some keys lying next the powder box, and she put them in with the other loose articles.

In the hall she met Kitty, who eyed her curiously.

"Where're you going?"

"To town," Kate replied curtly and ran down the steps.

The trip to town took less time than usual, and had she thought about it, she would have been glad that in this emergency she had the use of a powerful car.

She parked the car along the courthouse square and almost ran across the short lawn and into the sheriff's office. A young girl who chewed gum loudly sat at the desk and told her the sheriff had gone home to dinner and that she didn't know when he'd be back.

Disappointed, Kate turned back into the dingy hallway. As she came out a group of players seated on the sunny end of the gallery called to her.

"How about that fox hunt you promised us a few weeks ago? Would it bother you if we came out there next Monday night?"

"Fox hunt?" Kate dimly recalled the promise she had made that afternoon she had met Kitty. "Of course you may come."

"Sure we won't be in the way, 'specially at this time?"

"No, come whenever you want to."

"That's mighty nice of you. We kinder thought we'd ask that young man boarding with you. Reckon he'd like to go with us?"

"Yes, I'm sure he would." Kate was anxious to get away.

"Saw him go into church with Miss Lucy a while ago. I'll ask him when he comes out."

"That'll be fine." Kate backed away and crossed the street to the bank building. She bit her lip nervously as she climbed the dark stairs to Leigh's office on the second floor.

His secretary was a neat middle-aged woman whom he had inherited along with his practice from Alicia's father. She greeted Kate with a friendly smile.

"Is Leigh here, Miss Mattie?"

"No, he's not, Kate. He had to go out into the country this morning and he hasn't come back. Is it something important?" she asked sympathetically. "I can call his house and see if he's there."

"Will you, please? I've got to see him right away," Kate begged.

Miss Mattie took up the phone, cranked the bell, and spoke finally to the cook. Even before she returned the receiver to its hook Kate knew the answer. Leigh wasn't at home, and they didn't know where he was.

"Is there anything I can do?"

"Thank you, Miss Mattie, I guess not." Kate turned away, her shoulders drooping with discouragement.

Outside on the sidewalk she heard a voice address her and, turning, looked into Judge Brewster's beaming face.

"It's a good thing you don't live in a big city any more, young lady. If you don't watch where you're going you'll get run over one of these fine days."

"I'm sorry, and thank you for saving me." Kate tried to smile, but her face was stiff. "Judge, maybe you can help me. Leigh wasn't in his office and I need a lawyer."

"You need a lawyer?" Judge Brewster sounded surprised.

"Yes, dreadfully. Come over to the car and I'll tell you about it. It's rather a long story."

They crossed the street, and the judge eased his rather ponderous weight into the seat beside her. He listened attentively while she told him of Jeff's arrest, not once interrupting her.

"So you see I need a lawyer," Kate concluded. "I don't know why they've taken Jeff and I couldn't get a thing out of that office girl except that Mr. Bill had been in and had gone home for lunch."

"You know I don't practice law any more. I've turned all that over to Leigh."

"But Leigh isn't here, and I need somebody to find out about Jeff right now. You should have seen Mrs. Gaines when she told me. She was really pitiful."

"She's a pretty good woman," said the judge, much to Kate's surprise. "And if you ask me, the major didn't do so bad when he married her."

Kate vaguely remembered that her father had said much the same thing at the time. It had been her mother who had been cold and aloof about the marriage.

"You've just got to find out about Jeff for me, Judge. Find out why they have him in jail at least."

"I don't know whether that's such a good idea." The judge shook his head. "But you wait here and I'll go in and find out what I can."

The judge was a big man, over six feet tall, but the amount of fat that covered his body made him seem only average in height. It was easy to see why Alicia was tall, and it was probably a fear of also inheriting his rotundity that kept her watching her diet with an anxious eye.

Kate moved restlessly on the leather seat and opened her purse in search of a cigarette. Finding none, she pressed the button of the dashboard compartment and, turning over a rag and a clothesbrush, found what she wanted. It was somewhat stale, but it gave her something to do to pass the time while she waited.

The judge was not gone long. She caught sight of him coming out of the front door. For all his size and weight he had a very dignified appearance. He lived in comfort at the local hotel, having given up the home as well as his private practice when Alicia married. Some would have it that he was more comfortable than he had been since he married.

"I couldn't find out much, Kate," he said as he leaned his arms against the door. "I talked to the sheriff on the phone. Jeff has been held for questioning and will probably be charged with Brock's murder."

Kate gasped, and her eyes were wide with horror. The judge patted her arm.

"Don't take it like that," he said kindly. "But you'd better know the worst. The sheriff says that, to say the least, Jeff found Brock before you came along. He even admits hearing the shot and going over to the place. But he says the murderer was gone when he got there and that he went to the house to get help. Only he was frightened and didn't."

"Oh no, no." The words, were breathed rather than spoken.

"You go on back home and I'll get Leigh to see Jeff. He'll do whatever he can."

"I must see Jeff."

"Well, Bill said you could see him if you insisted. But the jail isn't exactly the place for a lady. Better let me see about it first."

"I must see Jeff. Even before you talk to him." Kate was decisive.

"I was afraid of that." The judge let out a wheeze which was intended for a sigh. "The sheriff will meet us there in fifteen minutes."

Kate turned the key in the ignition.

"You've got some time yet," the judge assured her. "The jail isn't a good hotel. Jeff might talk to us more easily if we tended his bodily comforts."

Bodily comforts were important to the judge, and he went with her to the drugstore and helped select a few articles.

The sheriff was waiting for them when they drove up in front of the jail twenty minutes later.

"I can't keep the judge out if he's going to be Jeff's lawyer, and there's no real reason why you can't see him, but if I were you I'd let him alone. He's in a mean mood."

Kate's mouth set in a straight line, and her jaw squared.

The sheriff had already learned the significance of what he called that "bulldog Leigh look."

"I want to see him now—and alone. If he killed Uncle Brock I won't raise a finger to save him. But I must be absolutely sure."

Kate spoke with a deadly calm that evidently impressed the sheriff, as he merely shrugged and led her to a dingy, smelly room, where he left her. In a few minutes he brought in Jeff, sullen and defiant, and closed the door.

Kate flew to him and for the first time began to cry as though her heart would break. Jeff held her close and over her head shouted at the top of his voice to the sheriff.

"Why in hell did you bring her here!" He followed with a string of invectives that astonished even the hardened warden. They were strong enough to drive the others from the room and leave the two alone.

Jeff was as gentle with Kate as he had been harsh with the men. And under his soothing, awkward pats she became calmer.

"I'm sorry I made such a fool of myself," she sniffed and brushed the tears from her face with the back of her hand. "I came as soon as I found out where you were. Leigh wasn't in the office, so I brought Judge Brewster with me. But you can have any lawyer you want. This is so absurd."

Jeff held her tear-streaked face in one hand, and there was an odd expression of wonder in his eyes as he looked down into hers.

"You have such great faith, Kate."

"You didn't do it."

There was a question in her tone, and Jeff turned away from her. She watched him with fear mounting in her heart.

"You might have hit a man, Jeff, but I don't believe you would shoot one."

"What's the use of saying I did or that I didn't? Proof is the only thing that will be of the slightest use to me. They haven't much against me; it's circumstantial evidence at the most." He swung round to face her, but his eyes shifted under her steady gaze.

The room was still as Kate waited for him to explain. He began instead to pace from one end of the room to the other.

"Will you talk to the judge? He's outside now. I brought him along with me to arrange bail."

"There isn't going to be any bail. The sheriff made that perfectly clear when he brought me here this morning." Jeff's voice was harsh and thick with anger.

"Shall I ask the judge to come in and talk to you?"

Jeff hesitated, then shrugged and said almost indifferently, "If you like."

Kate still waited expectantly. This was the way Jeff talked to other people but never to her. Slowly she walked to the door, then turned. "I brought you a few things I thought you might need. I'll get whatever you want from your home. Is there anything else I can do?"

"Yes, don't come back here."

Color mounted her cheeks. His words were like a slap in the face. Even then she was uncertain and spoke again. "Jeff." But he didn't reply. She went out of the room and closed the door quietly behind her.

13

The weekend was not a success. The hours dragged by in endless minutes. Worry over Jeff's arrest sat heavily on Kate's slight shoulders, and when she called Judge Brewster his news was neither encouraging nor enthusiastic.

Lucy and Alex apparently accepted the arrest as the closing of the case, and for the first time in over a week the sheriff did not come to Cliff's Edge. Kate herself was uneasy and uncertain. In spite of the fact that the deed seemed alien to the Jeff she knew, a nagging doubt always tugged at the corners of her mind.

As for Kitty, there was no knowing what she thought—or knew. She was more silent than usual, but there was a secretive, sly quirk to her mouth, and she spent hours in her own room, writing.

It rained all Saturday morning, pouring down in thick sheets, and in the afternoon a fog rose from the river, wrapping the house in a damp gray blanket. Kate felt that they were cut off from the outside world, and even the Negroes were subdued and quiet and gloomy.

The wind rose that night, and the house was filled with strange noises. Kate lay in her bed, waiting for sleep that seemed never to come. Somewhere in the house a door creaked in opening, and Kate slid her bare feet to the floor and went softly to her door.

She saw Kitty standing at the head of the dark well of the back stairs. She moved quietly, almost furtively, as Lucy came in sight on the steps. Kate held tightly to the door, waiting as Lucy tiptoed across the hall into her own room, closing the door behind her, and turned the key in the lock. Farther down the hall another key turned in another lock.

Sleep was out of the question then, though sometime after dawn Kate did lose consciousness and woke with a start when she heard people moving in the hall. The morning sun was beaming through her window.

Leigh and Alicia drove out to Cliff's Edge on Sunday afternoon. Alicia wore a new spring dress of soft green which reflected its color in her eyes but did nothing for her sallow skin. Kate thought Leigh looked tired, and there was something lacking in his usual charm.

"I wonder if I can go through some of Uncle Brock's papers, Kate?" he asked soon after they arrived.

They were all in the garden, where Lucy led them to see the latest blooms. Kate's feet dragged as she followed the group down the path. Lucy diplomatically walked between Kitty and Alicia. But they all turned when Leigh spoke.

"Can't you let your business wait even on Sunday?" asked Alicia.

"Yes, do," Kitty put in, her eyes bright and speculative.

"You needn't bother," Leigh said. "If Kate will just give me the key to the office . . ."

"Haven't you got all the papers you need yet?" Kitty asked.

"I don't know why you always have to run off as soon as we get somewhere." Alicia's tone was cool, but Kate knew she was angry

Little beads of perspiration began to show at the roots of his fair hair, and Leigh muttered, "I didn't mean to make an issue of it."

"Come along. I'll get the key for you." Kate tugged at his arm. She felt sorry for him, so agreeable and pleasant when things were going right, but so lacking in force of character when things went wrong. Now he was being torn between two women, one clinging tenaciously to a possession, the other not really wanting him but merely striking through him at a woman she despised.

He followed Kate into the house and waited at the foot of the stairs while she went for the key.

"You needn't come with me," he said as she rejoined him.

"I don't want to see the garden. Besides I've been moving things about in the office and I may have to show you where to find the papers you want."

Leigh bit his lip as he followed her. Probably just then he would have liked to live in a completely womanless world.

"What do you want?" she asked as she opened a window to let in the afternoon sun and warm the chilly room. "I thought you had taken most of Uncle Brock's papers into town."

"Nothing in particular. I just wanted to be sure I hadn't overlooked anything. I'd like to get the estate settled as soon as possible."

Kate smiled understandingly. She thought it most likely only an excuse to get away from Alicia and Kitty. Leigh never could think up good excuses.

"Don't let what Kitty keeps saying worry you. She's just bent on trying to stir up trouble." Kate sat down and lit a cigarette as he opened the safe and swung back the heavy door. "I wanted to ask you about Jeff anyway. Why hasn't he been released?"

"There's no use in getting yourself so upset, Kate. After all, there wasn't much I could do Saturday and nothing today. I'll get him released on bail tomorrow." He glanced through some papers and then added, "You know that I'll have to pull a few wires to get him out. The sheriff is convinced that Jeff did it."

"Yes, I know. And thanks for doing all you can. It's just— just— Oh, I don't know. Everything seems so twisted and turned upside down these days."

"That's pretty damning evidence against him." Leigh replaced some papers and took out some others.

"Those are my letters from Pete," Kate said, and he put them back quickly. "He might be telling the truth."

"Maybe. He won't tell me anything, or the judge either, so far as I can find out. There's a space of time he can't or won't

account for. And that little omission can bring him to trial—
and even convict him."

"Why didn't he give the alarm, Leigh?"

"He won't say. That's the whole trouble. He claims he heard
the shot and thought somebody was hunting on your place and
came over to stop them."

"You think he did it." Kate's eyes were accusing, and Leigh
turned away.

"I don't know. We may be able to raise a reasonable doubt.
Look here, darling, you're worrying yourself to death, and Jeff
isn't worth it. Everything points to somebody who could come
and go without raising suspicion, and if not Jeff, who?"

The words echoed in her ears. If not Jeff, who? Lucy, Kitty,
Alex, the Negroes?

"Tell me the truth, Kate; aren't you a little doubtful about
him? Aren't you—?"

The telephone shrilled jarringly, and Kate went to the desk
to answer it. But it was only Kitty, talking from the house, making an appointment with the president of the bank for Monday
morning. Kate replaced the receiver slowly. Kitty's words had
been clear and distinct in the stillness of the room.

"I only want Jeff to have a fair chance," she said. "If you're
through now, suppose we go back to the house."

Leigh waited while she locked the door of the office, and
there was a frown creasing his forehead as he followed her
back to the house.

The others were in the parlor, where Alex had joined them.
Kitty was more animated than she had been in the garden
and moved restlessly about the room. Kate saw that Alex was
watching her and that he frowned and was quieter than usual.
There was a look of malicious triumph in Kitty's small black
eyes, and she laughed a little too freely, as though mirth effer-
vesced within her and spilled easily from her painted lips.

She carried the conversation, relating several amusing anec-
dotes and finally offering to play for them. Kate was afraid,
recognizing the subtle danger of her mood. Still the afternoon

passed pleasantly enough, and nothing ruffled the surface calm of their conversation. Alicia and Kitty seemed to have formed a truce, though each was on guard.

Fancy opened the door to tell Kitty she was wanted on the phone.

"It's them telegram comp'ny agin, Mis' Kitty." Fancy grinned, displaying a new gold tooth which almost matched the gold of her skin.

Kitty threw a half-smoked cigarette into the fire and with an irritated jerk of her shoulders left the room.

Lucy surveyed the colored girl for a minute, then said somewhat severely, "Isn't that one of Miss Kitty's dresses you're wearing, Fancy?"

"She give it to me," the girl answered sullenly.

When the door had closed behind her Lucy exploded.

"Well! I must say I don't understand it. That looks like a fairly new dress to me. If that's what she's doing to get Fancy to wait on her hand and foot—"

"If she's giving away creations like that, I might be persuaded to serve her breakfast in bed some morning," said Kate.

"Her things wouldn't be becoming to you." Lucy threw back her white head.

"You look very pretty just as you are," Alex said, and for the first time that day Kate felt warm and happy.

"I must say Kitty has always had good taste when it comes to clothes," Alicia commented grudgingly. "Come along, Leigh; it's high time we were starting home."

There was some confusion as they all rose, and Alex helped Alicia with her coat. In the hall they called good-bye to Kitty, who was still seated at the phone, and she did not come to the door as they left.

It was a peculiar Sunday evening. After a light supper which none of them ate they sat quietly in the parlor. Soft music from the radio, the low murmur of the fire were casual accompaniments to their occasional conversation. But their talk was sporadic; they were too nervous for the things that might ordinarily have

been said. The sheriff afterward called it the lull before the storm.
It might have been better if they had cried aloud their tension,
their doubts and suspicions.

Kitty was more nervous than the others, and at times her
voice rose to an almost hysterical note. But if the others noticed they made no comment.

It was barely nine when Lucy left the room, taking Kitty
with her. Kate was changing the radio program and did not
know how it was managed, but that it was managed; she was
certain.

Left alone with Alex, she felt almost shy, like a girl with her
first beau.

"Sit down over here," Alex suggested, pulling a small sofa
closer to the fire. He lit a cigarette for her and settled himself
comfortably beside her with his pipe.

"This is the sort of thing I used to wish for," he said.

"It must be very quiet here to you. When I first came back
the quiet kept me awake. I kept listening for the rumble of the
elevated and the hum of all-night traffic. Down here the frogs
croaked and the crickets cricked—or whatever they do. That
first night it seemed louder than anything I ever heard in New
York. It's funny"—she smiled at him—"I don't know when I
began to get used to the country again."

Alex listened to her voice, as clear as running water, alive,
effortless.

"Do you miss it—the city, I mean?"

"Of course. I liked living in New York. I liked the excitement
and the people." She leaned forward, elbows on her knees, her
chin resting in her hands, and stared dreamily into the fire. "I
go back for a week or two every year. Pete and I had lots of
friends, and they're nice enough to show me a good time while
I'm there."

"Have you ever thought of going back to live?"

"Yes, but I don't suppose I ever will. Somebody has to be
here, and it's impossible for my brother to come. Besides,
Cliff's Edge helped me a lot when I first came. So much space
gives you a better perspective."

"It's very beautiful down here," Alex agreed quietly.

"I don't suppose you see it as I do. We're such good pretenders about things we love. Maybe everybody is; I don't know. Anyway, we have lots of fun here in the winter. There's nearly always a houseful from October through February. We always have a big party out here on Christmas Eve. And in the summer our friends come out and we go swimming in the river and then come back to the house to cut watermelons."

"Aren't you afraid to swim in the river?"

"Oh no. The river is part of us. Most of us have been swimming in it ever since we were children. I suppose the danger gives us a little added thrill."

"It's still too dangerous."

"You've seen it only after the spring rains. It would be very dangerous now, but in the summer it's lazy and warm."

Alex rose and knocked the ashes from the pipe onto the dull embers left on the hearth.

"I'm sorry I had to tell the sheriff about Jeff," he said at last.

"You! What did you have to tell him?"

"I told him that Jeff knew Mr. Brock had been shot. You hadn't told me that." Alex dropped his eyes from the baffled hurt look in hers.

"Oh. I didn't know that."

"The sheriff was talking to me, and before I knew it I had told him."

"Yes. Mr. Bill has a way . . ."

Kate rose and switched off the radio. "I have a dreadful headache. Don't you think we'd better go to bed? It's getting late."

Alex helped her turn off the lights in the parlor and followed her up the curving stair. In the darkness of the upper hall she whispered, "Good night."

"I love you."

Kate went to her room, not knowing whether she had really heard the words or only imagined them. With only the moonlight shining through the window she leaned close to the old mirror and stared at her own reflection. No miracle had happened; it was her own face, the moonlight tracing the outlines, reflected in the shadowy depths.

There was a gentle rap on the door, and she heard Lucy's voice low and careful. "Kate?"

"Come in." She turned to switch on the bedside lamp, but Lucy stopped her.

"No, don't turn on your light. I just came to tell you to lock your door."

"Lock my door!" Kate was incredulous, amazed.

"Yes," Lucy whispered. "Somebody tried to get into Brock's room again last night."

Kate sat down abruptly, remembering Lucy's stealthy tread on the back stairs and Kitty's silent watch.

"Someone tried to get in through the window. I found the screen loose this morning and I'm pretty sure someone tried to get in through the door too. I've been keeping it locked, but with old locks like these almost anything will open them."

"Are you sure?" Kate was still inclined to be skeptical.

"Of course I'm sure, and you lock your door." Lucy no longer whispered, but she left with that final word of warning.

14

Kate tried to work all Monday morning. She woke with a headache which even aspirin did not drive away. Nervous and out of sorts, she spoke shortly to the Negroes and then couldn't bear the hurt, bewildered look in their soft black eyes. Lucy's silence was a rebuke, too, so that at last she went to the office to work alone.

She scanned the farm ledgers, conscious that she would have been of more use in the house, where Lucy had begun the annual frenzy of a thorough spring cleaning.

From the office window she saw Kitty leave the house. She told no one where she was going but simply appropriated the station wagon and left. It wasn't until they sat down to lunch that Fancy gave them word that "Mis' Kitty done gone to town and won't likely be back for lunch."

Alex was pushed firmly out of doors, and since it was a warm sunshiny day he went without too much urging. Kate was so evidently avoiding him that he dared not join her in the office, so he gladly accepted the company of a mongrel hound with baleful eyes, apparently the sole property of Eph.

Kate did not see him, but she could hear the bang of the back door and once, as she watched, she saw Lucy peer cautiously from the window of Brock's room.

The telephone rang.

"Hello. . . . Yes. . . . How are you? . . . Of course I remembered, but thank you for calling to remind me. . . . Yes, I'll be glad to tell him. . . . What time are you planning to start? . . .

Oh, I'm always glad to have you. I just wish I could ask you to come back to the house afterward, but I'm afraid that's impossible this time. . . . Of course. . . . Good-bye."

She replaced the receiver with a sigh. It wasn't very convenient to have men chasing a fox over the plantation roads, but she couldn't refuse. These men had hunted there with her father and grandfather, and Kate had no thought of breaking tradition. After all, it would mean one less fox to kill the chickens. Perhaps Alex would enjoy it.

Her eyes danced merrily at the thought of what was in store for him. She knew what he expected: men on horseback streaking over the open fields through the moonlight; horses clearing fences and coming in on a kill, surrounded by the dogs; perhaps he even looked forward to a few pink coats.

She lit a cigarette and threw back her head, thinking of what he would really see. Black-belt fox hunts had little in common with their English predecessors. Men and women arrived at an appointed place in their cars, rattletrap Fords or new Chevrolets, and then raced as fast as possible over the plantation roads, bumping carelessly over the muddy ruts and laughing in the darkness.

Kate had known these hunts always. As children, she and her brother had hung from an upstairs window and listened to the musical baying of the hounds that floated through the stillness, growing loud as they struck the scent, and dying away as the fox circled and dodged through the woods and over the fields. Sometimes she wondered if the fox himself didn't enjoy the run, for most often he bested the lot of them. The sport was not in catching the fox but in keeping within the sound of the dogs.

Kate tossed her cigarette into the fire and laughed aloud at the disillusionment in store for Alex, the Yankee, and with the laugh some of her good spirits were restored.

She rose as the telephone rang again and picked up the receiver.

"Hello. . . . Hello, this is Cliff's Edge. . . ."

There was no sound from the other end, and she tried again. "Hello. . .

There was an almost imperceptible click, and the connection was broken. Kate held the receiver for a moment, then slowly replaced it. Her brow was knit in a puzzled frown. It was strange, for undoubtedly someone had been at the other end of the line.

Shrugging her shoulders, she locked the office door. She paused outside in surprise. She could see the sheriff in earnest conversation with Will, but strain her ears as she would, she could not catch his words. There was only the faint rumble of the sheriff's voice and the vigorous nods Will made in agreement.

Finally she went into the house through the dining room, where Fancy was setting the table.

"Is lunch ready?" she asked.

"Mis' Lucy ain't give us time to fix nothin'. We's havin' what was left from yisterd'y. She done had us takin' down cu'tins all mornin'." Fancy was never enthusiastic over the extra work involved in spring cleaning.

"Well, it'll be over in a week," Kate assured her.

In the hall she found Lucy outside Brock's room. Lucy started nervously when she saw her and pulled the key from the lock with a jerk.

"Tomorrow I want to clean the parlor," she said, putting the key in her pocket. "Zack will have to polish the floor, though much good it will do. All the floors need revarnishing." Lucy hurried up the steps.

"I'll help you after lunch," Kate called up to her.

Lucy's reply was lost to her. Alex had come in the front door.

"Oh, hello. Did they run you completely out of the house?"

"Well, it was either walk out or get swept out," he replied with a laugh. He looked at her as though she were a complicated piece of mechanism. Sometimes she was as friendly as the spring sunshine, and again she retreated into a cool reserved world of her own.

"I was told to remind you of the hunt tonight," she said. "I expect you'll find it—different, to say the least."

"Night does seem a queer time to go fox hunting," he agreed.

"I won't spoil your fun by telling you about it. Here's Cu'un Lucy, so I guess lunch is ready."

Lucy took her seat opposite Kate. "In a house like this you never get it all done," she sighed. "Kate, I do wish you'd wash the chandelier in the green parlor this afternoon. I got the room cleaned this morning, but I was afraid to trust even Zack with that. He's dropped everything he's picked up. And you can keep an eye on Fancy while she dusts the furniture."

"We have to do this thing a room at a time," Kate explained to Alex. "And the chandelier is a very prized possession. Uncle Brock took us to New Orleans for Mardi Gras last year, and we found it in an antique shop in the French Quarter. It was so appropriate for the room, we couldn't resist it."

"I think I'll write and see if we can't get something for this room too. It needs it more than any other in the house." Lucy held out an empty cup for Zack to refill.

"We'll get round to the other rooms sooner or later."

When lunch was over Alex followed Kate to the parlor.

"Suppose you let me help you get it down."

"If you can take it down without breaking the prisms I'll be delighted," she said.

Alex brought a ladder and, carefully unhooking the tiny pieces of glass, handed them down one by one to Kate. For a time they worked in silence, broken only now and then by the coy giggling of Fancy, who whisked a cloth over the surface of the furniture until a frown from Kate sent her to her knees to dust the legs of the chairs and tables.

The parlor furniture was probably the oldest and best in the house. It predated Victorianism and had escaped the rococo style that marred the other pieces in the house. It had recently been upholstered in a soft green damask with a silvery stripe. The plastering was new and had been tinted a pale green, harmonizing with the color scheme of the room. Over the marble mantel which matched the one in the opposite parlor hung the portrait of a young man in a claret-colored coat, one arm resting stiffly on a table which faded vaguely into the dark background. The room had an atmosphere of its own—formal, dignified, cool, quiet.

"You'd better let me put them back. I'll have to wipe off the rest," Kate said.

Alex descended and held the ladder for her. He handed her the pieces one by one and watched her as she put them carefully back in place.

"Fancy, you'd better take the pan back to the kitchen. Be careful not to spill any of the water on the floor."

Fancy picked up the basin and with a knowing toss of her kinky head left the room.

"Someday I'm going to fire her." Kate stopped her work. "She can do more to provoke me than any darky I've ever known. If she weren't Ella's granddaughter I'd have fired her long ago."

She stepped down quickly, and her foot missed the rung. Alex's strong arms caught her and lifted her to the floor. For a moment they stood silent and close. Kate could see the throb of a vein at his temple and felt the quick hammering of her own heart.

"Well!"

Alex dropped his arms from Kate and turned.

Kitty stood in the open door. The black silk of her dress melted eloquently against the curves of her body, and on her head she wore an absurd hat, a piquant wisp of a veil topped with a bunch of blue velvet violets and yellow daisies. She stood there, watching them, the fine lines of her eyebrows raised in an inquisitive arch.

"Hello, Kitty. You're just back from town?" Kate's voice was cool. "Alex, put the ladder in the hall for me. We're sure to need it tomorrow." Kate walked toward the door and took Kitty's arm firmly. "I don't believe I've seen you wear that hat before. Surely you didn't get it in town today."

"Now you know very well, Kate, they never have anything fit to wear in that place. Besides, I didn't go shopping today."

Kitty's voice was excited, and the words flowed quickly. "It was a very satisfactory day. I learned so much; you'd never guess."

"Don't tell me you picked up a new scandal in town."

"I mustn't tell you about it yet," Kitty replied slyly and laughed.

It was an unpleasant sound, and Kate was glad when they reached the top of the steps. Lucy was in the upper hall, several curtains draped over her arm.

"Supper will have to be early if Alex is going on that hunt tonight."

"Hunt?" Kitty asked.

"Yes. I forgot to mention it to you," Kate said. "I promised Mr. Bob a few weeks ago they could have a fox hunt out here, and they'll be out tonight. They invited Alex to go with them."

Kitty frowned and mumbled something about complications, but the other two paid no attention. Abruptly she turned and went back down the steps.

It was nearly time for supper when they all met again in the parlor, though the last rays of a red sun still gave a vermilion tint to the trees outside the windows. Conversation was brief. Only Lucy seemed not to notice the strained silences. Kitty twisted the rings on her fingers and nervously paced the floor while they waited. There was something of the caged panther in the lithe grace of her walk.

"I cleaned Brock's room thoroughly this morning," Lucy announced, her eyes darting from one face to another. "I've packed all his things and cleared the room."

A sudden blare came from the radio where Kitty was standing, and she quickly turned it down. Kate stared at Lucy, wondering what she was trying to do. Before she could decide Zack came to tell them supper was on the table.

At the table the clatter of dishes and the clinking of glasses and silver covered their silences. Kate even began to wonder if the sinister cloud that she felt hovering over them might not be only her own vivid imagination.

They were just pushing back their chairs when they heard cars in the drive. They hurried to the front door, Lucy leading them. There were perhaps fifteen men on the steps and the front lawn.

"We're going to have a fine moonlight night for our hunt," called a white-haired man sitting beside a younger edition of himself.

"Couldn't have been better," said another, and to Alex added, "You'll be hearing some of the finest hounds in the county tonight, sir."

"Alex, you go get your coat," Lucy said. "It'll be cold out there, tearing over the roads with these wild men."

"Now, Miss Lucy. I bet you'd like to go 'long with us," Judge Brewster rumbled. He was enthroned on the back seat of the car, his enormous size taking up most of the space.

Kate saw Leigh alone in his coupé and went over to him.

"What have they done about Jeff, Leigh?"

"Jeff?" His mind wasn't focused on her words. "Oh, the sheriff let me arrange bail for him this morning. He's out."

Alex came out of the door then, a coat over his arm, and Kate stepped back. He would have preferred going with Leigh, since he was the only man he knew. But Leigh's car was already moving forward, so he climbed into another car whose door was held hospitably open for him.

"This is Bill Denton," Kate introduced him. "He's our rising young doctor."

"Glad to meet you." The doctor had an engaging smile. "I told Jenny to telephone you if I got a call tonight, Kate. Hang a lantern in the tower if I'm needed, will you? I'll come bounding back in a hurry."

"Silly." Kate wrinkled her nose at him. "We've got an electric light up there now. But I'll turn it on if you're called."

There was a sudden bark of a dog, and with a burst of speed the men were off down the road, and the lights became faint flickers in the darkness.

In the hall the telephone was ringing, and Kate went to it.

"Hello. . . . Oh, hello, Alicia. . . . Yes, he came with the others. . . . Yes, I'm glad he did. He's been working so hard lately. Why didn't you come with him? . . . Well, I can't say I blame you; they do stay so late. . . . Come out any time. . . . Good-bye."

"Who was it?" asked Lucy as Kate joined them in the parlor.

"Alicia. She just wanted to know whether Leigh had managed to get out to the hunt."

"Why don't you two go to the movies?" Kitty asked.

"Well!" exclaimed Lucy. "After all, there's been a death in the family, Kitty."

Kitty shrugged and lit a cigarette. Kate suggested double solitaire, but Kitty declined and continued to prowl around the room.

"We must begin by plastering the dining room this summer." Lucy took up her knitting and settled herself comfortably by the fire.

"It certainly needs it," Kitty commented satirically. "I expect the ceiling to fall every time I sit down to the table. If you aren't able to keep this house up you ought to sell it."

"We aren't exactly paupers," Kate said calmly. "We'll get it all done in time. Old houses cost more to repair than new ones."

"This room could be done too," Lucy continued, trying to ignore Kitty.

"We might get it painted a soft salmon pink," Kate replied. "Do you suppose Will and I could do the painting and maybe fix the floors?"

"Will's not to be trusted with a job like that, and you know it. I intend to buy a rug for either this room or the dining room.

"No, Cu'un Lucy. Don't do that."

"Stuff and nonsense!" The diamonds in her ears caught the firelight as she tossed her head. "If I wasn't living out here I'd have to keep my house in town instead of renting it."

"Buy something for your own room then," Kate suggested.

The two of them fell into an animated discussion, and Kate got a discarded bridge score pad and listed the things they might do. Kitty yawned openly to show how utterly bored she was, and twice she wandered to the window and peered searchingly out into the darkness. When the clock struck ten and they were still deep in their plans she rose.

"I think I'll go to my room." Neither of the other two looked up, apparently unaware that she had spoken.

But when the door closed Lucy leaned forward and whispered, "It was Kitty who was searching Brock's room."

"How do you know?" Kate's eyes widened in surprise.

"I just know." Lucy bobbed her head up and down.

"What on earth would she want in there?"

"I don't know—yet. I went through everything this morning. Ella helped me, and we packed all his clothes in a box and I took it up to my room. I'll go through them more thoroughly the first chance I get."

Kate did not answer, but she knew again that cold chill of fear. Something alien had entered the house, yet she could not know just what she feared. Lucy's nocturnal wanderings, the locked doors, and Kitty's stealthy watch over all of them were things she did not understand.

The old house creaked and settled again, like a plump old lady sinking tiredly into her chair after a day's work. But there was something sinister in even the casual noises of the house.

The clock tinkled and recalled them to the present. They turned off the lights and, leaving a dim one burning in the hall, slowly mounted the stairs. The upper hall was dark, but a faint light came from the transom over Kitty's door at the far end of the hall.

Kate said good night and went to her room. In the stillness she heard the lock click in Lucy's door. She undressed and climbed into the great bed. The cool air blew in from the window, and she huddled closer under the covers. The fire was only a glow in the grate, and even its light faded and she slept.

She did not know what waked her, waked her with shocking suddenness from a sound sleep. She sat upright in bed, holding the covers to her shoulders. Her eyes were wide open in the darkness, and she listened with concentrated attention. There was a faint humming noise, and she heard a car engine start. She was very still, but her ears caught no other sound.

She threw her feet over the side of the bed and, groping in the darkness, found her old flannel bathrobe. She moved toward the door and stood there, listening. The house creaked and groaned, and then she heard a door open quietly. She opened her own and saw the light go out, then heard Alex climbing the steps, heard the creak of the fifth step, and saw him emerge at the top, holding aloft a lighted match which burned out in his fingers.

Relieved and satisfied, she closed her door and went back to bed.

15

"I want to get started on the dining room this morning," Lucy said and began counting off tasks on her plump fingers. "Zack will have to clean and wax the floor. Will can brush the walls and wash the windows. We ought to get the pictures down now."

Lucy bustled forward, and Kate followed. Over the mantels of the dining room were big steel engravings, and Kate's eyes followed the crack in the plaster which one of them did not quite hide.

"I'll wash the glass and wipe the frames."

"No, Zack can do that. I want you to help me with the china."

"Oh, Cu'un Lucy," Kate groaned, "not the china too."

"Certainly. Ella will wash the shelves, and you don't expect me to put dusty china back on clean shelves, do you? And I certainly won't trust the darkies with the best china."

Kate shuddered as she looked at the corner cupboards filled with china and glassware.

"You needn't act that way," Lucy told her. "It's a job that has to be done. It's your china, and you know we always have to wash it ourselves."

"All right," Kate sighed. "Has everybody finished eating?"

"Alex hasn't come down yet. Neither has Kitty."

"You might as well let Alex stay in bed a little longer, and Kitty would only be in the way if she came down here."

Lucy snorted. "I do wish everybody in the house would eat at one time. Alex is paying for service, but Kitty—" She broke off and called to Will, who was in the yard near the back windows. "Will! Come here, Will."

"Yas'm?"

"Get the ladder from the hall and take down these pictures." Lucy opened the china-closet doors and began to remove the glasses. She picked up two and carried them to the kitchen and returned presently, followed by Ella's massive bulk.

"Clear the table now, Ella, and get these dishes done just as soon as you can. Fancy ought to be upstairs now. Has Zack finished mopping the hall?"

"Yas'm. He done finish' the steps an' he'll be throo the hall terreckly." Ella began loading a tray. "Whut yo' goin' do 'bout Mist' Alex an' Mis' Kitty?"

"I'll answer for myself." Alex spoke from the door.

"Give him his breakfast," Lucy said resignedly. "You'll have to eat in a hurry. I want to start with this room today. Thank goodness I had Eph take down that sign by the gate or we'd be sure to have some tourists in here at any odd hour."

"Is it always like this?" Alex asked Kate as Lucy once more retreated to the kitchen.

"Always." She smiled at him. "We go through it twice a year, and everybody's thoroughly exhausted when it's over. Have a nice time last night?"

"It was fun, and certainly different." Alex shook his head. "In fact, that was the weirdest fox hunt I was ever on."

"They used to hunt on horseback. I used to go all the time myself, but since I came back here to live I don't go so often."

His mouth was full of battercake and molasses, and he washed it down with a gulp of coffee.

"Is there anything I can help you do this morning?"

"I don't think so. I'm relegated to the kitchen," she added with a grimace. "We're going to wash all the china."

Kate picked up some plates and went out into the hall, where she met Fancy.

"You'd better do Mr. Alex' room right away," she said. "As soon as I put these down I'll come up and straighten my room.

We won't try to do much. Cu'un Lucy will want to clean it thoroughly in a few days."

"Yas'm. She done already took down mos' of the cu'tins and sont word to Jawn to come up and wash all the windows nex' Thu'sday."

Kate put the plates in the kitchen and a moment later followed the colored girl up the back stairs. She could hear a young voice raised in song as she passed Alex's door.

She made her bed, fluffed the pillows, and straightened the bureau. The fire had been lit against the early-morning chill but was almost dead now, and she opened the windows to let in the fresh spring air.

From her own room she went to Lucy's. The room was as neat as its occupant and except for the disarranged bed looked undisturbed. The furniture was hideous, heavy black walnut of the late Victorian period which Lucy had brought with her to Cliff's Edge. The scrollwork which stood out in bas-relief over the high headboard of the bed was repeated over the mirrored doors of the clumsy wardrobe. The marble dresser top was covered with a linen scarf on which was set a silver mirror, comb, and brush. The room was prim and smug, very much like Lucy.

Kate made the bed, beating the heavy feather mattress so that the top stood up like a huge puff. When she had finished she surveyed her work and nodded her head with a satisfied air. She pushed a chair into place and opened the door.

Fancy came out of Alex's room at the same time, holding a battered coal scuttle in one hand and a small shovel in the other.

"Take up the ashes in these two rooms, and then you had better wake Miss Kitty. Be sure to mop all the floors."

"Mis' Lucy got 'nough for me to do downstairs 'thout I do all this too." Fancy was resentful, and her thick lips drooped.

"It shouldn't take you long to do this. When you've finished come downstairs." Kate continued her way down the stairs, oblivious of the black look the maid gave her.

"It's time you came," Lucy said as she came into the kitchen. "Here's a towel. Just put the things on that table and we'll take them back when Ella has finished washing the closets."

Kate took the cloth and picked up a glass, but before she could wipe it the door was thrown open and Fancy stood on the threshold panting.

"Mis' Kitty ain't in her room!" The words came in short gasps.

"Nonsense." Lucy barely looked up. She placed another glass on the rubber mat. "She's up, then, and somewhere in the house."

"She ain't slep' in her bed." Fancy's eyes were rolling with fright, and a white rim showed around their dark irises.

Kate stood still, towel in hand, and stared at the girl. She caught the fear in her face and brushed quickly past the others and raced up the back steps.

She opened the door to the empty room. The bed was smooth, just as it had been made the day before except for a slight depression near the head where someone had evidently sat. The windows were down, and the air was close. She stood there in the doorway until Lucy came up behind her.

"Fancy's right; she didn't sleep here last night."

"But she left us downstairs fairly early and came up here." Lucy was panting from her exertions. "Maybe she slept in one of the other rooms," she offered hopefully, but her words showed that she herself was unconvinced.

"We can see"—Kate was doubtful—"but—well, we might look."

Ella came puffing up the steps, and Fancy clung to her grandmother, unwilling to be left downstairs.

Together they went toward the middle room at the front of the house. Lucy opened the door timidly, but it did not take them long in the semigloom of the half-drawn shades to see that the room had not been used.

Kate walked quickly to the other end of the house and opened the door of the room which was directly above the one Brock had occupied. The two Negroes hurried after her, but

Lucy stood watching them from the middle of the hall. Kate went in and raised a shade, but she knew immediately that the room was empty. When she came out she shook her head in reply to Lucy's silent question.

"She must be in her room," Lucy said desperately, and they went back to Kitty's room.

But there was no one there. They looked in the closet and in the adjoining bath. Lucy even got down on her plump knees and peered under the bed.

"Could she have gone without telling us?"

Kate was standing in front of the dressing table and she picked up a silver mirror before she replied.

"She would hardly have left these if she had gone."

"What about her clothes? Is her traveling bag still here?" Lucy opened the large wardrobe which covered most of one wall.

Inside were Kitty's hats, carefully placed on the shelves, and at the top was a small traveling case. They searched the closet then and the dresser drawers, and as well as they could tell, nothing was missing; everything was in place.

Over the foot of the bed lay a thin nightgown and a satin dressing coat, as though they had been placed there in readiness for the night. Only the mules on the floor seemed to have been moved. One lay on its side, its high heel pointing toward the window, and the other stood crookedly propped against the leg of the fireside chair.

"What shall we do?" Kate's voice was scarcely above a whisper.

Lucy, white of face, sank down on the bed.

Still holding Ella's apron with one hand, Fancy looked at first one and then the other. Suddenly she screamed, screamed in pure terror.

Down in the dining room Zack and Will heard her and stopped short at the window they were washing.

And Alex, coming in from the garden, heard the high, hysterical screams. He took the back steps two at a time, his face clouding with worry as the sounds were suddenly choked into silence.

Only Eph, down by the stable, did not hear and went blithe-ly on with his task.

Alex reached the room to find Kate with one hand over Fancy's mouth and trying to hold the flaying arms with the other. Ella had a protecting arm around the girl.

"Kate! Kate, has anything happened to you?" he demanded breathlessly.

Kate looked at him and nodded, relief flooding her face. "We can't find Kitty."

Alex strode across the room and put his hands on her arms. "You're cold; you're shaking," he muttered.

"It's Kitty, Alex," Lucy said, and Alex turned toward her, the strong light from the window falling on the gray hairs at his temple.

"She doesn't—doesn't seem to have slept here at all last night." Kate was shaking again, and Alex held her firmly.

"Come out of here, all of you," he said. "She's somewhere around the place. We'll find her in a little while."

They trooped out of the empty room and down the front stairs. Zack and Will, who had followed Alex, brought up the rear with many furtive glances over their shoulders.

In the hall they held a brief conference.

"She must be around here somewhere," Lucy said.

"She couldn't have gone without letting you know?"

"I think not," Lucy replied with a reluctant shake of her head.

"All her things are in her room, Alex," Kate said. "Kitty wouldn't have left them behind."

"Then she's here somewhere," Alex concluded. "We'd better look for her. Zack, you and Will—"

"Now sir, Mist' Alex," Zack interrupted. "I ain't goin' to do no surchin'. She a debil incalculate, an' I ain't goin' round ova de house lookin' for her."

"It's no use asking them to look," Kate sighed. "Ella, you'd better give Cu'un Lucy some ammonia, and then all of you get back to work. She'll turn up in a little while."

"If you'll come with me I'll look for her," Alex said, and she nodded. She was pale, but her dark eyes were steady enough as they met his.

It was nearly eleven o'clock when Kate and Alex began their search. The sun was high and beamed brightly through a cloudless sky. They went first to the stable, but none of the horses were gone, and in the barn Alex's coupé and the family station wagon were still parked as they had been the night before.

They searched the house, beginning with the ground floor and working their way gradually to the roof. Kate led Alex through rooms, and he discovered new crannies he would never have dreamed existed. They opened closets and wardrobes, went through closed rooms, looked in every conceivable place a human might be expected to hide.

Finally they came panting up the narrow flight of steps to the boxlike conservatory that crowned the roof. Odd pieces of furniture leaned against the walls. A chair with a rocker missing sat drunkenly in a corner. The film of dust over furniture was undisturbed.

"We never use this now, except sometimes in the summer as a sleeping porch." Kate crossed the floor, and her tracks showed plainly on the bare boards.

She opened a glass door and went out on the narrow veranda that ran around the four sides of the room. Alex, following, found himself looking down on the treetops and gazing over the plowed acres of the plantation.

Kate shaded her eyes from the bright glare of the sun and walked slowly around the room. The trees, now in full foliage, concealed the close surroundings of the house. In the distance miniature people moved to and fro in a field, and a toy mule pulled a toy plow, leaving behind a furrow of red-raw earth.

"I—I don't see her anywhere," Kate faltered.

"No," Alex agreed, and then after a brief pause, "We'd better go back downstairs."

It was twelve-thirty when Alex called the sheriff. That was after they had discussed among themselves what should be done. It was after Kate had called Leigh to ask guardedly if Kitty had been in town that morning.

As Alex talked to the sheriff the others stood huddled together in the hall, strangely quiet. They knew by then that something had happened, that tragedy had struck again, silently and furtively. There would be nights in the future when they would wake suddenly with fear and feel death brush their faces, for none of them really doubted what had happened, and they were afraid.

The sheriff wasted little time with words, and thirty minutes after they called him his old car rattled to a stop before the broad portico of the house. He opened the door, and his long, gangling legs dropped straight to the ground. Three other men climbed out after him, and they entered the house together.

Sheriff Davies stood before them, tall, wiry, tireless. His clothes were unpressed and baggy, but his face was inscrutable as he listened to their story. He made Kate repeat the events of the previous night and took them over and over the frantic morning search. When he had exhausted them with questions he took one of the men and went upstairs to Kitty's room. The two left began another futile search of the house.

Lucy was white and had begun to show signs of collapse, so Kate sent her to bed, guarded by the faithful Ella. She and Alex went into the parlor to wait. Alex put an arm about her shoulders and pulled her gently to him.

"Oh, Alex, I'm so afraid," she whispered.

"There's nothing to be afraid of, darling." He soothed her for a while, and she let her head rest wearily against his coat. "I've fallen so completely in love with you," he said, his cheek against her hair.

Kate lifted her face and he kissed her. They stood there a moment, clinging to each other.

"Sit down here." Alex pulled her down on the sofa. "I must talk to you. I don't know what Kitty has told you."

"It doesn't matter," she said softly.

"It will, though, and I'd like for you at least to know the truth." She took his hand and linked her fingers through his.

"I married about six years ago. I'd known Eleanor always, and we sort of—well, drifted into marriage. There was never much love between us; we had so little in common. She wanted new thrills and began to play around with people who were willing to take any sort of chance. Part of it was my fault. I didn't care, and there was nobody else to stop her."

"Don't, Alex." She saw the pained, hurt look on his face. "You don't have to tell me that."

"I want you to know, because it was at my request that she finally went to Reno. I told her if she didn't get the divorce I would. God knows I had plenty of grounds. I suppose Kitty has told you the rest of the story. She said she would. I'd just like you to know my side too."

"Kitty didn't tell me anything except that you had been married—and that your wife had been killed in an automobile accident."

"She didn't?" Alex looked at her in surprise. "She said she would if I didn't— Well, Eleanor came back from Reno and called me up last December. She said she had to see me, and I was fool enough to believe her. I picked her up in my car, but she did the driving. She was in some sort of jam, I think. She wanted me to marry her again, again after that terrible hell I had lived through with her."

Alex broke off and was silent, gazing absently into the fire. When he spoke again his voice was harsh.

"Something had frightened her. She finally said if I didn't marry her she'd kill us both and then she drove like mad. She was insane that day. It wasn't an accident; she drove deliberately into that telephone pole."

He closed his eyes as though to shut out the picture of the tragedy. Kate did not say anything; instead she put up both hands and pulled his face down to her own.

At the door the shadowy Tom tipped quietly away from his listening post.

"You'll marry me as soon as you can?" he asked presently.

"Oh, darling, yes."

He toyed with the plain gold band on her left hand. "I've been so terribly jealous of this," he said with a short laugh. "I'm still a little jealous of Jeff—and even Leigh and that Dr. Denton I was with last night. He talked incessantly about you."

"You needn't—" Kate began but stopped as the sheriff loomed suddenly in the doorway.

"We've found her," he said quietly, looking over their heads.

"She's—?"

"Yes, dead. Murdered."

Kate put her hand over her mouth as though to choke back the scream that swelled in her throat, and Alex tightened his arm about her.

"Where—where did you find her?" he asked.

"In the brook, not more than a couple of hundred yards from the house." The sheriff's eyes were half closed, but now he watched every move, every expression on their faces.

"She was drowned?" Alex asked.

"No. She was choked to death. I don't know yet until the doctor has seen her, but I don't think he'll find any water in her lungs."

Kate's eyes were wide and dry, and without warning she began to laugh hysterically. Alex shook her until the uncontrolled sounds subsided into a mere whimper.

"Can't you see that the strain is getting too much for her?" he demanded angrily.

"You'd better sit down," said the sheriff grimly. "There's a lot we'd better talk over."

The intent of his words cut like an icy wind, and they argued no more. Their eyes, wide and incredulous, were fixed on his lean brown face.

"First of all," he said, "Miss Kitty wasn't killed down there by the brook."

"What—what do you mean?" Kate gripped the carved arm of the love seat until the knuckles of her hands were white.

"It looks mighty like she was dragged down there, part of the way at least. The ground don't tell much, but some of the grass is bent and the bushes broken."

"Couldn't she have gone down there herself? Gone there maybe to meet somebody?" Alex asked.

"No, I don't think so." Sheriff Bill shook his head slowly. "One of her shoes is missing, and it isn't likely she would walk down there in the woods with only one shoe on. We've looked for the other shoe, but it isn't anywhere around—the place where we found her."

This is all so strange, unreal, thought Kate. There was something she ought to remember, some small fact that just eluded her memory. She frowned a little in concentration and, looking up, caught the sheriff's alert eyes on her.

"We found this in her hand."

The sheriff extended his right hand palm upward, and Kate gazed down at a brown button, round and flat, such a button as men use on their suit coats.

16

One of the men came to the door, and the sheriff immediately got up and went over to him. For several minutes they talked in guarded undertones, and after the man left the sheriff turned to Kate.

"Will you tell Miss Lucy? I'd like to talk to all of you in just a few minutes."

"I got Ella to put Cu'un Lucy to bed. Must you talk to her now?"

"Yes, if she's able." The sheriff turned and without another word left them alone.

Alex put his arm around her comfortingly.

"Chin up, darling," he said and gave her a little push toward the door.

Kate smiled tiredly over her shoulder as she left him and went up the stairs.

Ella opened Lucy's door for her, and she entered a dim room, its shades half drawn against the sun. Lucy was propped up in bed, her small eyes closed. Even before she spoke Kate realized that Lucy already knew. That unaccountably accurate grapevine that runs its course through kitchens and up back stairs had already brought her the news. "Where will it all end, Kate?" she whispered.

Kate sat down beside her on the bed. "I don't know."

"She—she couldn't possibly have done it herself?"

"Sheriff Bill says not."

Ella mumbled something, rocking to and fro by the empty fireplace, and though Kate turned her head she could not understand what the old colored woman said.

"Cu'un Lucy, the sheriff sent me up here to tell you. He wants to talk to all of us again. Are you able to come downstairs?"

"Yes, I'll come. You must go back. Ella will help me."

"I could send him up here to talk to you."

"No, I'd rather come down there." Lucy sat up in bed, and in the dim light Kate could see that her face was drawn and old.

As she opened the door again Lucy said something strange. "There ought to have been some other solution."

Sheriff Bill was waiting for her in the parlor. Alex, who had been nervously puffing a cigarette, crushed it in the tray and rose when she entered.

"Cu'un Lucy will be down in a minute. But please, Mr. Bill"—her voice broke, but she quickly recovered her composure—"please try not to excite her too much. She's been under a terrific strain lately."

"I'll do what I can," the sheriff said kindly. "I just want all of you to help me a bit with what happened here last night."

"Last night?" Kate said in surprise. "I've already told you, nothing."

"Looks like plenty happened," he told her bluntly. "The doctor says she's been dead a long time, and you know yourself her bed wasn't slept in."

"She was dead—last night?"

"You would have a fox hunt out here with all sorts of folks traipsing all over the place," the sheriff grumbled. "Now—you folks came back in here after the others started off on that chase?"

"Cu'un Lucy and I tried to make some plans about what we could do to the house this summer. Kitty was bored and wandered around the room."

"Sort of restless-like?"

"Yes." The line between Kate's eyes deepened as she tried to remember. That little lost fact worried her; it was so near the surface of her mind, yet tantalizingly just beyond her grasp. "She went over to the window several times."

"She was looking for someone?"

"No," Kate replied honestly, "I didn't get that impression. She just wandered around the room, picking up the things on the tables and putting them down again."

"You said she went upstairs before you and Miss Lucy did?"

"Yes, she went up about ten o'clock."

"You didn't see her after that?"

"No. We stayed down here a little longer and then went to bed ourselves."

"Do you know what time it was when you went up?"

"I don't know exactly, but I imagine between ten-thirty and eleven."

"Could anybody have come in before then and you not have heard them?"

"Yes." Kate might have added more, but just then the door was opened and Lucy entered.

She was pale but composed. The white hair had been piled majestically on top of her head, and her small black eyes were bright with indignation.

"This is a fine how-de-do, Bill Davies," she said.

"I agree with you, ma'am, but we can't change facts," answered the sheriff affably. "Just sit down here while we talk all this over."

Alex held a chair and Lucy took it, back upright, as though a board held her rigidly in place. Kate perched on the arm of the chair and took Lucy's hand in her own.

The sheriff resumed his seat, and they watched him apprehensively. This gawky county sheriff might lack the scientific training and knowledge of the city police, but he made up for it in native shrewdness.

"You were telling me whether you heard anybody come in the house last night." He turned back to Kate.

"No, I didn't hear anybody. But I suppose somebody could have come in without us hearing him. The kitchen and dining-room doors were locked when the Negroes left, but I don't know about the side door." She turned inquiringly toward Lucy.

"I've only been locking that door recently. We never used to lock any of them. I didn't lock it last night; I forgot it."

"I didn't think of it either," Kate sighed and said to the sheriff. "So the side door was unlocked all night. We wouldn't have heard anybody come in that way while we were in here, and they could have used the back steps. I feel sure nobody came in the front door while we were still downstairs."

"And you locked the front door when you went up?"

Kate's hand tightened in Lucy's as the older woman answered.

"The front door was left unlocked, of course. Mr. Dexter was still out and had no key."

"Damn thunder and tarnation!" the sheriff swore under his breath.

Lucy lifted her thin eyebrows, and he hastily apologized. "What time did those d— those fox hunters leave the house?"

"Just after supper," Lucy told him. "We had it early on account of the hunt. It was just getting dark when the men arrived."

"Who was with you?" the sheriff asked Alex.

"I rode with a young doctor, Dr. Denton."

"Where'd you go?"

Alex shrugged. "Ask me something easier than that. I have no idea where we were from the time we left until we returned. It was very dark, and we bumped over what seemed to be a recently plowed field."

"With the doctor all the time?"

"Yes, though I doubt if I can prove it."

Three pairs of eyes, shocked, questioning, skeptic, were turned on him.

"We lost the dogs once, and all of us got out and there was a great deal of moving about there in the dark."

"Everybody?"

Alex met the sheriff's eyes candidly. "I don't know. There were several cars and, as I said, it was dark. Some of the car headlights were on, but there were plenty of men moving off from the light, trying to find some road they apparently had lost."

"How far from the house were you then?"

"I haven't the slightest idea."

"Are you accusing one of us?" Lucy threw back her head, and her eyes flashed with something of their old fire.

Kate was cold with fear. She could feel the small beads of perspiration on her forehead and along her upper lip, though she forced her cold hands to lie idle. She sat perfectly still there on the arm of the chair, but her brain was whirling as she sought frantically for an answer. She closed her eyes and could only see Alex standing there in a dark brown suit and she could hear Lucy telling him that a button was loose and that she would sew it on for him. A button—a brown button—and the sheriff had held one out in his hand for her to see. She tried to remember what Alex had worn last night, but she couldn't. Her mind seemed fogged, and she shook her head slightly as though to clear it. Only the sharp eyes of the sheriff saw that almost involuntary movement and wondered.

"It's somebody who knows this house right well," the sheriff mumbled.

There was a commotion in the hall, and the door was thrust open and Leigh and Alicia hurried into the parlor. Leigh was hatless, and the wind had tangled his hair.

"I couldn't stop 'em," said a deputy standing in the doorway, and the sheriff nodded.

"Cu'un Lucy, Kate!" Leigh exclaimed. "I came just as soon as I heard. I should have known there was something wrong when you called me this morning."

"Just what have you heard?" inquired the sheriff.

"Oh!" Leigh swung round to face him. "Why, I heard, of course, that Kitty had been killed."

"Yes indeed, it's all over town now," Alicia declared shrilly. There were high spots of color on her sallow cheeks, and her pale eyes were bright.

"Who called you?" The sheriff slid his eyes over the assemblage.

"I called him," Kate answered. "We thought Kitty might be in town and that if she was Leigh might have seen her."

The sheriff ground his teeth and stared at them belligerently.

"We got Jeff Gaines out here now, Sheriff." The deputy had come back and opened the door.

"You folks wait right here." He eyed them for a moment, then, evidently deciding that they did not need a guard, left them alone.

As soon as he had gone the others began talking all together. Lucy explained very briefly what had happened, interrupted by what sounded like squeals from Alicia. Leigh asked questions and promised them that he was there to protect them, that they did not have to answer the questions the sheriff asked them without his advice. Kate saw her opportunity and in the general confusion managed to slip away.

A hasty glance showed the front hall was empty, though she could hear the rumbling of voices in the rear. Quickly she mounted the stairs, stepping over the fifth step to avoid its telltale creak. The upper hall was quiet and deserted, and she ran across it to Alex's room. There still might be time; the sheriff's men had not yet had time for a thorough search.

She jerked open the closet door, sobbing under her breath at the sound it made. She pushed aside clothes hung neatly in a row: gray suits, blue suits, sports suits, and there at the back a brown suit. She dragged the coat off the hanger and brought it to the light. One button was missing.

The coat fell from her hands, and she gazed blankly down at the brown heap on the floor. And, standing there by the window, she thought of Kitty, vain, arrogant, greedy, reckless, of the way she had ruined the lives of so many others. She thought of how she had last seen her, her high heels tapping lightly over the floor. And she thought of Alex—and stopped. She mustn't think of him now. Slowly and deliberately she picked up the coat and, going to the closet, put it back on the hanger.

At the door she turned again and with a swift decision went back to the closet and jerked down the brown suit, flinging it over her arm.

The hall was still empty, and she hurried to her own room.

Her eyes traveled from wall to wall, picking out hiding places and discarding them. The house would be searched thoroughly and if it were found in her room would only confirm the sheriff's already aroused suspicions. She could hear people arriving downstairs. It was now or not at all. Suddenly she remembered the box of clothes in Lucy's room. Those clothes of Uncle Brock's that had been collected to be carefully gone over and then given away. Lucy wouldn't have much time to do it tonight, and if any of the searchers found a brown suit there it would seem natural. She tucked the suit under her arm and went back to the hall and into Lucy's room.

The box stood in a dark corner of the room, a large corrugated cardboard box. On one side, in even block letters, Lucy had printed: BROCK'S CLOTHES—TO BE SORTED. The clothes had been neatly folded, and Kate pulled up several layers and pushed the brown suit in somewhere near the bottom.

Opening the door, she glanced stealthily out into the hall, but no one was in sight. She let out her breath softly and crept down the stairs and back into the parlor. They were all there as she had left them—all except Alex.

"Oh, there you are." Lucy pounced on her at once. "We were wondering where you had gone. Do you think we should telephone or telegraph Kitty's husband? I think he ought to know it at once, and Leigh can't seem to make up his mind."

"I think we should call him on the phone." Alicia was decisive.

"But wouldn't a telegram be less of a shock?" Lucy asked.

"It's bound to be a shock either way." Leigh sounded tired and uncertain. Kate noticed the tired look of his eyes and the strained lines on his face.

"Better telephone him. There'd be more opportunity to explain," Kate agreed with Alicia.

"Then you'd better do it, Leigh," Lucy said.

"But I don't know him."

"None of us know him," Alicia argued. "He's X, the unknown quantity. I don't think I ever heard her mention him while she was here. She discarded husbands so lightly that we could scarcely expect to keep up with them." Alicia ended her words with a bitter laugh.

While she was talking Alex slipped back into the parlor. No one appeared to notice him, so he sat down quietly near the door.

"I'll talk to him myself," Kate said.

"Yes, maybe that would be best," Leigh agreed, and the others sighed, relieved not to have the unpleasant task.

"Do you know where to call?" asked Alicia.

"Yes, I know," replied Kate. It was one address that had been burned on her memory ever since she had carried a delayed letter in an old red sweater pocket.

"You'd better call him as soon as possible," Leigh said sharply. His brows were drawn together in a frown and his face sagged with worry.

Kate rose and went to the door, but before she could reach it a man came in and said:

"The sheriff would like to speak to Mrs. Allen." They stared at him uncomprehendingly and he added, "In the parlor across the hall."

There was a sharp intake of breath, clearly audible in the breathless silence. Then Lucy rose and followed him across the hall, and the door of the green parlor closed behind her.

Leigh was the first to move. He sank heavily into a chair and buried his face in his hands.

Alicia turned on him and demanded irritatingly: "Do something!"

"I—I don't know what to do," he almost sobbed. Kate eyed him with horror.

For the first time she thought she saw him as he really was, weak, sluggish, without brains or force of character. And, looking up, she caught the same look in Alicia's eyes. So Alicia knew too. Had probably known for a long time and had loyally hidden his incredible inability from the world.

They sat in silence then, dreading the ordeal which they knew must be met. There was courage in the pale planes of Kate's cheeks, singular dignity in the set of Alicia's shoulders, and Alex—the deep-set eyes were dark and turbulent. Once he moved to put an arm around Kate and comfort her, but she shrank from his touch and whispered, "Don't!"

All sense of time was lost. The little French clock on the mantel ticked busily, noisily, in the silent room. There was a new fear stealing over them, enveloping them in a misty veil of doubt and distrust. Though they struggled against it, it clung to their thoughts, choking out other ideas.

They did not hear the quiet little man come back to the door and so were startled when he spoke.

"The sheriff will see you now, Mrs. Frazier."

Kate managed to rise, but her knees were shaking.

"He can't do this!" Alicia cried hysterically.

It was then that the little man made the one voluntary utterance anybody heard him make during the entire investigation.

"He's doin' it," he said.

Alex put out his hand toward Kate, as though he would stop her, but she did not look at him. She followed the man across the hall, leaving the parlor door open as she left.

Lucy was not in the room, and it was a stern and determined sheriff who faced her, his back to the clean white marble mantel. There were other people in the room, but Kate was scarcely aware of them. She stood facing the sheriff, the fading afternoon light falling across her face, waiting for him to speak.

"You'd better sit down," he said at last, and without taking her eyes from his face she sank into a chair which one of the men brought to her.

"There's lots of things to say that are mighty unpleasant especially when there's been a murder," he began deliberately. "And there's one thing we've got to know—the truth."

"The truth . . ." Kate repeated.

"There's always a reason for murder too," he continued, as though she had not spoken, "however unreasonable it seems to the rest of us. And we've had two murders out here. As long as a killer's loose there's a chance he'll do it again. Murder breeds murder."

Kate was shaking with fright, and cold beads of perspiration glistened on her forehead. Her heart pounded madly.

"You want us to know the truth, don't you?" the sheriff asked suddenly.

"Oh yes . . ."

"You didn't see Kitty after she left the parlor last night?"

"No."

"Did you see a light on in her room when you went up to bed?"

"I didn't— Yes, I think there was a light showing through the transom of her door."

"You'd told her to leave, hadn't you?"

The blood drained from her face, and one of the men stepped forward, as though he thought she might faint. She sat rigidly in the hard, straight chair.

"Yes, I'd asked her to leave." Her voice was low but somehow steady.

"You hated her." It was a statement rather than a question.

"I hadn't thought—but perhaps I did."

"Look here, Kate." The sheriff leaned forward. "I don't think you did it. But you've got to face facts. Kitty was killed here. Mr. Brock was killed here. And still none of you realize the fix you're in."

Kate put a hand to her head to check the throbbing at her temple.

"What—what do you mean?" she asked.

"I mean I could build up a case against any of you." His words fell like hail on a glass windowpane—hollow, brittle. "Yes, you, or Miss Lucy, or Jeff Gaines, or even your precious Mr. Dexter."

"It couldn't have been one of us."

"Yes," the sheriff sighed and sounded utterly weary of the whole thing, "it could, and probably was. Now suppose you tell us some facts."

"But—" She checked herself. "What do you want to know?"

"Suppose you tell me everything that happened out here. Maybe you'd better start with yesterday morning."

"Why, nothing happened." Kate was puzzled. "Cu'un Lucy started spring cleaning, and everybody was busy with that. I was in the office most of the morning, but after lunch I helped too."

"And Kitty?" he prompted.

"She went to town sometime during the morning. I didn't see her, and she didn't tell us she was going. Fancy told us at lunch that she had gone. I—I thought she might be making arrangements to go back home."

"And did she?"

"I don't know. If she did she didn't tell me."

"I see."

Kate's tense fingers, which had been grasping the edges of the chair, relaxed. She hesitated before she spoke again.

"I don't know whether it's important," she said, "but there was a strange telephone call yesterday."

"A telephone call?"

"Yes. While I was in the office. It—it wasn't exactly a call. The phone rang and I answered, but there was nobody at the other end. At least nobody replied." Her black brows came together in a frown. "There must have been somebody on the line, though; I distinctly heard a click when the receiver was being put back."

"Was that all?"

"Yes. I thought it was—well, queer—but it doesn't seem important."

"Could it have been somebody up here at the house on this phone?"

"No, the phone out there wouldn't have rung if a call was being made from the one here. And I answered it immediately; it only rang once, so I don't believe anybody up here bothered. We answer if it rings repeatedly."

The sheriff digested her information slowly. His long legs were tucked awkwardly under the slender chair in which he sat, and he seemed for a moment to have forgotten that she was there.

"What time did Kitty get back from town?"

"In the afternoon. I don't know the time exactly, but it was around four. I was in here washing the chandelier." The blood rose to her pale cheeks as she remembered Kitty's sudden entrance.

"Did she say why she had been in town?"

"No. She said"—Kate met his eyes squarely—"she said she had a very successful day."

"What did you do then?"

"We went upstairs together, and Cu'un Lucy reminded us that supper would have to be early because of the hunt." Kate paused and then added more slowly, selecting her words carefully, "Kitty was a little upset, I think. I don't believe she had remembered the hunt. Maybe I had never mentioned it to her. She said something—I don't know what."

"Try to remember what it was."

Kate shook her head. "I wasn't listening. Cu'un Lucy might know. I think it was something about not knowing of the hunt, or why didn't they ask her? I really have no idea."

"What did she do after that?"

"Kitty came back downstairs and we went to our rooms. We had supper about six and had just finished when the men came for Alex."

"Kate, you've sat there and told me several times that nothing happened. But something *did* happen. Kitty was murdered here—in this house."

He waited for the full weight of his words to be felt.

"We've searched for the other shoe and haven't found it. Fancy says they are the ones she wore yesterday afternoon. And she was dragged part of the way to the brook. There's a piece of gravel from your walk imbedded in her forehead, and her clothes are torn. She was killed somewhere in this house, and I intend to find out where—and why."

Kate could not take her eyes from the determined face opposite.

"We haven't found any signs of a struggle yet," he said. "But you had all morning to arrange things."

"The elevator," Kate said clearly, and to her own ears the words sounded loud and harsh.

"The elevator?" the sheriff asked in bewilderment.

"Yes. It woke me last night." Kate was suddenly relieved, for at last that eluding memory had come back to her.

"What are you talking about, Kate?"

"Last night. I woke up. I thought it was only Alex coming in. But it was the elevator. I heard it."

The sheriff was skeptical and looked at her in exasperation. "I don't understand a thing you're saying."

"Of course," Kate replied simply. "It was the slave elevator. Leigh and Uncle Brock oiled it, but it still had a sort of humming noise."

"Are you trying to tell me that you have an elevator here in this house?"

"Yes."

"And you heard it last night?"

"Yes, of course." Kate frowned, irritated by the sheriff's obtuseness.

"Where is this elevator?" the sheriff demanded, rising so suddenly that his long legs seemed to push him upward in their sudden process of unfolding.

"Between the dining room and the kitchen." Kate got up, and one of the men opened the door.

Across the hall Leigh and Alicia and Alex watched them troop out of the green parlor. It was a silent procession, but there was something electric in the air about them.

Kate went directly to the small space between the kitchen door and the dining-room wall. There a long, narrow panel ran up to the ceiling, exactly matched by a similar panel at the other end, beside the door of what had been Brock's room. There was no effort to conceal the small door. Indeed, a small white knob turned easily under Kate's fingers, and the door swung forward, disclosing a dark gap.

The sheriff stepped forward and struck a match. The tiny flame showed a coil of new rope, and on the center of a rough wooden platform was the missing shoe.

17

It was Alex who finally called Kitty's husband. Kate and Lucy were utterly exhausted by the questioning and the climactic discovery of the evidence in the elevator.

It took some time for the Washington operator to locate Ralph Bolling and more time for Alex to explain to a bewildered husband that his wife was dead. The conversation was ended only when Bolling said he would charter a plane the next day and wire them the time of his arrival.

Kate drove alone to the near-by airport to meet him early Wednesday afternoon. She was glad of this opportunity to be alone. The house had been in an uproar for the past twenty-four hours with people coming and going. The doctor had given Lucy a strong sedative so that she was quiet, almost peaceful, in her room. But Kate had not been spared. A man stationed at the gate turned visitors away, but the sheriff and his deputies were in full possession. They came and went—searching, questioning—until Fancy was in hysterics, and even the calm Ella showed signs of breaking under the strain.

The second murder had become a Roman holiday for the press. One reporter had slipped through the police cordon strung around the house and frightened Zack when he took a flash picture. The sheriff himself sent the reporter away, and no more came to disturb them that day.

Leigh came but was so wholly inadequate in the crisis that Kate, watching him, felt her contempt turn into sympathetic pity. Alex would have been a pillar to lean upon, but she was filled with too many doubts and suspicions to fully trust him now.

Strangely enough, it was Jeff who took command of the situation. The sheriff questioned him again and again, but in between he gave quiet orders to the Negroes. He patted Kate gently on the shoulders but offered no words of sympathy. For once he was clean and sober, but the tight lines about his mouth showed that he fully understood his danger.

The sheriff talked to Kate and Jeff together before lunch.

"You and Kitty weren't on very good terms, were you, Jeff?" he asked dryly.

"No," Jeff replied and then, facing him squarely, added, "I hated every little bone in her body."

"Enough to kill her?"

Blood rushed to Jeff's sunburned face, but he answered quietly, "Probably, if I had hated her at just the right moment."

Kate shifted uneasily in her chair, and her eyes went from one to the other.

"Look here." Jeff leaned forward. "I may have hated her, but I'm honest enough to say it. I didn't happen to kill her, but she was as worthless a trollop as I've ever known. It's my opinion that the world is well rid of her, and if she alone was involved, I wouldn't lift my little finger to help you find her murderer."

"I'm not asking for your opinions," snapped the sheriff angrily. "I'm looking for facts, and Fancy told me that Kitty came back from your house one afternoon with the story that you had threatened to kill her."

Kate rose abruptly and went to the window, where she stood fingering the heavy brocade drapery, her back to the men. There was a brief pause before Jeff answered.

"I'm not surprised that she said that," he said, and his voice was dead and tired. "Kate can tell you all about it. She was there too."

Kate let the curtain swing back into place. The room was hot and close, but the palms of her hands were cold and damp with sweat. The sheriff seemed to be waiting for her to speak, and she turned slowly and faced him.

"I did tell you. You were here when I came back."

"Oh, that day. But you didn't say anything about a threat."

"Jeff didn't mean anything. We all threaten people when we're angry, and Kitty—Kitty had been unpardonably rude."

"Maybe you'd better tell me the story again and leave off the whitewash this time."

"Yes, he'd rather have the story from you." Jeff's lips were pressed tight, and he gave a harsh laugh. "He'd come nearer believing you."

Kate turned puzzled eyes toward him, but he nodded and she told the sheriff about the meeting on the steps of The Laurels. As near as she could remember, she repeated what each of them had said.

"I hit the horse so that she would go," she concluded. "I thought there had been enough accusations for one afternoon."

"That's the way it happened," Jeff said.

"Mr. Dexter had known her before he came here, hadn't he?" The sheriff addressed Kate and she nodded.

"The darkies say he had a quarrel with her one morning. What do you know about that?"

Kate was silent, refusing to answer, and the sheriff let them go soon afterward. Later in the morning she saw him talking to Alex and realized he was thoroughly checking every small detail and filing it away in his mind for future reference.

Kate thought of all these things as she drove to the airport. The car kept pace with her thoughts, now going smoothly, now jerking unevenly along with short spurts of speed. Farms and country stores plastered with Coca-Cola signs and patent-medicine advertisements sped by, and along the road the tall grass bent sharply in the current of air created by the car. She paid little attention to the roadside. It was familiar enough and she kept her eyes fastened intently on the concrete ribbon of the highway.

Her newest guest was waiting in the small bare building when she arrived, and Kate could not conceal her start of surprise as he came forward to meet her.

"You're Kate? I'm Ralph Bolling."

She took his extended hand and for a moment was at a loss for words. He was not the sort of man she had pictured as Kitty's husband.

He was a man of mature years, probably somewhere in his fifties. His white hair was silky and brushed smoothly back from a high forehead. His face was a healthy color, but the deep seams beside his mouth showed a man of experience. He was stockily built, with broad shoulders, but was trim and neat in appearance.

He smiled at Kate, and she suddenly realized that this was just the sort of choice Kitty would have made. Her first two husbands had undoubtedly been on the romantic side, but in marrying Ralph Bolling, Kitty had chosen social position and a man who would demand little and give much.

"I'm glad you are here," she said, and there was a sincere ring to her words. "I'm only sorry that it was a tragedy that had to bring you."

"Thank you." His eyes dropped to his feet, and Kate felt a shock of surprise that this man was really grieved, that he had really loved Kitty.

"If you'll put your bag in the car we had better start. It's about fifty miles to Cliff's Edge."

"I'm sorry to have made you come so far. They told me in Washington that this was the nearest field."

"It's been no trouble at all." Kate smiled at him. "I frequently come here to meet people coming to Cliff's Edge. Modern traffic more or less passed by our little part of the world."

On the homeward journey Kate told him something of the story, keeping to the bare facts of the case as best she could. It was not easy to tell, but he seemed to understand when she halted and stumbled.

"Thank you for telling me," he sighed when she had finished.

"I hope it will all be cleared up very soon. Our sheriff is—is very capable."

There was no more real conversation until they drew up in front of the white pillars of the house. Ralph got out of the car and stood for a moment looking up at the old house.

"So this is Cliff's Edge," he said softly. "Yes, it's very much as I imagined it." He turned to Kate. "Kitty really loved this place."

"Kitty loved it! No, you're mistaken. She hated it."

"You may have thought that, but I'm right. I've heard her talk about it to our friends. Of course," he added frankly, looking at the peeling paint and weather-stained boards, "she exaggerated it somewhat, but she was proud of it. I think she was jealous of you because you owned it."

"I never knew that." Kate looked up at him in amazement.

Zack came out on the porch, and Kate told him to take the bag from the car. She led the way into the broad hall and up the curving stair, stopping at the door of the room next to the one Alex occupied.

"This will be yours while you're with us." She opened the door and crossed the room to lower the shade against the glare of the afternoon sun. "No," she answered his unspoken question, "this wasn't her room. She had the one across the hall. I know you'll want to freshen up a bit now. Zack will show you where everything is. I'll be downstairs when you're ready to come down."

Smiling, she left him. The hall was quiet and dim and cool. It had the apparent happy serenity of a home, but there were still secrets lurking in the dark corners and slipping up the stairs. Kate hurried to her own room, took off her hat, and slung it on the bed. She washed her face and hands and, returning, surveyed herself in the old mirror.

It was a pale and worried face that looked back at her, and the dark eyes seemed wider and the square jaws more set. She dusted powder lightly over her nose and ran a comb through the black hair, pushing it back in a loose wave from her face.

Downstairs in the hall she found Jeff wandering absently about the place. His shoulders drooped, but he smiled when he saw her.

"They've got Alex in there now. Been at him for some time."

"What—what are they asking him?" Kate could feel the pounding of her heart.

"Probably going over every shred of his life with him. They took me over the jumps from the cradle—well, till I'm almost ready for the grave. Don't worry so, Kate; he'll get along all right."

Kate felt the blood rush to her face.

"I don't know what you mean."

"Yes, you do. Come out on the front steps. I'd like to talk to you. Out there we can watch the approaches so that we can be assured the little shadow isn't listening."

"The shadow?"

"That little man that follows Mr. Bill around and never says anything. I don't know his name, but he's definitely the little man who's there."

The corners of Kate's mouth turned up in amusement as she followed him to the door. Jeff took out a handkerchief and dusted the step before he allowed her to sit on it.

"Why, Jeff, it's been a long time since you were so gallant."

"Has it? Then I must mind my manners a little better in the future. Cigarette?"

Kate took one from the crumpled pack and leaned forward for him to light it. He lit his own before he spoke.

"I never have told you how much I appreciated what you did for me. I was rather rough on you. Down there at the jail, I mean." He lowered his eyes and fastened them on the cigarette which he was absently rolling between his fingers. "I hated you coming down there."

"That's all right."

"I'd be there now if they had anything extra on me. The only trouble is that nobody liked Kitty, and what evidence they have will apply equally to a lot of people."

He took her hand and swung it in his own. Kate bit her lip but said nothing.

"You brought her husband back. Tell me what he's like."

"He's old. That is, much older than Kitty. I liked him; he's kind and real. Do you know what he said, Jeff? He said Kitty loved Cliff's Edge. That she was jealous of me because I own it."

"Yes, I think she was," was Jeff's surprising answer. "She tried to wheedle your grandfather into leaving it to her that last summer before he died."

"What!"

"Yes, she did. She was furious with him afterward and left rather suddenly. I think that summer she was engaged to me it was The Laurels she really wanted, and when she saw the way things were over there she broke away as quick as she could."

"This is all news to me," Kate said. "I can't even picture her living here."

"Oh, she didn't want to live here. Her idea was merely to bring people down and impress them. Kitty always wanted to play the grand lady, but she never quite measured up to it."

Kate flicked her cigarette out on the gravel walk and turned with a startled movement to see Alex standing behind them in the open door. He turned quickly and went back into the house.

"You're in love with him, aren't you?" Jeff asked gently.

"No," she denied, but not very convincingly.

"Then you're both giving a good imitation of it. He looks like he'd be all right for you, Kate." He put his hand under her chin and pulled her face around. "Don't worry, plain Kate. Everything will be all right."

He took her hand and without another word drew her to her feet, and they went back into the house together.

Alex and Ralph joined them in the hall, and Kate introduced them. Avoiding the hurt look in Alex's eyes, she led them into the parlor.

Before long Alex and Ralph had discovered mutual friends in Philadelphia and talked about them. Kate was glad enough to relax in silence. Jeff stirred the fire, for with the coming of evening there was a chill in the air. Already the tall shadows of the trees slanted in the late-afternoon sun.

When the fire was burning brightly Jeff went out to speak to the sheriff. Presently he returned and said to Kate:

"I'm going home now. But you're not to worry any more. I'll look after the farm for you, and pretty soon well see if we can make it a really good one."

He left almost at once, and Alex soon followed, casting a worried look in Kate's direction.

"I'm not at all what you expected, am I?" Ralph spoke unexpectedly, and Kate jumped, so far away her thoughts had wandered.

"Well, no, not exactly."

"I knew you were surprised. You know, Mrs. Frazier, I loved Kitty very much, but I never had any illusions about her. She was so pretty and vivacious, wasn't she?" he asked wistfully.

"Yes." Kate was sorry for this man who had loved Kitty and had at the same time understood her so well.

"She didn't love me, and I demanded very little from her. So you see we were better matched than you would think. We each had something the other wanted."

Kate was embarrassed by the candor of his words and was glad when the sheriff interrupted them.

"I know you will want to talk and I should go up and see about Cu'un Lucy." She rose hurriedly and left the two alone.

She was breathless when she knocked on Lucy's door a moment later. Lucy was awake and called to her to come in. She was propped up in the bed by two enormous pillows. Kate climbed up on the bed and sat beside her, swinging her legs over the side.

"You brought Kitty's husband back?" Lucy asked.

"Yes. He's been here a few hours now. I knew you were sleeping when we came and I didn't want to disturb you. You can meet him tomorrow."

"Yes, that would be better. Dr. Denton says that if I'm perfectly quiet today and tonight I'll be all right tomorrow. Bill Davies came up and talked to me for a while, but otherwise I haven't seen anyone."

"We all need a good night's rest," Kate said. "Cu'un Lucy, do you suppose we will ever get everything and everybody cleared?"

"No, dear, not everybody. But don't worry, Kate; everything will be all right soon."

Kate thought Jeff had said the same thing earlier. Her eyes fell on the box of old clothes, and she asked in a small voice, "Have you been through those clothes yet?"

"No, of course I haven't." Lucy showed her surprise. "It won't matter when they're done. There's plenty of time to give them away."

"Oh yes, indeed," Kate agreed hastily and tried to push down that little nagging mistrust of Alex. "Is there anything I can get for you?"

"No, I don't know of anything now. Just tell me a little about Mr. Bolling."

Kate tried to describe him as best she could.

"He must have made Kitty a very good husband," commented Lucy when she had finished. "He was the sort of balance wheel she needed. Not that I think she would ever have settled down; she was always flighty, even as a child."

Kate pulled at the hem of her dress. "He loved her very much, Cu'un Lucy. But I think he knew all her faults."

"Poor Kitty lacked integrity." This seemed to be the last word that could be said about Kitty, and Lucy changed the subject. "You run along downstairs now, Kate. Ella will bring me a light supper. And try to get a good night's rest. Everything will be all right in the morning."

Kate planted a soft kiss on the withered cheek and left her.

18

The house was overrun with people on the day that Kitty was buried. Ralph had made the decision. She was to be placed in the family plot, next to a new grave that was still not two weeks old.

"I would like to think of her here, and I know this is where she would rather be," he told Kate. "She never had a home."

Kate regarded him with interest. His face was marked by his grief. She thought with a sort of dull surprise that grief was curiously out of place, as nobody else seemed to care what happened to Kitty.

"I may not have this opportunity to talk to you alone again," he continued. "The sheriff tells me that she recently inherited some money which will come to me if she made no will. I don't think she did. Kitty wasn't the sort to give death a thought. I—I don't want it; I want you to take it and apply it to the house if you will."

"Oh no." Kate drew back, as though what he offered was tainted.

"Please," Ralph pleaded. "I have enough for myself and I had no one to give it to but her. I wish now I had given it all. . . ."

They were interrupted before he could explain what he had meant. Flowers must be placed, and friends and relatives arrived, offering guarded sympathy, for Kitty had never been popular in the neighborhood, especially among the women. Lucy came downstairs to help Kate. There was an almost instantaneous mutual understanding between her and Ralph

Bolling. They had a common ground in that they belonged to the same generation.

During a lull Kate slipped out of the parlor. She was tired, and the crowd and the heavy scent of the flowers made her head ache. At the side door she was startled when a hand was laid on her arm.

"Kate," Alex said, "Kate darling, what's the matter?"

"Nothing." The word was low, barely audible.

"Yes, there is. You've avoided me as though I were a plague for the past two days. Now you won't," he said as she tried to pull away. "I want to talk to you."

Still holding her arm, he held the door open and took her to the far end of the garden.

"Now tell me what's the matter," he demanded.

Kate turned her face away, afraid of what he might read in her eyes.

"Really, Alex, nothing's the matter. You have no right to drag me down here."

"I have every right." The hard lines about his mouth deepened, and there was suppressed violence in his words. "I love you and you told me you loved me. That gives me every right in the world to know what's happened to make you avoid me, to make you pull away from me as though you're afraid to have me touch you."

He pulled her to him and kissed her angrily, hungrily. Kate tried to push him away but found herself responding to his passion. When he let her go she was breathless and shaken.

"I knew you loved me," he exulted. "And you know it too. Something happened that made you act like this. But don't worry; everything's going to be all right."

"Don't say that!" she cried.

"You're trembling. Sit down." He pulled her down on the grass beneath a lilac bush. He tried to kiss her again, but she turned her head, and his kiss fell lightly on the tip of her nose. He took her hand in his, holding it firmly, and said in a serious tone:

"Tell me what's bothering you. We haven't had time to really know each other. We just know we're in love. We've the rest of a lifetime. . . ." He laid a hand on her cheek and pulled her face toward his.

Steel-blue eyes met black, and Kate could see a small muscle beside his mouth jerk spasmodically.

"Kate, what happened? What made you suspect me?"

"The button," she whispered, almost involuntarily, impelled by the unyielding determination in his eyes.

"What button?"

"The brown button. The one from your coat."

"So that's what you were doing in my room."

Kate was frightened. He wasn't even denying it.

"Kate, you darling little fool," he said at last and smiled into her tense face.

"But—but the button was off your coat?"

"Listen to me, Kate," he said harshly. "God, I thought you at least were different! I thought you had a little faith in me!" He laughed mirthlessly.

"I found your brown coat in your closet." Her words were flat and lifeless. "There was one button missing, and the others were just like the one the sheriff showed us. I—I hid your coat."

He looked at her in silence for a moment, then, picking up a stick, scratched absently in the ground. "I didn't kill her, Kate. I don't know whether I can make you believe me or not. You must be right about the button, but I didn't know I had lost it. I haven't worn that brown coat for days. I didn't like Kitty, but I wouldn't have killed her. Not even after she tried to blackmail me."

"Blackmail? Oh, Alex!"

"She knew I was in love with you and she wanted money. It's generally thought I was driving the car that day—that day Eleanor was killed. Kitty said she wouldn't tell you if I'd give her a thousand dollars."

Kate's hand tightened on his arm. "You must remember," he continued, looking at her earnestly. "I bumped into you just afterward. I told her to tell you and be damned. I intended you should know the truth and what other people thought too."

"Why did Kitty need so much money, Alex? Her husband must have plenty."

"I don't know. I was so furious I couldn't even think. But it's probably back of her own murder."

Kate flinched at the brutal word. "The sheriff thinks it was one of us," she said.

"That's very obvious," Alex said grimly. "He's cross-examined us often enough. I don't know whom he's picked for his victim."

"But, Alex, one of *us*. I've known these people all my life." Kate stopped abruptly.

"All of them except me. That's what you were going to say, isn't it?"

"It could have been any one of us. Jeff or Cu'un Lucy or me. . . ."

"Hush." Alex put his hand over her mouth. "It's Mr. Brock's death you have to remember. Kitty was very obviously killed because she knew who did that. Maybe she tried to blackmail him too."

Kate shivered, and he put an arm around her shoulders.

"You mustn't be afraid, Kate. I'll never let anything happen to you," he said gently. "But there is one thing I'd like to know. . . ."

He had no opportunity to finish his question.

"Kate!" Lucy called from the open doorway. "Kate!"

"Oh, damn! She's seen us," Alex muttered.

"Yes, Cu'un Lucy."

"Kate, you're needed up here." Even from a distance they could hear the irritation in Lucy's voice.

"I'm coming." Kate rose swiftly and hurried up the narrow garden walk. As she reached the steps she turned and smiled almost gaily at Alex.

In the house the front rooms were again filled with people whose eyes avidly devoured the family for an answer to the tragedy. Kate felt a close bond to Alicia when she heard her telling one person that she would be a hypocrite if she said she was sorry. And there was the policeman in the hall. . . .

Finally Kate gave orders for Zack to stand at the door and tell people that the family was resting. Then Jeff came and she saw him moving quietly at the rear of the house. Once he came to her and asked for the keys to the office.

"I'll take this chance to look through some of Uncle Brock's books," he said when she gave them to him. "I'll be out of your way unless you want me."

"Thanks, Jeff. I must get Cu'un Lucy upstairs to rest or she'll really collapse. The books you want are on the shelves to the left of the desk."

For some reason she was glad that Jeff was there. He knew and understood the whole situation as Alex didn't and probably never would. She knew the sheriff still had his eyes on Jeff, but he had been such a help. If I eliminate Alex and Jeff and Cu'un Lucy and myself, she thought, and the Negroes, because I somehow can't see . . . She saw Alicia and Leigh come out of the parlor and forced her mind into a blank.

As it turned out there was little chance for rest before Ella called them to lunch. The meal itself wasn't a success. Zack passed the dishes and, prompted from the kitchen by Ella, recommended various tidbits which might tempt their appetites. But the people at the table were not interested. They ate little, and what they did eat was scarcely tasted.

After lunch the house was quiet, and Kate went to her room and threw herself on the bed. There she tossed restlessly, finally climbing down to lower a shade, but the dimness of the room did nothing to calm her nerves.

She had beat her pillow out of shape before she discarded all hope of sleep. She got up and bathed and dressed carefully. A navy-blue dress would satisfy the proprieties, and she slipped it over her head. Pinning a towel around her shoulders, she smoothed powder over her face and applied a touch of rouge along the ridge of her high cheekbones. There were deep shadows beneath her eyes which she could not hide.

There was still time to spare when she had finished, and she took her hat, bag, and gloves from the wardrobe and placed them on the rumpled bed. When she had done that she stared about her, looking for something else to do. She stood at her window, trying to see whether Jeff was still in the office, but the angle of her window did not give the depth of view necessary. She thought she saw someone slide around the building, but when he did not reappear she decided it was only a shadow.

The hall was empty when she opened her door. Her feet made only a whisper of sound as she went quietly down the back steps and out the side door toward the river's edge.

She was curiously in need of the solitude which the turbulent waters of the river gave her. She stood there, her back against the rough bark of a tree, and gazed down at the water. She picked up a rock and threw it into the river, listening to the remote splash it made and watching the widening circles as it cut the surface.

It was there that the sheriff found her.

"Kate," he said.

She turned quickly, startled, and his hand caught her arm so that she would not lose her balance.

"This is a dangerous place for you to come."

"I love the river, Mr. Bill."

"Then don't stand so near its edge. The Indians didn't name it the coffinmaker without reason." He took a newspaper from a sagging pocket of his coat and spread it on the ground. "Sit down here," he said. "I want to talk to you for a few minutes."

Kate sat down, wondering why he had come, why he had chosen this moment to question her again.

"I only want to ask you one question," he said as though he read her thoughts, "and ask you to help. Kate, do you want this whole thing cleared up today?"

His keen blue eyes searched her face while he waited for a reply, and evidently he was satisfied with what he saw, for he gave a slight nod.

"Yes."

"I thought you would." He fumbled in his pockets again and after several tries found his pipe and tobacco and lit it.

Kate watched him silently and tried to collect her thoughts. She knew that she did want the case closed, regardless of the result. The strain and fear under which they had all been living were more unbearable, more terrible than the truth.

"Mr. Brock's murder is the key to the whole thing," the sheriff was saying, and she remembered that Alex had said the same thing just that morning. "Kitty's is easily explained. But Mr. Brock's was planned and the ground prepared. You've all told me he was cross and irritable, so he must have known something, something that made him that way. He knew about the trouble, but he didn't realize the danger, and that gave the killer a chance. His death was probably planned to appear as a suicide. Why, even his own gun was used. But the murderer was frightened and bungled it. He remembered to wipe off his fingerprints, but he forgot to put Mr. Brock's on the gun. Maybe he heard you or Jeff—who says he got there pretty soon after the shot—something must have interrupted him. Maybe it was pure panic, because he left the scene before he had completely set the stage."

The sheriff paused and drew on his dead pipe, then absently stuffed it into his pocket.

"Things must not have gone so well after that. Though why they didn't is more than I know. All of you helped. You told me the truth, but you were so busy protecting each other you didn't tell me all of it. You destroyed evidence." He turned on Kate, and there was an accusing look in his eyes that frightened her.

"And on top of that, not one of you had a conceivable alibi and you had a motive. Any one of you could have done it, man or woman; the murderer didn't need much physical force. Do you want me to go on?" He broke off abruptly.

"Yes."

"Well, Kitty didn't stay satisfied—if she ever was. She never was one to mind her own business. She must have found out who did it. And once a person's killed there don't seem to be anything to keep him from killing again."

"You mean that somebody else—somebody—"

"Yes. That's why we have law. I don't particularly like hunting people, but the rest of you would always be in danger. Protecting society, you might call it."

He picked up a stick and broke it while Kate watched him, fascinated.

"That's why I want your help," he continued. "I know who did it and I reckon you would, too, if you'd just think. I don't want to scare you, but I want it stopped—now, before it goes on any further. I've got a little evidence but no proof, and a really good lawyer would twist it all out of shape."

"I'll do whatever I can."

"Wait till you hear what I want before you say that. I want you to be a bait. Willing to take a chance?"

"Yes, I think I am."

"You're a good girl, Kate." The sheriff laid his rough hand on hers. "I don't think there'll be any real danger. I'll be around to prevent that."

"What do you want me to do?"

"When you get back to the house go out to the office and get one of those farm ledgers. Got one in the safe?" he asked abruptly.

"Of course not. Why should I put that in the safe?"

"Then is there a small account book in the safe?"

"No, I don't think so. There's an old notebook with some lists of seeds in it. I think I stuck it in the safe the other day, though I don't know why."

"That's just fine. Is it small enough to go in your handbag?"

"I guess so. But what do you want with it? Surely it's not important."

"That won't make any difference. Now you go out to the office and get it and put it in your purse and carry it every-where you go, no matter how silly it seems to you."

Kate was completely bewildered. What the sheriff was say-ing didn't make sense.

"You understand about that?" There was mounting excite-ment in his voice. "All right. Then you're to speak very confi-dentially to several people. You just tell 'em you've got to see me as soon as the funeral's over, that you've found something important. I want you to watch 'em but don't let 'em know it. Can you do it?"

"Yes, but—"

"All right then." He reached in the inside pocket of his coat and pulled out a paper on which nine names had been written.

Kate took the paper and stared at the names in amazement. "You can't suspect all of these. I don't believe it!"

"I certainly can. Only one did it, but the others are hiding something. Each one of them had plenty of opportunity, and I can think of a good reason. Maybe some more than others. I want the truth, and these people have lied or concealed something. You just watch 'em. If I could do it myself"—he rose and stood towering above her—"I would. But since I can't I'll have to trust you to act as my deputy."

He held out his hand and helped her to her feet. His shrewd eyes were almost dreamy, and the perpendicular lines between them were deepened like two dark exclamation points.

"If you do your part we'll know the truth tonight."

"I will," Kate promised. She read the names again and then, crumpling the paper into a hard ball, threw it over the bluff into the river.

"Just one more thing, Kate." The sheriff was serious and he spoke with great emphasis. "After you've talked to these people don't go anywhere alone. Don't go into a room with any one of them. And stay with as many people as you can. I'll always be somewhere around, but there's no use taking unnecessary risks."

Without another word he left her, slipping away quietly along the river's edge.

Kate was unbelievably frightened; her hands were trembling, and she put one against the tree trunk to steady herself. Suddenly she threw back her shoulders and lifted her head. She must not be afraid; there was so much to do and so little time left in which to do it. She glanced at the watch on her wrist and with a startled exclamation hurried back to the house.

She did not go directly in but circled around it and went into the office. She paused for a moment by the door and forced herself to breathe more slowly.

Jeff was seated at the desk and he looked up in surprise as she entered.

"Given time and a little variety, and I think we can make something really big out of this plantation," he said, and there was a spark of ambition in his voice.

"Good," replied Kate and knelt down in front of the old safe and twirled the dial.

"What are you looking for?" he asked.

"Just something I remembered. Oh," she breathed as though in relief, "here it is." She held up a small notebook and opened it, quickly scanning one or two pages.

"What is it?" Jeff rose and looked toward her, but she shut the book immediately.

"Just something I remembered was in the safe. I must give it to Mr. Bill." She spoke absently and turned toward the door.

"Wait a minute, Kate. . . ." But he finished his sentence to an empty room. He followed her to the door, a deep scowl on his face. But Kate was already up the steps and at the kitchen door.

She leaned against the door and breathed hard. The blood was racing through her veins. She had made a beginning.

Two black faces stared at her sudden and unexpected arrival, the whites of four eyes startling against the black background of skin. Zack and Will, clad in their somber and Sunday best, were waiting in the kitchen.

"Whut—whut yo' doin' in here, Mis' Kate?" stammered Zack.

Kate caught her breath and whispered in an almost conspiratorial tone, "Sh. . . . I've been out by the river. Are people beginning to come?"

"Yas'm."

"Have either of you seen the sheriff?"

"Naw'm," Will denied vehemently. "We ain't seen him a-tall terday. He ain't comin' round here now, is he, Mis' Kate?"

"I want to see him. I found something that's important." Kate moved the notebook slightly so that it caught their attention. "I want to give him this. If you see him anywhere tell him I'm looking for him, will you?"

"Yas'm," they agreed, but as she opened the door into the hall she noticed that they moved a little closer together, as though for mutual protection.

"Where have you been, Kate?" Alicia came toward her. "We've been looking everywhere for you. The family's going to stay in Cu'un Lucy's room until the service begins." She spoke in a whisper and took Kate by the arm and led her to the back steps. "People are already beginning to come, and we couldn't find you anywhere, so Leigh and I were sent to look."

Alicia panted a little as they climbed the steep stairs. She wore a mustard-colored suit which made her skin seem more sallow than ever. Her eyes were glittering with excitement, and Kate noticed that she, too, had dark circles under her eyes.

She followed Kate into her room. "Put on your hat and we'll go on to Cu'un Lucy's now. What's that you've got in your hands?"

"It's something important. I must show it to the sheriff just as soon as possible." Kate lowered her voice and continued in almost a whisper, "Alicia, I think I've found the answer to all this."

"You have? What is it?"

"No, I mustn't tell you now. Where can I hide it? I want to be sure it's safe."

"Give it to me." Alicia held out her hand. "I'll keep it for you."

"No, no. . . ." Kate held it back.

"Mis' Lucy sont me to see of yo' was ready." Fancy entered the room without knocking.

"You go on, Alicia," Kate said. "Tell her I'll be there in just a minute."

"Well . . ." Alicia's eyes were still on the small notebook Kate held. "All right." She turned suddenly and left them.

"Whut's the matter with Mis' Alicia?" Fancy asked when the door had closed.

"Nothing. She's just upset like the rest of us," Kate answered. "Is my slip showing?"

"Yo' looks all right." Fancy was indifferent. She watched Kate open and shut the small drawers of the bureau with growing interest. "Whut yo' lookin' for?"

"Some place to hide this." Kate showed her the small book and with growing excitement added, "I know what Miss Kitty knew, Fancy. I've found out who did it."

Fancy's eyes rolled and she uttered a scream as she backed toward the door, opened it, and fled down the steps as though bats out of hell were after her. Kate waited, then she shrugged, and put the notebook carefully into her purse. If the sheriff was after reactions, he was certainly getting a variety. Kate wondered dully what he would do when she reported to him.

Picking up her gloves, she closed the door and quietly crossed the hall to Lucy's. The family was assembled in full force, not only those closely related, but also some of the more distant cousins as well. The room was crowded.

Lucy sat near a front window, and Ralph Bolling stood behind her, staring vacantly down at the people on the veranda below. Leigh came to Kate and led her to a chair in a far corner of the room. He took her hand and whispered something which she didn't hear because she was busy watching Alicia, who was working her way through the maze of people toward the door. Then Lucy called to her and Kate went over and laid her smooth cheek against the withered one. Lucy patted her hand sympathetically, silently acknowledging it was an ordeal for both of them.

"It's almost time to go down, Kate," Leigh whispered and touched her arm.

She noticed that some of the people were indeed going. Ella hovered over Lucy like a mother hen with an only chick, and Alicia—Alicia had gone.

"I'd better wait and go with Cu'un Lucy, but you go on down," Kate whispered, but as he turned she called him back softly. "Leigh?"

"Yes?"

"Have you seen the sheriff this afternoon?"

"No. Surely he wouldn't be out here now."

"I just hoped." Kate dropped the lids over her eyes. "I found something that I know's important and I must give it to him right away."

"You mean you've found some new evidence?" he whispered, and Kate nodded. "What was it?"

"A little notebook that belonged to Uncle Brock."

"Good God, Kate!" Through her lowered eyes she could see sweat standing out on his brow. "Don't tell anybody what you've told me! Don't you realize the danger? You might tell the wrong person. Promise me you won't tell anybody else. What have you done with it?"

"I hid it in my room," Kate lied, her voice shaking from fright, which was partly reaction and partly due to the warning he had given her. "I won't tell a soul."

She went back to Lucy and Ella while Leigh stood uncertainly at the door, but she gave him a slight nod and he went out.

"I'll be glad when the whole thing's over," Lucy said. "What made you disappear so suddenly this afternoon when we needed you?"

"I—I remembered something important," Kate said.

"It couldn't-a been that 'portant," Ella stated flatly. "We had ever'body out lookin' for yo'."

"Yes, it was," Kate asserted. "I found some notes that were Uncle Brock's."

Lucy turned her head so quickly that the diamonds in her ears flashed, and Ella's garrulous flow of reprimands was stopped.

"Are you sure?" Lucy asked.

"I haven't had time to read all of them very carefully," Kate said, watching them, "but I think when I give them to the sheriff he'll know what to do."

The room was so still that Kate could hear the muffled sounds of the people in the room below. A car drew up outside, and the sound of the closing door came with peculiar clarity to their ears.

Lucy smoothed the front of her black silk dress, and when she spoke her words were thin and detached and resigned. "Whatever is, is best, no matter what the outcome."

Without looking at the girl again she went to the door. Kate followed her into the hall and down the steps, where Ralph met them. He gave Lucy his arm and she looked up with a vague smile on her lips. To Kate, at least, it was heartbreaking to see her there, a ghost of her former self. She wished heartily that she had never seen the sheriff or agreed to his plan. She might have turned then and rushed back to her room, but she caught sight of Alex standing in the doorway, waiting anxiously for her to come.

19

The afternoon was like a dream, unreal and terrifying. Kate clung to Alex while the rector read the solemn words of the burial service, the phrases drifting over her head unheard. Once a woman sobbed, and Kate turned toward her in annoyance. Her own eyes were dry and bright, her head high, and she stood rigid, unaware that Alex was watching her with a strange expression on his drawn face.

Afterward they walked the short distance to the hill which had been the resting place for generations of Leighs. It was set in a grove of trees and enclosed by a wrought-iron fence. The intricate tracery of the gate bore the name Leigh, and the marble monuments were ghostly guests. Kate shivered, and Alex pressed her hand reassuringly.

"It will soon be over, darling," he whispered.

"Yes, I know that."

He tucked her gloved hand into the crook of his arm. "I want to take you away just as soon as I can."

"That may be sooner than you think."

He looked down into her upturned face. "What do you mean?"

Kate motioned, and he lowered his head to catch her words. "I found out who did it this afternoon. I'm going to tell the sheriff as soon as we get back to the house. You see, I found a notebook that belonged to Uncle Brock and I—"

Lucy touched her arm and Kate turned to her, but not until she had seen Alex's face frozen into a mask of horror. He was like a stone beside her. She let her hand drop from his arm, but he did not move.

Afterward she could not remember what was said and done there by the open grave. It was only with great effort that she controlled her own jerking muscles and strained nerves. Her heart was pounding madly, sounding to her ears like the beat of a savage drum. She bit her lower lip and was unconscious of the sickening taste of blood.

"Let's go back to the house now," Lucy whispered, and she jumped. "I don't want to be here for the final part."

Judge Brewster walked with them and, looking back, Kate saw the little group of people who had come with Kitty to the grave slowly disintegrate.

The house was quiet and deserted when they entered the hall. Kate pulled off her hat and put her hand to her throbbing sorehead. She murmured a word of apology and went back to the kitchen. The Negroes had gone and she opened the refrigerator and, taking out a bottle, poured herself a glass of water.

When she returned the hall was empty. As she climbed the steps she had the eerie feeling that eyes were watching her, and she quickened her steps. She closed her door and with trembling fingers turned the key in the lock.

As she looked about her at the familiar objects of the room something seemed curiously out, of place. Her eyes fell on the corner of a handkerchief caught as a drawer had been too hastily closed. She stared at it until her hands were clammy with fear, knowing that what she had dreaded was true. The sheriff's plan had worked. Her room had been searched. She had talked to the murderer!

As her eyes moved restlessly about the room she saw other signs of search, vague but unmistakable. She covered her face with her hands, but the picture remained clear cut and brilliant before her eyes. It seemed incredible that her story had been believed, but there was the handkerchief in the drawer, the pillow replaced smoothly, the wardrobe door slightly ajar. She picked up her purse which she had dropped on the table as she entered and took it to the window. She opened it and took out the small notebook. It was all so absurd. The little black book contained only dates and the amounts of seed cotton and corn which had been bought for the plantation with such notations as: *Try Mr. S.'s seed cotton next year. Not sufficient yield from this lot.*

Kate replaced the book in her purse and unlocked the door. The hall was dim and empty, yet she could not be sure. The late-afternoon sun slanted at an angle through the window at the far end of the hall, leaving the back steps a well of deep shadow.

Her footsteps sounded loud to her own ears as she crossed the hall to the front steps. Uncertain, she looked about her, peering into the dark corners. Did that shadow move or was it only her imagination? With her hand on the stair rail, something impelled her to turn quickly and look again, but she saw no one. I'm imagining things, she told herself. For a moment she stood there, listening intently, but if she had heard a sound it was not repeated, and she walked quickly down the steps.

The parlor, too, was empty, and she crossed the room and put her purse on the mantel. The glow of the low fire was a cheerful note in the silence of the place. She picked up a box from the table and selected a cigarette. She was just lighting it when the door opened.

"I thought I would find you here."

Kate put the still-burning match in the ash tray and smiled confidently. She sat down on the arm of the sofa and drew on her cigarette before she asked, "Where is everybody else?"

"Upstairs or out in the yard."

"The strain is beginning to tell on all of us." Kate nodded. "I even imagined someone was watching me as I came downstairs. You needn't smile," she added, putting down her cigarette. "The sensation was quite real while it lasted."

"I can easily imagine that."

Kate looked up, suddenly afraid, and her eyes widened with horror. She could not tear her fascinated gaze from the glittering eyes of the malicious face opposite her. She knew with a violent shock that she was facing the murderer.

"I want that evidence you've been boasting about," the voice went on, and there was a deadly urgency in the words. "It's there in your purse, and I must have it."

"No." Kate's word was a mere whisper. "I hid it. I don't have it."

"I'm not a fool. I searched your room while everybody was downstairs, and it wasn't there. I've kept my eyes on you every second since you told me and I know you haven't had a chance to hide it."

"I gave it to the sheriff."

"I told you I'd been watching you. You didn't imagine that in the hall." The murderer laughed, and Kate felt as though she had suddenly plunged into icy water.

"The way you clung to that purse all afternoon made it quite evident what was in it. I might have known you wouldn't leave anything in the house. Now give it to me. Give it to me!" The hand held a small but deadly revolver.

"I haven't got it. I haven't got it," dimly she heard her own voice repeating monotonously.

"Oh yes, you do have it." The murderer laughed again. "Just repeating that won't save you. I've killed before to keep some-one from talking. One more means nothing to me. It's your own fault. I knew as soon as you told me you had the notebook I'd have to kill you too." The last words rose hysterically.

Kate had backed away from the pointed gun. Where was Mr. Bill and his promised protection? Why was the house so strangely silent? That small gun the hand held was so well oiled, so smooth and cold, and so very deadly.

"Oh, why did you do it?" Her voice broke so that her words were almost a sob.

"I watched and waited for my chance. Why should I be sorry to kill two people I've always hated?"

"Uncle Brock never harmed anybody in his life."

"You don't know everything, no matter how much you think you do. And I'm safe. Perfectly safe. When you're dead nobody will know."

"Sheriff Bill knows."

"If he knew I wouldn't be here talking to you."

Kate stood frozen. Only her mind worked feverishly, but all efforts to, delay long enough for help to come seemed futile. She knew that she was actually facing certain death.

"You're right," she said. "I haven't had time to give it to Mr. Bill. It's here in my bag and you can get it."

The eyes watching her narrowed with cunning. "There must be only your fingerprints on it. Get it and give it to me." The gun motioned toward the mantel.

Kate stepped backward and felt along the mantel until her fingers touched the purse. Still the gun did not waver. Watching her opponent, she fumbled with the clasp and drew out the notebook. Holding it tightly, she moved in a wide semicircle, trying to get to the door, but the gun followed her every move.

She knew there was no escape.

Suddenly she threw the book squarely at the hand that held the gun. She heard the instantaneous explosion as two shots rang out in rapid succession, and there were people in the room crowding through the door.

She never knew what really happened; she only had small pictures of scenes: Alicia sobbing brokenly, her hands over her face; Lucy standing in the doorway white and shaken, and Jeff and the sheriff holding Leigh, who was screaming in a maddened rage. Kate felt Alex's arms around her protectingly, and she buried her face in his coat and sobbed.

"Get a doctor. Can't you see she's hurt?" Alex was calling frantically.

He picked her up and carried her to the sofa, and Kate saw that there was blood on her left sleeve. He put her down carefully, gently.

"Oh, darling, I tried to stop him," he whispered. "If that damn sheriff—"

"I—I don't think it's much." Kate smiled crookedly. Since he had called her attention to it her arm was throbbing painfully.

The sheriff came over to her then, and his body kept her from seeing them take Leigh away, but the struggle and scuffle were sounds that not even the hysterical weeping of Alicia could drown. The sheriff slit the sleeve of her dress.

"It was ruined already," he apologized, holding a ragged edge. "It's not so bad, Kate. The shot just grazed your arm and cut the skin. I've sent for a doctor, but until he comes Miss Lucy can fix that, can't you?" He turned to Lucy, who came to life when she was given something to do.

"I certainly can. I've been fixing gunshot wounds for darkies and white folks as long as I can remember."

Sheriff Davies turned to Alicia, and there was real sorrow in the lines of his face. He waited without speaking as she made a gallant effort to control her sobbing.

"I'm—" he began.

"Please don't say it." Alicia stopped him. "I don't think I could stand your pity. I—I guessed it—was as it was."

"Yes, I thought you knew," the sheriff replied kindly.

"I'll look after Alicia, Sheriff." Jeff came forward.

Alicia looked up without really seeing him.

"Will you take me home? Oh, I forgot. . . ." Tears rolled unchecked down her cheeks, streaking the powder and blurring her eyes. "I forgot—I haven't a home now."

"I'll take you to your father," Jeff said.

"Yes, Father. . . ." Alicia rose, and Jeff put an arm around her waist to help her. At the door she turned back to the sheriff and said, "Please be—"

The front door was thrown open, and two excited men motioned to the sheriff, who went out to them immediately, closing the parlor door behind him. Alicia stood rigid against Jeff, and Lucy paused with a stained piece of absorbent cotton in her hand. Kate clutched Alex's hand and clung to him. They did not have long to wait, for almost immediately the door opened again and the sheriff returned.

"I'm sorry, Mrs. Randall," he said. "Your husband is dead."

Alicia uttered a hoarse cry and fainted.

In the confusion that followed Kate was only aware of Alex as he stood beside her, never leaving her for a moment. Lights sprang up all over the great house, and the voices of men on the lawn were loud and shrill. Jeff and the sheriff worked with Alicia, and Lucy quickly bandaged Kate's arm and convinced

Alex that it was only a clean surface cut, then directed him to get Kate up to her room.

"It's not my leg, darling," she protested when he would have picked her up. "It's only my arm. And I doubt if you could manage me up all these steps."

In the hall the sheriff came out to them.

"The doctor ought to be here any minute. Take her upstairs and get one of the darkies to put her to bed," he said to Alex. "She's more tired and frightened than hurt."

"You won't leave until you've told us what happened?" Kate halted with one foot on the bottom step.

"I'll come talk to you the first opportunity I get," he promised.

It was, however, some time before he came back to talk to them. The doctor had come and dressed Kate's arm, pronouncing it only a scratch. Alicia was more of a problem, and the doctor gave her a strong sedative and left Ella to put her to bed in the small upstairs room next to Lucy's. Given something definite to do, Lucy had rallied and bustled busily through the house, efficiently directing and supervising.

Kate was content to have the time alone with Alex. She refused to be put to bed, and they went downstairs when the doctor had gone. Kate averted her face as they passed the closed door of the parlor where they usually sat, and Alex took her into the opposite room, where he lit the fire and brought some warmth to the cool green-draped room.

"He might have killed you, Kate," Alex said for the hundredth time, holding tight to her hand. "And that fool sheriff held me outside the door."

Kate put her head against his shoulder, and he bent to kiss the cloud of black hair. She closed her eyes as though to shut out the horror of death that had kept step with her all afternoon.

"You were such a fool to go around telling people that you knew something," Alex continued. "I tried to keep as near you as I could, but you ran from one place to another and I didn't hear you leave your room when we came back, so I thought you were safe in there, until I knocked at your door and found it empty."

"Were you watching me, Alex?"

"God, how I tried!"

"I thought somebody was watching me when I came downstairs. It was the sheriff's plan. I didn't really have anything, only an old notebook with the amounts of seeds Uncle Brock had bought for the plantation."

Alex swore long and loud, condemning the sheriff and his methods, until Kate put a hand over his mouth.

"It worked, darling," she said, "and everything is all right. Mr. Bill was watching me too. He couldn't foresee that he would have a gun and that I'd throw my purse at it. We talked it all over while I was down at the river."

"I saw you come back, but you went straight to the office. And I knew Jeff was out there."

"Alex, you were jealous!" Kate turned her face to him and laughed happily. "But I had told you I loved you."

Alex kissed her.

"Well!" Lucy stood in the, doorway, her mouth a thin line of prim indignation. Behind her Jeff and the sheriff were grinning.

Alex sprang to his feet, the blood mounting to his cheeks in an embarrassed blush. Kate caught his hand and held it. Her eyes were bright; and happiness warmed her skin like the glow of a light through a translucent shade.

"Our intentions are entirely honorable," she said, and Lucy's mouth relaxed.

"I've been expecting this for a long time," Lucy said and kissed them both.

There was a flurry of excited congratulations, and Alex was surprised by the warmth of Jeff's handshake and the sincerity of his words. Lucy cried a little but reiterated how happy they had made her, until the sheriff significantly looked at his watch.

"Sit down, everybody," Kate ordered, "So Mr. Bill can tell us what happened."

There was instant stillness as they were brought back to the tragedy that had shrouded them for the past few weeks.

The sheriff fumbled for his pipe but put it back into his pocket unlit before he began his story.

"I guess you've all put some of the pieces of this puzzle together by now," he began. "Those pieces you so conveniently forgot to tell me, until it was almost too late. Mr. Brock's death had been planned, and I expect the gun was taken before that afternoon, though there's no way now of telling. You told me that Mr. Brock was grumpy from the time Kitty came, and you thought that was the cause. But actually the day Kate went to meet her was the same time Mr. Brock got his papers from the bank. He must have had some suspicion of what was happening and that afternoon he learned the truth."

"But I gave you the papers, and you didn't find anything," Kate said.

The sheriff stretched his long legs before him, and a little mud that had dried on his boots fell on the carpet. Lucy made an involuntary movement, but nobody noticed her.

"Some of the papers were missing. Mr. Brock didn't have a list," the sheriff answered Kate. "I had no way of knowing anything was gone. Leigh handled the investments and had used some for his own purpose. People always think they can put back what they've stolen before they're discovered, so that's what he must have figured. He'd made some wildcat investments and lost everything he had and he didn't dare go to his wife for money. I don't know, of course, but Mr. Brock must have threatened to expose him."

"Yes," Kite said suddenly: "They were quarreling the afternoon Leigh and Alicia came out to see Kitty."

"You didn't tell me that."

"I didn't think anything about it. Uncle Brock was quarreling with everybody. I had been out to the stables"—her eyes turned to Jeff and his dropped—"and when I came in I met Kitty in the dining room. We heard them quarreling there in Uncle Brock's room. . . . Oh, maybe Kitty had been listening. . . ."

"I expect she had. Mr. Brock must have telephoned Leigh to come out here that afternoon when he found that most of you would be gone. Maybe they arranged to meet somewhere, since nobody seems to have seen him come to the house. That gave him his chance. He made up his mind that afternoon before he came out here. I still think it was intended to look like suicide, and it would have if you hadn't interrupted him." The sheriff turned to Jeff.

"I interrupted him?"

"Yes. Suppose you tell us the whole truth about your part that afternoon."

"I—well, Uncle Brock and I had had a quarrel the night before, and I came over to apologize. I knew it wouldn't do any good; he hadn't much use for me. But I had just enough corn liquor in me to give me the nerve and I came over to talk to him. I heard the shot and started running toward the sound. I thought somebody was hunting, just like I told you. There wasn't anybody there when I got to—I got there. I just stood and stared and then I got sick." Jeff hung his head. "I was pretty sick out there in the woods. When I heard Kate coming I knew I mustn't be found there and I ran away."

"You didn't touch anything?" the sheriff asked.

"No. He—he was so still I knew he was dead." Jeff shivered in recollection.

"Then Kate came along." The sheriff took up the story again. "She found Mr. Brock and she found your tobacco pouch under his body when she touched him." He looked straight at Alex and added dryly, "That's why she burned it when she got back to the house."

"But why my pouch?" Alex asked.

"Miss Lucy explained that to me." The sheriff smiled at Lucy. "None of you remembered much about it, but Miss Lucy actually saw Leigh pick it up. She didn't know he had taken it. You put it down on the piano when Kitty was playing, and I suppose he took it, thinking it might be useful at some time."

Kate smiled at Alex, and he gripped her hand more firmly.

"Kitty was really smarter than the rest of us. She realized almost immediately what the motive was. The rest of you didn't seem to know or even suspect that Mr. Brock had more money than Leigh had accounted for. That is, all except Mrs. Randall. I think she knew and that she began to suspect her husband then. She watched him closer than even he suspected and she knew he had lost all his money. She was waiting for him to come to her for help."

"Alicia has known that long?" asked Lucy.

"Yes, she knew her husband's weakness and she was a very jealous woman. She loved him and meant to hold him. In her own way she's just as ruthless as he was. I don't know when Kitty found out, but it must have been pretty soon after she came that she realized the truth."

"She searched Brock's room," Lucy said. "I watched her and saw her go in there."

"But she was watching you!" Kate cried in surprise.

"She watched me?"

"Yes, it was Saturday night. I saw you come up the steps, and Kitty was at the top. She went back down the hall before you got upstairs. I thought—" Kate dropped her eyes, and Lucy fumbled with her handkerchief.

"I had been waiting for her to come back down there," Lucy explained. "I waited that night and the next, but she didn't come. I kept the room locked and saw to it that she didn't get a chance to go in there during the day. If what Kate says is true she knew I was watching her and of course didn't try."

Kate relaxed, glad that at last Lucy's nocturnal prowlings had been explained.

"That day Kitty went to town"—the sheriff picked up the thread of the story—"she went to all the places that Mr. Brock went and talked to the same people. I'd done that, too, but I couldn't see anything significant in talking to the president of the bank and old Judge Brewster. The judge began to suspect the truth, too, but he kept quiet for his daughter's sake."

"The judge did a lot more to help me than Leigh did," Jeff said, and the sheriff nodded.

"I expect his conscience was giving him some trouble. Then Kitty was killed, and that time there was no effort made to cover up a murder. I figure she was killed up there in her room. Leigh must have come back here to see her after the hunt got started."

"Then she was really trying to get rid of us that night," Lucy exclaimed.

"But when did she have time to plan to meet him that night? She didn't know about the hunt until she came back from town," Kate said.

"She was talking over the telephone when I came upstairs to change my clothes," Alex suggested.

"That's right." Kate nodded in agreement. "She went back downstairs as soon as I told her about the hunt."

"I reckon that's the way it happened," said the sheriff. "He must have tried to hide her to keep her from being found too soon. He knew the way you all felt about her and that you wouldn't make much effort to find her if you discovered she wasn't in her room that night. Alex came back while he was in the upper hall, and he had to get rid of her quickly. You told me yourself, Kate, that it was Leigh and Mr. Brock who had put the old elevator back into running order, so he knew all about it. In the darkness he must not have known that she had lost a shoe."

Kate shuddered, and Alex drew her closer to him.

"He chose his time nicely"—the sheriff took out his pipe and lit it—"when there'd be a reason for being out this way and with plenty of others around at the same time. She must have met him and taken him up to her room, since you were down here. Was she trying to get some money out of him?"

The sheriff addressed his question to Ralph, who nodded and spoke for the first time.

"Yes, she had some huge gambling debts." Ralph's face was haggard and almost as white as his hair. "That was what we quarreled about when she came down here—to Cliff's Edge. I refused to pay them, hoping to cure her. And she thought by going away she could force me into giving her the money."

"You could never have stopped her," Lucy said gently, and Ralph gave her a grateful smile. "She had to have excitement to live."

"I did a lot of checking up on that night," the sheriff said. "I talked to a lot of people who went on that hunt. You'll be glad to know"—his eyes twinkled at Alex—"that that young Dr. Denton swore to your alibi. He was keeping an eye on you because his wife wanted to know all about you, as the news has been going around the town that you were going to marry Kate. And several people remembered seeing you that time you all stopped for a drink, but nobody remembered seeing Leigh. That was one of the things that made me concentrate on him. Kate"—he turned to her abruptly—"what did you hide that afternoon when you went upstairs?"

Kate could feel the blood rush to her face. Only a few times in her life had she blushed, but never had she been so acutely embarrassed.

"She hid my brown suit," Alex answered for her.

"I thought as much"—the sheriff nodded, pleased that he had been right—"when Zack couldn't find it in your closet. Leigh had a brown suit we couldn't find either. Jeff here doesn't own one. Mrs. Gaines sent all his clothes to the jail, and they were still there on Monday night, and you didn't leave wearing a brown suit."

The sheriff had allowed his pipe to go out, and he put it back into his pocket before he continued. "You see, all this evidence was pretty circumstantial, and that was why I asked Kate to help me this afternoon. I had some deputies helping me watch her all the time, so I didn't think there was any danger. But I *had* warned her not to go into any room alone. We saw Leigh go to her room during the service down here. His wife caught him in there. She went up right behind him and waited until he came out and went back downstairs. I don't think he ever knew he'd been seen."

"She tried to get me to give her the notebook when I told her I had it," Kate said.

"What was in the notebook?" Jeff asked.

"Nothing at all. It was just a little book that Uncle Brock used to keep the amount of seeds and the prices he paid for them from year to year. I'll give it to you, and maybe it will help you order for next year."

"God alive, girl!" he exclaimed. "You ought to have had better sense than to go around telling people you had something important, regardless of what Mr. Bill said. I tried to call you back and tell you to put it back in the safe, but you ran from me like the house was on fire."

"I'm sorry, Jeff," Kate said meekly.

"If I'd had any idea of what you were up to I'd have taken it away from you by force if necessary. I thought you only told me because I saw you get it." Jeff took out a handkerchief and mopped his forehead.

"I kept an eye on Kate when she came back to the house," the sheriff defended himself. He reached into his pocket and took something out, weighing it lightly in his hand. "One of the deputies followed her down to the burial place and came back with her. I saw her go up to her room and heard her lock the door, but after a while she came out and went back downstairs. Leigh must have been watching, too, because he followed her. I was right outside the door all the time with a witness to hear what I expected to be his confession. Alex here nearly ruined it. It was all I could do to keep him from busting in and spoiling everything."

Sheriff Bill rose awkwardly, his heavy boots and untidy clothes making him appear out of place in the quiet elegance of that parlor. He held out his hand, and they saw a flattened bullet in the center of his palm.

"I got this out of the door. There'll always be a dent in it, but I don't think it's ruined. I guess that's about all," he concluded.

"But Leigh—" Kate began.

"We had handcuffs on him and thought he had calmed down some, but he broke away from my men when they got to the car." The sheriff hesitated and then added quietly, "He jumped over the cliff. He never hit the water. His head struck a stump or a rock, and he was dead before he got to the bottom. The doctor says he didn't suffer."

He crossed to the door but turned at the threshold and spoke to Alex. "I meant my congratulations a little while ago.

There ain't many people in these parts any better than the Leighs, and Miss Kate was always my pick of the lot. But of all the high-tempered, bullheadingest—"

Lucy rose quickly. Her head jerked back and her eyes flashed so that the sheriff left his sentence unfinished. They heard the front door close. Jeff looked significantly at Kate and literally herded Lucy and Ralph out of the room.

"Love me?" Alex caught her chin in his hand and pulled her face toward him.

"You know I do," Kate whispered.

"Temper and stubbornness and all?"

He read the answer in her eyes, for his arms went round her and he kissed her upturned face.

AFTERWORD TO
MURDER RENTS A ROOM

PERSONAL REFLECTIONS ON
A SOUTHERN MYSTERY NOVEL

DEAN JAMES

Having grown up on a farm in Grenada County, Mississippi, in the 1960s and early 1970s, I found Sara Elizabeth Mason's debut mystery, *Murder Rents a Room* (1943), fascinating in its depiction of the setting and the relations between the races. The attitudes and behaviors depicted in the novel brought back memories from my childhood and adolescence, both of which occurred during two decades of rapid change and civil turmoil. Though the book is set around 1940, when my father would have been fifteen, I found much that was familiar.

My father's farm had never been a plantation—it was not quite 400 acres—but the James family had been established in what are now Grenada and Webster Counties since 1831. My fourth great-grandfather, David James of Pitt, North Carolina, started moving westward with his wife and children, with stops in South Carolina, Georgia, and Tennessee before settling in Mississippi. The James family were farmers, evidently substantial ones, because by the time of the 1860 slave census, David and his son John Culpepper James, between them owned fifty-two slaves. Over the generations, with prolific births over the years, land got dispersed or fortunes declined after the Civil War so that the Jameses became small farmers rather than plantation owners.

My father and his siblings grew up on the small farm that my father eventually took over from his father. The landscape was picturesque, set among gently rolling hills and fertile fields. The nearby Baptist church stood on land originally given to the community by my third great-grandfather, John Culpepper. The original wood church burned down in the 1950s, to be replaced by the brick structure that still stands today as Pleasant Grove Baptist Church. There were numerous farms in the area, some of them owned by families either closely or distantly related to the James clan.

Black and white families lived in fairly close proximity when I was growing up but on their own land and in their own houses, unlike the workers in *Murder Rents a Room*. By the 1960s they were not uniformly agricultural workers, however, though all the men who worked alongside my father on the farm were black. So were the women, children, and adolescents who helped pick cotton when it was ready to harvest. I remember going with my mother to the fields to pick cotton. I even had my own small custom-made cotton sack, but at the time the cotton stalks were probably taller than I was. Not long after, I believe, my father was able to buy a cotton picker. Workers still went behind the picker, however, to pick every last scrap of cotton from the bolls.

In some ways I was no doubt oblivious to the more unpleasant aspects of relations between black and white in the 1960s, the decade of my childhood. I can't remember ever hearing the word *darkie* coming from my parents' or my grandparents' lips, but the word *Negro* and its far less polite synonym I heard frequently. I remember the prevailing assumptions about the differences between the races. Blacks were fundamentally lazy and had to be prodded into doing a day's work, whereas whites (most of them, anyway), were more industrious and hard-working.

I remember the paternalism, too. Black people were often considered childlike and needed guidance. The men who worked on our farm came to my father with their problems, and he did what he could to help them. Both my parents worked long hours, my father on the farm, my mother in Grenada at the hosiery mill and later as a waitress, so when one of my mother's younger sisters wasn't available to look after me, one of the black women in the community did. She also helped with housework.

My family didn't have the cadre of house staff and farm workers that the Leighs of Cliff's Edge employed, but in general they had the same attitude toward their black workers that Kate, Cu'un Lucy, Uncle Brock, Kitty, and the others demonstrate in *Murder Rents a Room*. These attitudes, and the subsequent treatment of black persons, will appall readers today. They certainly do appall me, even though I am familiar with them. They haven't gone away either, sadly.

Popular fiction, particularly mystery fiction with its emphasis on restoration of order after disruption by violent death, often provides a window into the time period in which books were published. Sara Elizabeth Mason provides a window into rural and small-town Alabama circa 1940 in *Murder Rents a Room* with considerable skill. I found the characters and the setting convincing. Everything rang true to me. In a sense, all was familiar, though some of it made me squirm, as it will others. If readers are interested in the daily life, the mores, and the attitudes, of eras gone by, however, they can find excellent guides in the work of talented writers like Sara Elizabeth Mason.

PREFACE TO
THE CRIMSON FEATHER

THE CRIMSON FEATHER (1945)

CURTIS EVANS

A soft fine mist beat against the thick windows of the train. Outside, a blurred and indistinguishable landscape sped by, with here and there a bleak, bare tree standing out in silhouette against the grayness of the afternoon. . . . [A]s the train rumbled southward an occasional light shone murkily though the gloom from the houses and shacks by the road . . . it was too dark . . . for her to see the familiar landmarks that pointed out the approach to her old home. She grimaced, thinking of the sunshine and dryness that Dr. Timmons had ordered when he sent her South. It was strange what peculiar ideas people had about the "sunny South." She might just as well have stayed there in the little apartment [in Chicago] not far from Lake Shore Drive.
  —*The Crimson Feather* (1945)

The train had left the echoing passes in the high hills during the morning and now for some time had been rolling through the vine-hung woods standing in yellow water. Suddenly it came out on a plain of red clay land sparsely overgrown with sedge grass. "Tuscaloosa, folks, Tuscaloosa," shouted the conductor.

—*Stars Fell on Alabama* (1934), Carl Carmer

Like Carl Carmer's celebrated book *Stars Fell on Alabama*, published to great acclaim and sales just over a decade earlier, Sara Elizabeth Mason's third detective novel, *The Crimson Feather* (1945), opens with the tale's protagonist, Ann Bartley, traveling from her home in the northern United States to the small city of Tuscaloosa, Alabama (population 27,493 in 1940), home of the state university. After an absence of five years, during which time she attended the Art Institute in Chicago and attained some measure of success as an illustrator of children's books, Ann, the daughter of a deceased chemistry professor at UA, has returned to Tuscaloosa in order to recuperate from a bout with pneumonia and give succor, if she can, to her married adopted sister, Jean Tolliver, who recently sent her a distressed and something less than coherent letter, reading in part: "I've begged and begged, oh so many times, for you to come back home. I need you, I desperately need you now. I'm so afraid. . . ."

Before Ann left Tuscaloosa, on account of a failed love affair with Hugh Scott, her sister Jean had married Bill Tolliver, whose sister, Lou, Hugh eloped with a week before Jean's wedding, though he was engaged to Ann. (Talk about the late unpleasantness!) Not helpful in this trying situation was Bill's and Lou's imperious and status-conscious mother, Helen, wife of lumber mill owner William Tolliver, who made it clear to all and sundry that by her lights the orphaned Bartley girls were decidedly beneath the Tollivers socially. Absurdly attuned to picayune matters of social standing, Helen many years ago as a new bride "had attempted to have her husband return to the old English spelling of their name and had gone so far as to have her calling cards engraved 'Mrs. William Tolliaferro.' But her husband had been adamant, saying that people would never learn to pronounce or spell it and that his grandfather had simplified it for that very reason. She had accepted with ill

grace but afterward explained the change at every opportuni-
ty." Once back in Tuscaloosa, Ann quickly discerns that Helen
Tolliver remains hostile to Jean and is desirous of keeping
Jean's and Bill's young son, Chip, out of Jean's hands.

Three other individuals complete the social circle which
forms around Ann upon her return to Tuscaloosa: Helen Tolliver's sister, thin and self-effacing Amelia Langdon, who slips
silently in and out of rooms "like a wraith"; Dr. Hans Steigler,
a German immigrant and professor in the UA chemistry department, who, standing in the place of Ann's and Jean's late
father, his good friend, gave Jean away when she wed Bill Tolliver; and Major Paul Forrest, a handsome young doctor with
whom Steigler is working on a new anti-malaria drug to aid
Americans battling the forces of Imperial Japan in the islands
of the South Pacific. Paul contracted the disease himself when
he was in the Army at Guadalcanal and New Caledonia, and he
had to be sent home from the front. As for "Dr. Hans," as Ann
and Jean call him, he escaped another sort of contagion, this an
ideological one, when he fled Hitler's Germany, where earlier
in the Thirties the Bartleys, father and daughters, had used to
visit him and his own son and daughter, now regrettably Nazi
myrmidons.[1]

When William Tolliver is found dead under odd circumstances during a day's hunting in neighboring Greene County,
it is the county sheriff, wily old Bill Davies, veteran sleuth of
Sara Mason's previous detective novel, *Murder Rents a Room*,
who declares that something is exceedingly rotten in Dixie. Yet
Sheriff Davies has no legal authority in Tuscaloosa and he is
forced to conduct his criminal investigation on the sidelines,
as it were, while the malevolent Mrs. Tolliver, now widowed,
points an awful accusing finger at Jean, whose very sanity she,
along with others around her, professes to hold in doubt.[2] A
second death soon takes place, however, and this time there
can be no doubt that the crime is murder! Can Sheriff Davies
stop a crafty killer before he—or she—slays yet again?

For Alabama readers *The Crimson Feather* has especial interest for its wartime Tuscaloosa setting. When Sara Mason

writes of "the long L-shaped business district [of the city],
brilliant with neon signs, the broad street with cars parked on
both sides, and then the wide avenue that led from the heart
of town past the brick buildings of the university with their
classic facades, now blurred like art photographs in the rain,"
she clearly is writing of downtown Tuscaloosa and the University of Alabama in the 1940s. In correspondence many years
later Sara Mason conceded that the novel was set in Tuscaloosa, primarily in a "residential area there called 'The Highlands.'" Today one of the most desirable of older residential
neighborhoods in Tuscaloosa, "The Highlands" in the 1940s
was, as Sara Mason skeptically puts it in the novel, "an exclusive residential section, a little raw, perhaps, with the smug air
of the newly rich." Sara Mason takes care to note that the fictional home of William and Helen Tolliver, though "beautiful"
and "built in the old Southern tradition" with white paint that
glistens in the sun and a two-story portico supported by six
fluted columns, is not in fact an antebellum mansion, as visitors frequently assume (pleasing Mrs. Tolliver considerably),
but rather a cunning exercise in 20th century architectural
artifice. So too is *The Crimson Feather* a cunning exercise—in
the fine art of murder.

NOTES

[1] There are also several black house servant characters
in the novel, though they play a much more recessive
role here than in Sara Mason's first mystery, *Murder
Rents a Room*. We may regret Ann's observation that the
servants can be ruled below suspicion of murder on the
grounds that they lack the "necessary intelligence" to
carry it off successfully, yet Ann also interestingly comments that Helen Tolliver's sister, Amelia Langdon, "did
a great deal of the work in the house"—that is, "whatever the Negroes left undone, a fact of which they were
completely aware."

[2] The Tuscaloosa hunting party was shooting on the grounds of the Allen plantation, which presumably is owned by relatives of the Leighs, who themselves confronted foul play at their plantation house in *Murder Rents a Room*; happily Sheriff Davies solved the crime and caught the killer.

THE CRIMSON FEATHER

For S. B. M.

1

RETURN OF THE PRODIGAL

A soft fine mist beat against the thick windows of the train. Outside, a blurred and indistinguishable landscape sped by, with here and there a bleak, bare tree standing out in silhouette against the grayness of the afternoon. The day was dark, and as the train rumbled southward an occasional light shone murkily through the gloom from the houses and shacks by the road.

Ann had stared through the window for hours, resisting the conversational attempts of the middle-aged woman who had shared her compartment since they left Chattanooga. The Pullman was crowded, as all railway cars were in December, 1944, but Ann might have been alone, for she heard only the rhythmic click-clack of the wheels on the rails.

Her eyes caught the name of the station as it flashed by and she knew she had almost reached the end of her journey. She picked up the small alligator case and the paper bag that contained her hat. The woman across from her looked up from the baby sack she was crocheting and asked, "Almost there?"

Ann nodded and, rising, lurched down the narrow aisle to the dressing-room at the end of the car. It was empty and she put the case on the shelf and hung the coat of her suit carefully over the back of a chair.

Fifteen miles and maybe ten minutes before I get there, she thought, *and just five years ago I left the same station, solemnly vowing I'd never set foot in it again.*

She took a towel from the rack, pulled one of the small chairs forward, and sat down. Opening the case, she took out a brush and, after draping the towel over her shoulders, brushed her hair with vigorous strokes that made her scalp tingle. The soft light overhead left no shadows on the face reflected in the big mirror. It was not a conventionally pretty face; the skin was too white, the greenish shadows under the eyes too deep, but there was fine bone structure under the almost transparent skin. There were people who had called Ann Bartley beautiful. Under the hard strokes of the brush, coppery hair shone with the luster of fine silk. She laid aside the brush and with a comb arranged the curls and waves.

It had taken Ann years to realize the advantages of the brightness of her hair and the strange yellowish eyes with dark flecks in the irises. She had spent a tortured childhood filled with taunts of "cat eyes" and "redheaded peckerwood," years in which she had vainly sought to subdue the bright color with dull, drab clothes. But five years in a city had taught her much, had given her a smartness of style that was distinctive and individualistic.

She applied powder lightly, dusting off the excess with a piece of cotton, and added a touch of rouge along the edge of her cheekbones, stroking it toward the corners of her eyes. She opened her purse and took out a lipstick which she ran over full lips, blotting them with the edge of the towel. Dropping the lipstick back in her purse, she took out a small vial of amber liquid and with it smoothed down her eyebrows and touched the lobes of her ears.

She pushed back the chair at last and slipped on her coat, buttoned it, and straightened the collar. The mirror showed a tall, slender girl in a severely tailored green suit. A small gold ornament on the lapel reflected the glint of her hair and the color of her eyes. She was the sort of girl who would always draw a second glance from any man who passed. A little thin, perhaps, but that was to be expected after two weeks in a hospital and only twelve days' convalescence from pneumonia.

As an artist, Ann appreciated the color scheme of her costume and she nodded her satisfaction as she pulled on the darker green hat and adjusted it at the proper angle. It gave her courage to face the ordeal of coming back to the place she used to call—home.

"You ought to get away for a while," Dr. Timmons had told her that last time he had come to the apartment she shared with Beth Arnold. "Chicago's a fine place, but all this dampness and smoke won't do you any good. You need sunshine and plenty of fresh air. Isn't there somewhere you could go for a month or two?"

"Of course there is," Beth had seconded him. "I've been telling her the same thing, and it's not as though she were tied down with a regular job like I am. She's got a sister in Alabama who's been hounding her to come back there."

"I can't go back," Ann had protested weakly.

"You can't afford not to," the doctor declared. He glanced around the well-furnished room. "You don't know what a lucky girl you are. Take your pencils and paints with you, if you like. But don't touch them for the first month. After that you can do as you like if you take it easy. Don't come back to Chicago before next spring. You'll have a relapse if you stay here and I won't take that responsibility," he added threateningly.

"I'll pack her things and put her on the train," Beth said with a determined tilt of her pointed chin. "She'll go."

Even then they might not have persuaded her if she hadn't been so dreadfully tired and weak. And if she hadn't got Jean's letter. It was really the letter that decided her. It was there now in her purse and she took it out and read it again.

Ann darling . . . I've begged and begged, oh, so many times, for you to come back home. I need you, I need you desperately now. I'm so afraid. . . .

The words were very black and in Jean's characteristic writing that was half printing. Jean needed her. Jean was afraid. Though nearly two years younger, Ann had always been the stronger, the leader of the two. Wondering a little at the urgent tone of the letter, Ann tore it into shreds and, dropping it into the metal hair receiver on the shelf, struck a match and burned it. It wouldn't do to keep such a letter. She would see Jean in just a few more minutes and find out what was wrong. She snapped the lock of the alligator case and picked up her purse.

Several pairs of eyes followed her progress back to her seat. The porter had already taken her bags and there was only the fur coat and her gloves left on the plush seat. Mist clouded the thick plate glass of the windows but it was too dark anyway for her to see the familiar landmarks that pointed out the approach to her old home. She grimaced, thinking of the sunshine and dryness that Dr. Timmons had ordered when he sent her South. It was strange what peculiar ideas people had about the "sunny South." She might just as well have stayed there in the little apartment not far from Lake Shore Drive. Maybe she could see Jean, talk to her, and then go straight back to Chicago —or to Florida, or anywhere else but here.

"Someone's meeting you?" the middle-aged woman was inquiring.

"Yes, my sister," Ann replied as she picked up her gloves and draped the coat over her shoulders.

"How nice."

I haven't been polite to her, Ann thought as she walked down the aisle to the door. Several other people were getting off here too, and she waited, not really wanting to leave the safety and impersonality of the train. At last it was her turn and the conductor held out a hand to help her down the steps. She stood there, peering into the rain, searching for a familiar face.

There was a crowd at the station and she could see the gleam of rain on the umbrellas clustered like a bouquet of sequins at the edge of the shelter. The dampness of the air rushed toward her, cold and fresh against her face. She could hear the soft slur of Negro voices, a sound she had almost forgotten. It was like being in a dream world where people floated about in a confused mist.

"Here she is," a voice said almost in her ear.

She turned quickly and saw a man who was a perfect stranger to her. He was tall and dark, with a square face, broad shoulders, and an erect carriage. He smiled down at her, his lips parted to show strong even teeth.

"It *is* Miss Bartley, isn't it?" he asked as he put a hand under her elbow.

"Yes."

"I knew it. Here she is, Bill."

Another young man loomed beside her and said, "Hello, Ann," as he leaned forward and kissed her cheek. "Take her to the car, Paul, and I'll see about her luggage."

"You might introduce me first," Paul said. "I can see she doesn't remember me."

"Oh yes. This is Paul Forrest, Ann. You ought to remember him. He visited us once when we were kids." Bill picked up the case at his feet.

"It was a visit to remember," Paul said with a laugh. "You gave a party and a pretty redhead slapped my face for telling her she had very beautiful hair."

"I didn't understand Spanish then," Ann murmured.

"So you do remember! Only it wasn't Spanish. It was Portuguese. We lived in Brazil. It was the first time I ever had a compliment answered with a slap," he added ruefully.

"There's always a first time," Ann said.

"Your temper still matches your hair."

"Where are your checks, Ann?" Bill broke in before Ann could give a ready retort. "How many bags did you bring?"

"A small locker and a rather large bag, I'm afraid," Ann said apologetically. She opened her bag and gave him the check stubs.

"I'll get them." Bill disappeared almost instantly.

"The car's this way." Paul put a hand on her arm and guided her.

Ann had a feeling of disappointment. She had not realized how she had counted on Jean being there at the depot. And it did seem a little odd that her only sister had not come after writing her so often, begging her to come back to this place.

She began to wonder if she had made a mistake. Bill hadn't sounded especially cordial and his welcoming kiss had been almost perfunctory. Southerners always greeted people effusively, particularly those they had not seen for a long time.

Paul must have sensed her disappointment, for he said, "Jean's at home, and we're going straight there."

We're going, he had said. So he was to be included, Ann thought wearily, a little puzzled at his position. He opened the door of the car, helped her inside, and then took the seat beside her. "We'll let Bill sit up front with the bags," he said.

Ann turned to look at him then. He was pleasant-looking, though not handsome, and his black hair was a little grizzled at the temples. There were deep lines about his mouth and at the corners of his eyes, as though they had been exposed to the blinding glare of the sun for a long time. She knew in all reason he must be in his early thirties, but he looked older.

The lights of a passing car swept over them and she saw her companion clearly in the brief glare. His uniform fitted him to a nicety and there were the golden oak leaves of a major on his shoulder and the caduceus on the lapels of his dark olive blouse. The light was too brief for Ann to recognize the service ribbons over his left breast. Another doctor, she thought without interest. She had seen more than enough of that profession in the past month.

Paul Forrest and his brother had created quite a stir in their high school circle that September they had visited their cousins, the Tollivers. Ann began to recall the time quite clearly. The brothers had been sent back to the States for college and had spent two weeks here in Alabama before their school opened. She remembered Jean's fluttery excitement, though even then Bill had been labeled as her special property. At a gangly and awkward fourteen Ann had not been greatly impressed.

Bill came back to the car followed by an old Negro man and together they put the bags in the luggage compartment of the Buick.

"It's nice having you here with us, Ann," Bill said as he slid under the steering-wheel and started the motor.

"It's nice being here," Ann replied politely, knowing that they were only making conversation. She was already running over reasons in her mind which she would presently produce to excuse herself so that she could be on her way somewhere else, anywhere else but here.

"Jean had to stay with Chip," Bill explained. "We have a nurse, thank goodness, but she goes home at five. Say, you ought to see that boy!" He chattered on, answering her occasional questions.

It was warm and comfortable in the darkness of the back seat and Ann was lulled by the drone of the motor and the steady swish of the windshield wiper. It was so familiar, as though she had been away only a day, not five years. There was the long L-shaped business district, brilliant with neon signs, the broad street with cars parked on both sides, and then the wide avenue that led straight from the heart of the town past the brick buildings of the university with their classic facades, now blurred like art photographs by the rain.

At last they turned through two brick posts into a side road and presently Bill stopped the car beside a spreading white brick house which Ann recognized from Jean's descriptions. This was 22 Briarcliff Circle, the address to which she had written for the past few years. The road formed an inverted U with the center a narrow park. Now, at the beginning of winter, there were only the evergreen shrubs, but spring would bring new leaves to the trees and bright flowers would make an attractive view from the front windows of the houses on either side. And always the trees and shrubs would insure some privacy for all.

"Run on in, Ann," Bill said. "We'll take your bags in the back."

She got out and walked up the shallow brick steps alone. The door was thrust open immediately.

"Ann!" Jean's arms were around her, pulling her toward the light, welcoming her home.

Warmth and tenderness crept over Ann and some of the tenseness went out of her body. She hadn't known how glad she would be to see her sister.

"Oh, Ann darling, it's so good to see you again." Jean was smiling at her through tears and Ann's eyes were wet too. "Come inside where I can see you so I'll know you're really here."

Ann laughed to cover her nervousness, dropped her coat on a chair by the door, and put an arm about her sister's waist. "I'm here," she said shakily as she followed Jean into the living-room.

"Oh, Ann!"

"This must be Chip," Ann said, seeing a three-year-old boy seated in the middle of the floor watching her with wide-open blue eyes. "He's very much like you, Jean."

"And like Bill too," Jean said quickly. "Come here, Chip. This is your aunt Ann."

Chip rose on short, stubby legs. "Tan?" he asked.

Ann chuckled. "You're right. That's a very good name for me." She stooped and blew softly on his plump neck and he giggled.

"Do it again," he demanded.

Ann obliged and there was instant liking between them. Ann loved children and some sixth sense always told them this, which was very fortunate as she made her living sketching them, illustrating children's books.

"He's been waiting for you," Jean explained. "I promised him he could stay up if he'd be good and eat his supper and let me put him to bed afterward. Come along now, darling. Martha has your supper waiting."

"Want Tan with me," Chip said, clinging to Ann's hand.

"No," Jean said firmly. "Tan is tired and we'll have our supper and you can come back and tell her good night."

"I could go with you," Ann suggested, looking at her sister, but Jean avoided her eyes.

"No. You're company for one night at least. I'll feed him and get him to bed."

In her excitement, forgetting that she had not taken Ann to her room, Jean picked up the still protesting Chip and carried him away, leaving Ann alone. For a moment she stood there, a

puzzled frown creasing her forehead. Slowly she drew off her
gloves and hat and laid them beside her coat.

She was in a cheerful room, modern but not too modern.
The plaster walls were a pale soothing green which blend-
ed with the color scheme. At one end was a large fireplace in
which a log burned brightly on the polished andirons, but it
was mainly for decorative purposes, as there were low radiators under the wide front windows. Over a white mantel a
gilt-framed mirror reflected an attractive combination of the
old and new. The sofa Ann had never seen before, but the big
chair opposite it was the same old comfortable one her father
had used, though Jean had covered it with flowered chintz.
And the table beside it had belonged to their mother. A small
baby grand was also a relic. Ann remembered how excited they
all were when it had been bought, and yes, there was the scar
of the Coca-Cola bottle which she had thoughtlessly put on it;
afterward she had had to bribe Jean, into forgiveness with a
new pair of silk stockings.

"All alone?" Paul asked, opening the door from the hall.
"Where's Jean?"

"Giving Chip his supper," Ann replied. "I wonder if you can
show me my room?"

"Jean must have been excited! Come along this way. Bill
and I put your bags in there for you." He led her into the hallway and opened the first door on the left, snapping on the
lights as he did so.

"Thank you." Ann waited until he had gone, then crossed
the room and laid her hat and coat on the bed.

It was very definitely a guest room, pretty and dainty. The
striped wallpaper was matched by the flowered drapery and
bedspread, material Ann herself had selected at Marshall Field's
from the description and samples Jean had sent her. There were
ruffled organdy curtains at the windows and hooked rugs on
the floor which gleamed from a recent waxing. The bed looked
soft and inviting with its eiderdown comfort folded across the
foot and Ann could think of nothing better than to crawl into

it and sleep dreamlessly for the next twelve hours. She sighed audibly, crossed the room, and opened a door. It was a closet and padded hangers were waiting for her clothes. She closed it quickly, tried another, and found that it led to a shining pink bathroom. She shuddered at all this pink but she knew it was Jean's favorite color.

She fluffed her hair with her fingers and, getting the keys from her purse, opened a case and took out a plush rabbit she had brought Chip. Then she sat down at the dressing-table and added powder to her make-up, carefully covering the shadows under her eyes that told how tired she was.

Paul and Bill were in the living-room waiting for her.

"No use waiting for Jean," Bill said, handing her a cocktail. "She'll be along in a minute. Right now we need this to get the cold out of our marrow."

"I like your house," Ann said, taking the glass and sipping her drink.

"Jean really did it. For a year, every night when I got home, she had pictures and color cards and rough sketches ready for me to see."

"I wonder why Dr. Steigler hasn't come?" Paul said, glancing at his watch.

"Dr. Hans?" Ann asked, putting her glass on a table.

"This is a real celebration—in honor of the prodigal sister." Paul made a mock bow in her direction.

"I had no idea I was in the least prodigal."

The hall door opened and Chip pattered across the floor, followed by his mother. His blond hair was fluffed about his round face, giving him an angelic appearance which was far from natural. He clambered up into Ann's lap, threw his arms about her neck, and planted a moist kiss on her cheek.

"You've made quite a hit," Jean laughed.

"In that case I can give you this rabbit to keep you company tonight." Ann handed him the plush toy. "I saw him in a case and he was so miserable-looking. I told him I was coming to see you and presto, he turned green with envy. So I said he might as well come along too."

Chip crowed with delight. "Bunny, bunny, bunny," he said.

"Time for you to go to bed," Bill said, and leaned over to pick up his son, but Chip clung fiercely to Ann.

"Want Tan with me. She can put me to bed."

Ann laughed. "Get out of my lap and then I'll go with you. You're on the heavy side and I can't carry you."

Bill removed his son without further discussion, swinging Chip in a high arc before he put him on the floor. Seen together this way, Ann realized their close resemblance. Their faces were the same shape, though Chip's was still rounded childishly, and they had the same sturdy bodies. Bill's eyes were a warm brown and the child had inherited the long lashes that surrounded them. Chip made the rounds then, kissing everybody good night before he came back and caught Ann's hand and led her to, the hall.

Ann listened while he recited in a high treble, "Now I lay me down to sleep," and followed it with a long exhortation to bless "Mommy an' Daddy an' Tan an' Grandma an' Grandpa an' Aunt Lou an' Uncle Hugh an' everybody I love."

"Up you go." Jean lifted him into his bed and pulled the covers about him. "Put the window up a little, Ann," she directed. "I'll open it wide later. Here's your green bunny."

Ann did as she was told and then came back to the bed to give Chip another kiss before she left his room. "See you in the morning," she whispered.

2

A PUZZLING TENSION

As they re-entered the living-room a man got up from the big chair by the fireplace and came toward her.

"Ann Bartley at last," he said, catching her hands and holding her of so that he could see her.

"Dr. Hans!" Ann exclaimed with delight.

He was a short, fat man with a round, moonish face and wide-open blue eyes that blinked owlishly behind thick-lensed glasses. His thin white hair had been brushed across the bald spot on the top of his head and the dark gray suit he wore was wrinkled and baggy at the knees. He was always too busy peering into microscopes or watching the reaction of his chemicals to be concerned with his appearance. Now he pursed his lips and his short nose twitched with pleasure.

"*Feu d' Automne*," he said. "It is good to smell it again." He spoke precise English with only a trace of a guttural accent.

"Of course," Ann replied. "I'll never use anything else."

"What's this?" Paul asked. "Don't tell me you have a dark secret in your past. I'd never have suspected it of you, Doctor."

Ann put her arm through Dr. Hans's and drew him to the sofa. "Give me my drink and I can explain all," she said. "I'll have you know I'm the woman and it was no lurid past either." She laughed and it was a warm, intimate sound.

"Spill it," Paul said out of the corner of his mouth as he gave her the glass.

"The drink or the story?" she inquired, raising her eyebrows.

"The story, you idiot!"

"What a thing to call me," Ann grimaced. "My father had a sabbatical and we all went with him to Leipzig. It was a glorious summer. Of course there were lots of Nazis around but they weren't so obnoxious then. Dr. Hans had the most wonderful garden in Germany and he made Jean and me some perfume."

"In exchange for lessons in American slang," Dr. Hans added. "I give the girls the formula and I learn to speak the beautiful language. All of which has been most helpful to me here."

"I knew you'd need it," Ann said. "To a glorious summer." She lifted her glass toward him and sipped. "He could speak beautiful, precise English but nobody would ever have understood him. His vocabulary was made up of all the wrong words," Ann said to Paul. "It was too much trouble for us to learn German so Jean and I taught him Americanized English."

"And he gave you the perfume in return?"

"Yes. Jean and I went to school in Paris that year and we selected the names then. We've never used anything else."

"Finish your drinks," Bill ordered. "Martha has already glowered at us once from the dining-room and these days a good cook is worth her weight in gold."

At the table conversation was general. All of them tried to give Ann the news, bringing her up to date on her old friends. They told of the changes in the university; who was still there and who had gone. From all the bits of disjointed information she finally learned why Paul Forrest was there, why he was so intimate with Dr. Hans.

"The Army sent him to me after I had showed them what I was doing," Dr. Hans explained, placing his hands spread-eagle over his fat stomach. "I had not studied medicine in years and had not had the actual experience necessary to finish the experiments."

"What are you doing?" Ann asked.

"We're working on a new drug for malaria," Paul took up the explanation. "I had it myself and had to be sent back home. Since the Japs took most of the quinine supply the Army has been working on the problem day and night. We have atabrine and plasmochin, but the after effects are bad and they're not cures."

"And you have a cure?"

Dr. Hans shook his head. "It is too early to make such a claim. We need to be exact," he said. "We experiment, we learn something is wrong, we experiment again." He shrugged his stooped shoulders. "It is work that requires patience. But it is good to know that we are working to save lives, not destroy them. There is too much of that already." His voice was sad and there was a faraway look in his eyes.

"They have cages of rabbits and dogs. The place is overrun with them," Jean commented.

"You're still living in our old house?" Ann asked.

"Where else could I live? I have my laboratory near at hand and no neighbors to be bothered with all the noise, and now I have Dr. Forrest for company. He can keep up the work while I run across the campus and give my lectures."

The sentences ran together in Ann's ears. Although her father had been a chemist, the technicalities of his work had never bothered her. Vaguely she heard talk of coal-tar derivatives, or drugs that might belong to the sulfa family, of the different types of malaria.

"Was that what you were doing in the Army?" she asked Paul.

"You have no idea what a scourge malaria is out there in those Pacific Islands. I was on Guadalcanal for a while and then on New Caledonia and I saw plenty of it." His thin lips were pressed tight and his fist clenched and unclenched at the memory of the suffering. "We were fortunate that it was a benign type of the disease, but men were out of the front line. It was as bad as the Japs themselves. I tell you, malaria is as much a problem today as yellow fever was in 1898."

That would account for the deep lines on his face, the sallowness of his skin. Now Bill was talking excitedly of the war and conditions at home and abroad. Ann caught Jean watching him while she moved the food about on her plate, scarcely touching it. Perhaps that was what was worrying her sister.

Bill was going into the Army and Jean was afraid for him. Ann breathed a sigh of relief. Somehow she had got the idea of an intangible fear, but if this was all, she could talk Jean into accepting the inevitable within a few days. She glanced thoughtfully at her sister.

Jean had always made Ann think of the porcelain figurines they had seen in Europe: a shepherdess with golden hair, pink cheeks, and blue eyes. There was still that air of fragility and brittleness about her. She was much thinner than she used to be and very nervous. All her movements were jerky and fluttery. She was laughing too much and there was a shrillness about the sound that was unnatural. Five years ago she had been a happy, dainty, traditionally blushing bride, but now she seemed tired, almost shrinking from contacts with other people.

"Have you forgotten where you are so soon?" Paul was standing beside her chair.

Startled, Ann saw that the others were standing, waiting for her. She quickly pushed back her chair and rose.

"I'm sorry," she apologized. "I must be getting absentminded."

"That is a professor's prerogative." Dr. Hans wagged a pudgy finger at her. "I have eaten all that I could of the good Martha's dinner."

In the living-room Ann sat down as soon as possible. The furniture had a tendency to whirl when she stood and she wondered if the one cocktail she had drunk before dinner had gone to her head. Her mouth was hot and dry and she ran her tongue over her lips, moistening them. Bill went to the fire and added another log and Ann got up and moved to the other end of the room.

"It's stopped raining," Jean said. "I think Lou and Hugh will be able to come after all. Lou said they would. They want to welcome you home, Ann."

Ann took the blow standing. Her back was to the others and the only sign of her emotion that they could see was the twisting of the big sapphire ring on her right hand.

So they knew.

Hugh Scott was the reason Ann had left home. Five years ago she had been engaged to him and the wedding set for a time as soon as Jean's honeymoon was over. And then, without warning, Hugh had eloped with Bill's sister a week before Jean's wedding. Ann had wanted to run away then, but Jean and Dr. Hans wouldn't let her. They had made her stay and wear the blue satin bridesmaid's dress and carry the heavy flowers; made her stay and walk up the aisle of the church, past the smiling bride and groom. As soon as Jean had gone Ann had packed her bags, gone alone to the station, and vowed never to return.

She had done very well for herself in those five years. A year in the Art Institute to finish the training she had already begun, then a few commissions for illustrating until she had gained some reputation as an illustrator of children's stories.

There had been plenty of men in Chicago, too, and Ann had known her share. In particular there was Dick Martin, who had proposed regularly every Saturday night, sometimes over the phone, sometimes in a crowded restaurant, sometimes when they were alone and looking out over the waters of Lake Michigan. Now that he was in the Navy he sent cables from all over the world. And he always asked the same old question.

Somehow, just when she got herself keyed up to say yes, Hugh Scott's face would rise before her eyes like a desert mirage and she would see his tanned cheeks, his laughing brown eyes, and almost feel the thrill of his lips on hers.

"Do they live near you?" Ann asked, and was a little surprised that her voice was cool and steady. She turned and saw that Paul Forrest was watching her closely.

"On the other side of the Circle. Father Tolliver gave them the lot when he gave us ours."

Ann sat down on the piano bench. It was the nearest place and she knew she would never be able to walk across the room just then. "Come play something for me, Jean," she said. "Remember that Brahms piece that Pops used to love?"

"I'll go put up Chip's window and then be right back," Jean said.

"I'll do it." Bill was on his feet instantly.

Jean sat down beside Ann and ran her fingers over the keys before she dropped into the soft lullaby. Paul came over and stood beside them.

"Play some of our old favorites so we can sing," he suggested.

"Find the book then," Jean said.

He picked up a book, leafed through the pages, then propped it on the rack. He had a fair baritone voice and when Bill came back he joined them.

"Come on and sing," Paul urged Ann as he turned to *Drink to Me Only with Thine Eyes*.

She shook her head. "I can't carry a tune."

"You can whistle," Bill said.

"Some other time." She got up and joined Dr. Hans by the fire. He was seated in the old chair, his legs spread out in front, his hands folded in their characteristic pose over his stomach. He opened his sleepy eyes as she sat down opposite him.

"I come over very often to see that she keeps in practice— and of course, to get one of Martha's dinners too," he said, chuckling.

"I'm glad." Ann relaxed her tense body in a soft corner of the sofa.

"Talents aren't meant to be hidden. How is your work going?"

Ann shrugged and lit a cigarette. "All right, I suppose. I have as much as I can do."

"It is very good. I have the one you did of the dragons."

"What would you be doing with a fairy story?" Ann smiled.

"Fairy stories are meant for all ages."

"How is Franz?"

The doctor's face lighted with real pleasure. "He is a good boy." His words were more guttural when he spoke of his son and Ann thought for a moment that he would lapse into German. "He is on a mine sweeper, I think. He writes me letters and occasionally when he gets to a port he sends a cable or a telegram." Dr. Hans sighed. "That is what comes of papas making plans. I had wanted him here at the university with me, but no, off he had to go."

Ann flipped her cigarette into the fire. "He can do that later," she said. "What about Bill? Is he going now?"

"Yes," he replied sadly. "All the young men are going."

"When?"

"After Christmas, he told me the other day. He has had his examination and been accepted. After that, who knows?"

"And Jean? Is she worried?"

He dropped his eyes quickly. "Aren't we all worried?" he asked evasively. "I am glad you have come back to be with your sister."

Ann opened her mouth to tell him that she would be here only a few days, that she would be on her way somewhere else as soon as possible. But before she could say anything the door chimes sounded and Jean's fingers crashed discordantly on the piano. For an instant there was complete silence in the room.

"That must be Lou and Hugh," Jean said. "Move, Bill, so I can get up."

As Bill opened the door Ann stood up but she rested her hand on the back of the sofa. It was something solid to hold to in the farce that was about to be enacted.

"We didn't interrupt you?" Hugh Scott asked as he pulled off his overcoat and hat. "Weren't you playing, Jean?"

"We were only marking time until you came."

"So you've come back." Lou came toward Ann.

She was a plump woman with too many curves in the wrong places. Her eyes were a pale watery blue surrounded by short, colorless lashes that were now thickly coated with mascara. Her black dress was expensive but there were superfluous ruffles here and there on it. Lou's taste was one that never should be trusted. Beside the clean lines of Ann's suit and Jean's daintiness she looked frumpy, though her clothes had cost more and she had spent over an hour dressing for this appearance. An ugly red spread over her face, showing through the thick overlay of powder, as Ann's eyes swept coolly over her.

"Hello, Lou," Ann said indifferently.

She felt Paul's hand clamp down heavily on her shoulder but she shrugged it off. She and Lou had matched wits before and Ann had never come off second best. They had always hated each other, even before Lou had stolen Hugh.

"Hugh darling!" Ann turned to him and extended both her hands. She could feel her heart pounding madly and for a moment she forgot the others in the room. Her eyes sparkled like champagne and she laughed.

"More beautiful than ever, Ann." He held her at arm's length and looked at her.

"She's thin as a rail," Lou said acidly.

"Have you given up dieting completely?" Ann asked, turning directly to Lou.

"Let's have a drink," Bill broke in quickly. "We were just waiting for you to get here. Come help me, will you, Hugh?"

Hugh followed his brother-in-law—reluctantly, Ann thought, but her attention was sidetracked.

"Couldn't you be a little more subtle?" Paul whispered fiercely.

"Why bother?"

"Have you put Chip to bed?" Lou asked Jean. "Then I'll just run back and peep at him."

She had closed the door before Jean could go with her. Ann sat down again on the sofa. If there was going to be a battle of the sexes that night, she was going to do her fighting sitting down. After all, she had been out of bed only two weeks and she could feel weakness stealing up through her legs.

Paul dropped down beside her, drew out his case, and offered her a cigarette. As he lit it he said, "Don't let it come to physical violence."

"There's nothing to be amused about," she said curtly.

"No, but it's funny just the same to an innocent bystander like me. Only Lou has you outclassed when it comes to weight."

"I can take care of myself."

Paul might have said more had not the dining-room door opened and Bill come in laden with a tray of glasses. Hugh was behind him.

"Put it on the coffee table, Bill," Jean directed as she cleared the way by removing an ash tray.

"Where's Lou?" Bill asked as he passed the drinks.

"Here I am. He's sleeping like an angel, but really, Jean, you shouldn't have the window so wide open. The room was damp and cold."

Ann was watching her sister and saw the slight frown that crossed Jean's broad forehead. Jean started to say something but evidently changed her mind and turned to Hugh.

"Help me move this chair over to the others."

"Chip had a toy right in his mouth," Lou continued as she took the drink from Bill. "A silly green rabbit. I put it on the chair."

"Ann brought it to him," Jean said.

Lou turned to Ann. "You ought to have known he'd stick it in his mouth. Dye is poisonous, especially green."

"Round 2," Paul whispered with a chuckle.

"Would you like me to give you the chemical reaction of paints and dyes?" Ann asked coolly. "Or had you forgotten that I'm a professional on the subject?"

Blood rushed to Lou Scott's face again. It was not a becoming blush, but purplish red splotches that faded slowly. She sat down abruptly in the chair Bill had pushed up to her and drank hastily from the glass she had in her hand.

Ann laughed sarcastically and turned to Paul. "Do you live with Papa Hans?" she asked.

Dr. Steigler gave a deep rumbling chuckle. "Nobody has called me that in a long time. Here is the mud in your eyes." He held his glass toward her.

"That completely dates you," Ann said. "I'll have to teach you to speak all over again."

"Don't," begged Paul. "I'm just now beginning to understand his little peculiarities of speech."

"I speak beautifully," Dr. Hans protested.

Hugh had slowly inched his way toward the sofa and now he tried to sit down beside Ann. Paul must have been watching him, for he slid toward her so that Hugh was forced to take his seat on the other end with the young doctor between them. At another time Ann might have been amused, but tonight she was too tired to match wits with Lou, who watched them with glittering eyes and thin, pressed lips.

There was an awkward silence, broken suddenly by the door chimes. Jean was on her feet instantly and Bill went with her to the door. Ann leaned her head against the high back of the sofa and wondered if somehow she had suddenly been transported to Soldiers' Field. This room was growing crowded.

"Hello, Mother," Bill said. "This is certainly a pleasant surprise. Come in, all of you. Let me help you with your coat."

By merely turning her head Ann could see the three new arrivals. There was, first of all, Mrs. Tolliver, a tall, big-boned woman with snow-white hair that was fashionably and professionally piled high on her head. Her dark blue eyes were alive and piercing beneath heavy brows and seemed to take in every detail of the room in one quick glance. A large beak of a nose dominated her thin lips. Altogether it was an austere face and it fitted her. Helen Tolliver was handsome without being beautiful, the sort of woman who commands respect rather than love. She had the imperious carriage of an aristocrat and an enormous pride in her background. When she had been a bride she had attempted to have her husband return to the old English spelling of their name and had gone so far as to have her first calling cards engraved "Mrs. William Tolliaferro." But her husband had been adamant, saying that people would never learn to pronounce or spell it and that his grandfather had simplified it for that very reason. She had accepted it with ill grace but afterward had explained the change at every opportunity.

William Tolliver stood behind her, his arm hooked through Jean's. He was a little taller than his wife and his long face was heavily seamed, but his eyes were kind and gentle. His broad shoulders were stooped as though he were accustomed to carrying heavy burdens. He allowed Jean to help him with his overcoat, which he took from her and laid over a straight chair by the door.

"We can stay only a few minutes," he said. "But we did want your sister to know how glad we were that she was here."

Mrs. Tolliver came toward the fire, limping a little and leaning heavily on an ebony stick. "I can't tell you how surprised we were when we heard you were coming, Ann," she said in a beautifully modulated voice.

"Mother's not half expressing our delight," William Tolliver added, taking Ann's hand and patting it. "Jean has talked of nothing else for the past few days."

"Do sit down, Amelia." Mrs. Tolliver addressed the third arrival. "You make me nervous fluttering around the room."

Ann had hardly noticed this woman who had come in like a pale shadow behind the others. Nobody ever paid any attention to Amelia Langdon. She slipped in and out like a wraith, accomplishing many things quietly, for which she got no credit as they were seldom observed. She stood, uncertain now, alone and back from the others, still wearing a rusty black cloth coat with a worn fur collar. Wisps of gray hair escaped from the black velvet toque which had not been in style for several years. She was small and thin and bore little resemblance to her sister, so that Ann wondered again how it had been possible for the two of them to have had the same father and mother.

Amelia made small fluttery motions with her hands and let her eyes wander vaguely in search of a chair. Dr. Hans went to her and bowed with an Old World grace.

"Let me help you with your coat," he said and she smiled wanly in reply. He led her to a narrow bench which was placed in front of the three front windows, then went to get her a glass of ginger ale.

"I'd like to see Chip," Mrs. Tolliver said.

"He's sleeping," Jean said quickly. "I'll help you back to his room."

"My son will go with me," Mrs. Tolliver said coldly as she took Bill's arm. She patted Lou's shoulder as she passed but did not speak to her daughter.

Ann raised quizzical eyebrows as much as to say: *What goes on here?* Paul shrugged in reply, which was no answer to what she warned to know.

William Tolliver extended large blunt hands toward the fire. "It's really good to have you back, Ann," he said in a soft drawl. "And I know you're glad to get away from the snow and ice you've been having. I saw in the paper tonight that they were having a small blizzard up in the Dakotas. Of course you picked a rainy day to arrive, but tomorrow we'll order good sunshine for you. You're looking a little peaked."

"I haven't seen much sunshine lately."

"This rain never lasts; it's just trying to remind us that this is December. You'll see. Tomorrow the sun will come out and we'll have some of October's bright blue weather." He laughed and sat down in the chair which Dr. Hans had vacated.

"Put their coats on the guest-room bed, Hugh," Lou ordered. "There's no room for them in here. I told you, Jean, when you built this house, you ought to have a coat closet. I have one in my house," she added to Ann.

"Dad," Jean broke in, "why don't you all go hunting real soon? Bill's been talking about it for the past few weeks, and it might be his last chance to go for a long time."

"Yes, his last chance," Mr. Tolliver said sadly. "I think it's a very good idea. How about it, Paul? Could you and the doctor get off for a day soon?"

"I'd like nothing better," Paul said doubtfully. "We're pretty busy now."

"It is nonsense," Dr. Hans interrupted. "I will be there to see that things are going right. You're working hard and it seems to me that I used to hear Jean and Ann coax their father out by telling him something about all work and no play making Dr. Bartley a dunce cap." He beamed on the two girls as he spoke.

"You're going with us too," William Tolliver said decisively. "We wouldn't think of leaving you behind, would we, Hugh?"

"What's this?" Hugh asked.

"A hunt Dad's planning," Lou explained.

"I'm still not a very good shot," Mr. Tolliver said to Ann. "We'll have to take you boys along to kill us enough quail for dinner. Then we can have supper that night at our house. What about it, Amelia?"

"Yes." Amelia half rose as though she intended rushing to the kitchen that very minute. She looked about her vaguely and sank down again on the bench.

"Make it one day week after next and I think both of us can come," Paul said. "I've been wanting a hunt ever since I got here and if it's at all possible you can certainly count on me."

The door at the end of the room opened and Mrs. Tolliver came across the floor, her stick making muffled thuds on the thick rug.

"He's sleeping like an angel," she said.

Her husband helped her to the big chair opposite Ann, and Bill brought a small needlepoint stool for her lame foot. Ann wondered at this. She did not remember Mrs. Tolliver as being crippled and Jean had never mentioned it. It must have happened recently, but there was no sign of a bandage under the silk stocking.

"I have dogs," Dr. Hans said plaintively, "but they are all the wrong breeds. They will do us no good."

"Don't worry about that," Mr. Tolliver said. "Have you a license, Paul?"

"No, but I'll get one."

"Why not go to the old Allen place?" Bill asked. "It's still one of the best-stocked fields around here."

"Isn't that too far?" jean asked.

"We could take only two cars."

"If I go," Dr. Hans said, "I must take my car. I would not be able to stay the whole day."

"You must have breakfast with me," Jean invited.

They were all looking at her with peculiar expressions in their eyes. Ann struggled to understand this sudden tension which she felt all about her, but her head was too light for coherent thinking. The highball Bill had mixed for her was practically untasted, but there were leaden weights on her eyelids that dragged the dark lashes down to her cheeks. Her hands were wet with perspiration and the room seemed unbearably hot. She tried to move away from the heat of the fire but her muscles refused to answer the message from her brain. Her head was a drum and their words were muffled beats that hammered in her ears.

"We don't want to put you to the trouble," Mr. Tolliver said. "We can all make ourselves some coffee at home and Amelia will put us up one of her lunches. We'd better be going, Mother. It's getting late."

He held out his hand to his wife and helped her to her feet. The others got up instantly, as though they were suddenly released from chains that bound them to their chairs. Ann tried to rise too, but her legs doubled under her and she sat down quickly. Paul's fingers grasped her wrist while with his other hand he roughly pushed her head into her lap.

"Too rapid," he said tersely.

Ann never lost consciousness, though the room was swimming dizzily around her.

Quite clearly she heard Lou say, "Trust Ann to be dramatic."

"She won't faint," Paul said, still holding her head down. "Have you a thermometer, Jean? She has some fever. I thought something was wrong with her." He bent down toward her. "What's the matter with you, Ann?"

"Pneumonia. I've been up for two weeks, though." The words were muffled, but he heard them. He picked her up as he would a child, his arm under her knees.

"I'll put her on the bed," he said. "You'd better keep her there for a while."

3
A TERRIBLE ACCIDENT

"Ann! Ann, wake up!" The only response Ann made was to turn over and pull the eiderdown comfort closer under her chin. But she underestimated the persistence of her sister. Jean shook her.

"You're awake, Ann. It's time to get up."

Ann opened one eye. The room was dark. There was no hint of dawn through the windows.

"I've just gone to bed," she said, her voice blurred with sleep. "It's only midnight."

"It's five o'clock," Jean said crossly. "The others will be here in half an hour. Please get up and come help me in the kitchen."

"All right." Ann pushed herself up to a sitting position and yawned.

"I've pulled down your windows, but you'd better dress in the bathroom. It's warmer there." Jean hurried through the door.

Ann reached out and switched on the light beside her bed. She blinked in the sudden brightness and waited a minute for the pupils of her eyes to contract. Then she swung her feet over the side of the bed and padded, barefoot, across the room.

Cold water on her face helped wake her and she came back to get her clothes which she had placed on a chair in readiness for this morning. It was an odd assortment which she and Jean had collected for this occasion. Jean's old jodhpurs were a little too large at the waist and there was a small tear near the ankle, but the pull-on sweater was her own. Hunting was the last thing she had expected to do when she came to Alabama, but when Paul had suggested, last Sunday, that she go with them, Jean has been enthusiastic and Bill offered her the use of a small gun.

She dressed hurriedly against the chill of the room, then sat down at the flounced dressing-table, turned on the light, and with extreme care applied powder and lipstick. Her cheeks were still somewhat hollow, though two weeks' rest had erased the shadows under her eyes. As she rose she picked up a slender, clear crystal bottle and with the long glass stopper dabbed perfume behind the lobes of her ears. She grinned at her reflection, and her face took on a gaminlike appearance. Nothing could be more absurd than using perfume when she was going hunting, but it had been automatic, a thing she did whenever she dressed.

"Autumn Fire," she murmured, tracing with her finger tips the name etched across the flaring base.

She was very fond of the bottle. She had given its mate to Jean last Christmas, and evidently her sister had shared her liking, for she had mentioned it several times. Ann hadn't seen it on Jean's dressing-table so she must have put it away from Chip's reaching hands.

Ann stood up. Her heart was beating faster at the thought of seeing Hugh again. She had rested for the first few days and then her old friends had begun to come to see her, dropping in at odd hours. She had slipped easily into a routine of small bridge parties and luncheons. It had been good to see them, but for some reason Hugh had not come. Not since that night she had arrived. She was excited at the prospect of being with him this morning. She felt alive again.

The kitchen was warm and smelled pleasantly of frying ham. Jean was busy measuring coffee. "Fix the oranges for me, will you, Ann?" she said without looking up.

"You oughtn't to have asked the whole tribe over here for breakfast. You didn't have to go to all this trouble."

"I like having them."

"Anything I can do?" Bill asked from the door.

"Yes," Jean replied with a cook's harassed tone. "Fix the oranges and let Ann do the table. I've put the dishes out," she added to her sister, "and the mats. I thought all of you could crowd into the breakfast room."

The breakfast room was not the usual cubbyhole. It was really a small, informal dining-room with a rose-colored tile floor and two walls of glass brick. Jean kept her most prized pot plants and ferns in it during the cold months and their greenery made a pleasantly tropical background. In the center was a long glass-topped table and the rush-bottomed chairs were painted and decorated with bright stenciled flowers.

Ann moved them into place about the table. "How many?" she called to Jean.

"Five. Dr. Hans won't be here and I'll eat later."

Before she had finished setting the table Paul arrived and came to help her.

"How's the weather?" Bill asked.

"A little foggy. I think it'll clear up later."

"Where's Dr. Hans?" Ann asked. "Jean says he's not coming."

"He'll meet us later. Somebody has to feed the dogs and rabbits. It's one thing we can't persuade our black angel to do for us. She won't go near them. Says they have 'communicant disease.'"

"That sounds like Adeline. Is she still taking care of Dr. Hans?"

"We couldn't live without her."

There was a knock on the back door and Bill opened it to admit Mr. Tolliver. "Good morning, Dad. Looking forward to the hunt?"

"As soon as I wake up I'll probably feel like a schoolboy playing hooky." Mr. Tolliver yawned and stretched. "Can't understand why I'm so sleepy. I had a cup of coffee before I left home."

"Breakfast is about ready," Jean said. "Go on in and sit down, Dad. I guess Hugh will be here in a minute."

As if in answer, the door chimes tinkled in the hall.

"I hope the noise won't wake Chip," Jean whispered to Ann. "Don't you want me to stay and help you? Lily had such a terrible cold yesterday. Chip ought not to be around her."

"Lou asked for him," Jean replied. "He's spending the day with her."

"Good morning, everybody," Hugh greeted them. "Breakfast ready?"

He was the only one dressed in the proper clothes. The others wore mismatched coats and trousers, but Hugh might have posed for a sporting goods ad. He was like that. He had expensive tastes. He was almost too handsome, Ann thought as she picked up her orange juice to avoid the smile she saw in his eyes. Now that she had seen him again, Ann tried to tell herself that she was no longer in love with him, but there still lingered about him an aura of romance and old-time fascination.

Jean poured steaming coffee into big cups.

"Pass me the sugar, please." Mr. Tolliver took the bowl from Ann.

"You ruin the taste," she told him as he poured three heaping spoonfuls into his cup.

"I like it sweet."

They ate hungrily as they chattered about the morning's hunt. Only Mr. Tolliver took little part in the conversation. He slouched drowsily in his chair, yawned again and again, and seemed to have to rouse himself to eat.

"What about Dr. Steigler?" he asked Paul. "What time will he join us?"

"I don't know just when," Paul replied. "He has an eight o'clock class and he'll have to feed the dogs."

"Oh yes, I remember now he said that." Mr. Tolliver put down his empty cup.

The thin barking of the dogs could be heard in the darkness outside.

"Hook the trailer to your car, will you, Bill?" Hugh asked. "I'm taking mine and the hook doesn't fit."

A few minutes later Ann saw the reason for Hugh's request. His car was a shiny new convertible and he was not the sort of person to run the risk of any damage, no matter how slight, to his possessions.

"I'll ride with Hugh. You two go with Bill." Mr. Tolliver made the decision for them all.

The dogs were milling frantically within the small confines of their cage, which Paul and Bill attached to the Buick. It was still cold and dark. The lights of the car had been turned on so that they could see to load and pack their equipment. Ann felt the clammy dampness of a heavy fog that made it impossible to see more than a few yards away even with the headlights.

At the last minute she turned back to her sister. "Are you sure you don't want me to stay with you?" she asked.

"Of course I don't want you to stay," Jean replied. "I wouldn't have you miss this for the world. Run along and have a good time."

Paul helped Ann into the front seat and, crowded there between the two men, she was warm and comfortable. It wasn't quite so dark now. There was a faint grayish light in the sky and she could tell that the fog was slowly lifting. The windshield wiper fanned across her vision, scraping away the mist that collected on the glass.

The Allen plantation was a long distance from town and Bill drove slowly, almost feeling his way. As the sky turned pearl-colored Ann could see the broad open fields filled with dead cotton and cornstalks, like barren skeletons now that their fruitful season was over. A heavy frost whitened the hollows between the rows and touched with icy fingers the grass on the side of the road.

Bill stopped the car in front of a sagging barbed-wire gate, and Paul got out of the car and opened it. When he had closed it and got back into the car he said, "The others must have got here ahead of us. There were tire marks on the frost."

They bounced over a rutted wagon road, finally turning from it into what was no more than a faint trail. Bill had to give all his attention to driving but he got plenty of advice from the other two, which he took with a good-natured grin. At last they emerged from a small wood into a cleared place filled with tall grass and a few straggling bushes. A car was parked to one side under a huge oak tree and Hugh and Mr. Tolliver came toward them.

"We're going to have a good day after all," Hugh said, glancing up at the sky. "The sun will be up in a little while."

"Let the dogs out, son," Mr. Tolliver directed.

As the wire door was opened four Irish setters bounded out of their cage and raced madly in circles about the hunters. They were a beautiful sight, their long silky ears flopping as they ran, their sensitive noses close to the ground. Bill called to them and they came back, barking with excitement and jumping on the men in their eagerness to be off again.

Mr. Tolliver hung a bag over his shoulder and picked up his gun. "I suppose Dr. Steigler can find us?" he asked Paul.

"There's no use for us to wait for him. Ann and I will come back to the cars after a while and see if he's come. Anyway, he wanted most of all just to be out in the country and it's quite likely he won't even remember to bring his gun."

"Let's get going then," Bill said impatiently.

They moved forward slowly and cautiously, watching the dogs, waiting for them to flush a covey. The briers and underbrush were thick and Ann was soon panting with exertion. Paul must have seen this, for he dropped back, shortening his pace to one that she could match. They had gone only a little way when Bill cried out that Duke, the best trained of the dogs, had found a covey. Ann and Paul stumbled forward quickly to where they could see the dog, frozen into position, until his master should send him for the birds.

Bill called to Duke and as the birds rose in fright three sharp reports broke the stillness of the air. Ann had raised her gun but her hands shook so with excitement that she could not pull the trigger.

The sun had risen and it was warm on their heads and shoulders. Somehow, after those first shots, Ann and Paul got separated from the others, though occasionally they heard the reports of the guns and the excited barks of the dogs.

"I think I'll go back and wait for Dr. Hans," she said, stopping and resting for a moment against the scaly trunk of a cedar.

"Sit down here and smoke a cigarette and then we'll both go back." Paul dug in his pocket and produced a new package, which he opened and offered her.

As he held a lighter to hers Ann said impulsively, "I'm worried about Jean."

"Why?" he asked in surprise.

"What's worrying her? She won't talk to me. I never get a chance to speak to her alone. I think she's actually avoiding me."

"You're imagining things. Sit down on this log."

"It's not imagination," she denied. "There is something wrong. I can feel it."

He didn't say anything for a few minutes, just sat there beside her, relaxed and smoking slowly. "You've been sick," he said at last. "Maybe Jean's been worried about you."

"Then why did she write me that letter?" Ann burst out.

"What letter?"

"The one saying she was afraid. It came while I was still in the hospital and Jean didn't know then that I was sick."

"What did she say?"

"Just that she was afraid," Ann replied vaguely. "She said she needed me. Oh, it wasn't so much what she said, it was the whole tone of the letter. She sounded as though she thought she was going to die."

Paul laughed. "Of all the nonsense. Jean's as healthy a specimen as you could expect to find."

"She's not happy," Ann muttered half to herself. "I tried to talk to her Sunday afternoon. It was the first time I'd really been alone with her and then you came along."

"So that's why you were so reluctant to go with me."

"Well, you saw how she practically pushed me out of the house. She was relieved not to have me around."

"She only wanted you to get out in the fresh air. You hadn't been out much since you got here."

"That's not it at all," Ann said, frowning and closing her oblique eyes until there was only a glimmer of light shining through her dark lashes. "They watch her."

"Who?" he asked sensibly.

"All of them," she said. "Bill, the Tollivers—"

"Ann, you have the most vivid imagination!"

"Well, they do," she maintained. "They criticize everything she does. Mr. Tolliver isn't so bad and he seems worried too, but he watches her just the same. And they snatch Chip away all the time."

"Chip is an only grandchild," Paul said dryly. "Isn't it natural for them to want him? Most grandparents are that way."

"It's not the Tollivers so much as Lou."

"Well?"

"Oh, you!" Ann exclaimed in disgust as she dropped her cigarette on the ground and crushed it with the heel of her shoe. "You wouldn't see anything that stared at you from under your nose."

"And you're trying to make something out of nothing," he retorted.

"What about the things in my room being moved?" she demanded. "That's something."

"What are you talking about now?"

"Jean unpacked my bags and put my things away while I was still in bed," Ann explained. "She had everything jumbled together and when I got up I sorted them and put them in the right places. Then they got jumbled again and I straightened them a second time. That's happened three times."

"You mixed things up when you were dressing."

"I don't move handkerchiefs out of one drawer and put them in another," she said. "And I didn't put my little gold crab in with my stockings. Anybody in their right mind would know the sharp points would tear them."

"What gold crab?" he asked patiently.

Ann's lips were set grimly. "An ornament I wear on my coat. It was given to me and I never take it off. I had it on the night I came here and I'm sure it was still on the lapel of my suit coat when Jean hung it in the closet."

"Then the servants have been going through your things."

"But nothing's been taken. They're just moved."

"The servants were only curious."

"That's not it. It's—queer."

She looked away from him, her eyes clouding as she tried to solve her problem. She wondered why she had thought Paul could help her. Already she regretted confiding her own fears to him. She stood up suddenly.

"I think I'll go look for Dr. Hans."

He got up too. Looking down at her, his eyes wore a puzzled expression. "Give me your gun," he said. "I'll carry it for you."

"No, thanks." She hung it easily through her arm and started off in the general direction of the cars.

He followed her, walking with a sureness he must have learned from his fighting experiences. They came to a barbed-wire fence and he broke the strained silence. "Is this the right way? We didn't come through a fence."

"I—I don't know." Ann was confused. "I just thought I was going in the right direction."

"I'm not sure either," he said. "Let's turn back and see if we can find some of the others."

"Doesn't that look like the trees where we left the cars?"

Ann pointed to a small clump of pines and oaks.

"I don't know," he said. "Want to take a chance?"

"Yes."

"All right, crawl through when I get the wires pulled apart and be careful that you don't get snagged."

He pushed down one wire with his foot and pulled at the next one, leaving a gap through which Ann crawled. She stood up and held the wires for him.

"Don't get your hand caught. Those sharp wires can give you a nasty cut." It wasn't as easy for him as it had been for Ann, and a barb caught on the shoulder of his coat and tore it.

As they picked up their guns and turned they saw a man coming toward them. He was tall and slender, and his clothes were old and worn. An old felt hat was pulled low over his eyes and the big pockets of his leather jacket sagged with the weight of the accumulated paraphernalia of the hunter. He had been carrying his rifle loosely at his side, but now he threw it over his shoulder and advanced to meet them with long easy strides.

"Mornin'," he said as he came up to them. "Don't you know this place is posted?"

There was one bird in the bag which Paul carried and Ann glanced uneasily at it. "We had permission to hunt on the Allen place," she said.

"We got separated from the others," Paul put in, "and are trying to find the cars. Mr. Tolliver talked to the owner and I'm sure we had the right to hunt here."

"My name's Bill Davies. I'm the sheriff of this county," the stranger said, and there was a twinkle in his blue eyes as he watched their discomfiture.

"Are we still on the Allen place?" Ann asked. "We didn't come through a fence."

"Yes'm, this is the Allen place," Sheriff Davies assured her. He looked them over carefully. Their accents told him they weren't local products. Their words were a little too clipped for Alabamians. Under his skeptical gaze Ann grew restless and shifted her weight from one foot to the other.

The sheriff turned to Paul and began asking questions: who were they, where did they live, why had they happened to be this far away from town? Paul answered readily and went on to explain how they got separated from the others.

"Got your license with you, son?" asked the sheriff when Paul had finished.

Paul fished in his pocket and took out a billfold which he handed the sheriff, who read the enclosed paper and gave it back to him.

"What about yours, young lady?"

"I'm afraid I left it in the car," Ann said. "Bill gave it to me when we left the house this morning and I must have stuffed it in the glove compartment. I didn't want to carry it around in my pocket. And of course," she added with a whimsical smile, "I had no idea I'd run into the law and need it."

Sheriff Davies laughed and crow's-feet appeared at the corners of his eyes. "No'm," he said, "I don't expect you did. But if you're on your way back to the car, I'd like to see it."

"You'll have to show us the way," Ann said. "We're lost. We think the cars are over there." She pointed.

"I know this farm pretty well," the sheriff said. "Tell me where you left them and I can probably take you."

They described the clearing where the cars were parked and he nodded knowingly. Then he gave a shrill whistle and two pointer dogs rushed up to him. He leaned down and rubbed their cold noses affectionately.

"We can go this way," he said, and started across what must have been a pasture. There was less grass here and from a line of trees on the far side they knew there must be a creek. "You people just visiting?" he asked conversationally.

"I came down to see my sister," Ann answered. "Major Forrest is a doctor. He's working with one of the university professors on something that will cure malaria."

Sheriff Davies nodded. "That's a fine idea," he commented. "We got a lot of that in these parts."

"We need a cure more than ever now," Ann said, "with so many of our soldiers out in the tropics."

"I got a son-in-law somewhere out in the South Pacific," he said slowly.

They walked on then, talking easily. The dogs raced off in all directions, following faint trails they found but returning every now and then to their master. The sheriff became a self-appointed guide, evidently thinking that, as visitors, they should be told about the trees and shrubs and soil. Ann had the feeling that they were walking through a vast museum of natural science, for their guide seemed to have a great knowledge of his subject.

"Lots of old-fashioned herbs grow around here," he said. "I can remember my grandma used to doctor all the children with her own brews. She was pretty good at it, too," he added, his blue eyes laughing at Paul. "We never had to have a real doctor except once in a while."

Paul laughed in genuine amusement. "I guess the old folks knew a lot of remedies we've forgotten these days."

"We live longer now," Ann argued.

"She's been reading insurance statistics," Paul told the older man. "I expect she had a date with a salesman once."

The sheriff was not listening. His eyes were on one of the dogs that had stopped in front of them. "Watch it," he said softly.

He moved his gun and turned as Ann did the same. "I wouldn't if I were you," he warned.

"I'll kill something this morning if I have to go to jail for it," Ann declared recklessly.

"She has a license, Mr. Davie's," Paul assured him.

The sheriff shook his head but he was too intent on his dog to make any further protest. They walked cautiously until they had almost reached the dog.

"Get him, Joe!" the sheriff commanded, and the dog sprang forward.

There was a soft whir of wings and five birds flew up into the air. Almost simultaneously three shots rang out and one bird fluttered helplessly to the ground. The dogs were off instantly and a few minutes later Joe returned with the quail held lightly in his mouth.

As the sheriff took it he said to Ann, "It's yours when you show me that license."

"Do you really think I hit it?" she asked eagerly.

"Not a doubt about it," he lied gallantly.

"Let's hurry." Ann went on ahead of the two men and in a few minutes she called back to them, "I can see the cars now."

Breaking into a run, she pushed through the tall grass and brambles to the clearing under the trees. Her eyes were on the cars and so she stumbled over it before she saw the crumpled figure on the ground. Her mouth opened but no sound came from the constricted cords of her throat. Waves of nausea seemed to engulf her and she swayed like the last leaves on a tree in a winter wind. She was conscious not of fear but only of a paralyzing numbness that crept from her feet to her brain.

"There's something wrong!"

As from a distance, she heard Paul's shout. The sound of their footsteps was drowned by the pounding of blood in her ears.

Paul gave her only the briefest of glances before he dropped on his knee beside the still body of a man sprawled at her feet. There was blood on the matted gray head that lay crushed against a fallen limb but the face that was turned up to the sky was calm and peaceful. The arms were spread apart and one leg was pulled upward as though in a reflex of pain.

"What—what a terrible accident," Ann whispered through stiff lips.

"We'd better get the others as quickly as possible," Paul said, his fingers dropping to the cold wrist. "He's dead."

"Who is he?" asked the sheriff.

Paul looked up at him incredulously. "Mr. Tolliver."

4

SO MUCH CONFUSION

Everything was very still in the small clearing. A bright sun, shining through the leafless branches of the tree, warmed the cold ground, though there was still a hint of frost near the roots of the big oak tree. The sheriff's dogs were restless but they stayed close to him as though they understood that tragedy had invaded the peaceful quiet of the morning.

Ann heard herself muttering, "If only that limb hadn't been there, if only that limb—" She shut her eyes and tried to suppress the shudder that shook her body.

More experienced, the sheriff could take a dispassionate view of the situation. His bushy eyebrows drew together in a puzzled frown as he looked from the tree to the body and then on to the fallen limb. It was no new break; some early winter wind had torn it from the tree, but its position and the peculiar twist of the body were queer. He took a step forward, then suddenly stopped and picked up some small object that lay near the limb.

He held it loosely in the broad palm of his hand while he rummaged with the other in one pocket after another until he had found a small slip of paper. Folding it inside the paper, he carefully put it away in an inside pocket. His next action was even stranger. He picked up the dead man's gun, sniffed the barrel, and replaced it where it had been found.

"He hasn't fired his gun," the sheriff said.

"Are you sure?" Paul asked, but his attention was really on Ann. "Go sit in the car, Ann. We'll have to get the others and go back to town as soon as possible."

"No birds in his bag." The sheriff paid no attention to what they were doing. "His gun hasn't been fired and he hasn't got a bird."

"Hadn't we better call the others?" Paul asked again.

"Yes," the sheriff replied absently, without diverting his attention from the crumpled figure at his feet.

Paul walked away and, cupping his hands about his mouth, called to Bill and Hugh. His words echoed through the cold air but there was no answer. He called again and again, until the sheriff, apparently realizing for the first time what he was trying to do, raised his rifle and fired three times in rapid succession. As he lifted his gun to repeat the signal Ann put her hands over her ears and retreated to the car. Never had she felt so helpless, so inadequate, and now that she was standing still she realized how cold she was.

Although it seemed a long time to the three waiting people, actually it was only a few minutes later that they heard a thrashing in the underbrush and Dr. Steigler struggled toward them. His face was flushed with exertion and he carried his gun as though he were afraid of it.

"There's been a terrible accident," Paul told him. "Cousin William—"

"Mr. Tolliver, he has been hurt?" Dr. Hans asked in alarm, his eyes wide and distorted behind the thick-lensed glasses.

"He's dead," the sheriff explained.

Paul introduced them, and told the professor what had happened.

"How long ago did you get here?" Sheriff Davies asked.

"I do not know." Dr. Hans shook his head. "I had some difficulty in finding the place and I stopped once to ask a Negro the way. There was nobody here so I wandered around and found this." He held up a few stalks of a weed which he had torn from the ground. "It is very interesting. I do not know what it is, but it might be important."

The sheriff viewed the specimen with skepticism. Common weeds held no interest for him. To him, they were the farmer's enemy, things to be destroyed.

"Didn't you come out here to hunt:"

"I have brought my gun, as you see, but I have no instinct for the hunt. I do not like to see things killed." Dr. Steigler shuddered and his round face saddened. "I like the open country. Even the scientist must go to nature for his knowledge. Our greatest discoveries stem from the simplest observations."

"Then you haven't fired your gun."

"It isn't even loaded. Major Forrest cleaned it for me and I'm sure he put out some shells, but I didn't notice when I left home, so I brought none with me."

"What's that got to do with it?" Paul asked.

"It's just—" began the sheriff as a dog dashed toward them and began barking frantically.

"That's Duke," Paul said. "Bill must be coming back."

As if in answer, Bill came running across the clearing. He was panting hard and called to them before he could see why they were standing so awkwardly under the tree.

"What's the matter? Has something happened to Ann? I heard three shots."

Paul started toward him, but Bill saw his father before the doctor had a chance to speak. He stopped so suddenly that he swayed on his feet. Shock and amazement stiffened his face, then he gasped, dropped his gun, and stumbled forward. He knelt beside his father's body and lifted the crushed head on his arm.

"Dad—Dad!" he muttered. "Can't you do something?' he asked, lifting tragic eyes to Paul.

"Sorry," Paul answered gently. "We were too late. There was nothing that we could do."

In the car Ann turned her head away. She could not bear to look at Bill's grief-stricken face. Death is always a shock, she knew, no matter how well prepared you are, but when it is sudden and inexplicable you are more numbed and stupefied. The mere fact that life and death are sometimes beyond human control only intensifies the pain when you meet that fact face to face.

The sheriff, too, seemed to sense the shock that gripped the silent group. He was not unaccustomed to death, even sudden and violent death, but the sight of it always sickened him. Hunting accidents were not uncommon in this section, though they were seldom fatal, but he had never schooled himself into an objectivity that would accept such carelessness and waste of human life. He stooped and picked up Bill's gun and his blue eyes grew shrewd as he examined it carefully before he brought it back to its owner.

Bill had become calmer, though his face was white and his eyes were still clouded with pain. "I had no idea this would happen," he said. "Dad only said he was sleepy."

"He left you?"

"Yes. Paul and Ann had already dropped behind and he began to worry about Dr. Hans. He said he was tired anyway and would come back to the car and rest."

"He had no need to worry about me." Dr. Hans sounded distressed.

"Dad," Bill said with a weary smile, "Dad was like that."

"Yes," the little German replied. "He was a good man."

"His gun hasn't been fired," interposed the sheriff.

"I know," Bill said. "He raised it once or twice, but I don't think he fired. He left the real opportunities to Hugh and me."

"Did he look sick?" the sheriff asked. "I mean, didn't he say something?"

"No. He kept yawning and he said he was sleepy. I thought he'd come back to the car and maybe sleep until we got back here for lunch." Bill turned to his father and tears came to his eyes.

Sheriff Davies touched Paul's arm and drew him aside. They walked toward the car in which Ann sat forgotten, and she heard him ask, "Did he have a stroke?"

Paul frowned. "I don't know. It doesn't look like it, but you'd need a more thorough examination to really determine that. He might have had a slight dizzy spell or he could have stumbled."

"Would just falling be enough to crush his skull?"

"It's possible," Paul replied. "Naturally there would be other things to consider. He wasn't a young man and there might have been some heart condition or high blood pressure—any number of things could be contributing causes."

"It's funny," the sheriff muttered to himself. "Most people fall forward and he's stretched out there on his back." He shook his head as though he were not quite satisfied with the doctor's explanation.

One of the dogs howled and the others took up the cry. It was an infinitely lonely sound, this baying of the hounds. Ann lowered the window of the car and called to Paul, "Let's get away from here. Bill's almost at the breaking-point. And those at home will have to know."

"What about Hugh?" Paul asked the sheriff.

"Who's he?"

"Mr. Tolliver's son-in-law. We all came together."

"Call him again," Ann said. "If he doesn't come we'll have to go on without him."

It was some fifteen minutes later that Hugh came. Paul had shouted his name until he was almost hoarse. The sheriff explained that an accident had occurred and that they would have to go back to town. Hugh took the news quietly enough, though the big vein in his temple throbbed and his face darkened.

"I'm sorry," he said at last. "I didn't know. I heard the shots, of course, but I never thought of them as a distress signal. I didn't think of anything like this. . . . He only said he was sleepy." He looked at Bill and went to him and put an arm about his shoulders. "Let Ann and Paul take you home, Bill," he said. "They can take you in my car. I'll stay here and see about everything else."

Bill was dazed and seemed not to hear, so Paul touched his arm. "I'll take you now."

"You'll have to tell Mother, Bill," Hugh said, shaking him gently. "She'll take it better from you than from me. Go on with Paul and we'll come behind you."

Ann got out of the car and came to her brother-in-law, slipped her hand in his, and drew him to Hugh's car. There were tears in his eyes, though he fought hard to hold them back, and a dry sob racked his body as he turned once more to his father. She thought he was going to say something, but he only turned quickly back to her and walked slowly to the car. They waited there while Paul spoke to Dr. Hans and the sheriff.

With three of them on the seat it was a little crowded, but Ann didn't mind. Bill held her hand so tightly that she thought the bones would crack and she bit her lip once or twice to keep from crying out. Only once did Bill speak and that was as Paul turned the car and headed it for home.

"He looked so cold and uncomfortable," Bill muttered.

"But he looked peaceful too," Ann said comfortingly.

"Yes, peaceful—"

After that nobody spoke. When they reached the gate Paul got out and held it open while Ann drove the car through it. The way back seemed interminable now, though it had seemed short enough earlier that morning. Paul quickened his speed as they came to the paved highway and when they eventually reached the outskirts of the town he twisted and turned through back streets to avoid midmorning traffic. When they came to the brick posts of Briarcliff Circle Bill groaned aloud.

Paul glanced at him, shook his head slightly, and said quietly to Ann, "I'm dropping you at home first and I'll take Bill on to Cousin Helen's. Tell Jean to come over right away. He'll need her."

She nodded understandingly as he brought the car to a stop and opened the door at his side.

"Slide out this way," he said.

"I'll tell Jean," she whispered, "and come myself as soon as I can."

Paul smiled at her as he slid back into his seat. Ann stood at the curb and watched the car move slowly on and stop at the imposing Tolliver house which stood in the center of the loop, dominating by its very bigness the houses on either side. Bill's house was at one end of the Circle, where the road intersected with College Street, and Lou and Hugh had built directly opposite, across the small parkway. It was an exclusive residential section, a little raw, perhaps, with the smug air of the newly rich.

Ann walked slowly up the steps and opened the front door. She dreaded breaking the news to Jean, but she squared her shoulders and marched through the living-room to the nursery, where she found her sister on the floor, straightening Chip's toys on the low shelves under the windows.

"Ann!" Jean got to her feet immediately. "Ann, what is it?"

"There's been an accident—"

"Bill?" Jean grasped Ann's shoulders and shook her. "Has anything happened to Bill?"

"No, Jean, Bill's all right." Ann tried to pull Jean's hands away. The frantic fingers were digging into her arms. "It was Mr. Tolliver. He fell."

"I didn't have anything to do with it," Jean muttered. "I didn't—"

"What do you mean?" Ann asked. "He fell against a fallen log."

"He's dead?"

"Yes." Ann watched her sister anxiously. "We found him when we came back to the cars." She went on to describe what had happened. wondering as she did so whether Jean really heard what she was saying. There was a faraway, dreamy look in her eyes. "Paul took Bill on to his mother's," she concluded. "I think you'd better go to hire. He'll need you."

Jean frowned and shook her head as if to clear her thoughts.

"I'll get your coat. You'd better go right away." Ann went to her sister's room and Jean followed her. "In the closet?" she asked, opening the door. She soon found a dark sports coat and dragged it out. Then she stared at it in amazement. It was turned neatly wrong side out. "Well!" she exclaimed. "You're getting absent-minded."

Jean was looking at the coat in horror.

"What's the matter?" Ann laughed as she turned the sleeves. "You're looking as though it were a live snake."

Jean gasped, tore the coat from Ann's unresisting hands, threw it about her shoulders, and rushed from the room.

"Well!" Ann said again as she heard the front door slam.

She was completely bewildered by Jean's reaction and, shaking her head over the puzzle, she went back to the kitchen to explain to Martha what had happened. This done, she went to her own room, took a quick shower, and dressed.

Several cars were parked along the curved road, Ann noted as she walked to the Tolliver house a short time later. It was a beautiful house, built in the old Southern tradition. Its white paint glistened in the sun and the two-storied veranda was supported by six fluted columns. Visitors frequently mistook it for an ante-bellum mansion, which pleased Mrs. Tolliver very much. But in truth the effect had been achieved by the careful planning of an architect. It sat on a smooth carpet of winter grass and the whole place was conscientiously landscaped.

A stranger opened the door and Ann stepped through it into a once familiar hall. A graceful stair rose on one side and against the opposite wall was a large framed mirror, placed so that a person descending the steps would get a full view of her reflection. Under it was a Queen Anne lowboy on which someone had placed a crystal vase of yellow chrysanthemums. Though Ann had been many times in previous years, this was the first time she had been inside since her return.

"They're in the library," the lady beside her whispered, drawing toward the double doors on the left.

The venetian blinds were partly closed and the room was very dim. Several people looked up as the door opened and the low buzz of whispered conversation almost ceased. A quick glance convinced Ann that none of the family were here and she was ready to go out again when Paul came over to her. He still wore his hunting clothes and his face seemed strained and quiet. She noticed then the man to whom he had been talking. It was their lanky companion of the morning—Sheriff Davies.

"The family's upstairs," Paul said, linking his arm through hers.

"Hadn't I better see Jean? There might be something for me to do."

"Let's get out of here."

"How did they take it?" she asked when he had closed the doors behind them.

"They're mostly shocked. It was all so sudden. Lou's up-stairs now, still weeping buckets of tears, and Amelia's fluttering around like a wet hen. Cousin Helen took it as well as could be expected. They're trying to keep her as quiet as possible."

"What arrangements—?"

"I don't know. Hugh's seeing about that for them. Bill is still stunned and I don't think he's capable of making decisions yet."

"Jean?"

Paul frowned. "Jean was a little hysterical at first. No, don't go to her. She's all right now. Bill's with her and it's best thing for him. It'll keep his mind off the other. . . . Look here, Ann, it's way past lunchtime and I don't think anybody's thought of food. Could you—?"

"I'm not very experienced, but I'll do the best I can."

He followed her to the back of the house and into the kitchen, where they found a Negro man and woman.

"Flora," Paul addressed the cook, "this is Miss Bartley, Miss Jean's sister. Can you and John help her get some food fixed for the others? They aren't thinking about lunch, but just the same they ought to have something to eat."

"Yas sir," Flora answered, smoothing the starched front of her blue uniform. "We sho' will. Me and Jawn been wonderin' what to do."

"Don't you think we could fix some trays and take them upstairs?" Ann asked. "There are so many people in the house and so much confusion downstairs—" She trailed her sentence as both Negroes bobbed their heads in agreement. "What have you planned, Flora?"

"We got a roast chicken."

The four of them worked together smoothly. Trays and china were assembled and plates filled. Ann nibbled on a chicken leg as she worked and realized with a sort of wonder that she was really hungry. As they finished one tray John picked it up and was about to take it upstairs when the door opened and the sheriff came inside.

"I was just wondering," he said, scratching the side of his cheek, "what you'd done with those birds you shot this morning. They ought to be cleaned and put in the icebox."

"I don't know." Ann turned to Paul, who shook his head.

"I don't know where they are. Does it matter?"

"I thought I might clean 'em for you."

"They's still in the bags," John interrupted. "I 'spects they's on the back gallery where Mr. Hugh lef' 'em."

The sheriff's blue eyes brightened and it took only two strides of his long legs for him to reach the back porch. Through the glass panel they could see him bend over the bags and carefully lift out the birds, turning each one over in his big hands as though he was searching for something.

"Why is he here?" Ann whispered to Paul. "I wondered when I saw him in the library."

"I don't know."

"What's he looking for? Is there some law about the kind of bullets to be used on quail?"

"Not that I know of."

"He's looking for something," Ann insisted. "Go out and talk to him. How do we know he's really a sheriff? He could have been just somebody else out there hunting."

"Oh, he's a sheriff all right. But I don't know why he came back here. He was in the car with Hugh and went with him when they took Cousin William—downtown."

Ann gave him a push and, obediently, he joined the sheriff. Through the closed door Ann could hear the murmur of their voices though their words were indistinguishable. There were gestures from the sheriff and disagreement from Paul, then more talk. And all the time the strange tall man was busy with the birds. Just as Ann had made up her mind to go out herself and find out what was the matter the sheriff laid aside the last bird and both men rose and walked calmly out of the back door.

Ann was too surprised to do anything but stare at the empty back porch. Her eyes narrowed but before she could speculate further on their strange behavior the hall door opened and Jean came into the kitchen.

"I wondered who had taken charge down here," she said wearily.

Ann went to her, slipped an arm around her waist, and laid a cool cheek against Jean's damp one.

"I haven't done anything," she said. "Paul thought you'd want something to eat."

"That's all right, Flora," Jean said to the servant. "The rest of us can just eat something here in the kitchen."

"How's Mrs. Tolliver?" Ann asked politely.

"Aunt Amelia's with her. I think she'll try to rest this afternoon. Hugh's seeing to things."

"Jean," Ann asked suddenly, "where's Chip?"

"Chip? I hadn't thought—I guess he's still at Lou's."

"Who's over there with him?"

"I don't know."

"Well, I'm going to get him and take him home."

5

A HORRIBLE ACCUSATION

"An' a fire engine, an' tricycle, an' a nairoplane an'—" Chip paused for breath. Ann squeezed the mittened fist that clung tightly to her hand. Chip's stubby legs danced excitedly beside her and the wind had whipped color into his cheeks. Short hair turned up like duck feathers around the dark blue beret he wore.

"Where will you hang your stocking?" she asked.

"On my bed. Aunt Lou's gonna make a big red stocking with bells on it and I'll put it on my bed an' then in the mornin' Santa Claus will have it filled with . . ." He went on with his enumeration.

Even Ann was becoming fired with his enthusiasm. There had been too much gloom, too many tears during the past two days. It had been left to her to explain this unusual behavior of the adults to a puzzled child. Chip had not understood but he accepted her fumbling efforts to divert him. Mr. Tolliver was being buried this afternoon and Ann had volunteered to take Chip for a walk as Lily was still at home with a cold. Bill had wanted his son with him but had finally given in to the pleas of Ann and Jean.

She was really enjoying being out of doors. The air was warm and pleasant though, to her, anything would have been better than the chill dampness of a church filled with the heavy scent of funeral flowers. She had a vivid imagination and there had been no dull moments for either of them since they had set out from the white brick house in search of buried treasure.

Except for her trimly shod feet and the straight seams of her stockings, Ann might have been mistaken for one of the college girls, dressed as she was in her fur coat and a bright peasant kerchief over her head.

"Let's select our tree," she suggested. "What kind do you want?"

"A great big one." Chip measured as high as he could reach. "Most a hundred feet high."

"Won't that be too big?"

"Well, it'll have to be as tall as my daddy."

"What about that one?" she asked, pointing to a fir that stood at the corner of a small white house. "We could come back at midnight and cut it down."

Chip stopped and eyed it critically. "Where would we put it?" he asked seriously.

"Maybe it's too big. We'd probably have to move the piano to get it in the living-room."

"I want a big one," Chip asserted stubbornly.

"I tell you what, we'll get Daddy to take us out in the country Sunday and find just the tree we want. We'll put a tag with your name on it and the Sunday before Christmas we'll go back and get it."

"Is Sunday tomorrow?"

"No," Ann laughed. "What will you put on it for Mommy?"

Chip thought for a long minute. "I think   get her a hat," he said at last.

"A hat! Why?"

"She cried today."

"But why a hat?"

"Because it was funny," Chip explained. "She took it out and cried."

"What was wrong with it?"

"It was funny," Chip explained vaguely.

Something wrong with a hat; so that was why she borrowed mine, Ann thought. Chip's interests were already running in another channel and he fired questions at Ann, who answered them absently. Some of the pleasure of making their plans for Christmas was gone.

A car drew up to the curb and Hugh rolled down the window and called to them.

"Get in," he invited, "and I'll drive you back to the Circle."

"Is it over?" Ann asked, surprised at seeing him alone.

"Yes," he said tersely and then, as though he realized he had sounded rude, he added, "Lou sent me to town for some aspirin tablets. She had a terrible headache. Come on and get in."

Ann hesitated. There was really no reason for not riding with Hugh, but she knew it might complicate matters. Lou was the possessive type and, though there had never been any love lost between them, Ann had no desire to make things more unpleasant for Jean.

"All right," she said, and helped Chip into the front seat with them.

He immediately crawled into her lap so that he would be elevated enough to see out of the window. *Well,* thought Ann, *no chance for Hugh to make a pass at me with Chip squirming all over the seat.*

"I never see you alone, Ann," Hugh said as he put the car into gear. "Have you been avoiding me?"

"Of course not," she denied quickly. "Why should I?"

"You know why."

"That was five years ago."

"Sometimes I've thought I was an awful fool," he muttered.

"Oh, Hugh," Ann said with a shake of her head, "don't make it more difficult than it is."

"All right, if that's the way you want it."

Ann glanced at his handsome profile through her lashes. She wasn't at all sure she was still in love with him, but he still had the power to make her blood race madly and she had the queer sensation that butterflies were playing tag on her heart. Maybe women always feel that way about their first loves, clinging to them, feeding the last embers of a fire that has long been dead.

Chip lunged forward then and Ann caught him to keep him from falling. "There's Aunt Lou," he shouted, fumbling with the knob to roll down the window. "Aunt Lou! Aunt Lou!" he called.

He was right. Lou stood on the front walk leading to her home. She was coatless and the black dress she wore was unbecoming and made her skin look pasty. Hugh was driving slowly and Ann could plainly see the concentrated fury on Lou's face. The wind had whipped the curl out of her hair and it hung limply about her face. As Chip called, she turned suddenly and walked into her house.

"Put us out here, Hugh," Ann said. "We'd better walk on home."

"All right," he said through tight lips. "Maybe it would be better."

"Thanks for picking us up. No, Chip, we're not going in here. We have to hurry home." She caught his arm and dragged him along with her.

Poor Hugh. The last five years couldn't have been easy for him either. For the hundredth time Ann wondered why he had married Lou, why he had done it so suddenly and without warning. In the old days Lou had never quite been one of their exclusive little clique. She had been older, though so had Hugh, but somehow she had never seemed to belong. She had been too anxious, too ingratiating, and it had been a shock when she married Hugh. Ann's lips twisted bitterly at the memory.

"That's Daddy's car," Chip shouted, and broke away from her.

Before she could stop him he was up the walk and on the porch of his grandmother's house. Ann followed him more slowly. It was Bill's car, parked there at the curb, so probably he and Jean had stopped here before they went home.

The white flowers had been removed from the door, Ann noticed as she rattled the shining brass knocker.

There were hurried footsteps and Amelia opened the door for them.

"Hello, darling," she said to Chip. "Come on inside out of the cold."

The warm air of the hall swept toward them as Amelia closed the door. She was smiling and somehow looked more alive than Ann had ever seen her. She had always been just in the background, a quiet, efficient, and unpaid housekeeper. Now her eyes were shining and her cheeks were flushed with excitement. Ann looked at her critically, as though seeing her for the first time, and decided that, dressed differently, Amelia might actually be pretty.

"Oh, Ann, have you heard?" she asked in a soft rush of words.

"Heard what?"

"He really appreciated all I did for him," Amelia whispered. "All these years he must have known. He never said anything, but he remembered."

"Remembered what?"

"Remembered all the things I've done," Amelia explained patiently. "Didn't you know? But of course not. You weren't here this morning when Mr. Holmes told me. William's left me some money. It's all my own and I can do what I please. Mr. Holmes said it was in the will."

"Didn't you know?" Ann asked.

"Well—I wasn't sure," Amelia said vaguely. "Chip, honey, somebody sent some cookies. They're in the kitchen. Do you want one?"

"Yes'um." Chip had a healthy appetite and never turned down an opportunity to eat.

"Where are the others?" Ann asked as Amelia took the child's hand to lead him to the back of the house.

"Oh, they're in the library," Amelia answered. "Go on in there, dear."

Ann opened the double wooden doors quietly. As she entered she heard Bill say, "I can't do that, Mother. Jean is my wife—for better or for worse."

He was standing with his back to the big open fire, his hands thrust deeply into the pockets of his coat. His face was drawn with strain and a frown wrinkled his forehead. Mrs. Tolliver sat in the wing chair a few feet from him, her hand resting on the head of the black cane. A lamp on the table beside her shed a soft radiance over her, touching the silvery white hair. Behind them were shelves of handsomely bound books that gave the room its name, though they showed no evidence of having been read.

"It certainly is for the worst," Mrs. Tolliver replied. "For your own protection, and for your son's, something must be done. If you are too weak to take the necessary steps I will."

"What steps, Mrs. Tolliver?" Ann asked, advancing to the center of the room.

If Helen Tolliver was startled by Ann's sudden entrance she covered it nicely. Her cold blue eyes rested on Ann's flushed face briefly before she said, "Sit down, Ann." She pointed with the stick to the chair across the fireplace from hers.

The thick pile of the rug muffled the girl's footsteps and she untied the kerchief under her chin and pushed back her coat before she sat down in the chair. Her tawny eyes glittered dangerously as they met Mrs. Tolliver's, as though she sensed the animosity in the older woman.

Bill turned his back to them and, resting his arms on the mantel, stared intently into the fire, where bright orange and blue flames curled about the logs. He took the brass poker and jabbed at the fire so that the log snapped and sent a myriad of sparks up the chimney. Ann's lips tightened as she realized he was making no effort to defend his wife.

"What is it?" she asked.

"There is no reason why you shouldn't know," Helen Tolliver said coldly. "Bill has a mistaken idea of chivalry. Something should have been done long ago."

"What should have been done?"

"I've just told him that the necessary steps *must* be taken to protect all of us from your adopted sister—"

"My sister," Ann corrected.

"Your adopted sister," Mrs. Tolliver repeated.

"Ann." Bill turned and interrupted their conversation. "Do you know anything about Jean's parents? Weren't there any papers? Didn't your father know something about her?" His voice had a desperate note and his eyes burned feverishly.

Ann turned hard eyes on him and he seemed to flinch under the contempt she made no effort to hide. "No, why should he?" she said quietly. "My mother and father adopted her. They gave her my mother's name. Isn't that enough? She *is* my sister."

"We have every reason to believe she's insane."

Ann gasped at Mrs. Tolliver's words. Never in her wildest imagining would she have thought she would sit in a chair and hear her sister called—insane. The room seemed to rock and the furniture was out of focus.

"You're crazy yourself," she said in a choked voice.

Mrs. Tolliver smiled frostily. "That is just what I would have expected you to say."

"You're damn right! Do you think I'm going to sit here and have you malign my sister and do nothing about it? Is that what you were saying to Bill?" Ann's voice shook with anger and she turned bright eyes on her brother-in-law. "And you stand there and let her say those things about Jean!" she spat at him contemptuously. "No wonder she was frightened. She had every right to be. It was time I came home."

"Your manners haven't improved a bit," Mrs. Tolliver interposed harshly. "You were always a little unconventional, even as a child. A little too impulsive. I suppose now you call it temperament." The thin lips curled.

Ann stood up and the kerchief dropped from her lap to the floor. The light on the big red flowers made them look like bright bloodstains on the dark rug. Her cheeks were blazing and her throat was burning with every breath she drew. She could not remember ever being quite so angry before. It was only with a great effort at self-control that she did not snatch that walking stick and break it over the smart coiffure of the woman who still sat calmly in the chair.

"So," she said with a dangerous softness to her words. "So Jean had good reason to write me that she was afraid. She could expect no help from her own husband." Pausing a moment, she turned on him. Bill met her eyes and then dropped his head. Ann turned back to his mother. "And you are trying to railroad her into an asylum. For that's what I suppose you mean by 'the necessary steps,' isn't it? You were always slightly drunk with the power of your money and position. Your children have nearly always done what you wanted. What has stopped you this time? Was it Mr. Tolliver? Or was it Bill?"

"You are being very foolish," Mrs. Tolliver snapped. "Your adopted sister has been acting strangely for the past three years, ever since the baby was born." She shrugged her black silk shoulders. "We know nothing of her inherited tendencies. I wanted Bill to investigate them, for the sake of his son. We have the right to know what sort of undesirable characteristics we must combat in him."

"Jean is my sister."

"Only an adopted sister." Mrs. Tolliver permitted a cold smile to play over her lips. "What do you know of her? Nothing."

"Aren't you a little late thinking about that? She married your son five years ago."

"It's only lately that Jean's been acting like this."

Bill's face was tortured, but Ann felt no pity for him.

"So she's convinced you too," she said slowly. "One of the last things you said to me before I left was that you would take care of Jean. You said, 'I'll love her and protect her always, Ann. Always.' Do you remember?"

"Oh, God!" Bill buried his face in his hands and turned away from her.

"Your defense is probably commendable from your point of view, Ann," Mrs. Tolliver said. "Unfortunately there are so many small evidences to prove that I am right."

"Evidences?" Ann stood rigid.

"There were only small things at first," Mrs. Tolliver went on inexorably. "Objects moved and hidden, then mutilation of clothes." She stopped and eyed Ann narrowly. "Ah, so you have noticed things since you've been here. Then there was the poisoning of the dog."

"Poisoning of the dog?"

"Bill kept his hunting dogs in his back yard until three years ago. When Chip was born Jean suggested that he get rid of them. Of course there was no reason. She just disliked them.

Then one afternoon Bill was detained in town and telephoned her to feed them. The next morning one of the dogs was dead."

She paused, but Ann was frozen in horrified amazement.

"There was my accident too. Jean put one of the baby's toys on the stairs when she knew I was coming down." She tapped the stick at her side. "I will never be able to walk without this again."

"She doesn't remember anything about these things," Bill muttered.

Mrs. Tolliver turned to her son, pity written on her narrow face. "Naturally not," she said. "It is a clear case of mental derangement."

"You're crazy yourself," Ann retorted.

Mrs. Tolliver ignored this. "There is also her sudden and inexplicable adherence to the Roman Catholic Church. I know," she went on when Ann would have interrupted. "Your parents never gave either of you the proper religious training, but after her marriage Jean came into our church and for the first year or two she took an active part in it. Now she sneaks out and goes to mass and probably to confession too."

Ann was breathing hard. She laughed harshly and said, "That at least I can explain. Jean is a very good musician, or she was until she married. Not great, but good. Perhaps you've forgotten, or more likely you never knew, that some of the world's greatest music has been written for the Roman Church. When we were in school in Paris we went fairly regularly to mass. You might gain a little culture if you were more tolerant."

Mrs. Tolliver bit her lip and the fingers tightened about the stick. "Perhaps you would like to see this. It is by no means the first. We have all had them at various times. And goodness knows who else gets them. Sometimes they come by mail and sometimes we just find them."

She took up a folded sheet of paper from the table beside her chair and handed it to Ann.

The stillness in the room was so complete that a dropped pin would have sounded like the firing of a cannon. Slowly Ann unfolded the paper. Her eyes were on Mrs. Tolliver as though she expected some trick. On the whiteness of the paper were the black letters, the characteristic half printing, half writing, that Jean used.

> *Ask your sister why she always got up to fix your husband's breakfast. Ask her if she put anything in his coffee that last morning. She's free of you at last.*

The black ink seemed to leap at her and Ann read it through twice, the words swimming together in a blur. Slowly she refolded the paper and deliberately tore it into shreds, letting the scraps drop from her fingers.

"There are others," Mrs. Tolliver said with a sly smile. "This is by no means the first. They have all been malicious. Quite evidently the work of an unbalanced brain."

Ann was trembling now with anger but her voice was calm and icy when she spoke. "I was raised in a scientific family, Mrs. Tolliver," she said. "I was taught not to believe anything until it was proved, until there was absolute and undeniable proof in my hands. You implied, a few minutes ago, that my home training was incomplete. I had some advantages, you know. You may find that they weigh rather heavily in my favor. So far as I can see, this may well be a forgery. Anybody with a normal amount of intelligence could imitate Jean's writing. What is there in this scrap of paper to make me believe somebody else didn't write it? I could have done it. So could you."

Mrs. Tolliver reddened angrily and for the first time that afternoon the composure slipped from her face.

"The only proof that I would accept would be to see Jean with a pen in her hand, writing such a note," Ann continued.

She turned and walked to the door and with her hand on the knob turned and said with deadly intensity, "You have two to fight now, Mrs. Tolliver. And I promise you it will not be easy."

There was a gurgling sound in Helen Tolliver's throat and she half raised herself in the chair. "You impudent hussy!" she shouted shrilly.

Ann slammed the door so hard that the wall shook with the impact.

6

COLD FINGERS OF FEAR

She collided with Amelia in the hall and then, almost as though she were pursued by the furies, she ran from the house. Down the steps and across the lawn she ran. The sun was gone and the brief twilight of a winter evening was already fading. There were lights in the houses but she did not notice them; her only conscious thought was to get away—as far away as possible.

She was scarcely aware of her sister's house when she passed it. Her mood was not one in which she could face Jean. Ann was well aware of her own faults: she was most apt to say and do things on the spur of the moment and think them over later. Her temper was intense and triggerlike and she knew that it was best that she be alone, otherwise there might be an explosion that would bring dire consequences to them all.

She was breathing in short gasps before she slowed her pace at the end of the loop. The wind had ruffled her hair and she could feel the cold of the tears on her cheeks. Automatically she glanced up and down College Street before she darted across it. She turned left and walked briskly, not going anywhere, just getting away from the horrible word that kept ringing in her ears.

Insane—Insane—Insane—

She couldn't think clearly. Everything was muddled and confused in her brain. And that word—*insane—insane*—kept hammering in her ears like the steady beat of a drum.

"I hate them, I hate them all," she muttered aloud.

She knew she must think, think of some way to get Jean away from them—and Chip too. They were all mad. Mrs. Tolliver was a monster and a devil, and Bill— Ann was appalled by his ineptness, his weak defense of his wife. Surely Bill knew Jean was sane. He should have protected her.

Ann brushed her hands across her eyes and pushed back the hair from her forehead. Her mouth was set in a grim straight line and there was a stubborn look on her face that people closest to her had learned to avoid if possible. The touch of her cold fingers brought her back to the present and she came to an abrupt stop.

She had reached the university. The long brick buildings were dark and deserted and the street lights reflected on the black and lifeless windowpanes. She recognized them immediately; they were Grant Hall for chemistry, Bibb Hall for physics, the Tuomey Museum of Natural Science. This had been her father's domain and Ann knew it well. And back of Grant Hall, down a narrow alley, which they used to call "Pasteur Lane," was home.

Ann threw up her head and walked forward with new purpose in her steps. That little house back of this dark building was no longer home, but it was a sanctuary. When Dr. Bartley died, the two girls had moved to their sorority house until Jean could be married, the following June, and the house had been turned over to their friend, Dr. Hans. Somehow it made their loss easier, knowing he was there, and knowing too that the door would always be open whenever they wanted to return. Ann had left him her share of the furniture, writing him from Chicago to keep it for her.

She looked up at the house at the light shining from the front windows. A man emerged from the shadows at the side of it but she did not see him. He walked quickly toward her and then stopped, watching her as she ran up the graveled walk.

Sheriff Davies started to follow her but, seeming to think better of it, turned around and went to his car parked at the end of the alley.

Ann raised her hand to knock on the door but before her knuckles could touch the wood it was opened.

"Why, Ann," Dr. Hans said. "Come in. You don't know what a real pleasure this is." He must have seen the tears which were again streaming down her cheeks, for he put his arm about her shoulders and drew her toward the small fire at the end of the room.

"Let me have your coat," he said. "You're nearly frozen. Sit down here by the fire until you get good and warm." Feeling in three pockets, he finally found a handkerchief, which he gave her as he bent to add more coal to the fire.

Ann blew her nose and buried her face in her arms and cried so that her whole body was shaken by her gasps for breath. Dr. Hans sat down beside her. Not knowing exactly what to do, he merely waited.

"This isn't like my Ann," he said gently.

Raising her drenched face, she said, "You don't know. They want to take her away. They were saying such horrible things—"

"You're too upset to do any talking now," he said, getting to his feet. "I'll bring you something and then you can tell me all about it."

He went out, closing the door quietly. Ann mopped her face and looked about her. It was all so familiar. The room was a little shabbier than it had been the last time she was in it and more than a little dusty. There were books and papers everywhere, spilling over the big table under the windows and piled on the floor and chairs. The mantel was crowded with photographs and she recognized one of her father, smiling and holding aloft a tankard of beer. It must have been taken long ago in his student days. And there was the small painted chest, one of the few things Dr. Hans had been allowed to bring away with him from Germany. It was not a beautiful room, but it was warm and friendly and comforting.

Dr. Hans came back in a few minutes, bringing with him a bottle of wine and two glasses. He poured the rich red liquid into the tumblers and set the bottle on the floor.

"Drink this; it will do you good. It is not much," he added with a smile.

Ann drank and could feel her blood grow warm. Some color came back to her white face and that lost feeling that had been wrapped around her heart was melting. For the first time since she had been back Ann felt really at home. All the while Dr. Hans sat there, patting her hand and beaming like a benevolent Billiken.

"Don't talk unless you want to," he said.

"I'm sorry I made such a fool of myself."

"We all do that. We would not be human if we were wise all the time."

Ann got up and put her empty glass on the mantelpiece. She picked up the picture of her father and looked at it a long time before she replaced it and turned to the man seated on the sagging sofa. "You were his friend," she said quietly. "Maybe you can help me."

"Don't tell me anything you don't want to." Dr. Hans took off his glasses and polished the lenses. Without them his pale eyes looked vague and troubled.

"I have to," Ann declared. "I have to talk to somebody. It's about us—about Jean." She fumbled for the right words, then plunged into the story, the words coming like a seething torrent.

He listened without interrupting as she gave him the details. His moonish face became somewhat flushed and the furrows on his forehead deepened. As she talked Ann paced up and down the room. There was a package of cigarettes on the edge of the table and she took one, lighting it without interrupting the flow of her story.

"And now they're trying to shut her up somewhere," she concluded, tapping her foot impatiently on the floor. "Well, they'll never do it. There would have to be papers to sign and I'll never put my name on them."

"Sit down, Ann. I do not know what to advise you to do. I had not realized that Jean was an adopted child."

"She's the same as my own sister—"

"Tell me what you know."

"Oh, it wasn't a secret. They adopted her because they had given up hopes of having any children of their own. They were in California then but they moved to Illinois and I popped up. I was three when Pops got the professorship here."

"Your father never had any adoption papers?"

Ann shrugged. "Not that I know of. People weren't so particular in those days. He and Mother were satisfied and that seemed to be enough." She threw her cigarette into the fire. "I can't understand Bill," she said petulantly. "He knew Jean when he married her and I'm sure he loved her. They were so right together. I can understand that old harridan stirring up trouble because she never liked any of us. But Bill—" She threw out her hand in a helpless gesture.

"Then she must be mistaken."

"Of course she is," Ann interrupted quickly. "That means that somebody else is doing all these mean little things. Just take that note, for example—" She broke off and looked at him in surprise. "You've had one of them too?"

Dr. Hans nodded his head slowly. "Yes, but I never thought anything of it. It did not seem like Jean."

Ann's eyes narrowed. Somehow she knew he was lying. He *did* think Jean had written them. The tenuous silence in the room was broken suddenly as a coal sputtered in the grate. Ann drew in her breath in a despairing little sound. Whatever she did now she knew she must do alone. There were kindness and pity and sorrow written on the doctor's face, but experience had taught him a fatalistic acceptance of facts. With a heavy heart Ann picked up her coat.

"Don't go feeling like that," Dr. Hans urged. "I will do whatever I can."

"It's all right," she said dully. "I'll do whatever has to be done. Even if it means killing somebody with my bare hands."

There was suppressed fury in her voice and her hands clenched and unclenched. Dr. Hans might have said something else, but the sound of a door banging and then quick footsteps in the hall accompanied by an off-key whistle made him hesitate until it was too late. Paul opened the door and came in, his face alight with excitement. He broke off his whistling when he saw Ann.

"Hello, Ann," he said. "I didn't know you were here. Why didn't you call me? And, Dr. Hans, did you know Cousin William left us something to go on with our experiments? Money with no strings attached. Now we can get that apparatus we wanted. It's a godsend, coming at this time. Did you know about it?"

"Yes. Yes, I knew."

"It's funny he didn't tell me," Paul said. "The sheriff was here a while ago and he told me about it."

"The sheriff?" Dr. Hans looked up in surprise.

"He came out to the lab to talk to me. Didn't he come up here too?" He broke off and turned to Ann. "You aren't going, are you? I didn't know you were here or I'd have been right in. Why on earth didn't you call me?"

"I have to go now," Ann said. "I only dropped in for a few minutes."

"It's black night outside," Paul protested. "Why don't you stay and have supper with us? I'm fairly certain Adeline left us something in the refrigerator."

"I have to get back to Jean."

"Then I'll get the car and drive you back."

"You needn't go to that trouble."

"It's no trouble at all, and I can't let you go wandering around alone in the night."

He took a coat from the old-fashioned hatrack by the front door and pulled it on.

"Paul, what did the sheriff want?" Dr. Hans asked suddenly.

There was a moment's hesitation before the younger man replied. "Oh, nothing much. He just came by to talk to me. I'll tell you about it when I get back."

He took Ann's arm and, slamming, the door behind them, helped her down the steps. In the graveled driveway beside the house was an old and dilapidated-looking Chevrolet. Paul opened the door and ushered her into it with a grand air. A moment later he slid in beside her. The engine did not respond immediately to the pressure of his foot on the accelerator and had to be coaxed.

"Beautiful is faithful but not very prompt," he said, his hand on the choke.

"Beautiful?"

Paul laughed. "That's Dr. Steigler's name for her. He says if you name a horse, why not a car?"

"Why not indeed?"

The car rather reminded Ann of an old, dumb beast of burden that might be oiled and greased only when it refused to go another step.

Paul went on talking excitedly, describing the new additions to the small laboratory in the garage which the sudden gift would make possible. There was always so much to do and so little time and money with which to achieve the miracles of modern science.

That makes two of them, Ann thought. *Amelia and Paul. They're only excited about what's happening to them.*

Cold fingers of fear began to claw at her heart again and she stopped even the monosyllabic replies with which she had punctuated his recital. But he gave no sign of noticing her abstraction. He drew up to the curb and went up the short walk with her.

"Are you sure you want to go home?" he asked anxiously. "There's no light in the house, so Jean and Bill probably aren't there."

"Yes, I'm quite sure."

"They might be with Cousin Helen. Would you rather I take you there?"

Ann could not repress a shudder. Paul was looking down at her queerly. "No, no—no!"

"Look here, Ann." He pulled her roughly to him and his lips came down on hers, warm and hard.

For a moment she clung to him, finding a calming security in the strength of his arms. In that moment fear and loneliness left her and, instinctively, she responded. Then, with a hand on his shoulder, she pushed herself away from him.

"I've been wanting to do that ever since you stepped off the train," he said.

"No, no—good night." She opened the door and went inside, closing it and leaning against its smooth wooden panels. She had the feeling that he stood there on the other side, a little puzzled, then she heard the sound of his footsteps on the walk, accompanied by his tuneless whistle.

She groped her way in the dark until she found the lamp on the long narrow table near the door. Its small glow did little to disperse the gloom, so, slipping off her coat, she advanced into the living-room, turning on other lights. She almost stumbled over Jean, who was seated on the blue velvet sofa.

"I didn't see you!" Ann exclaimed. "Why on earth are you sitting here in the dark—!"

Jean made no reply. Her blue eyes looked up at her sister but there was no indication that she really saw her. Ann was alarmed by the blank expression on Jean's face. She threw down her coat and shook her sister.

"Jean! What's the matter?"

Jean dropped her eyes when Ann spoke and when she answered her voice sounded dead. "What did you say to her, Ann? What did you do?"

"What did I say to who?" Ann demanded ungrammatically.

"To Mother Tolliver."

Ann's face hardened. "What's that got to do with it?"

"They telephoned and said she was sick—maybe a stroke, Bill's staying with her." The words were spoken in a dull monotone.

Ann sat down on the sofa and put her arms about her sister. Jean did not pull away, but neither did she respond. Her face was swollen as though she had been crying, but her eyes were dry.

"Don't, baby," Ann said. "I had to say what I did to her. You know she—you know she and I never got along together."

"Ann, I think I must be losing my mind."

Ann's arms tightened about Jean and she bit her lip in alarm.

"You see," Jean went on, "I really don't know who I am."

"Stop saying that! You're as sane as I am. Look here, Jean, Pops and Mother adopted you. We all know that. They *chose* you. Don't you see? They had to take pot luck as far as I was concerned, but they could choose you."

Jean smiled wearily. "That doesn't change things," she whispered. "I do things and then don't remember doing them afterwards."

"What things?"

"I—I move things. I put them down in one place and then find them in another—or I don't find them at all. I break things—that perfume bottle you gave me."

"What about it?"

"I broke it. It was in the middle of the rug in my room. Ann, it had been deliberately smashed, and I loved it. I—I sent the rug to the cleaner's and didn't even tell Bill about it."

"And you don't remember breaking it?"

"No. I couldn't have been in my right mind, could I?" Jean raised desperate eyes to Ann. "I'm so afraid—"

"So you wrote me that letter?"

"Yes."

"You remember doing that?"

"Yes, of course I remember it."

Ann got up, took a cigarette from the box on the coffee table, and lit it. She looked down at her sister and said, "See here, Jean, you wouldn't remember some things and not others. Not if you were crazy. And everybody moves things and then forgets where they've been put."

"I get worse all the time." Jean shook her head, unbelieving. "At first it was just little things, then they got more and more important."

"Tell me what you remember doing."

"I remember putting the toy on the steps," Jean said. "It really was an accident, Ann. I didn't mean to hurt Mother Tolliver. I wouldn't have left it there if I'd known she was coming down the steps. But the telephone rang and I started to answer it but there was somebody at the front door too, so I put the toy on the steps and went to the door. I was answering the telephone when Mother Tolliver came downstairs and fell over it. It wasn't intentional. I didn't mean it like she said—" Jean's voice was rising hysterically,

Ann crushed her cigarette in a tray. Beside her she could feel Jean trembling. It was just nerves, for there were no tears. Ann was thinking furiously. If this went on much longer they would drive Jean crazy. Not for a moment would she accept the fact that there was anything really wrong. She waited and presently Jean grew quieter.

"They say I poisoned Bill's dog too. But I couldn't have done it. I didn't want dogs around the house with a small baby, but I wouldn't have poisoned Queenie. She was Bill's, and I couldn't do anything to hurt him, I just couldn't!" She paused and then added fiercely, "Why, if I did that, I'd be dangerous!"

"Just what did you do, Jean?"

"I don't know. I thought I opened a can of dog food, heated it, and took it out to them. But the next morning Queenie was dead. She'd been poisoned."

"You didn't do it," Ann said with all the conviction she could muster. "It could have happened any time during the night. Were there other dogs?" Jean nodded. "Well, isn't it strange that only one of them died?"

Jean's eyes widened and for the first time there was a look of hope in them. "Yes, of course. I hadn't thought—" Then she shook her head and a note of despair crept back into her voice. "The notes—I must have—"

"You know about them?" Ann was distinctly surprised.

"Yes. I found a half-finished one in my desk. It was horrible—I must have written it. It was in my handwriting."

Ann was cold with anxiety. Jean actually believed all this terrible farce. Her mind had been filled with lies. She got up and went to her room, returning a minute later with a block of drawing paper and a pencil. She sat down and printed a note.

"See?" she said, thrusting the paper at Jean. "Your style is very distinctive but it's easily imitated. A little practice and I could make a perfect copy." She printed a few words and there was an impressive similarity between what she had done and Jean's writing. "It's not even hard."

"But you're an artist. You've been trained to draw and print."

"It wouldn't take much skill," Ann said, becoming absorbed in what she was doing. "If I had a sample of your writing in front of me I could do a very good job of this. As it is, this would pass as yours if it weren't questioned." She held the block at arm's length and surveyed it critically. "Who else can draw?"

"Nobody, except you."

"Hum," Ann said thoughtfully. "Well, it wouldn't necessarily take an artist to do it."

"What are you trying to say, Ann?"

"If you didn't write those notes, then somebody else did," Ann explained patiently. "I take it they're another of the things you don't remember doing? I thought not. Who could do it then? It's got to be somebody who knows you rather well and somebody who's in and out of this house fairly often. Who is it?"

Jean shook her head.

"I think we can rule out the servants," Ann went on ruminatingly. "I don't think either Martha or Lily has the necessary intelligence."

"Oh, no," Jean said quickly. "Anyway, they haven't been with me long enough."

"Then there's Mr. and Mrs. Tolliver—I suppose it couldn't have been him—and Amelia, and Lou or Hugh, and Dr. Hans, and Bill—"

"Not Bill!"

"Who else comes over here a lot?"

"There's Mary Temple. She lives next door. And Connie and George Evans."

Ann made a list of all the possibilities. "Not very probable," she said, looking over the names, "but I'll see what I can make of it. What about Paul? No, I suppose he hasn't been here long enough to qualify either."

"Oh, no, none of them."

"It's screwy. I can't see a reason why anybody should write notes and go around breaking things in this house or poisoning the dog. It doesn't make sense."

"Maybe I am doing it."

"Stop it! You never could have done a single one of those things. And whoever is doing them isn't crazy either. There's some reason. There has to be." She rubbed a hand over her forehead as though to clear her thoughts. "But for the life of me I can't see it." She got up and put the block of paper and the pencil on the piano. "Where's Chip?" she asked suddenly.

"Chip? He's at Lou's."

"Why?"

"Lou telephoned me about—she said you had left Chip there and that she was taking him home with her."

"He's your child, isn't he?"

Jean threw out her hand appealingly. "Can't you forget that, Ann? Hugh isn't worth it. Don't you see that if he'd been worth loving he wouldn't have done—what he did?"

"I'm not thinking about Hugh," Ann retorted angrily. "I'm thinking that they're trying to take Chip away from you."

"Oh." Jean's voice was very small. "Ann, promise me. If something happens to me you'll look after Chip, won't you? Promise me that you will." She was crying now and there was desperation in her voice.

"Get your coat, baby. We're going to get Chip and bring him home—now."

7

THE BLOODSTAINED FEATHER

The next three days were uneventful—or practically so. After that first night Bill came home, though he was aloof and slightly cool toward Ann. She avoided him when she could.

As a matter of fact, Mrs. Tolliver was not very ill. The doctor diagnosed shock but Ann was of the private opinion that it was merely temper. A trained nurse stayed for the first day or two and after that it was decided that Amelia was capable of waiting on her sister. She had done it for years and was much more easily bullied. Helen Tolliver kept to her bed and Bill and Hugh spent hours with her, explaining the business and making reports, for William Tolliver had left everything, with the exception of small bequests, to his wife. A codicil in his handwriting divided his vast lumber interests between his two children at his wife's death, but until then she had full direction. At once she had declared her intention of taking over the management of the business.

Nothing happened: they ate and slept and went out into the cold December sunshine. But they didn't talk; they avoided each other with a watchful wariness that was unnerving. That was it; it was quiet, too quiet, so that there was a false normalcy to those days. Everybody was trying to ignore the tension but it was there so strongly that you could almost touch it Afterward Ann thought of it as that great silence that precedes a tornado, a time when you expect the destructive winds but can only wait, doing nothing.

It was Sheriff Davies who first stirred those quiescent winds. That was on Tuesday afternoon, a week after Mr. Tolliver's death. Ann was alone, writing to Beth. She had sat for a long time, chewing the end of her fountain pen, not knowing what to say. She was even glad when the telephone rang, interrupting her.

She got up quickly and went into the back hall to answer it. Ann wasn't given to any extraordinary sense of premonition so she lifted the phone from its cradle without any feeling of nervousness.

"Miss Bartley?" a voice asked. "This is Bill Davies. I'd like to talk to you—alone, if I may. Is there somewhere we could meet?"

"I—I— You can come here," Ann said, surprised by his directness. "There's nobody here now but me. You may come here if you like."

"Thank you. I'll be there in a few minutes."

The metallic click told her he had hung up the receiver. Wondering at the reason for his call, she put the telephone back on the rack and went back to the living-room. She picked up her writing materials and carried them to her room, stopping long enough to examine the perfection of her make-up and to add a touch of perfume to her arched eyebrows.

It must be that license, she thought. *He's remembered that he never did see it and now he's decided to check up on me. Where did I put it? I haven't thought of it again, so it must still be in the car and Jean has that.*

She stopped to rearrange the bronze chrysanthemums in the tall vase on the table in the entrance. They had come close on the heels of Dick Martin's regular weekend proposal, this time from Jacksonville. The dried-up spinster who kept the florist shop had reason to bless him during those first weeks in December, for Dick believed in flowery reminders.

He's sweet, thought Ann, and instantly forgot him as she saw the muddy coupé drive up to the front of the house, and watched the sheriff's long legs slide swiftly to the curb without touching the running-board.

"Thanks for letting me come," he said as she opened the door.

"Not at all. Come in," she invited.

He wasn't ill at ease, but his long legs and big, wind-rough-ened hands looked ungainly and awkward as he took the chair she indicated. He dropped his hat on the floor beside him and looked at her. The blue eyes under shaggy brows were shrewd-er than she remembered and she picked up the cigarette box and offered it to him.

"I'd rather smoke my pipe, if you don't mind," he said, draw-ing a yellow corncob from his coat pocket.

But he didn't smoke after all. He just sat there, weighing the pipe in his hand.

"Maybe I'm making a mistake in coming to you," he said at last. "It's none of my business when you come down to cold facts."

"What facts?"

"If I wasn't so sure I was right," he muttered. "See here, didn't you think there was something funny about that acci-dent?"

"Funny? No."

"You didn't think it was queer that he died that morning?"

"No."

Sheriff Davies scratched his ear. "You're about the only one I know to talk to," he said. "The others either tune up and cry or else they don't know anything." He glanced up at her shrewdly for a moment, then put his hand in the inside pocket of his coat and drew out a dirty envelope. He shook its con-tents into his hand and extended it to her, palm upward. "What do you think of that?" he demanded.

"Why—why, it's a feather."

"It means Mr. Tolliver was murdered."

"Murdered!"

Her yellow eyes widened incredulously and for the first time she was really afraid. She had been angry and bewil-dered—but not afraid.

He hitched himself forward in the chair. "Yes'm, I think it's murder. We get huntin' accidents every year, but that wasn't an accident. If I hadn't been there—well, you look at that feather. It's got blood on it."

"But we were hunting," Ann protested.

"Not Mr. Tolliver." Sheriff Davies shook his head. "His gun hadn't been fired and he didn't have a single bird in his bag. Nobody shot any birds under that particular tree and nobody, except Dr. Steigler, claims to have been near it after you all got there. I've been asking questions," he finished.

Ann drew her brows in concentration until there was a deep perpendicular line between her eyes. She remembered how the sheriff had made such a point of looking at all the guns that morning. And he had been the one to dress the birds later when they came home. He had been persistent, and he had gone away with Paul. She had meant to ask about that but had forgotten it. "You're—you're accusing one of us?"

"Folks don't usually get murdered by strangers," he said dryly.

"But—but that feather can't mean anything," she insisted. "He was with us for two or three hours. He might have picked up one of the birds and the feather got caught on his clothes. He could have given the bird to Bill or Hugh or Paul. The feather can't mean anything!"

"Do you remember him handling any of the birds? I guess what you say is possible," he said slowly and Ann drew a sigh of relief. "But," he added immediately, smashing her momentary sense of safety, "but there's other things too. That log, for instance. It hadn't just fallen off that tree. It had been lying there on the ground for quite a while—and not just where we found it. It didn't fall off the tree and hit him and he didn't stumble on anything and fall on it. There wasn't anything there to trip him. Besides, Major Forrest says he didn't have a stroke. There wasn't an autopsy—"

"It's absurd, what you're suggesting," Ann broke in.

"It's not absurd. A man is dead."

"It was an accident."

He shook his white head. "Bloody feathers don't drop out of the sky. Logs don't move themselves. When things lie on the ground a long time they get little white roots stuck to the underside and worms. And that log—well, it certainly had been moved."

"But one of us," Ann whispered, wondering how her hands could be so cold when the room was so hot. She knew what he meant and the implication was terrifying. They were people she hadn't seen for a long time, but they were people she knew.

As though he read her mind he said, "You've been away for a long time but you know these people. Of course I may be wrong," he added, but his expression showed that he didn't think he was. "Suppose you tell me something about Dr. Steigler."

"Dr. Hans?"

"He's a German," the sheriff said seriously.

"Of course he's a German. What's that got to do with it?"

"I never met many Germans in my life," was the laconic reply, "but I'm interested in them. A lot of boys have been killed fighting them in Europe."

"Dr. Steigler is an eminent scientist," she replied stiffly. "He has an international reputation and the university is most fortunate in having him here."

"If I wanted to send somebody over to undermine Germany I'd pick somebody that had a good reputation. And I'd send him over a long time before I needed the information."

"Dr. Hans isn't a Nazi. He left Germany because of them and my father persuaded him to come here. Pops had a sabbatical in 1935 and he took Jean and me to Europe with him. Mother was dead and he wanted to do some work at his old university. He and Dr. Hans had known each other for years and when we went to Leipzig we got a house close to where Dr. Hans lived. It was a wonderful summer. We took trips to the mountains and once we took the steamer down the Rhine, Dr. Hans and Franz, Jean and Pops and I."

There was a nostalgic tone to her words and her eyes grew dreamy as if she were seeing the dark green forests, the broad rivers and the quaint towns of a peaceful Germany.

"Franz?"

Ann jerked her thoughts back to the present with an effort. She looked at the man seated across from her. "Dr. Steigler's son," she said simply. "He was younger than I and we thought he was a nasty brat. Hitler was in power then but his ugly, perverted ideas hadn't reached the university, at least not so that we could see it. It must have been underneath all the time, though, because Franz was always goose-stepping. Anna— Anna was away at some Youth Movement camp."

"Who is Anna?"

Ann's lips curled in distaste. "She was his daughter." Unconsciously she stressed the verb. "Later she married some local Nazi official and Dr. Hans has never spoken of her since. I don't think he's heard from her since he came to America."

"So you spent that year in Germany?"

Something in his tone made Ann shake her head. "You don't understand. Germany is, or was, a beautiful country. There were clean blue skies and flowers and friendly people. Jean and I went to Paris for the winter. We were in a very strict boarding-school for girls but Pops and Dr. Hans came occasionally to see us and to take us to the interesting places. Dr. Hans used to laugh about it and say they were educating us to be women of the world. Once he lectured at the Pasteur Institute and we had dinner with him and afterward he took us to the opera. It was wonderful."

Sheriff Davies scratched his cheek and seemed to wonder why anybody would spend time and money on an opera, and why a child would enjoy it. He had never been to one himself and in his own opinion he hadn't missed anything.

"We went back to Leipzig," Ann continued, "for the Christmas holidays." She frowned at the memory of that vacation. "Everything was changed. Anna was home, for one thing, and she'd become a very regimented Nazi. I think it worried Dr. Hans. One night I did an imitation of some of Anna's friends and she was furious. It wasn't a very flattering mimicry, Mr. Davies," she added candidly.

"I didn't think it would be," he said dryly but there was a sly twinkle in his eyes and he was more relaxed.

"I think Dr. Hans must have seen the difference between his children and us. We were used to saying what we thought. Pops noticed it too and I know that before we left the next summer he tried to persuade Dr. Hans to come back with us. We were all so glad when he wrote us the next year that he was thinking it over. Pops helped get him the professorship here at the university."

"I see." The sheriff was thoughtful.

"He and Franz stayed with us and when Pops died he was wonderful to Jean and me. He gave Jean away when she married Bill. Now don't you see how ridiculous it is even to think of him as a spy?"

"It don't seem likely. What's he doing here?"

"He teaches chemistry. He and Pops were particularly interested in plastics and they did a lot of experimental work together. I don't know enough about their work to explain it to you."

"Patented their discoveries?" he asked sharply.

Ann smiled. "Of course they did. Scientists aren't nearly so gullible as people seem to think."

He appeared to mull over what she had told him. She had no way of knowing what he thought, but she was growing more alarmed. The muscles at the back of her neck ached and she flexed her long sensitive fingers to ease their tension.

"Dr. Hans's gun hadn't been fired," she said, summing up her thoughts. "You looked that morning and I heard you say so. He didn't have any birds. I don't think he even had a bag."

"How long have you known Major Forrest?" the sheriff asked, changing the subject abruptly.

He's going to take us all one by one, Ann thought. *He's probably already asked about me. That means he'll eventually get to Jean and I'll have to be careful what I say.* Aloud she said, after a brief hesitation, "He and his brother visited the Tollivers years ago. I met him then. I hadn't seen him since until I came back here."

"Then you don't know anything about him?"

"No."

But I do, her thoughts raced on. *I know the way he smiles, the steady touch of his hands, and the warmth and strength of his arms.*

"Hum," the sheriff broke into her thoughts. "He's some kin to the Tollivers?"

She nodded, forcing her eyes to meet his without wavering.

"It's likely, then, that he got Mr. Tolliver interested in those experiments he's making with the professor?"

"Mr. Tolliver was always interested. He used to talk to my father by the hour, trying to figure something that they could make out of sawdust."

"Sawdust?"

"Mr. Tolliver's business was lumber. He had sawmills and they made doors and window facings, plywood—that sort of thing."

"Pretty good business," the sheriff said thoughtfully. "Who's going to run it now?"

"His wife."

"Well, she's got her son to help her."

"Bill's going in the army the last of this month."

"That's right. Anyway, she's got the other one. He'll be around." Then, seeing the look of surprise on her face, he added, "He's got a busted knee or somethin' and they can't use him."

"Hugh?"

"I made inquiries."

Inquiries! To cover her confusion Ann got up and took another cigarette from the box. She turned her back to him to light it as the hand that held the match wasn't quite steady. She blew out the flame and placed the burned stick carefully in an ash tray before she came back to her place on the sofa.

"Don't seem like anybody profits from his death," Sheriff Davies said musingly.

"That's it," Ann put in eagerly. "He was kind and generous and—and sweet. Everybody loved him. He liked people and they liked him. If you've been asking questions you must have found out that. There isn't anybody who would—would do what you're saying."

"Somebody did," he maintained stubbornly.

"Well, if you're so determined," Ann said irritably, "Mrs. Tolliver followed us out there and hit over the head with that stick she uses. She's got all the money now. Or Lou wanted a new fur coat and he wouldn't give it to her so she drove out there and killed him."

"Or your sister, or her husband," he said acidly. "We got plenty of opportunity and not much to go on as a motive."

"Then it was an accident."

He shook his head.

"Look here, Mr. Davies. You said that log had been moved. Why couldn't somebody have stumbled over it earlier? The cars were parked under that tree and we all got out there. One of us could have accidentally moved it then. Or the dogs could have done it. They were racing around the whole place when Bill let them out of their trailer."

"Did you stumble over it?"

"No."

"See anybody else?"

"No, but that doesn't mean it couldn't have happened. You don't notice things like that."

"It could be," he answered slowly, and turned the conversation to other things.

His next questions covered everybody—Mrs. Tolliver, Amelia, Bill, Hugh, Lou, Jean, Paul. He skipped from one to the other without apparent connection. The questions seemed meaningless and for that reason Ann was on guard. Especially when they touched her sister. She evaded him when she could or answered briefly when she had to. He was quick and persistent so that she had no time to delve into his reasons for asking for so many details. He hadn't been idle for this past week, for there was so much he already knew. He must have asked many discreet questions. He knew, for instance, why Ann had left five years ago. She realized this, for his questions about Hugh and Lou were veiled.

"Now tell me what happened that morning all of you went on the hunt," he said at last. "By the way, how did it happen you were the only woman in that crowd of men?"

"Paul invited me. He came over Sunday afternoon and said it would do me good. I'd been sick. And the others thought it was a good idea. I used to tag along with them whenever I could."

"What others?"

"Bill and Jean. We were all here in the living-room. Bill said he'd lend me a gun and Jean found some old riding-breeches that I could wear."

"Hum. Well, what happened that morning?"

"Jean waked me up and I went out to help her with breakfast. She'd invited all of them to eat here before we left. That would mean only one house would be upset."

"All of them came?"

"All except Dr. Hans. He stayed to take care of his lab animals and sent word by Paul that he'd join us later."

"Who came first?"

"Paul did. He helped me set the table while Bill squeezed oranges. Then Mr. Tolliver came in the back door and—well, I guess that makes Hugh last."

"And then?"

"And then—nothing. We ate breakfast and left."

"Was Mr. Tolliver all right when he got here?"

"Of course he was. Bill opened the door and he came in yawning—" She stopped suddenly and a puzzled look came over her face. "That's funny," she said slowly. "He said he was sleepy but he'd had a cup of coffee before he left home. That usually wakes up a person."

The sheriff sat up in his chair and when he spoke there was a note of excitement in his voice. "He said that? He said he'd had a cup of coffee before he left home?"

"You think that means—?"

"That he was poisoned? No, I don't think so. But I'd like to know a little more about that coffee business." He pushed himself up from the chair and picked up his hat. "Miss Ann, I'd like to get you to help me a little. I haven't any authority here. This isn't even my county. I haven't got any real evidence, only a hunch. I can't ask these people to dig up a body just because I think something's so. All I can do is use the brains God gave me. I still think it was murder." He shook his head and his blue eyes were troubled. "That's an ugly word, but murder's an ugly business. It's like mold. It starts in just one spot and then pretty soon it's ruined everything around it. I've seen it before and I know what I am talking about."

"What do you want me to do?"

"Just ask some questions for me. You might begin by finding out all you can about that coffee. Will you do it?"

Ann looked at him for a long time before she replied. "Yes, I'll ask."

She went with him to the front door and closed it carefully behind him, but before he was off the steps she opened it again and asked, "How do you know I didn't poison his coffee and then hit him over the head?"

"I was given to understand you were with the major all morning," he chuckled. "I figured you sort of alibied each other."

8

A CUP OF COFFEE

It was not easy to become a detective, as Ann soon learned. She was excited and a little flattered by the sheriff's request and it gave her a chance to pick up some extra information in behalf of her sister. She rather prided herself that she had given him no intimation of that other trouble that nagged her so constantly.

When he left her she had made a thorough search of the glassed-in bookshelves on either side of the fireplace. But apparently neither Jean nor Bill was a great reader. There was a smattering of recent biography, books on gardening, on furniture, on music, but nothing dealing with the science of detecting. Ann wished for her father's technical library, which might have had some information on chemicals and drugs, but these had been left for Dr. Hans, since neither of the girls had thought they would ever need such books.

After dinner she retired to her own room, settling comfortably in bed with fat pillows behind her and a pad of drawing paper on her knees. Her plan was to assemble the facts she knew and those she suspected, but Jean, thinking she was ill, kept interrupting with offers of a hot-water bottle or hot lemonade.

"Let me alone," Ann snapped finally. "I want to think."

"All right. Think!" Jean slammed the door.

Ann closed her eyes and tried. What her mind conjured up was a duel between Hugh and Paul, replete with swords and costumes of some vague period. It was a very pleasant picture but it wasn't getting her any nearer the solution of her problem. She opened her eyes and began sketching Mr. Tolliver with a cup of coffee in his hand. Then in turn she sketched the other dropping in the poison or striking down the victim with the fallen limb of the tree. The only satisfactory result was a diabolical likeness of Lou. Ann was quite pleased and, switching off her light, went peacefully to sleep.

In the morning she was no nearer the solution of how to extract cold facts from unwilling witnesses than she had been after her talk with Sheriff Davies. She had cut off her entreé into houses where she needed to go and she hadn't dared tell this to the sheriff lest he ask her why. That nasty note Mrs. Tolliver had showed her had intimated that Amelia had put something in the coffee, so maybe there was something in the old man's theory after all. *But,* Ann thought ruefully, *you can't go up to the door, ring the bell, and ask, "Did you put poison in Mr. Tolliver's coffee? And did you, by any chance, bash him over the head?"*

It was a cold, raw morning, not raining, but definitely very damp, and low clouds hung from a leaden sky. Twirling a pencil idly between her fingers, she sat now by her bedroom window, a sketching board on her lap. Chip was sprawled at her feet, drawing large designs with a red wax crayon on a piece of brown wrapping-paper. His tongue was caught between his small teeth and a frown of concentration crinkled his forehead.

"This is a tree and this is a cow," he said slowly, making strange marks on the paper.

"Chip, who else can draw? I mean besides you and me?"

He looked up in surprise. "Marcy can't draw," he said.

Marcia Temple was the little girl who lived next door and Chip's most intimate playmate. Ann was not interested in her artistic ability but she knew you had to be careful in questioning a child. Subtlety was lost on them and there was danger in a direct question. Chip was too apt to mention it, which would be embarrassing, to say the least.

She tried a new line of questions. "Who comes to see your mother a lot? Who's her best friend?"

Chip ignored her. "Marcy's got mumps," he said. "She's gonna give 'em to me just as soon's she's up. I'll look like I've got marbles in my mouth." He blew out his cheeks and his eyes twinkled with humor.

"Who comes here to see her lots of times?" Ann insisted.

"Oh." He turned back to his drawing. "Marcy's mommy comes over here most every day."

Chip wasn't going to be much help as a source of information, Ann saw. Anyway, members of the family would have had the best opportunity to arrange those little misplaced articles that Jean forgot or to write anonymous notes.

Resolutely she applied her pencil to the paper and sketched his new position. Chip was a willing model when he was being entertained as well and Ann was slowly filling a small portfolio which would be invaluable later in her work.

"Let's go for a walk," she suggested, putting down her pencil.

"Now?"

"Yes, it's too hot in here."

Chip glanced doubtfully out of the window but he rose to his chubby legs. Ann felt a twinge of remorse, but Chip could get in where she couldn't, and if things worked out right she could follow him.

Jean objected to the idea but Ann overrode her. She was almost too easily persuaded, but Chip adored Ann, so his mother merely satisfied herself that he was warmly clad in a ski suit and let it go at that.

The wind was biting and Ann was almost sorry that she had come outside. Certainly they couldn't stay long. She shivered and drew the soft fur of her coat closer about her throat. She took the back way, walking so briskly that Chip had to run to keep up with her. She had chosen this way deliberately, knowing that doors are more easily opened in the back than in the front.

An alley ran parallel to the curving street and they got the back view of garages, a servant's house or two, and the varied assortment of fences and hedges that enclosed the lots. As they reached the flaring edge of the Tolliver place Ann paused.

"I wonder if I could have left my kerchief here the other day? Have you seen it anywhere, Chip?"

"What hand'chief, Tan?"

"The one with the big red flowers. I wear it on my head."

Chip needed no encouragement. He was not bothered with inhibitions about entering his grandmother's house and skipped along ahead of her. He reached the steps before Ann did and rattled the doorknob by way of knocking.

Amelia peered through the glass panel before she opened it. "Come in, Chip, darling. Oh, it's you, Ann," she added flatly.

She was dressed in a cotton house dress and a ragged brown sweater that made her sallow skin look muddy. A small heap of dampened linen lay on a chair near an ironing-board. Amelia's limp hair straggled about her face, which was flushed from the heat of her work.

"I thought I might have left my kerchief here," Ann said. "The one I wear over my head. It has bright red flowers on it."

"I think I remember seeing it." Amelia's small eyes darted toward the kitchen as though she expected someone to come through it and scold her for even talking to Ann.

"Want to see Grandma," Chip said, blinking back the tears the wind had brought to his eyes.

"Yes, darling, in just a minute. Let me finish this and take it upstairs with me." Amelia picked up the iron, folded the piece of linen, and pressed the creases.

"It's very beautiful work," Ann said. "Is it yours?"

"Oh, no. Helen does this. I never was good with a needle. She makes her own designs too. It is beautiful, but so much work. We don't like to trust the laundries with these things. Not that I mind doing it myself, of course," Amelia added hurriedly.

Ann picked up a luncheon cloth and examined the finely drawn monogram and the intricate and delicate embroidery. Amelia almost snatched it from her hands and, turning, gathered up the other things she had finished.

"Chip, if you want to see your grandma, come along with me. You musn't stay with her long. She isn't well." She turned

back to Ann and coughed embarrassedly. "I'll bring your kerchief. I don't know—perhaps it would be better—"

"I'll wait in the kitchen," Ann assured her stiffly.

Amelia looked more uncertain than before and a frown
puckered the space between her eyes. She started to protest,
but apparently thought better of it, and followed Chip through
the door into the hall. Ann smiled cynically at the closing door
before she went into the kitchen.

It was warm and the redolent odor of cooking food made
it a pleasant room. Flora was bent over a marble slab, slowly
kneading biscuit dough. She turned with a start as Ann opened
the door and some of the flour slipped from her big hands and
spilled on the waxed linoleum floor.

"Law's a mercy! I didn't know who 'twas!" she exclaimed.

"I left a handkerchief here," Ann explained. "Miss Amelia's
getting it for me. Anyway, I wanted to ask you a question."

Flora's eyes opened wide, showing so much white that it
was rather startling against the darkness of her skin.

"Yes'm?"

"Do you remember whether Mr. Tolliver had coffee here on
the morning—on that day we all went hunting? He had breakfast with the rest of us. But I thought he might have had coffee
before he left home."

Flora dug strong fingers into the dough. "I disremembers,"
she replied.

"Was there a cup left on the table?" Ann pursued her cause.
"Or a coffeepot left half full?"

The Negress was so long in answering that Ann was about
to repeat her question when Flora finally mumbled, "I thinks
there was."

"Was what?"

"I washed a cup an' saucer before I fix breakfas'. An' I makes
some more coffee. They laks it strong an' fresh."

"Was there some coffee left in the pot?"

"Yas'm."

"What did you do with it?"

Flora's thick lips parted in surprise. "I pours it down the sink. 'Twan't much, not a cupful."

"Had you made it for him before you left that night?"

"Naw'm," she replied sullenly. "Jawn an' me was ahurryin' to the movies. Ain't no call fer us to do any more extry wuk."

"I'm sure there wasn't," Ann said quickly. "Who could have made it, then?"

"I ain't know, Mis' Ann."

"Did Mr. Tolliver make it himself?"

"I ain't know," Flora repeated.

There was a finality about her words and Ann had no desire to antagonize or frighten her. One fact had emerged, anyway. Mr. Tolliver *had* had a cup of coffee at home before he came to Jean's, and there might have been something wrong with it. Ann perched on a high stool beside the stove and tried to remember how he had looked and acted that morning. He had been sleepy, but that was natural. Certainly she herself had had to struggle to keep her eyes open so early in the morning.

And he had used three spoonfuls of sugar. If he did that habitually it was enough to kill the bitter taste of any drug that might have been added.

The swinging door from the dining-room was pushed open abruptly and Chip came in, followed by Amelia.

"I can't find your kerchief, Ann." Amelia sounded distressed. "I'm sure I picked it up that afternoon. . . . I know I put it away, but I can't find it now. Flora, have you seen it? I don't know what I could have done with it—" Her voice trailed vaguely.

"That's all right," Ann said, sliding from the stool. "It's not important."

"I'm so sorry," Amelia apologized again. "I remember picking it up—I think I put it on the table in the hall. I must have put it away somewhere else. I—I was so upset—"

Ann felt sorry for this futile woman and a little ashamed of herself for using the handkerchief as an excuse to get other information.

"It doesn't matter in the least. I only thought I'd pick it up as we were passing. We'd better be getting home, Chip. It's lunch-time and your mother will be worrying if we don't get there on time."

"I wanta eat with Grandma."

"Not today," Ann said firmly. "She's not feeling well and she'd want you to be especially quiet."

"But she'd love—" began Amelia.

"Jean's expecting him at home." Ann cut her short and took Chip's hand. "I think it's going to rain any minute. I'll bet I can beat you home and the last one there is a rotten egg."

Chip took this threat seriously and she had no trouble getting him outside. A few scattered drops of rain told her that there was really need for haste. She let him beat her and tried to pretend her horror at becoming a rotten egg.

Lunch was a quiet affair with Bill not at home. Jean spent most of her time feeding Chip, who sat in a high chair between the sisters. Afterward, in the living-room, Ann sat watching the rain beat against the windows while Jean, with Chip in her lap, read aloud *A Visit from St. Nicholas.*

"Now, Dasher! Now, Dancer! Now, Prancer and Vixen!
On, Comet! On, Cupid, On, Donder and Blitzen!"

As Jean read, Chip whispered the names of the reindeer and grew drowsy in the comfortable warmth of her arms. She closed the book at last and, lifting him gently, carried him to his room for his afternoon nap.

Ann kept her eyes on the window where rain had turned the shrubs a silvery green. They swayed and tapped invitingly against the glass. When the telephone rang she got up at once to answer it but Jean must have been in the hall, for she already had the phone in her hand.

"It's for you," she said, giving it to Ann as she went on to the living-room.

When Ann returned a few minutes later Jean was on her knees by the fireplace. She looked up and smiled.

"I thought it would be cheery to have a fire on such a dreary day. Turn off the radiator, will you? We'll get too hot with both."

After doing as she was told, Ann came back to stand by the fire. The fat pine kindling had caught and already thin blue flames shot up around the logs.

"It was Paul. On the telephone, I mean," she said. "He invited me to dinner tonight."

Jean caught Ann's hand and pulled herself to her feet. "I'm so glad," she said. "I think it would be wonderful," she added, her eyes dancing with merriment. "You could marry Paul and settle down right here for the next few years."

Ann was startled. After all, she hadn't seen Paul since that night he had brought her home and kissed her at the door. "Aren't you building castles in Spain?" she asked.

"You've got over Hugh, haven't you, Ann?" Jean asked, and as Ann did not answer but continued to gaze into the fire, she added in a soft rush of words, "I know you loved him, but that was so long ago. Really, he's not worth it. He's vain and—sometimes I don't think he loves anybody as much as himself. Paul's different. I like him."

"And you don't like Hugh?"

"Of course I do," Jean denied much too quickly. "But he's not as steady and dependable as Paul."

"Anybody that married that scientist would play second fiddle to a test tube for the rest of her life," Ann said dryly. "I don't recall seeing him hanging on my words or rushing around here for a sight of my beautiful face, either."

"Oh, that. Naturally he's interested in his work. All men are. He concentrates on it, but I noticed when you were sketching Martha the other day I had to speak to you three times before you heard me. Paul's doing something, Ann. Something big. Just think what it will mean if he and Dr. Hans are successful."

Ann laughed at Jean's seriousness. "Baby, I believe you mean what you're saying. Still, you'll have to admit he's not chasing me. Why, I've scarcely seen him."

"He's interested," Jean maintained. "He was dreadfully disappointed that night he came to see you and you weren't here."

"When was that?"

"The night you went to the sorority house to have dinner with Franny. He came here first and when we weren't at home he came on over to Mother Tolliver's.'

Ann sucked in her breath in surprise. "But that was the night before—before the hunt. I didn't know you'd gone out too."

"Oh, we didn't go anywhere. I forgot you weren't here when Dad called. You'd just gone and he said Aunt Amelia wanted us to come over for supper."

"Who was there?"

"Just the family—Lou and Hugh, and Paul of course. He came while we were still eating." Jean sat down in a chair, switched on the reading-lamp, and picked up a basket of darning. "And he was very disappointed," she added, a smile quirking the soft corners of her mouth.

Ann selected a cigarette from the box and lit it, trying to cover the suppressed excitement she felt. She took a pillow from the sofa, dropped it on the floor, and sat cross-legged in front of the fire. It was much too simple. Why on earth hadn't she just asked Jean instead of prying into a kitchen where even her presence aroused suspicion?

"Wear the brown velvet suit, Ann. It's very becoming and it does something to your hair." Jean held a needle to the light and threaded it.

"Jean, did you discuss breakfast?"

"What?"

"That night you had supper with the Tollivers. Did you talk about having breakfast here?"

"I suppose so. I think they talked about the hunt. Paul told me then that Dr. Hans wouldn't be able to come for breakfast."

"You didn't leave Chip here alone, did you?" Ann was taking a circuitous route to the questions she intended asking. There was no use in alarming Jean or even arousing her suspicions.

"We always carry him over there with us. I put him to bed in the guest room and Bill brings him home. He never wakes up."

"I wonder why Mr. Tolliver said he'd had coffee before he left home that morning? He came here for breakfast." Ann held her breath while waiting for her sister's answer.

Jean picked up another sock, ran her hand in it, found the hole, and thrust a china egg into it. "He always had a cup of coffee when he got up early. It was just as automatic as washing his face. He used to say that the greatest luxury he could imagine would be to have someone hand him a cup the minute he waked up."

Jean's mouth trembled and her eyes misted with unshed tears.

"Did he always have it, then? Every morning?"

"Not every morning, but whenever he was going on a hunt or something like that. Why?"

"It just seemed unusual. Men don't usually get up and make themselves coffee early in the morning."

"He didn't have to do that. Aunt Amelia did it. She went out to the kitchen to make it before we left that night. All he had to do was plug in the percolator and heat it."

Ann moved back from the fire and sat clasping her legs, her eyes on the bright flames. A log sagged and sent a shower of red sparks up the chimney. She was thinking frantically of the facts she had assembled. So the explanation was simple after all—granted, naturally, that the coffee had been drugged. Somehow she accepted that as a fact. That nasty note— Well, they were all there and they were not the sort of family that stayed put. They roamed from room to room whenever they came visiting. So any one of them could have slipped into the kitchen and doctored the coffee. Amelia had the best opportunity and she profited by Mr. Tolliver's death. Ann closed her eyes and tried to imagine it, but Amelia was so colorless, so quiet, that she couldn't even get a clear vision of her.

Next in order of benefit came Mrs. Tolliver, but she was the one person who didn't move around much. Still, it was possible. Then there was Paul. He was getting some infernal machine so he might have given Providence a little prodding. And he had a knowledge of drugs.

Cold chills played a tattoo on Ann's spine. She might have been kissed by a murderer!

"Are you cold?" Jean asked.

"No."

Ann got up from the floor and crossed to the window. She clutched the drapery and watched the raindrops hit the glass and roll slowly to the ledge.

There was a great gap in the sheriff's theory. Motive. Opportunity there was for plenty of people—but no real motive.

9

ACCIDENT OR MURDER?

"I came for you early," Paul explained as he held her coat, "because I wanted you to see the lab. We've made quite a few changes."

"It must be very interesting." Ann pulled on her gloves, wrinkling them at the wrist. "I have a key, Jean," she said, brushing her lips against her sister's check. "Don't wait up for me if I'm late."

"I'll see that she gets home safe and sound," Paul said.

"Have a good time, darling."

Jean closed the door and they went out into the darkness together. Paul's hand on her arm guided her down the walk and into the car. There was no rain now, but the atmosphere was still moist and cool. The sky was powdered with a sprinkling of stars but they seemed far away and their glow was dimmed by the distance.

"Adeline and the doctor have been in constant consultation all afternoon," Paul said as he started the car. "He's interfering with her cooking and she's convinced that there's going to be an explosion in the kitchen before the night is over."

"Then I'm being treated to one of her dinners?"

"Yes, with a little improvising on our part. We're having everything we like best tonight. Adeline says shrimp creole is your favorite and pecan pie is mine, and the Lord only knows what Dr. Hans is making. He doesn't know, but he assures me they always had it in the old country and that you ate it."

Ann relaxed against the worn leather seat and made appropriate replies when it was necessary. It was very pleasant, sitting here close to Paul. He wasn't so handsome or elegant as Hugh, but there was something substantial about his broad shoulders and the sharp planes of his cheeks and chin. Ann grinned to herself in the darkness. Wouldn't he be surprised if he had heard Jean talking this afternoon?

"Here we are," he said, bringing the car to a jerking stop that sent the loose gravel of the driveway spinning. "Let's go on to the lab first. I want you to see that right away. Besides, I can see that Adeline and the doctor are still busy fixing our dinner."

He led her to the back and stopped in front of a dark squat building that had once been a garage. Taking a large key from his pocket, he unlocked the door and pressed the light switch inside. As the door was closed Ann looked around her with curiosity. There had been an addition to the rear of the building, and there were numerous changes in the long room in which she found herself. "You've changed everything," she said. "If it weren't for the skylight I wouldn't think it was the same place."

"Like it?" he asked eagerly.

Ann turned to him with a smile. "It looks very efficient. I'm no scientist, Paul. Pops used to keep me out of here as much as possible. He said I was like the proverbial bull in a china shop."

He took her on a tour of the place then, proudly showing her the microscopes on the tables, the cases of slides, the filing cabinets for the records. There were shelves of specimens, a small refrigerator, and racks of test tubes.

He turned on lights here and there, to show her the excellent arrangements they had. Ann listened to his explanation of this machine and that, but when he had finished she knew little more than she had when she first entered the room. These experiments were so different from her father's that she hadn't had time to master the patter, so she wisely chose the course of silence.

In addition the building housed the cages of animals and Ann's lack of enthusiasm was noticeable even to Paul, so they returned quickly to the realm of pure science.

"We're still in the early stages of experimentation," Paul said. "Sometimes they work, more often they don't. But I think we're making some real progress. It's just that it takes so much patience and there's so little time. We're fighting that always."

"You'll make it," Ann said decisively.

"I'll talk about it the rest of the night if I don't stop now," he said with a laugh. "Let's get back to the house and see what the others are doing. I've worked up an appetite. What about you?"

"Mmmmm—" Ann said, wrinkling her nose.

He closed and locked the doors of the laboratory and led her back to the house. Ann saw at once that somebody had made mammoth efforts to straighten the cluttered living-room. Books were stacked neatly and the litter of papers had disappeared from the table. A bright fire burned cheerfully in the grate and as soon as Paul had taken her coat Ann went to it, extending her cold hands toward its warmth.

As if they had been waiting for a cue, Adeline and Dr. Hans appeared from somewhere in the back of the house. Dr. Hans was struggling with his coat, but Adeline waddled forward and held out her huge arms to Ann.

"It's my chile done come home," she crooned.

Ann thought the breath was being squeezed out of her by the hamlike arms, but she managed to gasp, "I was given to understand you were fixing all my favorites for me tonight. I'm starved, really starved."

Adeline laughed with real pleasure. "It sho' is good to be cookin' fur somebody what's got a healthy respect for their stomachs. Them," she said with a grunt of disgust, "they ain't no better'n yo' pa. They don't know what I'm givin' 'em half the time. Why, they can't tell real gumbo from canned soup," she finished as though this was the final outrage of her ability as a cook.

"Something's burning." Dr. Hans sniffed the air and Adeline turned immediately and disappeared through the door.

"You're evidently a great favorite with her," Paul said. "You'll be sick if you eat everything she's cooked."

"Hum! I never got sick from Adeline's cooking in my life. You have no idea what a good appetite I have."

"She's right," Dr. Hans concurred. "I never quite knew how she did it, but the fact remains that she could eat more than my son Franz. Which is saying a good deal," he added with a smile.

"Yo' all can come in to suppa now," Adeline called through the door.

They sat down to an old-fashioned round table. Lacking flowers, a large bowl of evergreens with shining apples, oranges, and tangerines adorned the center of the table. When Ann commented on its attractiveness, Paul claimed credit for the artistic arrangement. After that the meal became a hilarious affair; the food was delicious, the conversation easy and light, and the kitchen door swished back and forth as Adeline brought in one dish after another. The Negress had as much to say as the others. She seemed to think it was her duty to bring Ann up to date on all her kitchen gossip and the garrulous flow of words went on unchecked except for an occasional interruption by Dr. Hans or Paul.

As they finished, Dr. Hans got up and brought a bottle of wine from the sideboard. "This is my last bottle of Rhenish wine, Ann. But for this special occasion—" He poured the liquid into glasses. "Come get yours, Adeline," he called, and added to Ann, "I keep it under lock and key, for Adeline has the right instinct when it comes to food and drink." His blue eyes twinkled with merriment as he gave the servant her glass.

"This sho' be good stuff," Adeline giggled as she swished her starched calico skirt back to the kitchen.

"No more draps for you," Paul called to her, "if you don't have our breakfast ready in the morning."

"I'd almost forgotten Adeline's little penchant for a 'drap,'" said Ann.

"It's the way we bribe her to stay with us," Paul said. "When she comes to us with a tale of the high wages the laundries or the fraternities are paying we haul out the bottle and she shows up bright and early the next morning."

They were still seated at the table, smoking after-dinner cigarettes, when the doorbell rang. It rang again, insistently, before Paul dunked his cigarette in the remains of his coffee and
pushed back his chair. "I'd better see who it is," he said crossly.

Dr. Hans followed him and Ann picked up her wineglass,
drained it, and took the empty glass to the kitchen, where she
complimented Adeline on her cooking. The Negress took this
opportunity to regale Ann with the exploits of the young doctor, most of which Ann took with a grain of salt.

"All them animules," Adeline said with a grunt of disgust. "I
wouldn't tech one of 'em with a ten-foot pole. An' as for them
things they wuk with all day! I tells yo' Mis' Ann, I makes 'em
wash they han's as soon as they set foot in the house. Yo' neva
can tell what kind o' p'ison they on 'em."

Paul pushed open the door. Ann saw at once that something
was wrong. His dark eyes glittered and his mouth was set grimly. She slid from her stool and laid the stalk of celery on which
she had been nibbling on the sink.

"You'd better come up in front," he said tersely. "Lou and
Hugh are here."

"Lou and Hugh?" Ann was as surprised as if he had said
Dracula was standing beside her.

"Exactly. Hugh seems to have something to say. You'd better
come up and hear it."

She followed him through the dining-room and into the little sitting-room. Hugh was nervously pacing the narrow space
between the davenport and a refectory table.

"I had to find out what you knew," he was saying. "Hello,
Ann. Bill said you were here too. It's preposterous!" he exploded.

"What is, Hugh?" Ann asked.

"A Mr. Davies came to see us tonight, just before dinner,"
Lou said.

"You know, that man you and Paul picked up the morning
of the hunt," Hugh explained.

"Sit down, Ann." Paul pulled her to the davenport and sat
down beside her. "Now suppose you begin at the beginning,
Hugh. What did the sheriff want?"

"He has somehow got the most fantastic idea that Dad's death wasn't an accident." It was Lou who answered. The light fell directly on her face, showing the faint circles and tired lines under her pale eyes. "He wanted to know all sorts of things, whether Dad had complained of feeling ill that morning, and whether he had ever had a fainting spell in his life."

"But why—?" Ann began.

"Dad drove out with me," Hugh said. "And he was all right when we got there. You all know that. I can't see any reason for this sheriff snooping around. Haven't we got enough trouble without him adding to it? If this ever gets to Mother—well, I wouldn't like to be held responsible for the result." He took a package of cigarettes from his pocket and lit one, throwing the discarded match into the fire.

"I do not understand." Dr. Hans spoke for the first time from the shadowy corner in which he sat. "Is this the man who has been to see us?" He turned to Paul, who nodded briefly.

"So he's been here, has he?" Hugh asked. "What about you, Ann?"

"Yes, I've talked to him."

"What did he ask you?" Lou leaned forward as she asked her question.

"Much the same things he asked you," Ann said warily. "Give me a cigarette, will you, Paul?"

"I don't understand," Hugh muttered. "He comes to see you and he comes to see us. But Bill hasn't heard from him."

"What do you mean?" Paul asked quickly.

"Well, Bill was the last one to talk to his father."

"Weren't you with them at the time?"

"Dad said he was worried about the professor. He went back to the car to look for him."

"But Ann and I had gone back to meet Dr. Hans."

"I know. Bill told him that but he insisted on going himself. You weren't familiar with the place and he thought Dr. Hans would get lost without somebody to show him the way. Bill and I went on a little farther until he dropped back to wait for Dad.

I took one of the dogs and moved on." Hugh shrugged expressively. "No use for all of us to wait."

"Paul," Lou said, "what do you know? If you've talked to—to this man, you must know something about him. Who is he? Why is he asking all these questions, making these horrible insinuations?"

"I don't know very much about him," Paul answered rather abruptly. "He's sheriff in the next county."

"Then he hasn't any right to question us."

"I wouldn't be too sure of that, Hugh," Paul answered slowly. "The accident occurred in his county. I don't know anything about law, but I imagine he's perfectly within his rights. I've talked to him two or three times. I knew he wasn't satisfied with the appearance of the accident."

"Was it an accident?" Ann asked suddenly.

Paul frowned. "It could have been," he replied. "I went down to— I looked at Cousin William and there was only that terrible blow on the back of his head. Somebody could have hit him, but it could just as easily be explained that he fell."

"The sheriff thinks that log was a little too convenient," Ann commented almost to herself and the others looked at her sharply.

"It was the only fallen log in the clearing." Paul shrugged.

"Do you know what you're implying?" Lou demanded shrilly. She turned to her husband and said fiercely, "I didn't want you to go. I told you I wasn't feeling well."

Hugh's face turned red and Ann raised her eyebrows, wondering if her own presence hadn't been the main reason Lou had tried to keep Hugh at home.

"Aren't you taking too much for granted, Lou?" asked Paul. "There's no reason to believe it was anything but an accident. The sheriff hasn't any proof. He's just curious."

Ann bit her lip thoughtfully. Evidently the sheriff hadn't told anybody else about the bloodstained feather. And that was his proof, that little bit of evidence that somebody else had been there in the clearing besides Mr. Tolliver.

"You didn't see Mr. Tolliver when you got there, did you, Dr. Hans?" She turned to him suddenly.

He was startled by the abruptness of her question and as the light struck his thick-lensed glasses he blinked foolishly. "No," he said. "There was no one there when I arrived. I left the car beside the others and tried to find you."

"You didn't hear him call?" Hugh asked, and the professor shook his head.

"What time was it when he left you and Bill?" Paul asked Hugh.

"I don't know."

Hugh sat down on the edge of a chair and began cracking the knuckles of his fingers. It was an irritating habit and Ann noticed that Paul glared at him as he asked the next question.

"Can't you put it at some time? How long before you heard the shots?"

"I don't know, I tell you. Maybe forty-five minutes, maybe an hour."

"We found him at eleven o'clock," Paul said. "Have you any idea when you got there, Dr. Hans?"

"I am a slave to the alarm clock." The doctor shook his head. "I feed the animals, I make the lecture, and I come back to the lab for just a few minutes. I do not know what time I arrive, but there was no one at the place when I parked the car. I looked about to be sure."

The doctor's nearsightedness and preoccupation were well known to all of them. If something had caught his attention he might have wandered off without noticing either a noise or a person near him. Still, it hardly seemed possible that he wouldn't have seen Mr. Tolliver if he had been in the clearing at the time. These thoughts were apparently racing through the minds of all of them as they watched the guileless face of the scientist.

"I knew something would happen on that hunt," Lou said, speaking with surprising intensity.

"That's the first time I've heard of it." Hugh stopped cracking his knuckles and turned to her.

"Well, I did. I told you you shouldn't go."

"Headaches do carry a sense of premonition," Ann said, and had the pleasure of seeing Lou give her a sullen look. "By the way, wasn't Mr. Tolliver feeling all right the night before?"

"Certainly he was," Hugh answered her. "Why?"

"I was only thinking that if he'd been sick he wouldn't have gone. I thought he might have eaten something that upset him during the night."

"Well, he didn't," Lou said. "We had dinner with Mother and Dad that night and he was all right when we left. If you're looking for the last place he ate," she added acidly, "you'll find it a little nearer home. He had breakfast with Jean that morning, didn't he?"

Ann's hands clenched and Paul put his over hers as though he wanted to suppress the angry outburst that appeared imminent. Her yellow eyes were narrowed to angry, glittering slits.

"We all had breakfast there, Lou," he said sharply. "We're wandering from the point. He died from a blow on the back of his head which was either deliberate—or an accident."

"Then what's she trying to insinuate?" demanded Lou.

"Only this," Ann answered. "He came into the kitchen that morning yawning and saying he was sleepy."

"That's natural, Ann," Paul said. "It was early in the morning. I wasn't so wide awake myself and certainly your own eyes were drooping."

Ann looked at him for one long minute before she said deliberately, "But he had a cup of coffee before he left home." She shifted her gaze to Lou. "That usually wakes up a person."

Was it only her imagination, or had Lou turned pale? She sat there watching, as tense and still as a cat who has paused while stalking its prey. The room was very quiet, as though she had shocked them into numbness. A piece of coal in the grate cracked and the hiss of the flame broke the tension that had gripped them.

"Shut up, Ann," Paul said roughly. "Get any ideas that you may have that there was something wrong with him then out of your head. He was definitely not poisoned."

Lou laughed hysterically. Hugh took her hand in his and she quieted almost as soon as he touched her. She dabbed at her lips with a handkerchief but the pudgy fingers with their bright red nails were trembling.

"I didn't mean that," Ann said slowly. "I only meant that he might have had something that made him sleepy so that he would have stumbled over the log and fallen."

"You drove him out there, Hugh. Was he drowsy?" Paul asked.

"Yes, I think he was. He didn't talk much, but I didn't pay any attention to that. He certainly didn't go to sleep. Ann's let that sheriff get her imagination working overtime. She always had plenty of it anyway. It was just an accident." His voice lacked the conviction it had had when he had called it an accident earlier in the evening.

"So many strange things have been happening around here," Ann said softly.

"We were getting along very nicely until you came back," Lou said hotly.

"Were you?" Ann asked with a smile. "I'm really most interested in a little forgery that seems to be going on here."

Whatever effect she had hoped to create was lost as the doorbell rang stridently. Paul muttered a "damn" as he rose quickly and opened the door. He took a step backward and Sheriff Davies walked into the room.

"Good evening," said the sheriff. "I'm not intruding, am I?"

10

THE UNINVITED

"Come in," Paul invited grudgingly.

"You're having a family party?" the sheriff inquired, taking off his hat and struggling with the sleeves of his overcoat.

"There's been a death in the family," Lou said stiffly. "We aren't thinking in terms of parties now."

"Come over and sit by me," Ann said. She moved to a corner to make room for him.

"Are you making the rounds of the family?" Hugh asked sarcastically.

Sheriff Davies dropped down beside Ann. Seated there, he looked like an odd assortment of old clothes and bones that might fall apart when he rose. The heavy lids of his eyes drooped, giving his seamed face a melancholy look. "Well now," he drawled, "I just dropped around for a little talk."

Hugh stood up, his hands thrust belligerently into his pockets. "There's no use upsetting everybody. All this talk about an accident being a murder is just your imagination and nothing else."

"Think of my mother," Lou said. "Kept in bed by the shock. If any of this loose talk gets to her ears it might kill her."

"Stop being so dramatic, Lou," Paul said. "Cousin Helen's as tough as they come. It would only make her fighting mad."

"I won't sit here and let you insult my mother and me." Lou was indignant and she tossed her head so that one of the numerous hairpins that were supposed to keep her hair in place slid to her shoulder and caught in the ruffled collar of her dress. "Let's go, Hugh." She rose.

"Didn't know I was upsetting anybody," the sheriff said calmly. "Is your mother right sick?"

"Not very," Hugh answered him.

"There's no use anybody getting flustered," the sheriff said mildly. "I just think there is something funny about that accident. It wasn't like most hunting accidents and it sort of got me interested."

"What's funny about it?" Hugh demanded.

The sheriff threw one leg across the other and rocked his foot. "Well," he said slowly, "you told me this afternoon he seemed tired and sleepy that morning. Folks don't get sleepy out in the cold morning air. They move around to keep warm. Looks to me like the excitement of going on a hunt would be enough to wake him up. Mama says the only time I don't need an alarm clock is when I'm going huntin' or fishin'."

Lou sat down again abruptly. Ann, who had been watching her, turned to look at the sheriff. Despite the mildness of his tone, she seemed to catch an iron will behind his words. *Why, he isn't stupid at all,* she thought. *He's quite intelligent. He's like a bulldog who's sunk his teeth in something and will hang on come hell or high water.* She looked at him with new interest, at his untidy clothes, his bushy gray hair, his big nose over thin lips.

Sheriff Davies was not intentionally deceptive. He was merely a slow-moving country man. His duties were mainly routine, but they had not dulled the alertness of a shrewd brain. Other people besides Ann had been deceived by his placid manner.

"Mr. Tolliver didn't have anything wrong with him," Ann heard him saying. "He was sound as a dollar and that's saying a lot for a man of his age. Not many of us can say as much when we get over fifty." He paused and sucked in his breath thoughtfully. "So I can't see any reason for him having a dizzy spell and falling on the one log in that clearing. And I didn't know I'd upset you by saying something about it, Mr. Scott."

"It's not so much what you say as what you don't say."

"There were too many coincidences to be real," the sheriff replied with reasonable logic.

Ann twined her handkerchief around her fingers. Apprehension made her hands and feet cold and she stirred nervously on the seat beside the sheriff. In the silence that followed the sheriff's words the ticking of the old clock on the wall sounded ominously loud and wheezing. So many coincidences, he had said, but a bloodstained feather could hardly be classified as coincidence. She guessed then that she was the only one to whom he had confided the knowledge of the insignificant but so far only clue.

"That rather puts us on the spot, doesn't it?" Paul asked with a harsh laugh.

Sheriff Davies' eyelids drooped sleepily and he sighed. It was as though he knew too much about people, about their petty faults and weaknesses, that he was unutterably weary of dealing with the imperfections of the human race.

"I wouldn't go so far to say that," he replied, and turned to the professor to ask about his experiments.

With the conversation turned into safer channels, Ann tried to sit back and relax. A few deft questions had instantly diverted the two scientists, who seemed ready, at the drop of a hat, to discuss their problem, though they were reticent as to their exact solution. Even Hugh asked a few questions. Lou fidgeted in her chair to show that she was plainly bored by the topic.

It took some minutes for Ann to realize that the sheriff had a purpose, however obscure—that he was manipulating them as though they were wooden puppets, having them say certain things in order that he might listen to their words and perhaps find some hidden meaning back of their reactions.

"You have a fine place here for your work," Sheriff Davies said.

"It was Professor Bartley's," Dr. Hans replied. "His daughters were kind enough to let me have it after his death."

"Your father was interested in this sort of thing?" The sheriff turned to Ann.

"Not quite the same," she replied. "He was a chemist. Dr. Hans has carried on quite different experiments. There's much more to the laboratory now."

"Takes a lot of money for changes," he muttered.

The telephone rang, breaking into their conversation at a fortunate moment, or so Ann thought. Paul went into the narrow back hall to answer it and came back a few minutes later to tell Hugh that Bill wanted to speak to him. An awkward silence followed when Hugh had left the room, though with the door closed they could not hear what he was saying.

He was frowning when he returned and Lou immediately asked. "What was it, Hugh?"

"Oh, nothing," he replied. "Bill says Mother wants to see us again tomorrow."

"What does she want?"

"How do I know?" he said irritably. "She wants to ask some more questions about the business, I reckon. That's all she's been doing for the past week."

"Well, it's hers," Lou said.

"Oh, I know. But Dad knew Bill was going into the Army and I was to take over. This is going to make me look an awful fool. Everything was settled."

"I wouldn't worry about that," Lou said. "Hugh's been wonderful in the business," she added to the others. "Mother thinks it's her duty to know about things. She'll turn it over to you as soon as she's thought about it. I'll give her a hint."

"I expect you're right," Hugh said more cheerfully, and some of the troubled look left his eyes. "After all, I've had experience."

"We'd better be going, darling. It's time for old married folks like us to get home."

There was a complacency in her tone and she looked significantly at Ann, apparently hoping for some reaction to her barb. Paul picked up her fur coat and held it for her. With it wrapped around her, she looked like a short fat bear.

He opened the door with a little too much alacrity and as he closed it he caught a twinkle in the sheriff's eyes and had the grace to look embarrassed.

"Hugh's a good sort," he said apologetically.

"But Mrs. Scott—?"

"Oh, Lou's all right. Only she could do with more outside interests. All she wants to talk about is her home and Hugh and it gets rather monotonous when you've heard it all before."

"She's the kind," Ann put in, "who sits around a bridge table and talks about the servant problem and what she plans to have for dinner, and if she had a child she'd talk endlessly and unintelligently about child psychology. She's always telling Jean what to do with Chip."

"Hum," grunted the sheriff.

Paul looked hopefully at his other uninvited guest, but Sheriff Davies stretched out his long legs and settled himself more comfortably on the davenport.

"I think we might have some fruit," Dr. Hans said. "I am sure that Adeline has left us some on the sideboard."

He went into the dining-room and returned presently with the bowl that had ornamented the table and some large dinner napkins.

"This is right?" he asked Ann anxiously as he passed them. "We have so little company. Anna used to see about such things in the old days."

His voice sounded pathetic and Ann quickly took a tangerine, sat down in a chair by the fire, and spread the big linen square over her lap so that it looked like an apron.

"This is fine," she said.

"I'll peel it for you," Paul said, pulling up a chair beside her.

She gave him the fruit and turned to the sheriff. "I've been wanting to tell you something."

"Yes?"

"It's about the coffee," she said. "Mr. Tolliver did have some that morning before he came to breakfast."

"What's all this about coffee?" Paul asked, giving her two lobes which he pulled from the tangerine.

"Amelia made it for him." Ann chewed on the fruit, spit the seeds into her hand, and threw them into the fire. "The night before. All he had to do was heat it in the morning."

"I do not understand all this about the coffee," Dr. Hans said.

"Neither do I," Paul put in. "What are you trying to say?"

"That he had some coffee early that morning. At home," Ann explained patiently.

"Ann, you're barking up the wrong tree," Paul said with a hint of exasperation. "Cousin William was not poisoned. There were no symptoms. I'm a doctor and I know. He died from a blow on the back of his head."

He spoke slowly and distinctly as though she were a child, and not too bright a one at that. Ann listened to him silently while she ate her tangerine. She wiped her fingers on the napkin and shook her head.

"Then why did he say he was sleepy?" she asked. "He did say that, you remember. Oh, I didn't mean that he'd been poisoned. I know as well as you do how he was killed. But couldn't something have been put in his coffee to drug him? Something that would have made him sleepy even after he'd had his breakfast?"

"I suppose so," Paul admitted.

"But why?" Dr. Hans inquired. "Why should anyone want to drug him? Couldn't he have taken it himself? I do not know, but many people take some mild sedative to make them sleep."

"He'd hardly do that when he was planning to get up early the next morning and go hunting," Sheriff Davies said dryly.

"Then why?" Dr. Hans insisted. "If you accept the premise that he was drugged, then you must know why."

"I'm not saying right now whether I think that or not," the sheriff said, turning the apple he was eating round and round between his hands. "But I can think of two pretty good reasons why he could have been given something."

"What are they?"

Ann asked the question, but three pairs of eyes were turned eagerly toward the sheriff.

"First of all it might have been given him to make him sleep, so he wouldn't go huntin' at all."

He bit into the apple and Ann prompted, "And—?"

"It might have been given him so's he'd be sleepy and somebody could kill him and make it look like an accident. Whoever came up to him in that clearing was somebody he knew, somebody he had no reason to fear. There weren't any signs of a struggle. And that log had been moved," he finished grimly.

They were silent then, turning over in their minds what had been said. It was nothing new, nor was it unexpected, but all of them had tried to veer from even the thought of murder and its terrible aftermath. Nothing would be the same again; the even tenor of their lives would be torn apart. There would be questions and suspicions and doubts, for if their minds accepted the fact of murder they must also accept the inevitable corollary that the deed had been committed by one of them.

The sheriff had said as much.

"Any of them could have drugged the coffee," Ann said musingly.

"How?" the sheriff wanted to know.

"Ask Paul," she replied with a shrug. "He was there."

"Well?" Sheriff Davies turned his searching blue eyes on the young doctor.

"I don't know. I went to Bill's that night and when he wasn't at home I went on over to Cousin William's. I knew they must be there. They were still eating dinner when I arrived."

"Who?"

"Jean and Bill, Lou and Hugh, and of course Cousin William and Amelia and Cousin Helen. It was a family dinner."

The sheriff looked inquiringly at Ann.

"I had dinner that night with the house mother at my sorority. Jean and I lived there for a while after Pops died. Franny was especially nice to us then."

"Who made the coffee?" Sheriff Davis turned back to Paul.

"Amelia did, but that isn't going to help much. We were all in the kitchen. She had fixed a lunch for us to carry and we all went back to see it. I think even Cousin Helen came."

"Did anybody object to the hunt?"

"Cousin Helen said we were fools to go out in the cold and risk pneumonia. She said it was all right for young idiots like us but that Cousin William was getting too old for that sort of thing."

"Nobody else disapproved?"

"Well—" Paul hesitated and glanced at Ann. "Lou did. She didn't know until then that Ann was going with us."

"She would," Ann muttered.

"Who invited you, young lady?"

"I did," Paul said quickly. "She needed to get out in the open air and I thought it would do her good. Neither Dr. Steigler nor I planned to stay all day and I knew I could bring her home if she got tired."

"And Mrs. Scott didn't know until that night? Who told her?"

Paul frowned. "I can't remember. I suppose I did, or maybe it was Jean. Yes, I do remember. It was while we were all in the kitchen. Jean told Amelia she was glad we were going to have deviled eggs as Ann was especially fond of them. Lou asked what that had to do with it and I told her I'd asked Ann to go with me."

"Was there any sort of drug in the house?" the sheriff wanted to know next. "Something any of you could have used?"

Paul shrugged and shook his head.

"Yes!" Coming from Dr. Hans, the word sounded almost like a hiss and they all turned to him. "Mrs. Tolliver had something which she took to make her sleep. It was nothing." He spread out his hands deprecatingly. "Mr. Tolliver brought it to me once and asked me if it was all right. He was disturbed and thought it might be habit-forming. I tested it for him, but it was nothing, only a mild sedative that would induce drowsiness and make a person relax. I told him so and he seemed very much relieved."

"Hump," said the sheriff. "The doctor said pseudo angina. That means she don't really have heart trouble."

Ann smiled to herself now that her own belief had been confirmed.

"It was not that he did not trust his doctor," Dr. Hans insisted. "It was only that he wanted to be sure."

"He left you some money to experiment with?"

Dr. Hans blinked at this sudden question of the sheriff's. "I am a chemist," he said simply. "Mr. Tolliver hoped I would find something that could be made from his waste materials. I had been doing some work along that line before I began my experiments for a new malaria drug."

"But you're planning to use the money for this new thing, aren't you?"

"There were no strings attached to the gift," Paul put in.

"I do not think Mr. Tolliver would care greatly," Dr. Hans replied. "If we can only do what we must in time."

The sheriff was silent for a full minute as his jaws moved rhythmically, chewing the remains of his apple. He threw the core into the fire, where it sizzled faintly, and folded the napkin carefully along its original creases. "Just how sick is Mrs. Tolliver?" he asked.

"She's not sick at all," Ann said decisively. "She wants to be waited on and bed is the best place for that. She's got everybody running around doing what she wants without having to lift a finger herself."

"I wouldn't say that, Ann," Paul said. "After all, she's lame and getting old. But I don't think there's anything seriously wrong with her. I saw her yesterday."

Sheriff Davies nodded. "That's what her doctor said. I thought I'd better have a little talk with her. And I'd like to see that Miss Amelia you mention."

"You won't get anything out of her," Ann said.

"Why not?"

"She's so vague. She'll say almost anything you suggest to her. I don't think she has a brain cell of her own."

"Hump. I think I'll try just the same."

Ann glanced at the clock and got up immediately. "I didn't realize it was so late. I'd better be getting home."

"Oh, not yet," Paul protested, but she was already on her feet.

"I'm tired, Paul," she said, opening her purse and taking out her compact. "I think you'd better take me straight home."

"I wonder if you'd drop me at the hotel?" the sheriff asked. "I came up with some friends who had to see a doctor and they'll pick me up tomorrow night."

Ann, who had been wondering how he was able to spend so much of his time away from his own county seat, thought this a very neat answer to her unasked question. Paul helped her with her coat and they went out into the cold darkness of the night. There were no stars now and Ann was glad to have Paul help her find her way to the car.

"It's gonna rain tomorrow," the sheriff declared. "I'll get in the back seat. More room for my legs." As there was no denying this, Paul helped Ann into the front seat and, after a few protests from the motor, the car started.

The academic buildings were dark and empty but there were a few lights in the dormitories and in the fraternity houses as they drove down College Street. Traffic was negligible and most of the street lights turned green as they reached them. When they drew up in front of the hotel the sheriff got out, bade them a pleasant good night, and stood in the doorway watching the red taillight disappear around the corner.

"The next time I invite you to dinner," Paul said when they were alone, "I'll take you to the most crowded dining-room I can find. Then maybe we can be alone."

Ann smiled at the discrepancy in his statement but she said nothing.

"How was I to know," he continued, "that everybody would pick this night to drop in uninvited?"

He turned the car into Briarcliff Circle, drew over to the curb, and switched off the engine.

"Look here, Ann. Will you marry me?"

She was left breathless with surprise. A proposal was about the last thing she had anticipated. A kiss at the door was what she had expected, and she had already planned the right answer. She would take a sisterly attitude, kiss him sweetly, and tell him gently but firmly that she would be a friend to him always. It had sounded corny when she rehearsed it to herself that afternoon, but it had worked before and she had thought it would again. Now she was left without a proper cue. She didn't know what to say. She hadn't thought he'd ask her to marry him.

"Didn't you hear me?" he asked. "Will you marry me, Ann?"

"I—I—" She fumbled with the handle of the door and he put his hand over hers and pulled her to him.

When he released her, her brain kept telling her to say something, but somehow the words wouldn't come.

"All right," he said. "I'll take you in now. You might keep that in mind for future reference—and compare it with the others. If you're a very good girl I may ask you again sometime."

He took her up the walk, unlocked the front door and, as he gave her the key, told her good night and disappeared into the darkness.

Ann turned out the light that had been left for her and went to her room. She undressed slowly, mentally kicking herself for not saying no at the proper time, which was naturally what she was going to say. Naturally.

The sleeping house was quiet and she lay wrapped in the eiderdown comfort, letting the cold breeze from the open window sweep over her face. She tried not to think of Paul. Dick Martin, for instance, had never upset her like this. She forced herself to think of the serene security of the apartment not far from the lake. She'd better write Beth in the morning that she was coming home. Somewhere in the back of her mind her conscience pricked her, telling her she was running away again, running away from life. Excitement should have kept her awake, but she was tired and exhausted and her heavy eyelids finally dropped and she slept.

Just when she awakened she didn't know, but it was still night. The wind had risen and there was a spattering of rain on the hawthorn bush outside her window. She lay quietly, trying to orient the sound that had waked her, until she realized it came from the soft banging of her own door. She hadn't quite closed it when she came in, and the wind was blowing it back and forth so that the catch of the lock hit the door facing with irritating persistence.

Ann slid from under the warm covers and, barefoot, felt her way across the cold floor. As she reached the door she heard another sound, the sound of someone sobbing. With her hand on the knob she peered into the hall. A dim light filtered through the half-opened door of Jean's room. Ann started to call out to her but she saw Bill lead Jean from Chip's room across the hall.

"You are not to go in there," Bill said.

Jean was crying and her reply was muffled, though Ann strained to hear her.

"He's all right. Let him alone. If I hadn't happened to wake up—"

"I only wanted to see that he was covered and that it wasn't raining in his window," Jean sobbed.

Ann opened the door a little wider but was arrested by the thought that it wasn't really her problem, that Jean and Bill must work this out for themselves.

"He's so little, he needs me," Jean said. "He's my baby."

"He's mine too. Stay out of his room at night. I mean it. I'll lock this door if necessary."

The door closed and Ann was left staring into an empty dark hall.

11

THINGS CAN'T GO ON—

The hands of the traveling clock pointed to nine o'clock when Ann opened her eyes on a sodden, drenched world. It had stopped raining but water dripped ceaselessly from the barren limbs of the trees. It was a dark and dreary day. Low, dark clouds gave a promise of more rain.

Pushing back the comfort, Ann stumbled across the floor. As she sloshed cold water over her face in the bathroom she was nagged by the thought of something that she must do that day. Paul had asked her to marry him and she was to— No, that wasn't it. . . . Oh yes, it was to persuade Jean to go away with her immediately. Now, before anything else happened.

She dressed carefully, straightening the seams of her stockings with accustomed precision, while her mind turned over ways and means of broaching the subject to her sister. It wasn't going to be easy to persuade her to leave. Jean had always been pliant, except, of course, Ann qualified to herself, where Bill was concerned. And going away would certainly concern him.

She slipped a soft beige wool dress over her head and fastened the wide leather belt about her waist. Snapping on the light, she sat down at her dressing-table and arranged her hair three different ways before she was satisfied. She knew she was wasting time, but she didn't want to face the others until she was sure in her own mind just what she was going to say.

As she smoothed bright carmine lipstick over her mouth she became conscious that something was missing from the dressing-table. Powder, rouge, face cream—she ticked them off until she discovered that it was her bottle of perfume that was missing. She frowned at her reflection in the glass.

There was a soft rap on the door. "Ann? Are you awake?" Jean called.

"Come in."

Jean opened the door. She looked pale, almost haggard, and her blue eyes were red-rimmed as though she had been crying. Ann hardly noticed this, however, for in her hands was the missing bottle of perfume.

"What are you doing with that?"

"I—I found it on my dresser this morning," Jean apologized. "I—really, I don't remember moving it there." She bit her lips in embarrassment. "Your breakfast's ready whenever you want it."

Ann took the bottle, turned it in her hand, and replaced it on her dressing-table. There was a deep crease between her eyes and her mouth was set in a hard line. Jean was already busy pulling back the covers of the bed and Ann watched her thoughtfully. Turning off the light, she got up and linked her arm through her sister's.

"Come along with me," she said. "We've got to talk, baby."

"There are so many things I have to do, Ann," Jean protested weakly. "You know how busy my mornings are. I have to order some groceries and see that Lily gets Chip's clothes washed and ironed. Though how she'll get them dry today I don't know."

"That can wait," Ann insisted.

There was a stubborn gleam in her tawny eyes and Jean, seeing that it was useless to argue, shrugged her shoulders as much as to say: *Very well, let's get it over.*

Still holding her sister's arm, Ann led the way to the dining-room. "Bring Miss Jean some coffee too," she said when Martha brought her orange juice and toast. She sipped her fruit juice until Martha had left them alone. "That perfume was on my dressing-table last night when I left," she said.

Jean put down her cup. "I know. Really, I don't know how it got in my room. Maybe Chip thought it was mine and put it on my dresser."

"You know that isn't true," Ann said decisively. "Who was in this house last night?"

"Lou and Hugh came in for a few minutes." Jean smoothed the linen mat with her nervous fingers.

"Did they go in my room? Or yours?"

"I don't know, Ann. I was in the kitchen putting away the food. I heard the doorbell but Bill was in the living-room, so I didn't come up until I had finished."

"Then you don't know whether they went into the back of the house or not?"

"Both of them did. I heard Lou talking to Chip. He hadn't gone to sleep. And later Bill and Hugh went into the back hall to look over some papers Bill had brought home from the office."

"So either of them could have moved the perfume," Ann said slowly.

"But why? I can't see any reason for them doing that."

"I don't know," Ann confessed honestly. "Unless it was to complicate things, to confuse you."

"Ann, is it true what Hugh was saying last night?" Jean asked. "He said that the county sheriff was hinting that Dad's death wasn't an accident, that he was—killed."

"Yes, and it's more than a hint. It's true."

Jean gasped in horror and her eyes were wide with alarm but before she could say anything the swinging door to the kitchen was opened and Martha's black face appeared.

"Miss' Tol'ver," she said in a harassed voice, "how I gonna make them potato cakes? This here lard we got is ransomed."

"I'll have to telephone McGregor's." Jean pushed back her chair and rose. "I hate to make them come out on a day like this but Bill took the car and I can't get to town."

"Yo' wants I should borrow some?" Martha asked.

"No, I'll try to have it sent."

Jean left the room and Martha advanced to the table and began picking up the soiled dishes. Over her head she wore a brown paper bag that stood up stiffly like a chef's cap and the apron that had been pinned to her dress was stained and dirty.

"Can't make things fit to eat 'thout proper ingre'jents," she muttered. "Yo' through?" she addressed Ann.

"Yes." Ann hastily gulped the remainder of her coffee, put down her cup, and left the dining-room.

In the living-room she lit a cigarette and curled up comfortably in a big chair where she could gaze out on the dreary view from the front window. Clasping her ankle, she waited. She could hear Jean's muffled words first on the telephone, and then answering some question Chip had come to ask. When Jean came back it was only to roam restlessly up and down the room, to move the ornaments on the mantel, rearrange the books on the shelves, straighten the magazines on the table.

Ann stubbed out her cigarette and said, "Stop fidgeting, for heaven's sake! I haven't finished talking to you."

"What's the use? What good will it do to talk?"

"Sit down, Jean," Ann said more gently, and when her sister had dropped into a chair she asked, "Was there anybody else here last night?"

"Only Aunt Amelia."

"What was she doing here?" Ann asked in surprise.

"She came over to tell Bill that Mother Tolliver wanted to see him this morning. And Hugh too," she added.

"You mean she came out in the cold to tell him that? Why on earth didn't she telephone?"

Jean shook her head wearily. "Aunt Amelia never uses the phone if she can help it. I think she's afraid of it. Anyway, she never uses it. Mother Tolliver or Flora or John do all the necessary phoning for the house. Aunt Amelia makes out lists for them."

"Imagine that!" Ann breathed. "I wouldn't have believed there were such people."

"Lots of people have idiosyncrasies," Jean said defensively. "I think Aunt Amelia's sweet."

"Yes, but—can you tell me how she looks?" Ann asked abruptly.

"Well, she has blue eyes and gray hair and—"

Ann waited for Jean to finish but when she got no further she said, "Exactly. She's so vague and fluttery nobody ever notices her. You never give her a second thought. Don't you see that nobody else could move your things more easily than she could?"

"But she wouldn't do that!"

"Did she go to your room?"

"I don't know. I opened the door for her and she said she wanted to talk to Bill. She seemed to have something on her mind, so I went back to the kitchen and made the congealed salad for today. I heard her crying and after a while Bill came to ask me if we had anything that would quiet her. I told him there was some ammonia in the bathroom but when we had fixed it for her she had gone."

"Gone!"

"Yes. I carried it to the living-room but she wasn't there."

Ann frowned. "Did Bill tell you what was the matter with her?" she asked.

"Yes. He said she was upset because Mother Tolliver had told her she wasn't capable of handling the trust fund Dad had left her."

"And Mrs. Tolliver was going to do that for her?"

"I suppose that was the way of it. Bill didn't say. She wanted Bill to talk to his mother and see if he couldn't persuade her to let Aunt Amelia have it."

"There isn't much chance of that, is there?"

"No."

Ann ran her hand over the padded arm of her chair. "How much money is it?" she asked.

"About fifteen hundred a year. That's just a guess, Ann."

"Enough, though, to make all the difference in the world to Amelia," Ann said thoughtfully. "She could live on that very nicely."

"Yes, I suppose she could."

"At least that gives us a motive as well as an opportunity," Ann said slowly.

"But Aunt Amelia couldn't have killed Dad!"

Ann explained then about the coffee, about the possibility that it had been drugged. Jean's face reflected mounting horror as she listened.

"Mrs. Tolliver had some sort of sleeping tablets," Ann finished, "so it was easy to get them."

"Any of us could have done it."

"Yes, if you had a motive. It would have made Mr. Tolliver dizzy and he might have fallen. But that wouldn't explain the feather," Ann said with a puzzled frown.

"What feather?"

There were more explanations and then Ann added, "I think I'm the only one who knows about the feather."

"It's horrible," Jean said, running nervous fingers through her hair. "I can't believe it."

They sat in silence for a time, thinking furiously. Outside, the wind swayed the trees, sending a spatter of raindrops against the windowpanes. A car passed in the street, its headlights stabbing through the gloom. It was a depressing day, Ann thought, and it certainly matched their moods.

The telephone rang and with a startled gasp Jean rose to answer it. Ann lit another cigarette, picked up the morning paper, and glanced idly at the front page before she put it down. Black headlines screamed of death and destruction and beside such world-wide horror their trouble seemed insignificantly small.

"It was Lou," Jean said when she returned.

"What did she want?"

"She wanted to know if Chip was all right," Jean said with a worried gesture of her hand, "She thought he had a cold last night. I haven't noticed anything wrong with him, have you?"

"Anybody's liable to have sniffles in weather like this. I wouldn't worry about Chip. He's as healthy a child as I've ever seen." Ann tapped the ash from her cigarette into a tray. "Isn't Lou a little too possessive with Chip? She acts as if he were hers."

Jean smiled wistfully. "You don't understand. Lou can't have a child of her own and she adores him. It's terrible to want something so much and know you can't have it."

Ann watched her sister with a vague uneasiness as Jean prowled restlessly up and down the room. There was a brooding look on her pale face.

"Something must be done," Jean said suddenly with deadly intensity. "They don't tell me things any more. They treat me like an outsider."

"What do you mean?"

"I asked Lou about Mother Tolliver. I wanted to see her, Ann. They haven't let me go near her since—since that afternoon you talked to her. Lou said she didn't want to see me. They hold me off at arm's length, all of them—even Bill. I don't know what to do, I don't know what to do—"

Her voice had risen hysterically and Ann got to her feet and grasped her sister's shoulders. Jean winced as sharp nails bit into her soft flesh. "I know what we're going to do," Ann said grimly. "You're going to pack your things and Chip's and we're going away. On the first train we can get out of here."

"I can't. I can't go away!" Jean whispered with a catch in her voice.

"You've got to! We've got to get away before something else happens!" Ann shook her sister as if by violence the could convince her of the necessity for haste.

"I can't leave Bill."

Ann pleaded with her for the next fifteen minutes. She gave one excuse after another, arguing her points with a fierceness that had fear back of it. Through it all Jean clung to a single idea: she couldn't leave Bill. Ann went back to the beginning, repeating herself as she struggled against an impregnable wall of resistance with which Jean had surrounded herself. She walked up and down the room as she talked, and came at last to stand in front of her sister.

"You're not listening to half of what I'm saying," she accused as she sank, exhausted, onto the sofa.

"Yes, I've heard you," Jean said quietly. "You think there's some danger and you want to get me away from it. But you don't understand, Ann. I couldn't ever leave Bill. No matter what happens. There's nothing you can say to make me change about that."

She stared vacantly out of the window, absently creasing the thick folds of the drapery. Suddenly she turned back to Ann. "There's one thing you can do," she said slowly.

"What is it?"

"If anything should happen to me, will you take Chip? Bill will be in the Army. I don't mean for always; I just want him taken care of now. He's such a baby."

"Nothing's going to happen," Ann replied, struggling to keep her voice controlled.

"I don't think so either," Jean said, smiling sadly. "I just wanted to be sure. You're right about one thing. Things can't go on any longer as they have been." She walked toward the door.

"What are you going to do?" Ann asked, thoroughly alarmed.

"I'm going to talk to Mother Tolliver."

"But you can't!" Ann exclaimed, following her sister into the hall, where Jean picked up a coat that had been thrown across the chair beside the telephone. "You can't do that. You'll make matters worse!"

"Things can't be any worse than they are already," Jean said stubbornly as she thrust her arms into the coat. "I want this thing, whatever it is, brought into the open and settled once and for all."

"She'll browbeat you. She'll have you at a disadvantage where you can't fight back." Ann caught the coat sleeve as though to delay her sister.

"Oh, yes, I can." Jean shrugged off her hand and went quickly to the front door. "She's trying to take Bill away from me. And there's nothing that I won't do to get him back."

The door was closed with a bang and Ann was left alone. She went to the window where she could watch until her sister was hidden from view. Putting her hand to her forehead, she rubbed it, as though by that futile gesture she could clear her brain. She had never before felt so defeated, so helpless. It wasn't as though she knew why all these queer little things had been happening; it was their inexplicability that was frightening. She was haunted by a nameless and unknown fear.

From somewhere in the rear she heard Chip's voice raised excitably and then a rush of laughter. One thing at least they had been spared—panic that had seized adults had not as yet touched him. With sudden resolution she went back and spoke to Lily.

"Take care of Chip while Miss Jean and I are out. We'll be back in a little while."

"Where are you going, Tan?" Chip demanded. "Can I go too?"

"No, darling, not this time. We'll be back in a little while. You stay with Lily and be a good boy."

"I wanna go too." She heard him wail as she closed the door.

Quickly she got her own coat and slipped out of the house. The damp air curled her hair and plastered it about her face. She hugged her arms closer to her body as a cold wind swirled against her legs and spattered water from the trees. Her breath came in short gasps as she ran along the sidewalk.

It took strength of will to force her reluctant steps up the flagstone path that led to the Tolliver house. On the edge of the porch she paused and looked up at the tall columns that rose on either side of her as though by their sheer height they sought to awe her. She hesitated, wondering if, like Samson, she was blindly pulling down the pillars of destruction on her own head.

The door was partly open and that in itself was odd. People do not usually leave front doors open on cold rainy days. Jean must have been unusually careless to have left it that way. Ann entered and shut it, listening to the almost silent click of the lock.

The hall was dark in spite of the fanlight and glass panels beside the door, but Ann could see that there was no one in it. She took two steps forward and then was startled by a voice that seemed to speak almost at her side.

"We need it immediately."

It was Dr. Hans who was speaking, and after a moment Ann realized that he was in the library and that door was partly open. That was why his words were so clear and distinct.

"I tell you I can't do anything about it," Bill said shortly. "Dad made Mother executor and she has full control. I talked to her about the bequest and told her the need for it was urgent, but she says nothing can be done about it until the entire estate is settled and she fully understands the management."

"But we do not have the time to wait." Dr. Hans sounded desperate. "I must talk to your mother. Surely when she understands the need she will give it to us."

"I don't think that would do any good. Certainly not this morning. She's got something on her mind. She's already had me on the carpet for neglecting the business and she's had John telephone for Mr. Holmes to come out and see her this afternoon."

"But we have already ordered it. The bill will be sent to me when it arrives and I must have the money to pay for it."

"I'm sorry, but there's nothing I can do for you."

"If I could talk to Mrs. Tolliver for a little while I think I could convince her—"

"Haven't I got enough troubles of my own without adding yours to them?" Bill broke in irritably. "If you want that contraption you've ordered you'd better wait. She's in no mood to listen to you now."

There was a scraping noise of a chair being moved and Ann looked about her in panic. It would be both awkward and embarrassing for her to be caught here in the hall. She had been eavesdropping on what sounded like a very private and confidential conversation. She crossed the hall on tiptoe and opened one of the double-paneled doors directly opposite those that led into the library.

12
THE ODOR OF DEATH

This was the room Mrs. Tolliver euphuistically called the drawing-room. It was probably the only one in town, as less pretentious people would have spoken of it as the parlor or simply the sitting-room. It was almost never used.

The curtains were tightly drawn and Ann had to grope her way through a chilled semigloom in which the furniture loomed as darker shadows. Her sense of smell was particularly keen and it seemed to her now that the odor of funeral flowers still clung to this room though Mr. Tolliver had left his home for the last time a week ago. She would have liked to let the cold wet air sweep through the place, let it blow away this fetid odor of death.

As she heard the library door open and the low rumble of men's voices in the hall she drew back against a chair. Sitting down, she waited, biding her time until the hall should be empty again, listening for the outer door to open and close. Suppose Bill should decide to go upstairs and see his mother? Ann held her breath. She had sat there for what seemed an eternity before she realized that the house was quiet again. But she had not heard the front door close.

She rose and peered into the hall. The very furtiveness of her own movements was frightening her and she imagined that the shadows in front and behind her moved, that other people watched from hiding-places in the hall. Her hands were damp and sweat broke out in little beads along her upper lip. She shook her head, resolutely pushed open the door, and stepped into the hall, glancing up the dark well of the stairs as she did so.

"Oh, it's you, Ann."

She spun around to find Bill standing a few feet from her.

"Come in here a minute. I want to talk to you." He spoke flatly, without inflection, and he seemed preoccupied and worried.

Silently she followed him into the library. A lamp on the table threw a small pool of light over the floor, giving the room some feeling of warmth. After all, this was the one livable room in an otherwise formal house.

"Give me a cigarette, Bill," she said shakily. She couldn't say: *You scared me. I almost screamed. I didn't expect you to be in the hall.*

He offered his case and lit her cigarette for her, watching her as she inhaled deeply. As he took one himself he said, "You smoke too much, Ann."

"What if I do?" She slid out of her coat and draped it over a chair.

"That's not what I wanted to talk to you about." He frowned and picked up the morning paper, refolded it carefully, and placed it on the table. "I wanted to ask you if you'd stay with Jean for the rest of the winter." He waited and when she didn't reply he added, "Will you?"

"Why? Why are you asking me to do this now?"

He threw out his arms in a helpless gesture. "I have to go into the Army in a few weeks. I—I don't want to leave Jean alone, and she's always wanted you with her."

He was avoiding her eyes and Ann's mouth was set and grim. She had always liked this brother-in-law of hers, but now she wasn't sure of him. She almost disliked him.

Bill ran nervous fingers through his thick hair and sat down in a chair opposite her. When he looked up there was a beseeching look on his face and she noticed that his eyes were bloodshot and that there were tired white lines about his mouth. His suit was wrinkled and even it looked tired and drooping.

"I made a new will yesterday," he said dully. "If anything happens to—to me, I want you to know about it."

He almost said, "if anything happens to Jean," Ann thought grimly, hardening her heart toward him.

"I've made you and Hugh administrators—and guardians for Chip in case anything happens."

"What makes you think something will happen? Jean—"

"Of course," he interrupted. "It's just that we're living in such an uncertain world today, Ann. I'll be away and I'd like to know that Jean has somebody—" He broke off and sat silent, leaning forward with his elbows on his knees. "You wouldn't have to take any real responsibility if you didn't want to. Hugh would look after the financial end and Lou would take care of Chip."

"If you think I'd let anybody have my sister's baby—!" Ann exclaimed. "She's my sister."

"I know," he said with a weary smile. "I don't necessarily believe everything I've been told, Ann. Jean would never harm Chip."

"You don't—?" Ann leaned toward him, incredulity written on her face.

"No. But Jean almost died when Chip was born. She isn't very strong even yet."

"Why didn't you write me?" Ann demanded angrily.

"She wouldn't let me. You know how she hates sickness. She knew you'd come if you were told and she didn't want you for that reason. She made me promise."

Ann drew her brows together so that there was a deep line between her eyes. "I don't understand," she said slowly. "Look here, Bill, I want to take Jean and Chip away with me."

"No!"

"I don't know what's happening here," Ann continued almost as though she were talking to herself. "I don't understand it, but Jean is nervous and—afraid. I don't care how things appear, I know she's not responsible for these queer things that have been happening."

Bill threw his cigarette into the empty fireplace, where it glowed in a round pencil point of fire. Ann watched him compassionately, a little sorrowfully. He was in the unenviable position of not wanting to believe and yet not quite unbelieving.

"You'll have to make up your own mind one way or the other."

"I know." He spoke with a new firmness in his voice and as he stood up some of the lethargy seemed to drop from his shoulders, "I've been wrong. I'll have to tell Jean. I ought to apologize."

"I should think you would," Ann said, her mind going instantly to the scene she had witnessed last night in the hall.

A low rumble of thunder, ending in a reverberating clap as a streak of lightning zigzagged across the sky, resounded through the room.

"Oh!"

Ann turned with a start. Amelia stood in the doorway, her hands pressed tightly over her ears. Her thin lips twitched nervously and tears came to her eyes.

Bill went to her. "You aren't afraid of lightning, are you, Aunt Amelia?" he asked gently. "There's no danger."

"No," Amelia quavered, dropping her hands with a fluttery movement. "No, I'm not afraid. But I don't like thunder and lightning."

"That's all right then." Bill patted her shoulder and took a step toward the door. She put out a hand and caught his arm.

"Bill, did you ask her?"

"Ask her what?"

"You know. About my money. It's mine." Amelia's face was white and she blinked back the tears in her eyes. She looked a thin, stooped shadow of a woman, but there must have been strength and endurance back of that seeming frailty, for she did a great deal of work—whatever the Negroes left undone, a fact of which they were completely aware.

"I forgot it. Why don't you let it alone for a while, Aunt Amelia?" Bill said persuasively. "Mother's upset about something this morning and I don't think it would be a good time to mention it. She'll give you whatever you need."

"You don't understand," Amelia replied with utter despair in her words. "It's mine. William gave it to me. I haven't had anything that was all mine in a long time."

The cigarette burned Ann's fingers and she put it down quickly. She was sitting in plain view, but she had the feeling that either Amelia was too distraught to see her or she didn't care. It was an odd feeling, as though she were a disembodied audience watching the opening curtain of a drama.

"Helen is cruel," Amelia continued. "You'll be going away soon and I'm afraid I'll never get it."

"Hugh will be here to look after you. He'll take care of you," Bill said with a reassuring pat. "Besides, he's much better about persuading Mother to do things than I am."

"I'll talk to her again myself," Amelia said with a show of determination. "I've been doing for Helen all my life. Why can't she do this one thing for me? The money is mine. Why can't she give it to me?"

Bill put an arm around her shoulders and pulled her toward the door. "I'll talk to Mother if you feel that way about it," he said. "We'll talk it over and as soon as things have settled down a bit we can get everything straightened."

"Now?" Amelia asked, once again her timid self.

"Not right now," he answered. "I have to see Jean and talk to her first. There's something I must tell her."

His hand pulled the door to behind them and Ann was left alone in the library. "Well!" she said aloud. "That's that."

She got up and went to a window through the mist-clouded glass of which she stared at the blurred outlines of the fluted columns on the porch. She didn't quite know what to do next. She had come to this house to get her sister, and though Jean might have left during that interview with Bill she couldn't be sure. The floors were too thickly carpeted, the place too insulated against sound. The very moment you crossed the doorway you instinctively lowered your voice. Ann twisted the sapphire on her right hand, trying to organize her thoughts until she reached a decision. She had to be sure that Jean had gone.

Opening the door, she went quietly up the wide stairs, her feet making soft squashy sounds on the carpeted treads. At the top she hesitated, not quite certain of her way.

The upper hall was dim, lighted only by a big window at one end. Closed doors lined the narrow corridor. Ann was less familiar with this part of the house so, clutching the newel post tightly, she stood there listening for the sound of voices that would help her find her direction.

She turned toward the window, simply because at that end there was more light, and almost immediately heard the low murmur of voices.

As she pressed against the wall beside the closed door she heard Jean speaking quite clearly.

"Why have you been so against me? Almost from the day I married Bill you've hated me."

"We have been over this already," Mrs. Tolliver replied in her carefully modulated voice. "There are more important things for me to think about today. So if there is nothing else you have to say to me—"

"I'm not crazy," Jean said dully. "I know all about these things that have been happening, but I didn't do them. Somebody else did them, somebody who wants to persecute me in all sorts of small ways."

"That is usually the excuse of unbalanced brains."

Ann could imagine the prim and cynical smile that curved Mrs. Tolliver's thin lips. She clenched her fists so tightly that the nails bit into the palms, though she was unconscious of the pain.

"I might really have believed you if Ann hadn't shown me," Jean said.

"Ann has always been ingenious about twisting facts to suit her own purpose," Mrs. Tolliver replied with what sounded like a sneer. "She has always influenced you. You have always done whatever she wanted you to do. You are weak and that, I think, is not a very admirable characteristic." She paused and then added, "I cannot say that that influence has been good."

Ann put her hand on the knob of the door but she was checked from opening it by Jean's angry voice. "She's my sister!"

"Hardly that." Mrs. Tolliver seemed amused. "You don't really know who you are, do you? And as far as I have been able to discover, nobody else does either."

"So—" The word sounded more like a quickly indrawn breath.

"I am a very strong believer in heredity," Mrs. Tolliver went on. "I am able to say that the blood that flows through the veins of my children is the best. The very best."

"You really hate me."

"Hate?" There was a rising inflection in Mrs. Tolliver's laugh. "My dear young lady, it is not a matter of hating you. It is simply that I don't think you are suitable." She hesitated and then added coldly, "Neither as a wife for my son nor as a mother for his child."

"I'll never give him up." Jean's voice was rough with anger but there was a deadly earnestness about what she was saying. "He loves me. Yes, in spite of all the lies you've told him. Do you hear me? I'll never give him up! I'll kill you first!"

Mrs. Tolliver laughed again and the sound made Ann's spine turn to ice. "Are you threatening me, my dear? It's so utterly absurd. I can do what I please with you. You completely underestimate me."

Somewhere down the hall a door opened softly and Ann turned her head toward the sound. There wasn't much light, but she would have been able to see anyone. The hall seemed empty and Ann decided the tension of overwrought nerves had made her imagine the sound. Certainly it had not been repeated. She crossed the hall quickly to the steep back stairs. It wouldn't do any good for her to be caught there in the upstairs hall and there was a slim chance that she could slip back to the library, get her coat, and leave this place. She could wait for Jean on the porch.

"Well!"

Ann saw that she had been trapped here on this steep flight of steps. She hated pretense and subterfuge; tact had never been numbered among her virtues. There was nothing for her to do but brazen this scene through to its end. Running her hand lightly along the wall, she boldly descended the few remaining steps until she stood on the small back porch.

"What are you doing in this house?" Lou demanded.

Ann's eyes narrowed so that they looked like the topazes to which one fellow artist had compared them—cold and shiny. "I came to talk to Bill," she said tersely.

"To Bill?" Lou laughed harshly. "Didn't you think you'd find Hugh here? Did you think you could carry on a backstairs affair without my knowing it? You can't have him. I took him from you once and I'll keep him!"

"Living with you hasn't made him deliriously happy so far as I can see," Ann retorted. "I rather imagine I could have him any time I want him."

Lou's face turned purplish red with anger. "You're as crazy as your sister!"

"Oh, nuts!" Ann exclaimed in disgust as she edged toward the door so that she could get away as quickly as possible. "Let me tell you something for your own good, Lou Tolliver. Bill knows what you and your mother have been saying and he knows it isn't true. He told me just this morning when he asked me to look after Jean and Chip for him when he was gone."

"What did he ask you to do for Chip and Jean?" Lou clutched Ann's arm with a fierce grip. Her voice cracked with some new emotion that the girl didn't understand.

"Just the usual thing you'd expect under the circumstances." Ann tried to brush off Lou's hands but the fingers tightened on her arm. "Hugh and I are to be joint guardians in case anything happens to Bill. He wanted to be sure that Jean's rights were protected. Hugh will look after the financial end of her affairs."

"It's a lie!"

"Ask Bill to show you his will if you don't believe me." Ann pulled away as Lou's grasp loosened.

"Chip's mine," Lou muttered.

"Aren't you claiming too much? It seems to me that Jean's his mother." Ann raised her arched brows disdainfully.

"Jean's crazy. Everybody knows it. She couldn't keep him."

"Oh yes, she can—and will." Ann opened the door to the kitchen, then turned back to say, "If you and your mother have to be vindictive, take it out on me. I don't care. But I'm warning you, leave my sister alone."

Lou raised a hand as though to strike, but evidently thought it would do no good, for she let it fall slowly to her side. She gave Ann an angry glare and started up the stairs.

Ann clung to the doorknob and listened to the sound of those footsteps. It was like the thump of clumps of earth thrown on a coffin, slow and final. Then they stopped. Those back stairs were steep and dark, walled in so that they opened into the upper hall by a door. There was only one small window, high up on the wall. For a moment Ann thought Lou might have fallen, but there had been no sound—nothing. She took an involuntary step forward, then whirled around to find John and Flora watching her.

They stood in the middle of the kitchen and even the inscrutability of their black faces could not hide their curiosity and interest. There was no doubt that they had seen and heard everything. Their eyes were wide and popped and John's mouth sagged in amazement. Her abrupt turning on them caught them doing nothing, nothing except listening, and she knew the grapevine back to the Circle would buzz before the day was over.

Flora was the first to recover. She wiped the palms of her hands along her ample hips with a downward stroke. It was like watching a photograph turn suddenly into a movie.

"Yo' had oughta stay out of Mis' Lou's way. She sho' ain't lak yo' an' Mis' Jean."

"I don't like her either, and she'd better stay out of my way."

John's thick lips cracked to say, "Mis Lou got a mean disposition."

"Does she treat Miss Jean like this when I'm not here?" Ann asked.

"Naw'm." Flora moved to the stove, where she lifted the lid of a kettle. She stepped back as steam rose from the opening. "I's Adeline's cousin. Mis' Jean got me an' Jawn this job."

Ann was listening, straining to understand the rising inflections, the soft cadence of their voices, which are more the essence of the Negro dialect than the words they use. Five years ago she would have caught their meaning instantly, but now she wasn't sure.

Flora picked up a pot and carried it to the sink. "Us sho' is glad yo' come to look after Mis' Jean while Mr. Bill's away," she said flatly.

"Mr. Tol'ver sho' wuz a fine man," John said.

"Mis' Amelia all right," Flora added.

But they don't say anything about Mrs. Tolliver, Ann thought. She nodded in understanding. They were telling her something in their peculiar roundabout way.

John's eyes went beyond her and Ann turned to see that Lou had come back to the porch.

"Yo' wants to git outta the back do'?" he asked softly.

"I left my coat in the library." Ann shook her head. "I'll have to get it and go that way."

"Yas'm." Both Negroes bobbed their heads in relief.

Pushing the swinging door, Ann went into the dining-room. She was surprised to find herself trembling and she sat down in one of the chairs until she could think what to do next. She had to give Jean time to get out of this house and she didn't want to run into anybody else. The whole place seemed crowded with people, people who moved about soundlessly on the thickly carpeted floors so that you didn't know they were there until you came face to face with them.

Ann put up a hand and rubbed at the puzzled lines that felt like deep ridges across her forehead. She forced herself to take ten slow, even breaths before she got up and opened the door that led into the hall.

There was a man standing at the foot of the stairs and Ann drew a sigh of relief when she recognized Hugh. He had two large books tucked under his arm and was peeling off his gloves. He smiled when he saw her, put the books on a chair, and laid his overcoat over them.

"Good morning, Hugh," Ann said. "What are you doing here so early?"

He grimaced. "The command audience," he said. "Have you forgotten that Bill phoned me last night?"

"Yes, I had forgotten. I left my coat in the library." She was wondering if she could delay Hugh for a few minutes. She was fairly sure that Jean had gone by now, but it wouldn't hurt to let Mrs. Tolliver cool off after that interview. She smiled brightly and Hugh followed her like a homing pigeon to the library.

"I've never really had a chance to talk to you since you've been here, Ann. Are you coming back to stay?"

"No, I'll stay until after Christmas," she said slowly. "Then I'll be off again."

"Back to Chicago?"

"I don't think so. At least not until spring. The doctor said the weather there was too damp. And now look at what I find here." She waved her hand toward the window.

"This is unusual." He gave the invariable excuse people do when someone maligns their climate. "I wish you'd stay."

"Why?"

"Isn't it enough that I want you?"

Ann picked up an ash tray from the table, then nervously replaced it. "I—I don't know," she faltered.

"Everybody makes mistakes once in a while. But there's no reason to go on paying for them all your life. Life's too short for that sort of martyrdom."

"Are you sure you've made a mistake?" she asked curiously.

"Aren't you, Ann? You went away so soon and then you stayed. You've known other men during these past years, haven't you? And you've never married. You ought to know your own mind in five years. You must have loved me or you'd never have left. Why are you fighting it? It's something bigger than either of us."

Ann turned her back on him and the lamplight fell full on her face. Her head ached and she rubbed her temples as if to ease the pain. "I—I don't know, Hugh," she said. "It's all so complicated."

He put his hands on her shoulders and turned her so that her face was on a level with his and forced her eyes to meet his own. He didn't speak for a moment, just held her, staring at the familiar curve of her cheek, the oblique shape of her tawny eyes shadowed by their fringe of dark lashes. He touched her hair gently and said, "You weren't always so uncertain."

Looking into his face, Ann was swept by a strange feeling, tumultuous and so terribly sweet—yet somehow a feeling softened by a touch of sadness. Her mouth twisted in a wry smile. "Life wasn't so complex five years ago, Hugh. We had only ourselves to consider then. Now—well, there's Lou."

"I think that was a touch of madness." His voice shook and she saw that his face was pale, that little bluish beads of sweat glistened on his forehead. "I still don't know how it happened."

"But it did happen," she pointed out.

She turned her face away from him as she wondered why on earth she didn't take him now. It was her supreme chance to strike back at the woman who had humiliated her, but somehow she couldn't take this opportunity. Lou wouldn't be the only one to be hurt. There was Bill and, through him, her sister.

"You mustn't worry," Hugh said quickly, misinterpreting her movement. "It's my mistake and I suppose I must make the best of it. I'll—I'll find some solution."

"I must go." Ann picked up her coat.

"Ann!"

His arms were around her and he held her tightly and kissed her mouth. The coat slipped from her hand and fell to the floor. She felt only the hard, almost savage pressure of his lips on hers. It was like being drowned, with the waves breaking over her head in a dazzling white spray. For a moment nothing else mattered; there were only the two of them in the whole world, a world of bright lights and ringing music in her ears. It was madness and then, as he laid his check against her, she began to fight. The memory of another kiss intruded upon her thoughts. This one was different. In Paul's arms she felt a warmth, a tenderness, an enduring peace. That, Ann knew

now, was love. This was only infatuation, wild and fantastic—
and at long last she was rid of it.

Above the soft murmuring of Hugh's lips against her ear
she heard a sharp noise, the sound of a door opening and closing. She pushed him away, her hands pressing hard against his
shoulders. "Stop, Hugh! You're mad!"

He drew back from her in amazement and she immediately
turned. The door was closed, but she knew it had been opened.
She wasn't mistaken in the sound she had heard.

"Ann! What's the matter?"

She began to laugh in little gasps of hysteria. "I don't love
you. Do you understand that? I thought I did, but I don't."

"You don't know what you're saying! Ann!"

"I don't love you." She caught up her coat and ran to the door.

Her fingers slipped on the knob as it opened and Bill stood
there, his hair plastered wetly to his head.

"Where's Jean?" he demanded. "I can't find her."

Ann laughed and ran past him and up the steps without
any conscious idea of direction. She knocked briskly on Mrs.
Tolliver's door and, without waiting for a reply, pushed it open.

Mrs. Tolliver lay in the center of a big four-poster bed,
propped up on a pillow. Her eyes were open, fixed on some
point to Ann's left. One thin hand grasped the Marseille coun-
terpane so tightly that the veins stood out on it like thin blue
ropes while the other hung limply over the side of the bed. The
white hair which was usually so stiffly coiffured was frowsy
and a lock straggled over her high forehead.

Ann glanced over her shoulder, following the direction of
the old woman's eyes, but she could see nothing except a bare
plastered wall and a steel engraving of *The Stag at Bay*. She
turned back to the woman on the bed.

"Mrs. Tolliver," she said.

There was a little light in the room and what came through
the windows was dim and leaden. Yet the bed was covered with
papers, scattered helter-skelter over the white spread and piled
on the table and chair. The draft from the door caught one

piece of paper and it floated slowly to the edge, then dropped silently to the pillow that lay on the floor near the head of the bed.

There was something frightening in that movement, the only movement in the otherwise still room. Fear was a giant spider spreading its grotesque legs over Ann until she was paralyzed.

"Where's Jean?" The words were whispered and Ann ran her tongue over her dry lips.

Mrs. Tolliver made no reply and Ann bent toward her. The thin lips were slightly parted and the face was a ghastly blue. Something was wrong, terribly wrong. It was queer, and with almost superhuman effort Ann put a hand on the older woman's shoulder. At her touch the white head fell forward and the body slumped sideways in the bed. Ann drew back instantly. Her fingers were chilled by the touch of death. Stepping backward, she stumbled over the fallen pillow. For a moment she could do nothing, then she raised her other hand to her throat and screamed, a shrill, terrified sound that echoed eerily through the house.

13

NOTHING TO DO BUT WAIT

She backed away from the figure slumped in the bed, her hand still against her throat in an effort to choke back the screams that burned there in searing, aching flames. At the door she bumped into Bill.

"What is it? What's the matter?" He gripped her shoulders, shaking her roughly. Then his eyes went beyond her to the bed. He pushed her away and she would have fallen had not Hugh caught her. Everybody was there in the doorway or in the shadowy hall, but they seemed numb, unable to move, as they watched Bill cross the room and bend over the woman on the bed.

"I'm all right, Hugh." Ann leaned against the wall, breathing in deep, uneven gasps.

He looked at her closely and was apparently satisfied with what he saw, for he turned and followed Bill into the room. Bill looked up and then took his brother-in-law by the arm.

"Call Dr. Morrison. I—I'm not sure Anyway, nobody's to come into this room until the doctor's been here." His face was white and pinched and his voice sounded harsh. He closed the door behind him. "All of you go back downstairs. I don't want anybody in this room until the doctor gets here."

They went like stupid, dumb animals as one by one they turned to obey. Amelia caught Ann's arm and the girl was surprised by the strength in the thin old lady. Gray hair hung limply beside withered cheeks and her lips moved constantly as though she were speaking a piece, but there was no sound.

Bill followed them down the steps. "Call the doctor, Hugh. No, maybe you'd better let John do it," he added, his troubled eyes on Lou, who clung, weeping, to her husband. "And turn on some lights in this house."

"Yas, sir." John hastened to do as he was told. He and Flora were helpless in their fright. Their black faces were shiny with sweat and their eyes were wide and terrified.

Hugh pushed his overcoat and hat from the chair and got Lou into it but she still held fast to his hand. Tears rolled in a steady stream from her reddened eyes until her cheeks were blotchy and her nose was an ugly plum color.

"She's dead, isn't she?" Lou moaned.

Hugh glanced hastily at Bill before he turned back to her and said, "Hush. There's nothing you can do for her now. We're calling a doctor."

"I ought to go to her."

Ann sat down on the bottom step and leaned her head against the newel post. There was no other available seat. She felt Amelia trembling as she edged closer. Ann felt like a trapped animal. She wanted a cigarette, a strong drink. She wanted to get out in the open and feel fresh, cold air on her face. Some of the first shock was ebbing, but her feet were leaden blocks and she couldn't move.

The light was clicked on with a suddenness that was startling. It came down garishly from between the crystal prisms of the chandelier that swung on a glass bead chain from the ceiling.

"I—I thought she was better. She was going to come downstairs this afternoon."

Amelia's voice sounded dull and monotonous. Ann looked at her queerly. Hadn't she understood the implication of that closed door upstairs? Didn't she realize that Bill had deliberately pushed them out, these people who would so naturally have been admitted to the presence of death?

Amelia's darting eyes rested momentarily on the coat and hat which Hugh had pushed to the floor. Swiftly she rose, picked them up, and carried them to the closet under the stairs. Watching her, Ann wondered why she thought there was something strange about this. But Amelia was innately tidy—except in her mind, which was always fuzzy. She had spent a good many years in this house picking up after other people, putting things away in their proper places. Still Ann couldn't shake off the feeling that there was something wrong this time.

Bill was standing midway down the steps and Hugh looked up at him and asked, "Is she—?"

"Yes. There's nothing we can do now." Bill rubbed a hand across his face but could not erase the lines of worry that looked like deep scars about his mouth and nose. "I can't be sure that it's natural after what's been said about—about Dad. That's why I want the doctor. He can tell us."

"But her weak heart?" Hugh said quickly.

Bill shook his head. "Dr. Morrison told me only last week that there was nothing whatsoever wrong with her heart. He said there wasn't anything wrong with her."

Ann was struck by the absence of grief in this family. Though she herself had disliked Mrs. Tolliver intensely, she had supposed the family loved her. Their faces showed shock and worry, but in spite of Lou's tears she felt there was no real grief in them.

They were silent then until they heard the brisk clatter of the knocker. Flora opened the door and Dr. Morrison stepped into the hall. As Bill came down the steps to meet him the doctor put his little black bag on the floor and let Flora help him with his heavy over coat and hat.

"Put 'em somewhere they can dry," he said. "It's nasty outside. Can't remember when we've had worse weather. All right, son, what's the matter? John said to hurry."

The doctor was a small, shriveled old man. His shoulders drooped, his dark suit hung loosely on his body, and gold-rimmed glasses were hooked over prominent ears. Dr. Morrison was tired and overworked. He had planned to retire, but when the younger doctors had been called to the service of their country he had taken up his burden and gone back to his work. He was like a dray horse that carries on even after he had a glimpse of the green pasture.

"It's my mother," Bill said.

Dr. Morrison clicked his false teeth in what was meant to be a sympathetic sound, picked up his bag, and followed Bill up the steps.

Six pairs of eyes followed them as they climbed the stairs, then dropped covertly at the sound of the bedroom door being opened. For a time none of them spoke. It was as though they were trying to dovetail facts and surmises into something that was credible. From beneath lowered lids they eyed each other warily and all of them apparently felt the tension of overdrawn nerves.

"Go up there, Hugh," Lou ordered. "Go see what they are doing. And stop cracking your knuckles!"

He dropped his hands to his side self-consciously and bit his lower lip. "Yes, yes, I'd better go."

It was only about ten minutes before the men came back to them, though it seemed that hours had passed. The doctor came first and stopped for a moment on the steps. His thin lips were tight and he gripped the bag he carried in his hand, He must have read the question in their upturned faces but he marched past them to the telephone on the table back of the stairs.

Picking up the receiver, he said, "Give me police headquarters. . . . Morrison speaking. I am at the Tollivers'. Mrs. Tolliver is dead and it looks like murder to me. . . . Hello, Captain. . . . No. . . . Yes, I'll be here. . . . All right, I'll do that. . . . Certainly."

Slowly he replaced the instrument and came back to the others. "The police will be here in a few minutes." He took a slim gold watch from his vest pocket and peered at it. "Haven't had lunch, have you? I thought not. What about it, Miss Amelia? Can you feed all of 'em? Better eat something," he added more kindly. "You'll need it."

Amelia uttered a few inarticulate sounds and her hands fluttered nervously.

"That's right," said the doctor. "All of you go in the dining-room. You fix 'em something, Flora. Give 'em a lot of coffee."

"I—I'm going to my mother." Lou rose unsteadily to her feet.

Dr. Morrison shook his head. "Nobody can go up there."

Lou's sobbing broke out anew, growing in hysterical intensity.

The doctor's faded eyes peered myopically at her through his glasses before he opened his bag and took out a small bottle of white pellets. "Take her in the dining-room and fetch me a glass of water," he directed. "I'll give her something that will help steady her nerves."

Hugh put an arm around his wife's waist and Ann pushed off the lethargy which had held her rooted to the steps.

"I'd better go home," she said. "I'll have to tell Jean."

The doctor grunted and looked at her. "You'll have to stay here. You were the one who found her, weren't you? The police will want to talk to you."

"But I've got to go. I can't stay here."

"Telephone Jean if you must," he compromised. "But mind you, don't say anything about what's happened here. The telephone's no place to get such a shock."

Ann picked up the receiver but with the doctor and Bill listening she could only say that she wouldn't be home for lunch. She couldn't answer the swift rush of questions that came over the wire. All she could do was repeat, rather stupidly, that she wouldn't be home for a while. As she turned from the table she felt sure of one thing: Jean had as yet no intimation of the tragedy that had happened here this morning.

Luncheon was a ghastly meal. Bill, stern and old-looking, sat at the head of the table where his father had once presided. The doctor's pill had helped Lou but she still sobbed and sniffled occasionally into a crushed handkerchief.

The roast was leathery and dry from overcooking and the baked tomatoes were burned. Not that any of them noticed, for the doctor was the only one who tasted his food and he, with a wry twist of his mouth, pushed it away from him. Once a dish crashed in the kitchen and as the sound reverberated through the dining-room Amelia half rose from her chair. John brought them coffee with the cups rattling against the saucers, but the brew was weak and bitter. Flora had evidently spread a small amount by the simple process of adding hot water. There had been no blessing to make a miracle of this feast.

The silence in the room was heavy, and though the first terrible shock was wearing away, they were still nervous and afraid. There was no conversation to accompany the little ordinary sounds of a meal. Even when Amelia dropped her knife and burst into tears nobody spoke.

When the doorbell rang the doctor rose and said, "That must be the police. I'll go see them."

Throwing down his napkin, Bill followed the doctor and a moment later Hugh left the dining-room. Left alone, the three women looked at each other, their faces expressing their mounting suspicions. Then, almost with one accord, they pushed back their chairs and went into the hall.

A policeman stood near the foot of the stairs and above them they could hear the tramping of heavy shoes and the rumble of men's voices.

"You can't go upstairs," the policeman said in a loud voice.

"The mud," Amelia said, not looking at him. "Look at the mud you've tracked in. Helen won't like that."

She scurried away and a few minutes later returned with a small broom and dustpan. As she started up the stairs the policemen stopped her again. "You can't go up there," he repeated.

"I have to get the mud off the carpet. Helen won't like it."

He looked at her doubtfully. "All right," he finally agreed, "but you can't go up on the second floor."

She made a thorough job of it, brushing the loose wet earth into the pan. If the police had planned to get any evidence from footprints, Ann decided, they had been neatly thwarted. Not that it made much difference, because to her certain knowledge several people had been up those steps this morning.

"Don't bother with the rest of it," Ann said as Amelia finished the steps. "There will be other people coming in later."

"Yes, ma'm," the policeman said with evident relief, as though the woman made him nervous with her cleaning. "You all go sit down. The cap'n will want to see you."

Politely he opened the drawing-room doors, but the sight of the gloomy room made him shut them quickly and indicate the library. Lou sniffed audibly and with her head in the air marched past him. Ann held back, but when she saw the policeman watching her she followed the others.

Someone, either Bill or Hugh, had picked up her coat, for it was hung neatly over the back of a chair. She searched its pockets vainly for cigarettes until she saw a newly opened pack on the table. She took one, lit it, and inhaled deeply. The muscles at the back of her neck ached and she rubbed them with her hand, trying to ease the tension. Amelia was perched on the edge of the wing chair, her eyes on the door, as though she would run if anyone entered. Lou sat in the big leather chair, pulled her dress tight over her fat knees and, after a few heaving breaths that shook the ruffles over her breast, began to cry.

Other people came. They could hear the opening and closing of the front door and the policeman in the hall speaking, though they could not distinguish his words. They could hear the heavy, dull tread of feet going up and down the stairs.

Ann was on her third cigarette before the doctor came back to them. "I'm sorry," he began.

"It's—it's—?" Ann asked.

He nodded slowly. "Yes. It's murder. The coroner is here now and Captain Harkness is in charge. They don't need me any more."

"How—?" It was Ann who asked the question but Lou and Amelia were listening.

"Captain Harkness will want to tell you about it. He'll be down in just a little while."

"I—I ought to be with Helen." Amelia jerked to her feet.

"There's nothing you can do for her now, Miss Amelia."

"Wait! Wait! There's nothing for us to do but wait!" Lou shrilled.

Dr. Morrison's face reddened. "You won't do anybody any good by getting hysterical. There's nothing you could do upstairs. The police are in complete charge."

Either his words or the harshness of his tone had the desired effect, for Lou buried her face in her arms and sobbed in a more controlled sort of way.

The doctor turned to Ann. "The police won't let either you or Bill leave yet," he said. He sighed and added, "I've told Bill I'd tell his wife for him. Doctors are used to handing out bad news and at least I'm better than the telephone. She'd better come over here."

"Yes, I suppose so." Ann replied, frowning.

"What about the baby?" Lou sat up and demanded.

"They have a nurse for him," Dr. Morrison replied impatiently. "There's no reason why she can't take care of him for the afternoon."

"I could look after him," Lou offered eagerly.

The frown on Ann's face deepened and her eyes narrowed in thought. She couldn't quite understand why Lou jumped at every opportunity to get Chip. There was something wrong, something queer in the way she went about it.

"You'll be wanted here," the doctor answered Lou. "After all, you were here in the house. They'll want to know what you can tell them."

He slammed his hat on his gray head then and marched out, his stooped shoulders showing his vexation and disapproval of the whole business.

Left alone again, the three women could only wait, huddled in their chairs, listening to all the odd little sounds of investigation: the low telephone conversations, the muffled sound of police hoots on the carpeted floors of the hall. Without quite comprehending, they heard the terse orders of the law being put into force.

"I don't understand," Amelia said at last, breaking the silence. "Helen was so much better this morning. She was going to come downstairs this afternoon. And she had John call Mr. Holmes."

"Why?" Ann asked.

"I—I don't know," Amelia replied, and subsided into silence.

Before Ann could ask who Mr. Holmes was a policeman opened the door and Jean came in. "Ann! What are you doing—?"

With a warning shake of her head, Ann went to her sister and quickly caught her hand.

"Come over here and sit down." She led the way to a padded seat below the wide front windows. "I'll explain."

"But why?" Jean asked as Ann pulled her down onto the seat. "Dr. Morrison came and told me. Ann, what's it all about? I don't understand. He said Mother Tolliver was dead.''

"Hush!" Ann whispered. As quickly as possible she told her sister what she knew, keeping her voice low so that what she said would not reach the ears of others.

"But she was all right when I left her," Jean murmured.

"Don't tell anybody you were here," Ann ordered. "Nobody saw you, did they?"

"I—I don't know."

"Did you see anybody while you were here?"

"No."

"All right then. There's no use your being dragged into this mess unless it's necessary."

"How—how did it happen, Ann?"

Ann shuddered. "I don't know. She seemed to be all right. She was sitting up in the bed but when I touched her shoulder she fell."

"How dreadful." Jean's chin quivered and she squeezed Ann's hand sympathetically.

"I—" Ann began but the door opened again. This time it was Hugh with a policeman at his heels.

"What's happened, Hugh?" Lou demanded. "Why were you so long? Why are we being kept here? Why don't they tell me something?"

"It's all right, Lou." Hugh's brown eyes were clouded and he rubbed his cheek.

"Captain Harkness will be here in a minute or two," the policeman broke in. "My name's Findlay, Ed Findlay. The cap'n had to talk to the servants first but he said for you to be patient just a little longer and he'd be here as soon as he could."

Ed Findlay was a little uneasy in his manner. He had never been in such a quiet house. He had never known people who kept such rigid control over their emotions. When folks he knew died their families wept and wailed—or "took on," as he would have expressed it.

Because he was nervous and ill at ease he put his hands on his hips and surveyed them belligerently. "We'll need some more chairs, I reckon." He went to the door, called one of his fellow members on the force, and two more chairs were brought into the library.

With the policeman there to listen, there were no more whispered conversations. Hugh prowled restlessly up and down the room, avoiding the women's eyes.

"That's fine," said a voice outside the door. "We're through upstairs now, so he can have it. And tell Johnny to get those prints as soon as he can and rush 'em here to me if I don't get there first. And tell the chief I'll want to see him tonight."

Captain Harkness thrust open the door and walked to the center of the room, where he paused, much as a star actor does, waiting for the round of applause that greets his entrance on a stage. He was a big man, solid and muscular. His dark coat was buttoned tightly across a barrel chest. Black hair was brushed back sleekly from a round face with a high forehead and small black eyes. He stood there with his thumbs hooked over his wide leather belt and let his eyes move over each one of them in turn.

Bill was just behind him and he came at once to Jean, putting his arms about her as though he had to touch her to be sure that she was all right.

"I'll have to ask you some questions," Captain Harkness said.

"We haven't been told what happened," Lou interrupted. "As the only daughter, I demand to know what happened to my mother."

The captain looked at her then, his thin lips curling into an imitation of a smile. "You don't know? Your mother was smothered. With the pillow that was dropped on the floor beside her bed."

14

ORDEAL BY QUESTION

The ordeal by question had begun. It began quite simply with the asking of their names. Ed Findlay proved to be Sergeant Findlay, a shorthand expert. He pulled a stenographer's pad from his pocket, drew a chair closer to the table light, and prepared to take down their evidence. The swift movement of his pencil across the paper added a necessary realism to the scene.

Captain Harkness took a straight chair and placed it in front of the fireplace. It was an advantageous position, directly opposite the door so that he could catch any signal his men might care to give him, yet facing the family, whose chairs made a rough semicircle around him.

"Mrs. Langdon," he began, addressing Amelia, "I believe you make your home with your sister."

Ann looked up in surprise. She had forgotten, if she had ever known, that Amelia had once been married. She had always been "Miss Amelia" or "Aunt Amelia," an unpaid housekeeper in the Tolliver home. Whatever past she had had was unknown to Ann.

"Yes," Amelia replied, ducking her head timidly.

"Did you see your sister this morning?"

"I took her breakfast up to her at eight o'clock. I always do that."

"What was wrong with her?" the policeman put his question bluntly.

Amelia's eyes darted toward the others. "She—she had heart trouble. William's death was a shock."

"The doctor says there was nothing wrong with her heart."

"She—she liked to be waited on," Amelia whispered.

Sergeant Findlay threw his captain a despairing glance.

"You'll have to speak a little louder, Mrs. Langdon. Had she ever said anything that showed she was afraid of someone? Someone who might do her harm?"

''No, no." Amelia showed her nervousness in agitated jerks of her hands and shoulders. "Helen was so much better this morning. She said she would get up this afternoon and come downstairs. She told me to have John telephone Mr. Holmes. She wanted to see him."

"He was her lawyer?"

"Yes."

"Did you call him?"

"No. I—I don't hear well over the telephone. John called and Mr. Holmes was to come at four this afternoon. I went back upstairs and told my sister."

"Can you tell me what time that was?"

Amelia shook her head. "It was before Bill came," she said hopefully.

Harkness turned to Bill, who answered the unspoken question. "I came over here about ten o'clock. Aunt Amelia came in last night to tell me that Mother wanted to see Hugh and me this morning. I went by the office for about an hour and then came here."

"You saw your mother when you came?"

"Yes."

The policeman nodded thoughtfully, but instead of continuing this line of inquiry he turned back to Amelia. "Did you speak to your sister again this morning?"

"No."

"Did any of you see Mrs. Tolliver this morning?" He addressed the circle.

Ann tightened her grip on Jean's arm as a warning to say nothing.

"Why don't you ask Ann Bartley what she was doing upstairs?" Lou said. "She was up there earlier and she came down the back steps."

"Yes, Miss Bartley?"

His voice was as smooth as ribbon-cane molasses. Ann forced her eyes to meet his without faltering. She wondered why the police had the reputation of being always blundering, stupid men. It wasn't true; they weren't dumb. And it really didn't matter, for they had organization and training and experience back to them. They had tricks and they made a specialty of finding out things people didn't want to tell them.

"Mrs. Tolliver and I had a disagreement last week," she replied slowly, choosing her words carefully. "I came over this morning to talk to her and see if we couldn't clear up our misunderstanding."

"And did you?"

"No. I thought there was someone with her in her room, talking to her. I changed my mind and came back downstairs."

"Yes, sneaking down the back way," Lou sneered.

"Which one of you was upstairs then?" the captain asked with a distasteful glance at Lou.

None of them answered and Hugh said, "Look here, you make it sound as if you thought one of us did it. Somebody must have come in without our knowing it."

"Besides the six of you and the two servants, was there anybody else in the house this morning?" Harkness asked.

"Dr. Steigler was here," Bill answered. "I talked to him for a few minutes after I'd seen mother."

"You went with him to the door and saw that he left?"

"No, but I'm sure he left immediately."

Captain Harkness took out a small notebook and pencil. "What was that name again?"

Bill gave him the name and address and the policeman wrote it down. Ann tried to remember what she had heard while she waited in the darkened drawing-room. But there had been only a heavy silence. Though she had been listening, she had not caught the sound of the front door being closed. And there was the funny feeling she had had when she first went upstairs, the feeling that someone was in that narrow hall watching her. Dr. Hans could have gone upstairs, waited until Jean was gone, and then—

"Did you recognize the voice you heard, Miss Bartley?" The captain broke into her thoughts.

"No," she lied.

"Were the outside doors locked, Mrs. Langdon?"

"Oh, no," Amelia said eagerly. "We never lock them in the daytime. That would have been inhospitable. Of course we fasten everything at night, the doors and windows. I always do that just before I go to bed."

"So you think someone could have come in that way?" Harkness peered at her, drawing his thick brows together so that they made a heavy black line across his nose.

"Oh yes," Amelia gasped. "That must have been it."

"Did you see anybody on either of the stairs? The front or the back?"

"No, no, I didn't see anyone." Amelia's fingers picked at her dress and her pale eyes shifted from Bill to Hugh and back again. She was rapidly becoming confused and the policeman must have realized that she would be a hopeless witness under any sort of cross-examination, for he turned again to Ann.

"You quarreled with Mrs. Tolliver last week?"

"I didn't say I quarreled with her."

"What was the misunderstanding about?" He rephrased his question, but she could see from his expression that he had already decided it was a quarrel.

"It was purely a personal matter," she said.

Someone laughed harshly and the captain's eyes snapped with anger. He clamped his teeth together so that his jaws were squared with determination.

"Nothing is personal where a murder is concerned," he said with deliberate grimness. "You might as well know that. Mrs. Tolliver didn't die a natural death and—"

"Aunt Amelia's told you that the doors were unlocked," Hugh interrupted. "Some thief must have sneaked in and—and Mother caught him."

Captain Harkness glared at Hugh and they could all see the mingled dislike and disgust on his face. He hadn't had much experience with this kind of people. Drunks and bootleggers and crapshooters were more in his line.

"Anything been stolen?" he asked.

"How should I know?" Hugh shrugged. "We've been with you ever since you came."

Captain Harkness got up and went to the door. "Hey, Tom," he called, and a young man came to him immediately. "Mrs. Langdon, you go with Tom and see if anything's missing. Not that I think anything will come of it, but if it will satisfy you I'll try to oblige."

He stood for a moment talking to the policeman in the hall, then closed the door and came back to his seat before the fireplace.

"This quarrel—" he began, looking again at Ann.

"I was there," Bill interrupted. "It wasn't a quarrel. Ann was more or less taking me to task. She didn't think her sister looked well and she thought I ought to do something about it."

How long are we going to cover up for each other? Ann wondered. *We're afraid to tell the truth, and though we aren't deliberately lying, we're certainly giving the wrong impression.*

"Mrs. Tolliver resented my interference," she said aloud.

"So you came over today to clear up your—misunderstanding," Harkness commented dryly. "What time was it, Miss Bartley?"

"I don't know exactly. I suppose it must have been about a quarter of eleven."

"Who let you in?"

"The door was unlocked. Nobody had to open it for me."

"Why didn't you go straight upstairs?"

"I met Bill. We came to this room and talked for a while. He's going into the Army right after Christmas," she explained, "and he wanted me to stay with my sister."

"And did you agree?"

"I thought it would be better if we both went to Florida for the rest of the winter. I—I had pneumonia last month and my doctor had already advised me to go to a warmer climate. I thought that would be the best place for both of us."

"Hump!" Captain Harkness sounded disappointed. "Then you went upstairs?"

"Amelia came in to talk to Bill for a minute or two and when they had gone I went up the steps. There was somebody with Mrs. Tolliver so I came down the back stairs. They're opposite her door."

"Did you hear what was being said?"

Ann dropped her eyes. She was afraid that he might read something in them which she did not want him to know. "No, I only heard voices. Lou was on the back porch and we talk-ed for a few minutes. I spoke to the servants in the kitchen. I would have gone home then, but I'd left my coat in here."

"Did you hear Mrs. Tolliver speak when you were upstairs?"

"Yes."

"And you didn't recognize the other voice?"

"No."

"So Mrs. Tolliver was alive then. Can you tell me what time it was?"

"No."

"If Ann came straight up to the front hall, maybe I can help," Hugh said, "I'd just looked at my watch and it was elev-en-thirty. I'd given myself time for a talk with Mother before I went home for lunch."

"I met Hugh in the hall." Ann nodded toward the door, afraid to let the police ask detailed questions about this part of her story. "He'd taken off his hat and he came in here to help me with my coat. Bill came about that time," she added, slurring over the time she had been alone with Hugh, "and I thought he might have been with his mother, so I went back to see her. She—" Ann shuddered at the memory of what she had found. "I—I spoke to her. I didn't know—and I touched her."

"Ann screamed," Bill said. "I couldn't imagine what had happened so I went up. . . . I got John to phone the doctor. I thought Mother had had a heart attack."

"Were you the one Miss Bartley says she heard upstairs?" asked the policeman.

"No."

Ann's whole body was trembling and she clawed at the arms of the chair. It wasn't over, but as the captain started questioning Bill she felt that she would have a few minutes' respite.

"Why did your mother send for you?"

"It was about the business. My father had, of course, left almost everything to her. She'd been going over the books and papers for the last week. She wanted to know something about them, I suppose. I couldn't tell her much. Hugh looked after that part of the business. She said she wanted to talk to him and I told her I'd called him last night after Aunt Amelia had told us she wanted to see us today."

"Was she worried or afraid?"

"No. She was busy with some papers. She had them all over the bed." He ran his fingers through his hair. There was pain in his eyes and his face showed strain and fatigue. He had been his mother's favorite, and if anybody had loved her it had been her son. "She told me that she'd sent for Mr. Holmes and she wanted me to be here when he came this afternoon."

"Didn't she tell you why she had sent for you?"

"No. She only said she was busy and hadn't intended for me to come until later."

"Why did she call Mr. Holmes?"

"I don't know. I suppose there were some papers we had to sign. Hugh and I were helping her settle the estate."

"You came downstairs then?"

"I went to the kitchen to ask John if he telephoned Mr. Holmes. Lou came then with something for Mother."

"I'd made her some charlotte russe," Lou said, tears rolling down her cheeks again. "It was her favorite."

"I asked her about Hugh and she said he'd gone to town but was coming here to see Mother this morning."

"And then—" Harkness prompted.

"The doorbell rang and I said I'd answer it. I thought it might be Hugh but it was Dr. Hans—Dr. Steigler."

"Oh yes, the teacher from the university." Captain Harkness patted his breast pocket, where he had placed the little note-book with Dr. Hans's name. "What did he want?"

"He came about the bequest Dad had left him. For his experiments."

"What was it?"

"Dad left him five hundred dollars."

"To the university?"

"No, it was left to Dr. Hans personally, for private experiments. Dr. Hans is a chemist."

"Hump." It was no more than a grunt, and before he could frame his next question the door opened and Amelia came back, followed by Tom.

"She can't find nothing missing," Tom said. "We went all over the place except in that room. The one you said to keep closed."

"All right."

"And, Cap'n, what do you want we should do with those darkies? Keep 'em in the kitchen? They're out there now prayin' up a storm."

"Send them in here," the captain ordered. "We'll need them to corroborate some of the other testimony." He faced Bill again. "Why did this schoolteacher come over here this morning?"

"He wanted to talk to Mother about getting the money right away. He and Paul had ordered some machine for their work and he said they would have to pay for it when it came."

"Paul?"

"Major Forrest. The Government sent him down to work with Dr. Hans. They're experimenting with some substitute for quinine, something to cure malaria."

There was a low moan outside and Flora came in, twisting her hands and breathing hard. John followed her, shuffling across the room, the loose soles of his shoes making soft sibilant sounds as they flapped against the rug.

"Fo' the Lawd, us ain't know nothin'," Flora groaned.

"Yas, sir, us ain't know nothin'," John agreed. "Me an Flora ain't even been upstairs."

"Naw, sir," Flora broke in before the captain could ask them a question. "Us got our wuk down here, an' its aplenty."

They were badly frightened and their eyes were wide, like small white doughnuts with dark holes in the centers. Their spatulate noses quivered and they stood there, just behind Amelia's chair, watching Captain Harkness and shifting from one foot to the other.

"I'm trying to get the times when everybody came here this morning," the policeman explained. "I want to know who you saw."

John shifted his eyes to Bill. "I was finishin' up cleanin' in the hall when Mr. Bill come. Mis' Tol'ver's particular an' I cleans the front rooms an' then I had to polish the silva."

"You let Mr. Bill in?"

"Yas, sir. He went on up to see his maw an' terreckly he come down an' want to know if I done called the lawyer man."

"You'd done that?"

"I done it soon's Mis' 'Melia tole me to."

"You were talking to Mr. Bill when Mrs. Scott came?"

"Yas, sir. Flora, she opened the back do' to let her in. She'd brung her maw somethin' to eat."

"Mr. Bill was in the kitchen then?"

"Yas, sir," Flora answered this time. "Mis' Lou ast him 'bout Mis' Tol'ver an' he say she all right. Ain't nothin' wrong with her. An' then she ast him had he done what she tole him to an' the do'bell rang an' he say yes an' he'd answer it."

"You old fool!" Lou spat at the Negro woman. Her face was flushed with anger and the tears had dried on her cheeks. "I was asking my brother about some business," she said to Captain Harkness, who was watching her like a cat watches a mouse.

A pleased, cynical smile curled the captain's tight lips. "And then—" he prompted Flora.

"Mis' 'Melia come in then an' she an' Mis' Lou went in the breakfust room an' talk fo' a long time," Flora answered, rolling her eyes.

"Now that's something," Lou said harshly. "I talked to my aunt. And I suppose you want to know what we said? Well, I'll tell you. Dad left a trust fund for Aunt Amelia and she wanted me to get Mother to turn it all over to her. Can you imagine that? Trust Aunt Amelia with a lot of money when she'd never had a penny in all her life!"

"It was mine!" Amelia exclaimed. "William left it to me. He said I was to have it. It was in his will. You can ask Mr. Holmes. He read it to all of us. Helen had no right to it. She should have given it to me when I asked her."

"You'd already asked her for it?" Captain Harkness slid his question in easily.

"Yes." Amelia shrank back in her chair. Ann felt sorry for her, she was so obviously frightened.

"When?"

"Last night," Amelia mumbled, scarcely moving her lips.

"And she refused?"

"She—she said I didn't know how to handle money. She said she'd have to look after it along with the rest of the estate."

"You stayed here after you'd talked to your aunt?" he asked Lou.

Lou Scott's bosom heaved as she fought to gain control of her emotions. She wasn't clever enough or quick-witted enough to enter battle with her tongue. It was a trait she had always envied in Ann, and one reason for their long antagonism toward each other. As a child Lou had scratched and bitten, and now that she was older and could no longer use these tactics, she had to resort to deliberate and planned malice.

"I knew Hugh would be here this morning and I waited for him so that we could go home for lunch together."

"You stayed in the kitchen, then, until you heard Miss Bartley scream?"

Lou bit her lips. "No," she said, looking at Flora. "After Ann came sneaking down those steps I went up to be sure that everything was all right."

"Ah!" The captain leaned forward with interest and the others waited, almost breathlessly, for what was to follow. "You went up to see your mother?"

"No—no, I didn't. I went part of the way up the stairs but I heard my mother talking to someone."

"And what did she say?"

"I heard her ask, 'So you've had time to think it over?' I didn't hear any reply and then Mother said, 'Close the door. No use telling everybody what you've done.'"

"Who was with your mother?"

"I don't know. I tell you I didn't hear anybody but Mother speaking."

"But your mother was alive after Miss Bartley had come down?"

"Yes," Lou admitted sullenly.

"I think we've had enough of this," Hugh said. "You haven't any right to ask us all these questions as though you thought we were common criminals. We should have a lawyer."

"I'm not accusing one of you—yet," the policeman replied. "I'm trying to find out where you people were this morning. If you want a lawyer, get him, but I warn you that the police can jail every last one of you on suspicion and hold you, too."

Hugh bit his lip but said nothing more.

"Now, Miss Bartley," Captain Harkness said after a moment's pause. "When you left Mrs. Scott, what did you do?"

"I spoke to the servants in the kitchen for a few minutes and then I went to the dining-room and sat down."

"Why?" he demanded.

"I—" Ann wondered what she could tell him. Not the truth, certainly, not that she had wanted to give Jean time to get out of the house and home again, not that she had been shaken by her abrupt encounter with Lou. "I don't know. I was trying to make up my mind whether I'd just go on out the back door as Flora had suggested or whether I'd get my coat and risk running into some more people."

"Whom did you expect to meet?"

"Oh, I don't know," she said wearily. "Lou and I aren't exactly close friends," she added dryly. "We don't toss compliments at each other when we meet."

Lou gave a short laugh that was nearer a sneer. Captain Harkness paid her no attention.

"And how long did you sit there trying to decide which exit you would take?" he asked.

"I don't know. Not long."

"Do you realize, Miss Bartley, that while you sat there, while you were trying to make up your mind, a murder was being committed upstairs?"

"No, of course I didn't know that," Ann retorted. "If I'd had the least idea that was happening I'd have skipped out of the back door as fast as lightning."

Sergeant Findlay snickered but when the captain whirled on him angrily his face was bland and expressionless.

"You met Mr. Scott in the hall?"

"Yes. He was taking off his overcoat and we came in here for a minute or two." She slid her eyes to the others seated on each side of her. She was almost sure one of them had opened the library door. Had it been Amelia, or Lou, or even Jean on her way out? No, it couldn't have been Jean if Lou had spoken the truth about what she'd heard from the back steps. Mrs. Tolliver wouldn't have said that to Jean, so she must have gone earlier.

"If I'd only gone straight upstairs," Hugh groaned.

"You didn't go until Miss Bartley screamed?"

"No. Mother had sent for Bill and me every day for the past week. I didn't think it was urgent. When Bill came I asked him it he knew what she wanted this time and he said he supposed it was about some papers that she wanted us to sign as she'd sent for Mr. Holmes. We were in the hall talking when Ann started screaming."

"Did you meet anybody as you came in?" the policeman asked.

Hugh hesitated. "No."

"Did anybody go out the back way?" Harkness asked the Negroes.

"Naw, sir," John said. "Ain't nobody come down thata-way, 'cept Mis' Ann an' Mis' Lou."

"How did you get in the house, Miss Bartley?"

"The front door was open."

"You didn't ring the bell?"

"No."

"And you, Mr. Scott?"

"The door was closed when I came but it wasn't locked. Mother was expecting me, so there was no use making somebody come to the door to let me in."

"Mr. Tolliver," Harkness broke off his questioning of Hugh as if his answers were only routine and of no interest. But now his little eyes brightened and there was a tightening of his jaw line. "Mr. Tolliver," he repeated, "from the time you talked to Miss Bartley in here to the time when you came back nearly an hour later, where were you?"

Ann drew in her breath and held it. Beside her she could feel Jean moving. The police were narrowing their inquiry now to cover the vital time. There was a quickening tension in the room as though all of them realized that what they had already said was only preliminary, that what was to come was important.

"I left this house," Bill said.

His face was pale except for a burning color along the ridge of his cheekbones. His nostrils flared as he took short rasping breaths. One hand was closed over Jean's wrist and she winced as his grasp tightened.

"Where did you go?"

"I—I went home."

"And did you see your wife?"

"No!" Jean spoke clearly. "He didn't see me. I wasn't there. I was over here."

Somebody gasped and then there was dead silence. "Yes, Mrs. Tolliver," Captain Harkness said smoothly. "I knew you had been there. I was waiting for you to admit it."

15

THE TELLTALE HANDKERCHIEF

The absolute silence was painful. "My wife had nothing to do with this!" Bill said sharply. His face was a dull gray, the color of ashes in a grate where papers have been burned. A white, tense line was plainly visible about his mouth and nose.

"Mrs. Tolliver was here." Captain Harkness made the statement as he pushed back his chair and rose to his feet. There was a look of triumph on his face, a smug, foxy look.

"There was a murder here this morning," he said, speaking distinctly to all of them. "Upstairs. A pillow was pushed over Mrs. Tolliver's face and held there. Either a man or a woman could have done that. Lying there in bed, she hadn't much chance against someone standing over her and pushing down with all his strength. It wouldn't take long, a matter of a few minutes. And she couldn't scream for help. This was no accident. It wasn't like the other one."

It was the first intimation they had that the local police were interested in the accident of a week ago.

"All of you were in the house." His eyes swept contemptuously over them. "Any of you could have slipped upstairs and done it. Any of you. There's not one of you that has an alibi."

His words were inexorable. A shiver ran through the occupants of the room like an icy draft. It was as though they all felt that death—no, murder—stood at their sides.

"Look here." Hugh was on his feet protesting. "You can't—"

A sharp rap sounded on the doors and they never learned what Hugh thought the police couldn't do. The policeman who came in wasn't one they had seen before. A wide grin lighted his weather-beaten face and in his hands he carried a small box.

"We found 'em, Cap'n," he announced. "But not where they should-a been."

His eyes snapping with interest, Captain Harkness strode across the room, pushing the solid hulk of his body between Bill and Amelia. Necks craned to see what this new evidence might be, but Captain Harkness obstructed their view. After a brief and whispered conference there at the door he turned back to face them.

"That will be all for right now," he said. "Will you please wait in some other room? There's one across the hall, isn't there?"

With one accord they got to their feet and moved stiffly toward the door. Captain Harkness held it open, but they were not to be let off so easily.

"Just a minute, Mrs. Tolliver," he said to Jean. "Will you stay with me a while longer?"

It was a command rather than a request.

"Yes," Jean replied, squaring her shoulders.

"Then I'm staying too." Bill put an arm protectingly about her.

"That isn't necessary," Captain Harkness said.

"I'm staying."

Ann hesitated, stepped back, and let the others precede her. Jean was being thrown to the lions while she stood by helpless.

"I want to talk to Mrs. Tolliver alone," Captain Harkness said.

"Is she under arrest?" Bill asked. "Then I'm staying with her."

They measured each other with their eyes before the captain accepted the inevitable.

"That will be all for now, Miss Bartley."

He pushed her through the door and closed it so that no sound would be audible through the thickness of the wooden panels.

A policeman touched her arm.

"You'd better go with the others."

Almost in a trance, Ann walked across the hall. The double doors to the drawing-room were thrown wide open so that they could watch the hallway and instantly see if the library doors were opened. Someone had switched on the overhead light and it made an unmerciful glare from the big crystal chandelier in the center of the ceiling.

The room was coldly formal, done in soft blues and grays. There was no warming note of orange or cerise that would give it a homey touch. It was an elegant room. It was never used.

The furniture was antique—or a reasonable facsimile, Ann thought quickly. Somehow the satiny smoothness of the mahogany tables and cabinets lacked the patina of age. The chairs and sofas were upholstered in a brocaded damask and were set with an exactitude that left no doubt that they had been placed there by a professional decorator.

"Turn off that light," Lou said, pulling back the curtains. "You might turn on some of the lamps, Ann."

Gray light filtered through Nottingham curtains. It had stopped raining, but drops of water clung to the glass panes of the windows and rolled down in small rivulets. In the softer light of the lamps the people looked less ghastly, though nothing could hide the stark fear that gripped them nor the untold weariness of sagging shoulders.

Ann drew a Victorian needlepoint chair forward so that she could see and sat down.

"It's cold in here." Lou hugged her arms. "Hugh, get John to light the fire. There's no use for us to freeze."

John had little trouble with the fire. The logs were so dry they blazed easily, and quickly.

"How long has it been since you polished those andirons? I don't believe you cleaned this room since Mother's been sick." Lou ran a finger along the edge of a table. "Look at the dust."

John muttered some unintelligible reply and Ann knew why Lou wasn't popular with the servants.

When the Negro had left the room Lou spoke to her husband. "What happened upstairs? While you were up there with

Dr. Morrison. Couldn't you have persuaded him not to call the police?"

Hugh shrugged. "You forget that Bill had already decided something was wrong. Surely you haven't forgotten so soon how he kept us there on the steps."

Lou ignored the sarcasm in his tone. "What did that policeman find?"

"He made us stay in the hall while he talked to the doctor. It happened like he said. They found the pillow there at the head of the bed. The doctor said that was probably the one used."

He took out a silver cigarette case, lit one for himself, and then, remembering his manners, offered it to Lou and Ann.

"This room is still cold," he said. "Are you sure the radiators are turned on?"

"Oh, yes," Amelia answered him. "We always keep them on even though we never come in here. Cold isn't good for the furniture."

"Something must be wrong with the furnace, then. I'll see about it."

Hugh left them, and presently there was a knocking sound in the radiators and the hiss of escaping steam.

"Hugh is so good about fixing things around a house," Lou said.

"It's wasteful to have heat in this room," Amelia commented. "We never use it."

"How's it doing?" Hugh asked from the doorway. He wiped his hands on a handkerchief and put it away in his pocket as he tested the valve of a radiator.

"Hugh," Ann asked suddenly, "what was it that Captain Harkness found? What made him say Jean had been here?"

"She was, wasn't she?" Lou asked. "I might have known she was here when I saw you."

"That wasn't what you thought at first," Ann snapped. "What was it, Hugh?"

"I don't know," he replied between jerky puffs on his cigarette. "I was upstairs when Dr. Morrison was here and I certainly didn't see anything. And he was like a setting hen telling us not to touch anything. I don't know what it was unless it was something in all those papers on the bed. I've practically moved the office out here this past week. Mother wanted to see everything, accounts, bills, statements, contracts—everything. I might as well have closed the office downtown."

"Whatever it was, I'll guarantee Jean will say she can't remember," Lou said with a nasty laugh.

Ann held fast to the arms of her chair. This was no time to fight it out with Lou. She needed a clear head to think, but there was so little that she could say that would clear her sister. Everything she knew was damaging. She watched Hugh pacing the room. She would always be fond of him but somehow she wished Paul were here. She could talk to him.

"I don't believe we'll ever get things straightened now," Hugh said. "Why did Jean come here this morning, Ann?"

"I imagine she'll be able to tell you that." Ann got up and flicked her cigarette into the fire.

"Too many people here," he muttered. "Did you really hear someone talking to Mother?" he asked Lou.

"Yes."

"Who was it?"

"I've said I didn't know," Lou said briefly.

"Whom did you hear, Ann?"

Ann was watching Lou, trying to read something in the splotchy face, in the pale eyes that avoided her own. "I don't know. I didn't listen," she lied.

"There, you see." Hugh threw out his arms. "It must have been somebody from the outside. The door wasn't locked and if nobody heard you come in, Ann—or me— then anybody could have got in that way."

"Nobody seems to have heard Jean come in either," Lou said slyly. "And she admitted she was here."

The door from the library opened then and Bill came into the hall. His face was flushed and his hair stood on end as if he had repeatedly run nervous fingers through it.

"Hugh," he said. "Call Mr. Holmes. I won't let Jean answer any more questions until he gets here. This is absurd. Tell him to come immediately." The door closed with a slam.

"Well!" Lou exclaimed.

"I'd better telephone him," Hugh said.

They could hear a short argument with the police on guard outside the door, but evidently nothing was done to stop him. For the past hour the telephone had rung constantly and one man had been placed on duty there, giving noncommittal replies to the curious and listening obediently to officials. Whatever he had said, it was enough to keep the neighbors away, though they must be curious, for cars were parked at the curb and in the driveway and men were constantly coming in and out the front door. Perhaps the darkness of the day hid the sight of uniforms and the marks of officialdom.

Silently they waited for the lawyer to arrive. Occasionally a policeman came to the door and looked in but they were not bothered. The jangle of the telephone bell and the nimble of voices in other parts of the house sounded unnaturally loud.

When Mr. Holmes came Hugh met him and brought him to the drawing-room.

"What's this all about?" the lawyer asked. "I wasn't supposed to come out here until later this afternoon."

He was a big man, tall and broad or shoulder. Thick white hair curled back from a handsome face. His whole appearance commanded respect and confidence; this and the fluent resonance of his speech were the keys to his success. More than one jury had felt the powerful influence of his personality and had returned a favorable verdict. His eyes were keen and alert now as he bent his head slightly to listen to Hugh's explanation of what had happened that morning.

"This is terrible," he said sympathetically.

"Bill asked me to get you right away," Hugh continued. "Harkness has Jean in the library now. He's been talking to her for nearly an hour. Bill's with her, but he said he wouldn't let her answer any more questions until you came."

Mr. Holmes threw back his head in horror. "But I am not a criminal lawyer," he said.

"You've got to do something," Ann insisted.

"This is Miss Bartley, Jean's sister."

The lawyer acknowledged the introduction courteously but Ann could see bewilderment replace the look of horror on his face.

"Jean had nothing to do with this," Ann said. "She wasn't the only person in the house this morning."

"My dear Miss Bartley, my practice has been entirely concerned with civil law."

Ann had never felt more disappointed or more desolate. "At least you can keep her from making damaging statements," she said.

He picked up the briefcase which he had placed on a chair and started out of the room, but Ann put her hand on his arm, detaining him.

"You tell that policeman in there that if he arrests my sister I'll sue him for false arrest and defamation of character and—everything," she said.

Mr. Holmes smiled and patted her shoulder. He liked pretty women and admired spunk and this one with the red hair and the yellow eyes was unusually attractive. He sighed, wishing he knew more about criminal law. There were interesting aspects to this case—very interesting.

"Don't you worry," he said. "I'll see about everything."

"I don't like him," Ann said when he had gone into the library. "I don't think he knows what to do."

"He's the best lawyer in town," Hugh tried to reassure her: "He looked after all our legal business for years."

"Just the same I wish—" Ann broke off her sentence because she was wishing she could talk to that sheriff who'd been hanging around so much lately. He was homely and gawky but he seemed to know what he was doing. And then, too, he must have been talking to the police, for Captain Harkness had mentioned the accident as though there was some doubt as to its authenticity.

"Don't worry so much, Ann," Hugh said kindly. "They won't do anything to Jean. She could always plead insanity."

She whirled on him in sudden anger and Lou rose to her feet and took a step toward them.

"Jean is *not* crazy!" Ann said through clenched teeth.

"I—I didn't mean that," Hugh stammered.

"I don't care what you meant. Jean is just as sane as you are."

"Of course she is," Hugh said reassuringly. "If we only knew what they found upstairs."

Ann sat down abruptly. Fear was like a lasso that was slowly strangling her.

"Where's Aunt Amelia?" Lou asked, looking about the room.

They all looked then, but she was certainly not with them.

"How do you suppose she got out of here without our seeing her?" Hugh asked.

Remembering the timid, wraithlike figure, Ann said, "Nobody ever notices her. She hardly ever says anything and you're apt to forget her."

"But where do you suppose she's gone?" Lou voiced the question uppermost in their minds.

Hugh strode to the door. "Did Aunt Amelia go upstairs?"

"The little old lady?" a policeman inquired. "We ain't seen her. Ain't she in there with you?"

"Perhaps she went through the dining-room," Ann suggested. "She might have had something for Flora or John to do."

But she wasn't in the kitchen and the two Negroes, huddled in a corner, declared that they hadn't seen her. The police then joined in the search.

"She couldn't-a got out of the house," Ann heard one of them whisper to another. "We got somebody at both doors. The cap'n sure will give us hell if she's got away."

"He sure will."

"Reckon she's the one that did it?" the first asked. "I wouldn't put it past her."

"Dunno," was the reply.

The search was brief but thorough. Doors were opened and closets, lights turned on and off. Hugh was the one who found her, cowering in the closet of her own room.

"Here she is," he called to the others.

"Why didn't you answer when we called?" Lou demanded in exasperation. "Didn't you hear us?"

"I—I was afraid."

"What are you doing up here anyway?"

The others were crowding into the doorway and Amelia backed up against the wall. To Ann she presented a pitiful sight, like an animal that has been chased until at last it turns desperately to face its hunters.

"I haven't got anything to wear," Amelia said, her lips quivering and slow, silent tears falling from her pale eyes. "She's my own sister and I haven't anything decent to wear to her funeral. Everything I have is worn and old."

"Oh, good Lord," Lou said in disgust. "I'll give you something of Mother's. You can take it up enough to wear it."

"I want a dress of my own," Amelia protested. "I never have anything that's just mine."

"You can have a new dress." Ann stepped forward and put a comforting arm about the older woman. "Come downstairs with me and I'll get some clothes sent out and you can choose what you want."

"You certainly are rash," Lou said. "It won't pay you to encourage her."

"If she wants a new dress she shall have it," Ann retorted.

"You won't feel so noble when you get the bill."

"I'll have some money of my own," Amelia put in eagerly. "You know, William's money."

"That's right," Ann told her soothingly. "We'll telephone now." She took Amelia's hand and as if she were a child led her out of the room.

Ashamed of their excitement, the police went back to their posts. They were secretly glad that they hadn't disturbed the captain and were greatly relieved to find the library doors still closed.

"I suppose it is all right if I use the telephone," Ann said as she picked up the directory and looked up her number. Tom nodded permission and she lifted the receiver.

"This is Ann Bartley at Mrs. William Tolliver's, Mrs. William Tolliver, Sr. I want some dresses sent out on approval for her sister." She turned aside, putting her hand over the mouthpiece. "What size do you wear?" Amelia shook her head vigorously. "I should say about size fourteen. Better send two or three," she added extravagantly. "A black and perhaps a blue—an Alice blue," she said judicially with her eyes on Amelia. "Yes, I think that might do. When can you send them? . . . Thank you so much.

"They'll send them out this afternoon," she told Amelia as she put the receiver back on its rack. "You can choose what you like."

Amelia's face was more animated than Ann had ever seen it, showing that she must have been appealingly pretty as a girl. There was nothing about her of the handsome stateliness of her sister, but there was something of the gentle aristocrat in her manner. She belonged to a breed fast dying out all over the world.

Amelia's eyes were shining. "I haven't had anything of my own since I eloped with Jim Langdon," she whispered to Ann.

They were still in the hall when Captain Harkness opened the door. His face was flushed and his little eyes were bright. Beyond him Ann could see Jean slumped down in the big wing chair, her face buried in her hands. Bill knelt beside her, speaking in low tones.

"We're taking your sister to town," Harkness said grimly. "She wants to speak to you first."

"And I have something else to tell you," Lou said quickly. "I think this is important."

He put out a hand to stop Ann but she brushed it aside and went instantly to her sister.

"What are they doing to you?" she demanded.

"It's all right, Ann." Jean looked up, her white face strained with fatigue. "They aren't arresting me. I'm going to town to talk to somebody else."

"It's nothing really to worry about, Miss Bartley," Mr. Holmes said lightly. "She's going to talk to Tim Norton. He's our city solicitor. Bill and I are going with her."

"I wanted to speak to you about Chip," Jean said.

"They can't do this!" Ann tried to fight down hysteria.

"I'm looking after her, Ann," Bill said. "Nothing can happen to her. I know she had nothing to do with this."

"If you would just tell the captain why you came over here and what you had to say to Mrs. Tolliver," Mr. Holmes pleaded.

"I can't do that," Jean replied steadily. "She was alive and all right when I left her."

Mr. Holmes looked at Ann and threw out his hands in a helpless gesture as much as to say, *See for yourself. What can anyone do for her when she won't give you a truthful answer?*

"About Chip, Ann—" Jean began.

"Oh, darling, I'll stay with him till you come home."

"Lily must have put him to bed by now," Jean went on, "and I'd like for you to be there when he wakes up."

"Of course I will. But—"

"I believe I understand now why you can't remember very much." Captain Harkness opened the door and came back to them. There was a pleased and satisfied expression on his face, and if he had been a cat, his whiskers would have been coated with thick cream.

"What did Lou tell you?" Ann felt choked with fright.

"She just explained a few things to me." He rubbed the palms of his hands together.

"You can't believe a word she says!"

His jaws hardened and he looked at her intently, so that his eyes reminded her of a snake poised and ready to strike.

"If she hadn't testified that she heard her mother's voice after you came down those back stairs, you'd have a great deal more to explain yourself, Miss Bartley. A great deal more than you have."

"That still doesn't give you the right to take Jean away. She wasn't the only person in the house. What about the others? What was Lou doing? Where was Amelia? I was here and so were Bill and Flora and John."

They were facing each other, openly antagonistic, forgetting that there were others besides themselves in the room.

"He isn't arresting her," Bill said wearily. "We're all going down to the courthouse to talk to Norton. I'll bring her home within an hour. I promise you."

"But why are they picking on her? She wasn't the only one that was in Mrs. Tolliver's room. Lou didn't say it was Jean she heard."

"But she didn't say it wasn't," Captain Harkness said quickly. "I've given permission for you to go home and be with the little boy. One of my men will take you."

"That will be fine protection," Ann said sarcastically.

Captain Harkness's face darkened with anger. "Where a murder is concerned—and possibly two—we can't be too careful."

Ann's eyes became narrow slits. "You may be sure I'll take every precaution to take care of myself and Chip," she said coldly. "As long as you persist in taking an innocent person away and leaving a murderer loose, I'm well aware of our danger."

"I wouldn't be too sure, Miss Bartley," he said silkily. "We have proof."

"And what is it?"

"It's this." Before they could stop her Jean snatched the box from the table and took from it a crumpled linen handkerchief. "Look at it, Ann."

It was an ordinary white handkerchief, and in one corner, embroidered in Jean's handwriting, was her name. Ann recognized it at once. She knew her sister had a dozen like this. On her birthday last May, Jean had given her a similar dozen.

"We found it in Mrs. Tolliver's hand," the policeman said. "It was the one thing she could snatch and hold."

"Smell it," Jean commanded.

Ann raised it to her nose and her surprised eyes met Jean's. "But—" she began.

Jean's eyes warned her and she gave an almost imperceptible shake of her head.

"We've found the others. They were hidden in another room, but we found 'em." Harkness motioned to one of his men, the same one who had brought the cardboard box only an hour ago. "Keep an eye on the others. I'll be back in an hour or two and I'll want to talk to all of 'em again. You'd better go now, Miss Bartley. I'll want to see you later too."

"See about Chip, Ann," Jean whispered. "You understand about the other? Then you'll know what to do."

16

THE SHERIFF KNOWS

As soon as her sister had gone Ann left the Tolliver house. Only Jean's plea that she stay with Chip prevented her from going with them. Could it have been only this morning that Jean had said: "If anything happens to me, Ann, take care of Chip"? And Ann had promised.

Though it had stopped raining, the trees still wept silent tears as Ann left the sidewalk and hurried down the street, taking the shortest way home. The house was quiet but she could hear someone moving about in the back. As she hung her coat in the closet she was surprised to see that it was only three-thirty. So much had happened in the last four hours.

"Where's Chip?" she asked, meeting Lily in the hall. The girl's arms were filled with clothes she had just finished ironing and her nose twitched as though she smelled trouble.

"He asleep," she answered.

"Mommy!"

At the sound of his voice Ann hurried to his room. Chip was standing up in the center of his bed, his face flushed with sleep, his hair curling in damp ringlets across his forehead.

"Mommy and Daddy had to go to town," she told him as she put her arms about him and lifted him from the bed. "They'll be back home in a little while."

"I want my mommy!" wailed Chip.

Ann kissed the soft hollow under his ear and comforted him as best she could, trying to fight down her own fears lest he sense something was wrong.

"I betta be gettin' home 'fore hit storms," Lily declared with an uneasy glance out of the window.

"You'll have to stay until Mrs. Tolliver comes home," Ann informed her. "We'll take you home in the car if it's raining."

"When'll Mommy come?" Chip asked as he slid chubby arms into the shirt his nurse was holding. "Where she gone, Tan?"

Ann winked, at him. "Sh!" she cautioned, putting a finger to her lips and whispering, "It's a Christmas secret."

Chip chuckled delightedly. "Tan play with me."

"I've got to see Paul, but I have something for you and Lily to do."

"What?" he demanded, catching her hand.

She took him to her room and brought out a box of varicolored building-blocks. It had been intended as a later present, but if it would keep him happy for the afternoon it would serve a better purpose.

"Keep him busy with those as long as you can," she told Lily.

"Yas'm." The Negress was sullen but she did as she was told.

"Tan play with me too?"

"No, darling. You stay with Lily. I'll come play with you as soon as I can."

He went willingly, diverted for the moment by his new toy. Ann breathed a sigh of relief and picked up the telephone.

"Adeline?" she said a moment later. "Get Dr. Paul to the phone for me, will you?"

"He out with them dawgs. He sho' ain't lak me 'sturb him, Mis' Ann."

"I don't care what he's doing. This is urgent. Please call him."

She could hear Adeline grumbling as she put down the receiver. Tapping the table impatiently with her fingernails, she waited for him to come.

"Hello." He sounded irritated by the interruption of his work.

"Paul, I wouldn't have called you if I weren't desperate. Something dreadful happened this morning."

"What happened, Ann?" he asked, catching the concern in her voice.

"I can't tell you over the phone. But—oh, can't you come over here? I need you so much."

"I suppose so. Dr. Hans is home now. I'll come if you need me."

"Oh, Paul, I do." Her voice sounded like a prayer for deliverance. "And, Paul, can you get that sheriff that was at your place last night?"

"Sheriff Davies? I don't know. I thought he was going home today."

"Get him. I've got to talk to him too."

"All right. I'll do the best I can. Hold everything until I can get there."

She left the telephone and went directly to the front window where she could watch and wait for them. Behind her the clock on the mantel ticked on monotonously, but the minute hand seemed reluctant to move, making each second unendurably long. The house was hushed and still, as though it, too, waited, staving off the catastrophe until help could arrive. Even the gray sky glowered between dark clouds.

Ann was shaking, not from nervous reaction but from pure terror. She gripped the window ledge as though by holding something solid she could fight down her panic. Once she heard the thud of blocks on a bare floor and the low murmur of voices in Chip's room but she did not dare leave her post.

It was only a few minutes after four when she saw a car draw up to the curb and she went at once to open the door.

"I thought you'd never come," she said as Paul came up the walk followed by the familiar lean figure of Sheriff Davies.

"What's happened, Ann?" Paul gripped her arms.

"Better get inside out of the damp before we do any talking," the sheriff remarked.

"I had to see you," Ann said as they came in and Paul closed the door. "I had to talk to you and get you to help us."

"What's happened, Ann?" Paul repeated his question.

"Mrs. Tolliver was killed this morning."

Paul let out a thin whistle. "So that's what's happened. We'd better get off our coats and sit down."

"Murdered?" the sheriff inquired as he slipped his arms oat of his overcoat.

"You're shaking." Paul put his arm around Ann's shoulders. "Come on over here and sit down. Then you can tell us is hat happened."

He led her to the sofa and kept his arm about her as he sat down beside her. Some of the numbness that had held her rigid ever since she had found that lifeless woman on the bed seemed to thaw, and she spoke quickly, a little incoherently.

"They took Jean to town. Bill went with her. But I don't like it. They can't do that, can they?"

"Suppose you begin at the beginning, Miss Ann," suggested the sheriff. "I can't rightly say who can do what until I know what's happened already. You say Mrs. Tolliver was murdered?"

"This morning. I found her. I—I didn't know. I touched her and she fell." Ann's eyes were dilated and she felt Paul's arm tighten about her.

"Where was she?"

"In her room. In bed."

"Hump," Sheriff Davies grunted. "How was it done?"

"With the pillow. Somebody held it over her face. It was there by her bed when I went in, but I didn't know—"

"How'd you happen to go over there?" he wanted to know. "I kinder got the idea you and Mrs. Tolliver weren't on speaking terms."

"I hated her!" Ann exclaimed. "That's the truth. You talked about not having any motives before but there are plenty now. Nobody liked Mrs. Tolliver. She was mean and cruel and—but Jean didn't kill her."

"Somebody did, it seems." His drawl was more pronounced as it always was when he was excited.

"Not Jean. She couldn't have done it. Everybody was in that house this morning. It's big and dark and anybody could have got upstairs and done it."

"Now we're getting somewhere. Give her a cigarette, Major, and see if that will stop her fidgeting. Can't do anything till I can get some sensible answers to my questions."

Paul gave Ann a cigarette, lit it for her, and offered the pack to the sheriff, who shook his head and took out his old pipe. Carefully he tamped tobacco into the bowl, struck a big match on the sole of his shoe, and settled more comfortably into his chair.

"Now," he said, "let's get things straight. Who was in that house today?"

Ann named them quickly.

"Hump!" He drew a dirty envelope from an inner pocket and after some searching found a stubby pencil. "I suppose Miss Amelia was the first one who saw her this morning? Who was the next?"

Ann told him as best she could. He scrawled on the envelope as she talked and when he had filled it Paul got some clean sheets from the desk and together they worked out a timetable for the morning.

9:00 a.m.	*Amelia took breakfast to her sister and was told to telephone the lawyer, Mr. Holmes, to come that afternoon. Either then, or on the previous night, Amelia asked her sister to give her control of the trust fund.*
10:00	*Bill came to the house and talked to his mother. She did not tell him why she had asked for him, only intimating that she must first see her lawyer. He thought there were papers to sign.*
10:15	*Bill talked to John in the kitchen. Lou Scott arrived.*
10:25	*Doorbell rang. Bill admitted Dr. Hans and took him to the library.*
10:30	*Amelia talked to Lou in the breakfast room. Tried to persuade Lou to help her get her money.*

10:35   *Jean arrived and went directly upstairs to Mrs. Tolliver.*

10:45   *Ann came. Front door open. She hid in the drawing-room.*

10:47   *Dr. Hans left?*

10:50   *Ann met Bill in the hall and went to the library to talk to him. Bill told her he had made a new will appointing her as co-guardian for Chip. He also explained that he knew that Jean had nothing to do with the peculiar things that had been happening.*

"I'll have to know about those things," the sheriff said to Ann, and she nodded. "All right then. Let's finish this first."

11:00   *Amelia joined them in the library. Wanted Bill to talk to Mrs. Tolliver about the trust fund.*

11:05   *Bill and Amelia left the library.*

11:08   *Ann went upstairs. Felt that there was somebody else in the hall. Heard her sister talking to Mrs. Tolliver and went down the back stairs.*

11:10-11:15 *Ann talked to Lou on the back porch.*

11:15   *Lou went up the back steps. Heard someone talking to Mrs. Tolliver. Ann doesn't think it was Jean as Mrs. Tolliver is quoted as saying, "So you've had time to think it over? Close the door."*

"Does sound like somebody she'd been talking to earlier," the sheriff mused. "We only got Bill and Miss Amelia admitting they'd talked to her, but any of the others could-a been up there one time or another. That is, of course, if it wasn't Miss Jean."

"The door was closed while she was talking to Jean," Ann insisted. "And I thought somebody was hiding upstairs in the hall when I was up there."

"But you didn't see anybody, did you?"

"No," she admitted reluctantly.

"Well—" He bent over the paper again and moistened the tip of his pencil. He wrote slowly and painfully, his gnarled fingers wrapped about the stubby pencil.

1:15-11:30	*Ann in the kitchen talking to the servants. Left when she saw Lou come back. Sat down in the dining-room.*
11:30	*Hugh arrived and Ann met him in the hall. They went to the library. Ann thinks she heard the door open once while they were talking but she isn't sure.*
11:45	*Bill burst in, wanting to know where his wife was. Ann rushed upstairs.*
11:47	*Ann discovered Mrs. Tolliver dead.*

"I'm always the one," Ann whispered. "I always find them."

"Hush, darling," Paul said softly, and then (to the sheriff) added, "Aren't we forgetting the two Negroes? There's nothing to show that they didn't go upstairs."

"There's nothing to show that any of them didn't go up to that room," the sheriff replied thoughtfully. He folded the sheet of paper into a square.

"What's that second story like, Miss Ann? I know about the first floor."

"There are two bedrooms and a bath in the front. Mrs. Tolliver had the one over the drawing-room. The hall runs crossways and there are three smaller rooms at the back. Amelia must have the one next to the back stairs, opposite Mrs. Tolliver's. I think the middle room was used for sewing and storage. It used to be. There's another bath at the end of the hall."

"Kinder dark up there?"

"Yes. There's only one window in the hall." Ann leaned forward anxiously. "You don't think she did it, do you?"

"I can't say as yet," he replied slowly. "I'll have to know a lot more afore I can make up my mind. Now about these peculiar things—" He looked up at her.

"They aren't true," Ann declared. "Jean was afraid, so she wrote me a letter That's really why I came."

"What letter? When was that?"

"The letter? It came while I was in the hospital, about the first of November. Afterward, when I was so weak, the doctor and Beth persuaded me to come down here. But I wouldn't have come if I hadn't got the letter."

"Why was your sister afraid? Nothing's happened to her."

"So many things had been happening. I didn't find out what was the matter until I got here. And not even then till I insisted," she explained. "You see, it all began with a dog."

"What dog?"

'The one that was poisoned. They said Jean did it."

She went on then to tell him about the other curious happenings, about the broken perfume bottle, the toy on the stair, the misplaced articles, the anonymous letters. Now that she had decided to talk, she told him the whole truth as she knew it.

"Look at this." She picked up a piece of paper from the table and the sheriff gave her his pencil. She wrote slowly and handed him the result. "That's a fair imitation of Jean's writing. It's not hard to imitate and anybody could copy it with a little practice. At least enough to pass anybody except an expert or a bank clerk."

Sheriff Davies rubbed his bristling jaw. "Hum. Did you ever see one of these letters?"

"Yes, one. Mrs. Tolliver showed me one that afternoon after Mr. Tolliver's funeral. It hinted that Amelia had put something in his coffee. That was why we quarreled so violently. She had convinced Jean that she wrote the letters and then forgot that she had done it. Once Jean found a half-finished letter in her desk. I don't know why it was done unless they were intended to make Jean doubt her own mind. That and all the other things she couldn't remember. Just little things at first, but they kept on occurring. Jean really thought she had done them until I came."

"And she never remembered afterward?"

"She remembered leaving Chip's toy on the steps. She said the telephone and the doorbell rang at the same time and she put down the toy to answer them. Mrs. Tolliver stumbled over it and fell."

"When did that happen?"

"The last part of September or early in October," Paul answered. "Cousin Helen sprained her ankle badly."

"She didn't really need the cane, did she?" Ann asked, and as Paul shook his head she added, "I thought not." She paused and bit her lip before she continued to the sheriff: "Mrs. Tolliver said all this proved that Jean was crazy. You see, Jean isn't my blood sister."

"What!"

"No. My father and mother adopted her. They were in California at the time. Then Pops got a professorship at the University of Illinois and I was born there. We came to Alabama when I was about three years old. I've never seen any papers about the adoption. They must have been lost long ago—if there ever were any."

"Did Miss Jean know this?" the sheriff asked.

"Yes. There was no secret about it. We were sisters and we shared everything. There was no difference between us. Bill knew it and his mother used it as a threat. She never approved of the marriage. She told me that Jean began acting queerly after Chip was born." Ann's troubled eyes were fastened on his face and she leaned forward and spoke with compelling urgency. "You must believe me. Jean didn't do any of these things. Somebody else did them to make it seem that she was crazy. She half believed it herself—and so did Bill."

"You say he's changed his mind?"

"I don't think Bill ever really believed it. It was Mrs. Tolliver who kept harping on those things that happened. Bill was worried. He knew he'd have to leave in a few weeks and I think he wanted to be sure that I'd look after Jean." Ann closed her eyes for a moment and when she opened them again they were remote and pensive. "This isn't an'thing but an impression, but

I think Bill had made up his mind this morning to stick by Jean regardless of what happened. I mean, I don't think he was sure, but after she was accused of his mother's death he was sure. He knew she couldn't have done that."

"Ann, what made them pick on Jean?" Paul asked. "From all you've said, nobody saw her enter or leave the house. How did they know she'd been there? You didn't tell them."

"It was the handkerchief," she replied simply.

"What handkerchief?" the sheriff demanded.

"I want to show you something."

She got to her feet and left them. The room had grown dark and shadowy. Sheriff Davis reached a long bony arms up and turned on the reading-lamp beside his chair. He took from his pocket the timetable that they had made and spread it over his knees.

"Is it as bad as that?" Paul asked in an undertone.

"Well now, I can't say exactly," the sheriff replied cautiously. His knotty fingers smoothed the paper he was studying. "Lots more I'll have to know."

"Does this tie up with what happened last week?"

"Yep."

Ann returned as the sheriff made this laconic reply. In her hands were the slender perfume bottle from her own dressing-table and an old medicine bottle half filled with a golden-colored liquid. She placed them on the coffee table in front of the sofa much as a magician might arrange his equipment before his act.

Her eyes eagerly sought the imperturbable face of the sheriff but the deep seams of his lean cheeks and the heavy lids of his partly closed eyes told her nothing.

"I had some trouble finding Jean's," she said breathlessly. "It wasn't marked."

"What is it?" he asked suspiciously.

"The perfume," she said in surprise. "That was what was wrong with the handkerchief. They found it in Mrs. Tolliver's hand and it had Jean's name embroidered on one corner. But it had my perfume on it. That's what Jean meant. She picked it up and handed it to me and I smelled it."

She took out the stoppers and extended the two bottles to the sheriff, who took them and sniffed gingerly as though he expected some strong, unpleasant odor. He replaced the bottles on the table and looked at her for an explanation.

"I told you about this before," Ann said.

He shook his head and, scratching another match on his shoe, relit his pipe.

"That summer we were in Germany Dr. Hans made this perfume for Jean and me. He was experimenting with some coal-tar derivatives at the time. Naturally we were thrilled to have something so special. He gave us the formulas and since then all we've had to do was to take them to a chemist. We gave them names. I called mine *Feu d'Automne* and Jean's *Soupir de Printemps*."

Sheriff Davies raised his bushy brows and Paul quickly translated, "Autumn Fire and Breath of Spring."

"You can tell the difference, can't you?" Ann insisted.

"Perfume is perfume to me," he said. "When you stick both those bottles under my nose I can tell the difference but if I closed my eyes and you gave me just one wouldn't know it from something in any drugstore."

"You know them, don't you?" she appealed to Paul.

"I think I do." He smiled. "At least I'd know yours."

"You see," she said to the sheriff. "They're very different. And my perfume bottle was put in Jean's room last night."

"What!"

"Yes," Ann said patiently. "I used it when I went out to dinner and left it on my dressing-table. Jean brought it back to me this morning. It had been put in her room. That's what I've been telling you all along. It was one of those queer things like the others."

"I'm bumfuzzled, Miss Ann," Sheriff Davies said. "You'd better explain from the beginning."

"Last Christmas I bought two perfume bottles," Ann said, speaking slowly and distinctly. "I gave one to Jean. It was just like this one except for the name etched on it. Several times during the spring she wrote me how much she liked it, then it wasn't mentioned again. A few days ago she told me that one day last summer she found it smashed on the floor. It was part and parcel with the crazy things she was supposed to have done. It was always the things she liked best that were mutilated or destroyed. After that she must have kept it in this bottle. You see, it isn't marked."

"And last night your bottle was put in her room?"

"Yes."

"You think somebody stole one of your sister's handkerchiefs and put the wrong perfume on it?"

"Yes."

"That would mean that the person who did it didn't know that your sister's bottle had been broken."

"That's rather complicating it, isn't it?" Paul asked. "You're implying that two people are involved."

"Might be," the sheriff commented.

"I still don't see—" Ann began.

"Look here." Paul took a piece of paper and pulled his fountain pen from his pocket. Quickly he drew three lines down the sheet so that it was divided into four columns. "You've made a timetable for this morning. Why not make a list of those people who had the opportunity to do these things?"

They watched him as he wrote rapidly, pausing now and then to ask Ann a question. When he had finished he passed the paper to her. Across the top he had printed OPPORTUNITY; and beneath that was written:

FOR MR. T.'S DEATH	FOR DRUGGING THE COFFEE
Bill	Bill
Hugh	Mrs. Tolliver
Ann	Lou
Paul	Amelia
Dr. Hans	Jean
	Paul
	Hugh

FOR MRS. T.'S DEATH	FOR STEALING THE HANDKERCHIEF
Jean	Ann
Amelia	Jean
Lou	Bill
Ann	Lou
Bill	Hugh
Dr. Hans	Amelia
Hugh	Paul
Flora	
John	

"I see you haven't omitted anybody," Ann said as she handed the paper to the sheriff.

"I couldn't, Ann. I had to put down everybody who had a chance to do any one of those things."

"Hugh couldn't have killed Mrs. Tolliver," she said. "He'd just come in and was taking off his gloves. He left his hat and overcoat and the ledgers he'd brought on that chair by the steps and then he went with me to the library." She hesitated and ducked her head because she had the horrible feeling that she was blushing. Her voice was rough and unsteady as she added, "He was talking to me until I went upstairs—and found her."

"Oh, all right. Scratch his name, Sheriff. I'll admit I don't like him, but my reasons are purely personal."

Because Ann and Paul were looking at each other then, they failed to see the twinkle in the sheriff's blue eyes. The crow's-feet at the corners deepened and he chuckled, though he tried immediately to cover it by coughing.

"He doesn't think we did it either," Ann said.

"Doesn't he?"

"He told me we alibied each other," she said softly. With an effort she tore her eyes from Paul's face and looked at the sheriff. "You did say that, didn't you?"

Sheriff Davies didn't answer at once. His pipe had gone out and he rammed it into his already sagging pocket. The contrast between the two men was great. Paul's uniform fitted him with a perfection of knifelike creases while the sheriff's clothes looked as though he might have slept in them, which he frequently did.

"Murder's a pretty serious business, Miss Ann. It's been going on since Adam and Eve, and with all our civilization we haven't stopped it. All we can do is try to prevent it and find the person who's guilty and put him where he won't trouble people any more. Once a person's done something like this he's more likely to do it again. It ain't easy to stop him. That's where the law comes in."

His eyes burned with a sudden cold flame of anger. He had their complete attention. His words seemed to bring something eerie into the room, as though death itself had entered and stood beside them, its fetid breath hot and burning against their cheeks. It was a terrible, unbearable sensation, and instinctively Ann moved toward Paul, as though his nearness would break the spell.

"If you'd told me all this a week ago, Mrs. Tolliver's death might have been prevented," the sheriff said harshly. "You can't keep things secret when a murderer's loose among you."

"Then—then it's one of us?" Ann's lips were stiff and she spoke haltingly.

"It's most likely. I'll never be able to prove Mr. Tolliver was murdered. Goodness knows, I've tried hard enough this past week. But all I can say for my trouble is that it could have been an accident. I know it was murder but that ain't enough."

"You think its the same person this time?" Paul asked.

"Stands to reason. He might even have got away with it a second time. All of you thought Mrs. Tolliver had heart trouble, and smothering and a heart attack look something alike. But at least he's come out in the open now and the doctor's said it couldn't have been an accident."

"But why—?" Ann asked.

"There ain't but two possible reasons this time," the sheriff answered. "Either Mrs. Tolliver found out something about the other—well, about Mr. Tolliver, or she stood in the way of somebody getting something."

"She didn't know that Cousin William's death was anything but an accident," Paul protested. "She's been up there in her room ever since he was buried and you know, last night—"

"Last night I said I wanted to talk to her," the sheriff interrupted. "I said I'd see her today. Maybe somebody didn't want me to talk to her."

They sat silent under his accusing gaze. All the slow, lazy manner had gone from him like a copperhead shedding its skin in the spring. Ann knew then that it had only been assumed for their benefit, that he was grimly determined to find out the truth, and that he was possessed of the intelligent shrewdness to accomplish his aim. She was suddenly afraid of the truth but at the same time she knew she no longer mattered. All she could do now was wait—and pray.

"Plenty of people stand to gain now," Sheriff Davies continued as though there had been no pause. "Your sister gets something through her husband, and of course the motive applies to Mr. Scott. Miss Amelia and Dr. Hans get money that they want badly. There's nothing to stand in the way now. And most of all there are Bill and Lou Scott. They inherit the estate."

Ann gasped. "Bill's going into the Army."

"Yes, but the money will be there when he comes out, and if he doesn't there's your sister and his child."

"It's too horrible to think of."

His eyes rested on her hard and cold. "You're quite capable of murder yourself, Miss Ann. If you decided to protect your sister—"

"See here," Paul broke in instantly.

"I'm not saying all of them did it, Major, but one of them—"

He broke off abruptly as though some new thought had come to him. When he spoke again it was to ask Ann a multitude of questions. He wanted to know every word that had been said that morning while she was in the Tolliver house. She went over every step she took, answering detailed questions as to how people had looked, what they had worn, the very gestures they had made. There was nothing that the sheriff didn't want to know.

"How long did Mrs. Scott stay on the back stairs? Could she have gone into her mother's room? From the top step could she have heard what was being said?"

"There's a door leading from the stairs into the hall. It's just like all the others. If it were open she could have heard."

"Did you leave it open when you came down?"

"I don't remember." Wearily Ann plodded through more details about the morning. Fatigue had almost replaced the fear that had numbed her for the last few hours.

"When you screamed everybody came upstairs?"

"Yes."

"Nobody was on the second floor except you?"

Ann tried to remember. She wanted to forget it, bury it somewhere beyond her conscious mind, never to have the unpleasantness and horror before her eyes again. She knew it was a weakness. A doctor would advise just the treatment the sheriff was giving her. She closed her eyes but her tormented brain kept shouting the words "Remember—remember—"

"I backed into Bill at the door." She opened her eyes and looked at the sheriff. "The others were there in the hall just behind him, Lou and Hugh and Amelia. I think the servants were on the stairs. Lou was hysterical. After a while Bill came out and closed the door. We went back downstairs. Hugh pushed his coat and hat off the chair so Lou could sit down and Amelia picked them up and hung them in the closet. Then she came back and sat on the steps with me. I—I don't think Flora and John were ever in that upper hall."

"Where was Bill during that time?"

"He stayed on the steps, just above us, until the doctor came. John had telephoned him. Bill and Hugh went back—back to that room with Dr. Morrison."

She thought there would be other questions and she tried to brace herself, but surprisingly the sheriff turned to Paul to ask him about Dr. Hans, about the routine of the professor's mornings.

"He had an early lecture this morning. There was one at eight and another at nine. After that he'd be in the school laboratory. He had student assistants there to help him with the supervision. Those who're getting their masters' in chemistry."

"He could leave the school at that time?"

"I don't know much about that part of his work. I suppose he can, as several times when we were in the midst of experiments he's come home to see how they were getting along. That was one of the reasons I was sent here. Dr. Hans couldn't give his full time to the type of experiments we are making and I could be there all the time."

"Did he come home today?"

"No. I didn't see him from the time we had breakfast together this morning until he came home about an hour ago."

"He didn't come for lunch?"

"No."

His questions were cut short as Chip wandered into the room. Ann picked him up and swung him across her hip while he crowed with delight. Next to being tossed in the air, this was the playing he enjoyed most.

"He's too heavy for you to do that," Paul said.

"No, not yet." Ann set Chip on his feet. "Meet the cock o' the walk." She introduced him with false gaiety.

"Where's Mommy?" Chip asked, looking about him.

"She hasn't come home yet," Ann answered quickly. "Where's Lily?"

"She's gone, Tan. She said to tell you she ain't coming tomorrow." His big blue eyes were fastened questioningly on her face.

"Of course not. Tomorrow's the day we're going to find our Christmas tree."

His eyes sparkled. "Really and truly, Tan?"

She nodded gravely. "Shall we invite them?" She indicated the two men in the room, but Chip shook his head vigorously.

"Daddy go with us," he said.

"Well, now," drawled the sheriff, "I could tell you where to find some pretty cedar trees."

"You can come too." Chip responded instantly to the hint.

"Don't promise a child something unless you can keep it," Ann said, warning him with her eyes.

Sheriff Davies' long legs propelled him out of his chair. From his great height he looked down on the little boy with a smile. "I don't see why anything could keep you and me and him from going out tomorrow afternoon."

"You mean—?"

"Yes'm, you've told me who it is." He picked up his overcoat and rammed his arms into the sleeves, leaving Ann to stare at him in wonderment. "I got to go downtown and talk to Captain Harkness for a while and see about some other things, but I guess I already know the answer."

"Who?"

The sheriff ignored her. "Major, will you run me into town? Then you come back here and collect Miss Ann and Chip and take 'em over to the other house. Reckon you can keep everybody together until I can finish up a little investigatin'?"

"Jean—"

"Oh, I expect they'll be there already. If they ain't, Harkness will send Bill and your sister out here in a little while. I'd just want to be sure all of you were in one place. Suppose you can get Dr. Hans and keep everybody in one room?"

Ann nodded. "Yes. Yes, I'll do it."

17

LITTLE, INSIGNIFICANT FACTS

"Wait here, until I can come for you," Paul said as he left with the sheriff. With mingled feelings Ann watched them go down the walk and climb into the car. Perhaps she had been wrong to tell Sheriff Davies so much, but if it had been a mistake it was too late now to recall it.

"Where's Mommy?" Chip pulled at the hem of her skirt.

"We're going over to your grandmother's," Ann said, putting her hand on his head and ruffling the soft hair. "Mommy and Daddy will be there in a little while if they aren't there now."

"Will that man take me to get a Chris'mus tree, Tan? I want a big one, most as big as this room."

"We'll get it," Ann replied with more confidence than she felt. "Let's get some clothes together. We might be over there a long time."

"Spend the night?" Chip asked excitedly.

"I don't know, but we can be prepared."

Anything can happen, Ann thought as she gathered up his bathrobe, pajamas, and shoes. There was no predicting what the night would bring. Murder was like a great vulture and the shadows under its widespread wings were frightening and black.

Chip seemed untouched by the sense of foreboding that tightened Ann's throat. He was completely happy. To him, his grandmother's house meant extra cookies from the jar in the kitchen, extra attention from all the grownups, added indulgences. He brought a cardboard box out of his closet and announced solemnly that it was his luggage.

"Put my bunny shoes in it, Tan," he ordered. "I take my green rabbit too," he added matter-of-factly.

"All right, darling."

"Tan, did he really turn green before your eyes?"

"Why, of course. He was nice and white like any ordinary rabbit, and then I said I was going to see Chip and he just—zip! And he was green."

"Can I turn green?"

"I think you look just right as you are."

"Lily looks like my cocoa."

"Will you play right here in the living-room while I dress?" Ann asked. "It won't take me long."

"All right." His soft mouth drooped petulantly. He wasn't used to being left to his own devices.

Ann showered quickly and, putting on the green suit, smoothed the skirt over her slim hips. The light from the dressing-table made a burnished cap of her bright hair and her eyes took on a greenish tinge. She ran her fingertips over her eyebrows and added the finishing touches to her lips as Chip wandered into her room.

"Fix my hands, Tan?" he asked, reaching across the glass top of the dressing-table for the small bottle of nail polish. "Pretty."

"Oh, all right." Ann dabbed the paint on his small nails, to his open delight.

"I'm hungry," he announced, waving his chubby hands in the air.

"Maybe we'd better eat something," she sighed. "Paul hasn't come?"

Chip shook his head. "Why?"

"We have to wait for him."

Foraging in the refrigerator, Ann found the leftovers of a fried chicken, and with milk and a cereal their stomachs were somewhat satisfied. It was quite dark outside now. The minutes lengthened into hours since Paul and the sheriff had gone. The delay made Ann nervous. She had been so sure Paul would come for her immediately. And the telephone had been quiet—

deadly quiet. Surely, if Jean had been released, she would have called to find out about Chip. Panic again crowded into her brain and made a tight iron band around her heart. Chip was watching her curiously and she forced her rigid muscles to relax.

"I through. Go Grandma's house now?"

"Yes, my pet. We won't wait for Paul any longer." She helped him down from his high chair. "Get your coat while I put these things away."

She left the soiled dishes in the sink and took the milk back to the refrigerator. When she reached the living-room Chip had struggled into his coat and she knelt beside him and fastened the brass buttons.

"Go Grandma's house now?" he asked.

"Just as soon as I can get my coat."

Her suit was too bulky to wear a coat over it so she merely draped it over her shoulders. Gathering up Chip's bathrobe and pajamas, she took his hand and said, "Let's leave the lights burning."

The wind had risen and the Circle was dark. The street lights were wide-spaced and glowed dimly and inadequately as they hurried along the wet sidewalk. Chip danced happily beside her, tugging at her hand when her steps faltered. He couldn't know or understand with what reluctance she returned to the big house where twin lights burned brightly on either side of the entrance.

Almost before her finger had released its pressure on the bell a policeman opened the door.

"The others are in there, miss," he said, jerking his thumb toward the drawing-room. "The cap'n phoned just now that he would be out in a little while but Mr. and Mrs. Tolliver are on their way here now," he added, answering the question in her eyes.

Putting her coat on a chair, Ann followed Chip through the open doors. They were all there, she saw at a glance, and Chip had already launched into a long and complicated description of the tree he planned to get tomorrow. Lou was helping him with the buttons. In the light from the lamp beside her the thick overlay of powder made her face look ghastly. Her eyes were puffy and her mouth drawn but she fluttered over Chip like a hen with a single chick.

Hugh sat opposite her, his legs stretched out toward the fire. He looked up when Ann entered and a frown darkened the clean-cut line of his face. He threw the cigarette he had been smoking into the fire.

"So they made you come back and join us," he said glumly.

"I—" Ann began and stopped.

"Come and sit beside me." Dr. Hans spoke suddenly from a far corner.

She took the chair beside him and he pulled his a little closer and whispered, "What is it all about, Ann? Paul told me to come here but then he went away—immediately. Why are we all brought here together? Why did you bring the child into this room? There is so much hate here."

Ann shuddered. "The police," she whispered, "the police wanted all of us to meet them here."

"Ah!" Dr. Hans hissed. "The police. This is like the fifth act of a tragedy by Aeschylus in which the actors proceed to their inevitable doom. We are the actors and this room is the stage," he said quietly. "This time we are not an audience."

"You frighten me," Ann said.

"We are all frightened." He seemed hardly aware of her, so intent was he on his own thoughts. "I did not think when I came to America I would ever feel this way again."

"It's because we don't know," Ann whispered.

He turned his head and the light struck his thick-lensed glasses so that his eyes were hidden by the reflected glare. Ann turned quickly and across the room caught the eyes of Amelia, who nodded and smiled pleasantly. There was something different about Amelia, and it was a full minute before Ann realized that a new dress had wrought a seeming miracle. It was a delft blue and the lines were good. The stiffened silk rustled when she moved. Her ordinarily stringy hair had been fluffed into a soft frame for her face and there was color in her cheeks, whether natural or applied Ann could not tell from a distance.

She sat now, knitting placidly, and the bright red wool made a heap of color in her lap.

The front door was opened briskly and all of them rose at the sound of voices.

"Mommy!" Chip ran to his mother, who stood in the doorway.

Jean gathered him in her arms and held him closely as though she never intended to let him be taken from her again. His arms were tight about her neck and she rubbed her cheek against his hair as she carried him to the sofa and sat down.

"Mommy, me and Tan is gettin' a Chris'mas tree in the mornin'," he began chattering excitedly. "You buy me a present?"

"Oh, my precious baby, yes, yes, of course."

"What happened to you, Bill?" Hugh asked.

Bill shrugged. "Nothing much. We went to Norton's office and talked. Just Captain Harkness and the two of us. Then Sheriff Davies came and he took Harkness outside and talked to him. I don't know what he said but in a little while Harkness came back and asked us to wait until he could check something else." He took a cigarette from his pocket and lit it. "That was the hardest part—waiting. Then Paul came and said he could bring us home, that all of you were here. That's really all."

"I don't understand," Hugh said. "They've kept us here all afternoon. We could go anywhere in the house, but there was always a policeman somewhere near by. They haven't told us anything. I simply can't understand it."

Bill drew on his cigarette and frowned. "Harkness said he'd be out here sometime tonight to talk to all of us again. We were to wait for him."

Paul caught Ann's eyes and nodded briefly toward the door. She followed him immediately and he put an arm about her and smiled reassuringly into her troubled face. "I was going to get you just as soon as I'd left Bill and Jean here," he said. "I thought you'd wait."

"I couldn't. You were gone so long." She caught the sleeve of his heavy coat. "Paul, what's happening? I'm afraid."

He glanced over her head toward the open door. "I don't think there's any danger," he said slowly. "Not with all of you together."

"What's Sheriff Davies doing?" she asked. "What did I tell him?"

"I don't know, Ann," he replied wearily. "I've tried to talk to him but he's shut up like a clam. He's with the police captain now. They've got something up their sleeve."

"I'm afraid," Ann said again.

"Everything will be all right." Paul stopped and glanced over his shoulder before he added in a lowered voice, "Do you know what Hugh did with those ledgers he brought over here this morning?"

"No." She was bewildered by his question. "The last I saw of them was when he put them on that chair over there."

"All right then, just one more question. Do you know who it was that opened the library door while Hugh was kissing you?"

"How did you know?" She drew away from him.

"You were a little bit evasive on that part of your story," he said dryly. "It didn't take much imagination to tell me why."

"What if he was?" she retorted angrily. "It wasn't the first time."

There was a dangerous glint in Paul's eyes and his mouth was grim. "Who opened the door, Ann?"

"I don't know."

"Who did you think it was?"

"Lou," she replied instantly.

"It couldn't have been Dr. Hans?"

Her lips parted in a faint gasp. "I don't know. My back was to the door."

He looked at her steadily for a moment, then caught her roughly by the shoulders and kissed her. His mouth against hers was hard and demanding. There was nothing soft or tender about this kiss. He released her and she stumbled back against the wall.

"I'll be back with the sheriff," he said, and was gone.

Ann tried to move but her legs seemed to be made of butter and she sat down abruptly in a chair. Her coat slid softly to the floor and she gazed at it dazedly before she picked it up. Paul always seemed to kiss and run, and always he left her with this tumultuous weakness. He never gave her a chance to tell him how she felt. And he'd left her with a killer probably sitting in the other room while he went gallivanting with the sheriff. He'd even admitted there was danger. The more she thought of it the madder she got. She pushed up her chin and marched back to the drawing-room. Paul needn't worry, she'd stick to them like Scotch tape and maybe she'd even outsmart him and solve the case herself.

Bill and Jean were seated together on the sofa. Chip's heavy eyelids barely opened as she came in and he snuggled drowsily in his mother's arms. Jean looked up and smiled at her sister, then dropped her eyes to the sleeping child she held.

"Why don't you put him to bed?" Ann asked. "I brought his pajamas with me."

"No." Jean's arms tightened about her son.

Bill had caught the worried look in Ann's eyes and realized that she was trying to get the baby out of the way before something happened. "I think it would be better, darling," he said. "He's practically asleep now and he'd be better off in bed."

"There's a policeman in the hall," Ann said significantly.

Jean looked from her husband to her sister, then without a word she got up and took Chip out of the room.

"Giving her a chance to escape?" Lou asked sarcastically.

Ann gritted her teeth. "Nobody can get out of this house now."

"Why do you say that?" Hugh asked. "You sound as though you thought one of us would have some reason to leave."

"You may before tonight is over," she replied. "You know as well as I do that the police think one of us killed Mrs. Tolliver."

There was an instant's stunned silence before Lou shrilled, "You—you—"

"You needn't say it," Ann said shortly. "I know what you think of me and I can assure you it's reciprocated—with interest."

"Hugh!" Lou was breathing hard as she turned to her husband. "Are you going to let her say such things to me?"

"You started this fight," Ann said, "and we'll all be here at the finish."

"Really, Ann." Dr. Hans was on his feet, shaking his head.

Looking about her, Ann tried to imagine one of them as a murderer, for the sheriff had made it plain that it was one of them. They were all watching her; even Amelia had laid aside her knitting and was smiling vaguely as though she didn't quite understand what was going on about her.

"Why did you come back here?" Lou asked. "Nobody wanted you."

"I'll tell you why I came back. The Lord knows I didn't want to, but Jean was frightened and I came to find out why."

"So Jean's developed a persecution complex on top of everything else," Lou sneered.

"You should have read more than one psychology book," Ann snapped. "You'd know the difference between real and imagined fear."

"Please, Ann." Bill got up and caught her arm. "You're making things worse than they are."

"Yes." Lou twitched at the ruffles at her neck. "First thing we know she'll be accusing me of killing my own mother and father."

Bill's hold had tightened, forcing Ann to sit down again on the chair beside the professor.

"Go on and sit down, Bill," Ann said wearily. "I'm not going to do anything. Anyway, I don't think Lou could have killed Tolliver."

"I'll bet it nearly kills you to admit that," Lou said with a short laugh.

"Nothing would give me greater pleasure than to plant some good solid evidence on you, but you couldn't have done that. You were in the kitchen."

"What are you trying to say, Ann?" Hugh asked.

She smiled at him. Ha was nervously lighting a fresh cigarette from the one he had only partly smoked. The same old Hugh, she thought, suave and charming, but so apt to let you down in the end. He'd done that to her and now he was making no effort to help his wife. In time she might even grow to dislike him, forget his appeal to her senses.

"When I was upstairs—the first time I was up there," she amended, "there was somebody hiding in one of those vacant rooms. I heard a door close. That's why I came down the back steps. It wasn't Jean because she was talking to Mrs. Tolliver then. And it wasn't Lou because she was in the kitchen. So were Flora and John," she added thoughtfully.

She had their full attention now and it rather frightened her. She had started something that she did not know how to finish. She had to keep talking, make somebody admit something that would give her a clue that she could follow. Deliberately she took a cigarette from a pack in her jacket pocket, lit it, and twirled it between her fingers. Maybe they wouldn't notice how tense she was.

"Dr. Hans," she asked, "when you'd talked to Bill this morning, where did you go?"

"I—I went back to the university."

"You didn't go upstairs?"

"No!"

"Bill, when you left me to look for Jean, why didn't you go straight home?"

"How do you know I didn't?"

"You were gone too long. It wouldn't have taken more than ten minutes to find out Jean wasn't there. You were gone nearly thirty."

A muscle at the edge of his jaw twitched and when he spoke his voice was harsher than she had ever heard it. "I walked down to College Street. I didn't go straight home. And we'll let it go at that."

"You walked there in the rain?"

"It wasn't raining, only misting a little. That's all I have to say on the subject." He crossed his arms with a gesture of finality.

"Amelia?"

"I—I went—I really don't know." Her eyes darted around the room, looking for some way to escape.

"What are trying to do?" Lou demanded. "What right have you to ask us questions? We have only your word for it that somebody was upstairs. That is, somebody besides yourself," she said slyly.

"We have your word too," Ann said dryly, and crushed out her cigarette. "You're on record as saying there was somebody talking to your mother after I came down those steps. And you've also said your mother was alive then."

Lou's mind wasn't agile enough for very quick comebacks, so while she was still sputtering Ann went back to Amelia.

"Try to think where you were, Amelia. Did you go upstairs?"

"We've been over all this with the police," Bill said. "Aunt Amelia talked to Lou. Have you forgotten that?"

"She wasn't out there when I came down," Ann said stubbornly. "After Lou told you she wouldn't help you, did you go upstairs?" she asked Amelia.

"No, no, I'm quite sure I didn't," Amelia replied.

"Aren't you going too far, Ann?" Hugh asked. "You'll be wanting to know where I was next. I might as well say I don't knew."

"I'm not bothering with you right now," Ann said, drawing her eyebrows together in a concentrated frown. "I'm trying to figure out who had a chance to get upstairs without being seen."

"You might start with the person we know was up there," Lou said sarcastically.

Bill uttered an angry exclamation and started to rise but Ann stopped him.

"Let me handle this, Bill. If Jean says Mrs. Tolliver was all right when she left, I believe her."

"Your faith is most touching." Lou buffed her fingernails on her sleeve with exaggerated care.

For a minute Ann could not see clearly and blood pounded in her ears. She dug her fingernails into the arm of the chair, leaving a permanent scar on the wood.

"Lou, take that back! Every word of it!" Bill was on his feet and his face was menacing.

"All right," Lou said quickly, drawing back in her chair. "All right, I didn't mean it."

"You'd better watch your tongue." He strode angrily to the door but a policeman promptly barred his way.

"The cap'n sent orders you was all to stay in one place," he said stoically.

"I want to go to my wife."

"She'll be back in a minute. She's putting the boy to bed." The policeman's face broke into a grin. "Say, that's a swell kid."

Bill muttered something about the incompetence and pig-headedness of the police but he came back to his chair.

"Dr. Hans." Ann leaned toward him and lowered her voice. "What time did you come here this afternoon? Did Paul bring you?"

He shook his head. "No, he telephoned me. I thought he meant to come right away but instead"—he spread his hands and shrugged—"instead, I have just sat here and waited."

"In this room? Nobody has left?"

"We have all been here together. We had a light supper but even then we were watched. That policeman in the hall—"

"Is he the only one here?"

"I do not know. He is the only one I've seen."

"No." Amelia broke into their conversation suddenly. "There's a man in the upstairs hall. He was quite nice about it, though."

"Nice about what?" Ann asked.

"The dresses. They came soon after you left and I wanted to see them. There's this one"—her hand caressed the silk across her knees—"and a lovely black one I can wear tomorrow. I can't thank you enough, dear, for getting them sent. I always said you were sweet." Amelia's face was flushed with pride and excitement and, though she was still as muddled and vague as ever, she was no longer the drab household drudge that Ann had known from childhood.

"The policeman," Ann said, trying to bring Amelia back to the point. "You said there was a policeman upstairs."

"The policeman?" Amelia's hands fluttered and she looked at Ann in surprise. "Oh, yes. He was in the hall. But he stood outside my door while I changed. And he said I looked so much better," she added breathlessly.

"You're a sucker for flattery," Lou said.

"The Miss Amelia is a very handsome lady." Dr. Hans rose to the occasion gallantly.

"But he didn't stop you? He merely went upstairs with you?" Ann was growing desperate trying to keep them on the right track. "Are you trying to say that two policemen have stayed here and watched you all afternoon?"

"They let us get some supper," Hugh said mildly. "I think I see what you're trying to get at, Ann. You want to know what the police have been doing here."

"Yes," she said. "The sheriff made it plain to me that he thought he'd finish the case tonight."

"And find one of us guilty?" Hugh smiled. "Maybe we'd better get our heads together and see what we can do to protect our interests."

"What I'd like to know," Bill said fiercely, "is who planted Jean's handkerchief in Mother's room?"

For a moment nobody spoke.

"Planted?" Lou asked, raising her eyebrows. "Don't be absurd. Jean undoubtedly dropped it when she was in there. She's always forgetting things like that."

"Which one of you wrote those anonymous letters?" Ann asked.

"Oh!" Amelia stood up suddenly and placed her hand against her mouth.

"What is it?" Ann demanded instantly.

"I've just remembered." Amelia's pale eyes were blank with surprise. "When I came out of my room—that is after I had changed my dress—"

"Yes?"

All of them were watching her speculatively, and Ann shivered with cold fear. She could almost feel the ripple of emotion that spread from one person to another. Beside her Dr. Hans had grown tense.

"The police were taking all those books out of Helen's room," Amelia said. "You know," she appealed to Bill, "the ones you and Hugh had brought out for her to see. They had her papers and they asked me if she kept all her letters in the desk in her room, and if she used any other place to write."

"But—" Bill was plainly bewildered by this action of the police. "Those were only the mill accounts. They're all right. We've been going over them with her for the past week."

"She wrote those letters!" Ann exclaimed.

"No," Bill said with a harried gesture of his hand. "Mother wouldn't have done that. What reason could she have had for doing that?"

"I don't know," Ann said weakly. "But somebody did and it wasn't Jean." She got up and took a step toward Amelia, who shrank back at the cold feline look in those tawny eyes. "Those books," Ann said, speaking with deliberate slowness, "what time did they take them away?"

"I—I don't know!" Amelia gasped.

"Was it after five? Was there a phone call about that time?"

"Yes, I suppose so," Amelia said.

"The sheriff left me about then," Ann said musingly. "He must have telephoned. Did the police do any searching after I left?"

"Well, I should say they did," Lou said. "They've done nothing but prance from one room to another, upstairs and down. There were several here when you left, but finally most of them went away and left that one out in the hall."

"And the one upstairs," Ann said softly. Suddenly she was aware of so many things. Little, insignificant facts crowded into her consciousness as pieces of the puzzle began to fall into place. "Hugh?" She swung about to face him. "What did you do with those ledgers you brought this morning?"

"What ledgers?"

"The ones you had under your arm there in the hall. I don't remember seeing them again."

"I don't know what you're talking about. I didn't bring anything at all with me when I came this morning."

18

A HARD THING TO FIGHT

Ann gasped. For the first time, she was sure of a deliberate lie. She had seen Hugh with the books under his arm.

"But you did," she said stubbornly. "You were holding them."

Hugh met her eyes and flushed under the directness of her gaze. "Oh, those," he said. "I didn't know what you meant. I'd just picked them up from the hall table. I thought maybe Bill had left them downstairs."

"That was what the sheriff said." Jean spoke clearly as she came toward them. "It was when he called Captain Harkness out of the room. You remember, Bill. Mr. Harkness had just started over again with his questions and the sheriff came."

"I didn't hear anything that was said," Bill replied.

Jean came to him, slipped a hand through his arm, and rested her head against his shoulder. "I—I was listening," she said softly. "The door wasn't quite closed and I heard the sheriff ask if he'd found some books there in the hall."

"Did you tell the sheriff about them?" Hugh asked Ann.

"I—I suppose so. He asked me to describe everything I'd said and done in this house."

"Where are they now?" Bill asked. "I didn't bring any with me this morning and I don't remember seeing any around the house. Everything was in Mother's room."

"Maybe Ann knows." Hugh turned his back to them and lit a cigarette.

Ann rubbed the back of her hand across her eyes. "Yes," she said slowly, groping for the picture in her mind. "You put them down on that chair at the foot of the stairs when we went to the library."

"You couldn't wait for a chance to get him alone," Lou said, her eyes hard with concentrated fury. "Even in my mother's house my husband isn't safe from your scheming ways."

"Lou!" There was an appeal as well as anger in Hugh's voice.

"Let her alone," Ann said. Anger stained her cheeks red and her eye glittered, but otherwise she seemed calm and determined. "I rather suspected it was you who opened the door."

"And would you like for me to tell them what I saw?" Lou demanded shrilly. "Well, I saw you enticing—"

Hugh clapped his hand over his wife's mouth. "Don't say anything you'll be sorry for later," he said through clenched teeth.

"Oh, I don't know," Ann broke in. "It leaves Lou with such a nice opportunity to take those books you left in the hall. They were there when we went to get my coat, but they weren't there later."

"Are you sure, Ann?" asked Bill.

"Yes. I noticed that they were gone when Lou sat down in that chair. They weren't under Hugh's overcoat either because Amelia took it and his hat and put them away. They were gone then."

"So things get lost here too." Jean closed her eyes and spoke in a dead voice without inflections. "So many queer things. My handkerchief with the wrong perfume, the things that were always missing, clothes cut and mutilated."

"I don't see why you're all so bothered about those books," Hugh said crossly. "Mother's had everything in her room for the past week and if anything was wrong we'd have heard about it pretty quick."

"She might have been silenced for that very reason." Sheriff Davies spoke from the doorway.

Nobody had heard him enter. He stood there, his greenish overcoat spotted with drops of rain, drooping dejectedly from his shoulders. Behind him was Captain Harkness, looking as though he would give anything in the world to be somewhere else at this moment.

Ann's eyes went eagerly past them but Paul was not there. She hadn't realized until then how much she had counted on his coming back to her. He ought to have known how much she needed him.

"I see you're all here," the sheriff was saying. "Now if you'll just sit down again, there's some things I'd like to say."

He had taken off his coat but his heavy boots made muddy tracks on the gray carpet as he pulled up an ornamental chair, tested it, and sat down. Captain Harkness, too, looked ill at ease but he seemed to have delegated complete charge of this situation to the sheriff, though he plainly had no liking for it.

Sheriff Davies settled himself as comfortably as he could and spread out his one legs in front of him. He cleared his throat loudly. "Sit down, Miss Ann," he said mildly. "You're sort of obstructing my view."

Ann was startled but she obeyed him instantly, sinking down into her chair beside the professor.

"I kinder thought we could settle things between us and I persuaded the cap'n here to let me talk to you all together." Mild blue eyes swept over the people on either side of him, but there was a quick appraising gleam in them. "I reckon you know by now that what you've been calling accidents weren't real accidents atall. They were planned by some very calculating brain." He paused to let his words sink in slowly, then went on, "The Lord endowed me with more than my share of curiosity and I didn't have much else to start with except a bloodstained feather."

"Bloodstained feather?" Amelia asked.

"Yes'm. I found a bird's feather on the ground by Mr. Tolliver and it had a smear of blood on it. I thought that was kinder funny, especially since Mr. Tolliver hadn't even fired his gun. And he didn't have any birds with him either."

"Are you trying to say my father was murdered too?" Bill's voice cracked in spite of an obvious effort to control it.

"Yes, son," the sheriff said gently, "I know that wasn't much to start with, but it set me thinking something was wrong and I just naturally began asking questions. You told me things and most of what you said was true but you left out lots of other things. It wasn't until Miss Ann told me Mr. Tolliver was sleepy that morning that I began to get an inkling of what might have happened. Most folks are wide awake when they get up to go hunting no matter how early it is. So I began asking some other questions and found out he'd had breakfast with all the rest of you, but he'd also had some coffee before he left this house."

"I made that coffee," Amelia said. "I made it for him often."

"Yes'm." The sheriff nodded. "But lots of folks were in the kitchen when you fixed it."

"My father was drugged?" Bill asked, and his hand caught Jean's so hard she winced with the pain.

"Maybe," Sheriff Davies said.

"Why?" Ann heard her own voice asking.

The sheriff shrugged. "If he was drugged it could have been a real accident. Major Forrest had been right careful to point out to me that Mr. Tolliver *could* have stumbled over that log and that it *could* have been turned by his fall. But that still didn't explain why that feather was on the ground. Only it wasn't enough proof for anybody except me. I even talked to the police."

Captain Harkness felt their eyes on him and he moved uncomfortably in his chair. Ann remembered that the captain had mentioned it. At least his suspicions had been aroused.

"But nobody would want to harm William," Amelia protested. "He was such a good man."

"You got an income," the sheriff said pointedly. "And the professor gets some money for experiments."

Dr. Hans's mouth dropped in surprise, then he murmured, "It is such a little bit."

"You could have killed him easy. He wouldn't have been expecting it," the sheriff said hurriedly. "And then Mr. Tolliver's children profited considerably."

"Don't!" Jean choked on the word.

"What I have to say can't be pleasant, Mrs. Tolliver." He sighed and, pulling one long leg toward him, hooked the heel of his shoe over the rung of his chair. "Murder never is," he continued harshly. "It wasn't until Miss Ann decided to tell me what she knew that I really began to see what had been staring me in the face for a long time. By then, she'd waited too long. Mrs. Tolliver was dead."

Talk, talk, talk, Ann thought. *What is the man trying to do? He's frightening the living daylights out of me.* She looked down at the palms of her hands and found that they were sticky with sweat, yet she felt cold, so cold that she thought she'd never be warm again. She tried to focus her attention on what the sheriff was saying.

"She told me about all the queer things that had been happening to her sister. The poisoning of the dog, the switching of the perfume bottle, the anonymous letters that had been written."

"Well, if she told you that you ought to know where to look for our trouble," Lou said bitterly. "You had no right to turn her loose on us to make more trouble."

"You're right that I knew where to look for the trouble," Sheriff Davies said. "Mrs. Tolliver never wrote an anonymous letter. I found the evidence when I opened a locked drawer in your desk just now."

Someone was laughing shrilly, hysterically. Ann felt strong hands press against her shoulders and realized that Dr. Hans was shaking her violently, shaking her until her teeth rattled. Why, she was the one who was laughing.

"Stop it, Ann!" he commanded. "Stop it, I say! This is no time for hysteria."

The others scarcely noticed her. They were watching Lou.

"I only wanted Chip," Lou muttered. "She had everything. Everything! Stop staring at me as though I were a leper!" She buried her face in her hands.

Amelia came over to her and put a sympathetic arm about the bowed shoulders. "I know," she said. Then she looked up and caught the sheriff's eyes. "It's hard being thrown so constantly

with other people's children and not having any of your own. I
know. It happened to me."

Lou took Amelia's hand and raised her face. Without the
look of crafty conceit in her eyes and the sour, discontented
droop of her mouth, it looked shockingly naked.

"I didn't kill Dad—or my mother."

"I know that, Mrs. Scott." There was no softening in the
sheriff's voice. "You couldn't have left the feather beside your
father." He paused and then went on as though there had been
no break in what he had to say: "This afternoon Miss Ann and
the major went over everything they knew for me. You can't
fit the picture of murder together until you have all the pieces
and some of them are so small that you'd hardly notice them. If
you'd told everything you knew in the very beginning we might
have been able to save Mrs. Tolliver. She finally guessed what
had happened and that was the reason she—"

He stopped abruptly and looked toward the open doors
leading to the hall. Ann, following his eyes, hoped to find Paul
standing there. But it was quite empty; there was no sign even
of the policeman who had been in the hallway.

"For the past week Mrs. Tolliver had been trying to learn
the business. According to her husband's will she was left in
full charge, wasn't she?" He raised his eyebrows in the direction of Captain Harkness.

"That's right."

"You bring everything out here?" the sheriff asked Bill.

"Yes, but I don't see what that has to do with it. Dad went
over the books and we had them audited once a year. Dad
wasn't entirely retired."

"All of you could do with a little more money than you
have." Captain Harkness broke into the conversation for the
first time. "Every last one of you wanted more than you had."

"He's right, son." The sheriff brought his hand down on his
knee with a spanking sound. "Everybody wants money, only
some folks are willing to do more to get it. I don't suppose
you'll be sorry to know your wife and child are well provided
for in case anything happens to you. And there's Miss Amelia

and Dr. Hans and Mr. Scott." His voice slurred into a slow drawl as he continued. "He's not so lucky as you. Your wife has a little money of her own, but he didn't have anything but what your father paid him."

"This farce has gone far enough!" Hugh got to his feet and his eyes were hard and bright. There was an ugly twist to his mouth.

"It's gone too far, Mr. Scott." The sheriff had not moved but his voice had lost its drawl and was now grim and determined.

"You've accused each of us," Hugh said, "and you haven't an ounce of proof."

"You weren't at the office at all this morning."

"I had business to attend to at the mill."

"No," Bill said suddenly. "I tried to get in touch with you before I came over here and then later—that's why I walked down the street to the drugstore. I called the mill then and they said you hadn't been there."

Hugh threw back his head defiantly. "You have no proof."

"You came over here early this morning," the sheriff said. "Mrs. Tolliver had guessed the truth and she knew there was something wrong with certain entries in those ledgers. You hid in the upstairs hall after you'd talked to her and when Miss Jean left you went back and killed her."

"And where is your proof?" Hugh laughed. "Any one of them"—he swung his arm to include the circle of people in the room—"any one of them could have gone upstairs at any time and killed her."

"But not any one of them could have killed Mr. Tolliver," the sheriff said softly. "There were only three possibilities there: Bill Tolliver, Dr. Steigler, and you. This morning it didn't take very long. All you had to do was to shove a pillow over her face and hold it. Lying flat on the bed, she couldn't put up much fight. Then you came downstairs and met Miss Ann in the hall. That must have given you a start because you thought she'd gone. A while ago, when I talked to her, she finally remembered that when she met you you were pulling off your gloves. You'd been very careful. And you had those ledgers."

"You can't prove a word you're saying!"

"Oh, I know the books have been burned. When the police dug them out of the furnace there wasn't much left. But there's enough."

"Hugh!" Ann sat up quickly and her words sounded breathless. "Hugh went down to fix the furnace because he said it was cold in here. He could have burned them then."

"And you think you can prove something against me with some old burned books," Hugh said sardonically. "Maybe you thought you could bluff me into a confession."

"Those books were burned but not destroyed," the sheriff said flatly.

"Hugh!" The word seemed drawn from Lou. Their eyes met and the anguish in hers was met by contempt in his.

"You!" he said scornfully. "You with all your pretense and nagging. *You* told me your father would give you some money when you married me. Why else do you think I'd want to be saddled with a dull woman like you? *You* told me she was crazy. You kept harping on all the nasty little things she'd done and all the time you'd done them yourself. *You* told me that your father would turn over all the business to me when Bill was gone. And it was you who was always fussing about your mother's weak heart, fetching and carrying to curry favor."

Lou's face was mottled with anger and she was on her feet before he had finished speaking. Her ruffled collar rose and fell spasmodically with her breathing. "How dare you!" she choked. "I'll tell them what I know now." She turned to the others. "I heard Hugh talking to my mother when I went up the back steps. There's no reason for me to keep quiet now. He was in that room and he killed her!"

"He's got a gun!" Ann screamed.

The room was suddenly as quiet as a grave. They seemed frozen to their places like wax figures in a chamber of horrors. A small snub-nosed pistol was held steadily in Hugh's hand. Despite its size, it looked deadly.

He backed away from them toward the dining-room doors. "I won't hesitate to shoot the first one who makes a move. I've been ready to leave if things went wrong and I mean to do it. How was I to know that Jean wasn't really crazy? Nobody need have been hurt. And how was I to know that the old lady didn't really have heart trouble? I've been wanting to leave for a long time. This town is dead. I know better places and you'll never find me. Never!"

The sheriff almost rose but Hugh's gun was instantly trained on his head and he dropped back quickly to his chair.

"Don't you think I mean it? You'd be dead before you could get to your feet." Hugh laughed, a crazy, chuckling sound, and with his other hand felt for the doorknob behind him.

The door swung slowly open and Ann, who could not summon the will power to take her eyes off him, saw Paul loom silently in the black opening. He threw himself against Hugh, trying to pin his arms against his body.

The room was filled with confusion. Shots exploded and there were sounds of a violent scuffle on the floor. People screamed and men in uniform appeared from nowhere, crowding into the small spaces and overturning chairs.

Ann was only partly aware of what was going on about her. When she saw Paul she had buried her face in her arms and crouched into as small a ball as possible on the theory that there would be less of her that way to be hit. She didn't even open her eyes when she left Paul's arms about her and heard his voice murmuring things in her ear, things she wanted more than anything else in the world to hear. She just clung to him, shaking with a violence she had never known. Gradually the sounds subsided and she ventured to peer under his arm. They had taken Hugh away.

"It's all right now, darling," Paul said soothingly. "It's all over at last."

"Who—who got shot?" she asked shakily.

"Nobody." Paul brushed back the hair from her face. "So you can still talk," he teased.

"Talk!" Ann pushed away from him. "You didn't think six shots would keep me from talking, did you?"

"Two," he murmured. "There were only two shots."

"Six," Ann said sharply.

"What is this?" Dr. Hans inquired as he came from the dining-room, carrying a tray which he placed on a table. "I thought we needed this," he continued, pouring drinks into the glasses and adding soda water. "It will do you no harm."

"Where—where are the others?" Ann looked about her to find only the three of them in the room. Two chairs lay on their sides and a table was tilted crookedly on the arm of a sofa, its glass ornaments shattered on the rug.

"Sit down, Ann." Paul drew her to the sofa, straightened the table, and got her a drink. "You crumpled up so suddenly in your chair that I thought something had hit you."

"I was afraid to look," she said meekly.

Paul and the professor exchanged glances and Dr. Hans nodded and mopped his shining head with his handkerchief.

"Well," Ann said irritably. "You needn't think you can stand there and wink and nod and not tell me what you mean. I want to know what happened."

Dr. Hans shrugged and sat down. "Better tell her. She can ask more whys and hows than Chip can. And she'll devil the life out of us until she knows everything."

"Well, naturally." Ann sat back and sipped her drink. "Sit down here, Paul." She moved to make room for him beside her. "When did you decide you'd seen enough?"

"When you attacked Hugh," she replied promptly. Now that it was all over she was reviving quickly. The drink was even making her feel warm again. "I always knew Hugh did it," she added complacently.

Fortunately she wasn't looking and did not see the utter amazement in Paul's face. He started to say something, checked himself in time, and said, "Hugh's gun went off when I grabbed him. The shot went in the floor so it didn't do any harm. He fought like a trapped fox and the sheriff finally wounded him— in the leg, I think." He extended his own to show a neat hole through his trousers.

"You were hurt?" Ann asked immediately.

"Only a near miss," he said ruefully. "The police got him then and took him away."

Ann ran her hand along his leg to reassure herself. "You had no business trying to do that yourself. It's what we have the police for."

"That from you," Paul murmured. "We didn't know he'd try to get out that way. Policemen were stationed at the doors to see that he couldn't get away. They didn't want to bring so many inside the house because that would have given the show away too soon. Captain Harkness wasn't completely convinced in spite of the evidence, and the sheriff had to make Hugh admit it. They had a big argument about it downtown. That's why we were so late coming out here."

"He was thorough," Dr. Hans said. "I thought he suspected me. He kept watching me."

"But that's absurd," Ann said, forgetting her own suspicions.

"No," Dr. Hans said with a shake of his head. "It was a logical conclusion. I do not know where I was when Mr. Tolliver was killed and this morning I didn't go back to the school after I had called here." He pursed his lips. "Yes, I think I should have arrested myself."

"Don't worry," Paul said dryly. "You were thoroughly investigated. As a matter of fact, it was you who kept Jean from being put in jail and held. Captain Harkness knew you didn't go back to the university and it wasn't until after the sheriff and I got there that he found out you'd been to the express station."

Jean and Bill came in then, arm in arm. In spite of all the strain and worry, Jean looked happier than she had since Ann's return. It was in the lightness of her movements, in the shine of her eyes.

"Chip's asleep again," Jean said. "He woke up, of course, but we got to him in time to keep him from being too frightened. Oh, I do hope he's too young to understand what happened."

"He'll forget," Bill said comfortingly and drew her closer to him. "You gave me the worst scare of my life tonight."

"I did?"

"You jumped up so quick I couldn't be sure Hugh wouldn't get away from Paul and shoot you. There was too big a chance of a wild shot hitting you."

"Give him a drink, Dr. Hans," Paul said. "He evidently needs it as much as we did."

"I'm sorry," Dr. Hans mumbled apologetically. "I asked John where to find it."

"I'm glad somebody kept his head," Bill said.

Jean came over to Ann and, leaning down, whispered, "Has he asked you yet?"

"No chance."

"What are you two whispering about?" Paul demanded.

"Oh, nothing," Jean replied airily, but her eyes were bright and there was a smile pulling up the corners of her mouth.

Ann caught his hand and smiled up at him but before he could ask another question the sheriff appeared in the doorway. Water dripped from his hair and clothes.

"I came back to tell you everything is all right," he said. "The police have him in jail. They wouldn't trust him in a doctor's office but they've called one to fix him up. He ain't hurt much." He coughed but his blue eyes were twinkling. "The cap'n hasn't realized I shot him but I reckon he won't press charges." He shifted his weight to his other foot. "What I really wanted to say was that I'm sorry I had to do it this way. You see, I don't rightly have anything to say in this county. All I can do is just ask some questions unofficial like. Of course Mr. Tolliver was killed in my county but I never could have proved anything, so I just did a little looking around on the sly."

"If that's what you've been doing for the last few weeks," Paul said, "I'd certainly hate to see you when you have real authority."

"Somebody had to do something. And I found out Mr. Scott had a lot of debts all over town. People sort of let him have things because they knew the Tollivers had plenty. His ideas of luxuries kept on growin'." He shook his head and sighed. "Greed's a hard thing to fight."

"He didn't put up much fight," Ann said.

"No'm, I reckon he didn't. Miss Ann, there's one thing I'd like to know. What in heaven's name made you go upstairs a second time?"

Ann dropped her eyes quickly. "Bill came in wanting to know where Jean was. I wasn't sure she'd gone so I went upstairs to try to smooth things before Bill got there."

"Well, I guess that's all. Mr. Scott was asking for a lawyer and saying he hadn't confessed to anything, but I guess it won't do him much good. if you're ever in my county again, look me up."

They followed him into the hall to say good night. While they were there Amelia joined them.

"I don't know what to do about Lou," she said worriedly. "She just sits there and won't say anything. I don't think she's listening to what I've been trying to tell her. I want her to go away with me. I have some money now, haven't I? We could travel for a while."

"That's a good idea." The sheriff patted her shoulder. "You take her away so's she won't have to see people she knows."

When he had gone Amelia went back to Lou. Through the open door Ann could see her crouched and shrinking in a big chair. Ann almost followed Amelia into the library, then turned back and closed the door.

"I couldn't say it," she said in a muffled voice. "I couldn't tell her how much I hated her. I know I ought to pity her, but I don't. She's mean and sneaky and—and hateful, but she's paying for everything she ever did. She'll be so alone from now on. That's why I couldn't tell her. She'll be alone."

Paul put his arms around her and led her back to the drawing-room, kicking the door shut behind them. Jean tugged at Bill, forcing him to flatten himself against the door.

"What is it?" he whispered.

"Sh!"

No sound came through the doors for a long time and Bill grew impatient until he heard Ann say, "Paul, aren't you ever going to ask me again?"

"Ask you what?"

"Well—to marry you."

"Do you want to?"

"Ask me and find out for yourself."

"Love of my life, Ann darling, will you marry me?"

"Yes!"

There was another extremely long pause before Jean heard her sister say quite clearly. "Six."

"Two," said Paul equally as decisively.

"What do you suppose they mean?" Jean asked.

"You are entirely too inquisitive," replied her husband as he pulled her away from the doors.

COACHWHIP PUBLICATIONS
CoachwhipBooks.com

THE
SARA ELIZABETH
MASON
MYSTERIES

THE HOUSE THAT HATE BUILT

⋙ ⋘

THE WHIP

COACHWHIP PUBLICATIONS
COACHWHIPBOOKS.COM

COACHWHIP PUBLICATIONS

CoachwhipBooks.com

NARROW
GAUGE TO
MURDER

CAROLYN THOMAS

COACHWHIP PUBLICATIONS
COACHWHIPBOOKS.COM

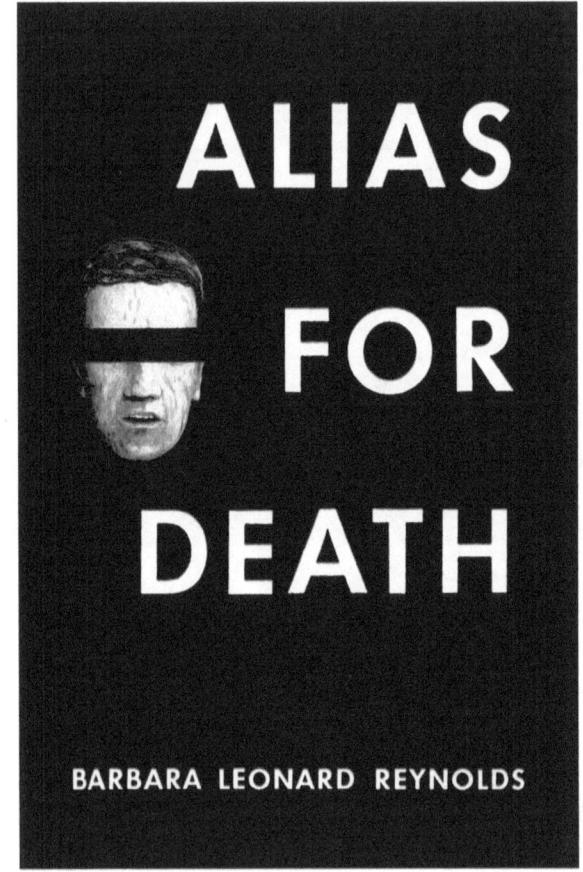

ALIAS

FOR

DEATH

BARBARA LEONARD REYNOLDS

COACHWHIP PUBLICATIONS
CoachwhipBooks.com

The Serpentine Club Investigates
Murder in Washington, D.C.

THE CAPITAL
MURDER

JAMES Z. ALNER

COACHWHIP PUBLICATIONS
CoachwhipBooks.com

A JUDGE MASSIE MYSTERY

THE CORPSE IS INDIGNANT

DOUGLAS STAPLETON
and HELEN A. CAREY

COACHWHIP PUBLICATIONS
CoachwhipBooks.com

www.ingramcontent.com/pod-product-compliance
Lightning Source LLC
Chambersburg PA
CBHW030845030726
47495CB00005B/1382